WILD LOVE, SWEET LOVE

Blake turned his head and looked at her as a parched man gazes upon clear water, almost afraid of the fierce passion, the tenderness, the wild hunger to possess that rose up like a geyser inside him. His hand trembled slightly as he cupped her face. "I love you, dear heart," he confessed huskily. "We won't be parted again."

Before she could speak, his lips moved on hers and his body covered her. His burning hands caressed her breasts, hips and thighs, each sweet, well-rememberd inch of her until they were both in a rapture of desire. In her turn, Alyssa explored him blindly, hungrily—his taut muscled back, lean hips, the hard strength of his thighs. "I love you," he repeated, "and I need you, sweet love. . . ."

IN THE COURT OF THE POISONED ROSE

Immured in the magnificent palace of Holyrood, there ruled a queen without a country, a woman without a future. She was the tragic . . .

Mary, Queen of Scots, a beautiful, winsome, tender-hearted monarch beset by cruel plots and bedeviled by capricious lovers. A desperate woman in a desperate situation, she relied on the strong arm of . . .

Blake Sinclair, a powerful Scots lord. Bold, handsome and shrewd, he was determined to keep Mary on her throne at any cost. But for all his loyalty to his sovereign, he had pledged his heart to . . .

Alyssa Dunne. Beautiful, willful and determined to discover the secret of her birth, she received Blake's fiery kisses but not his love—until her final confrontation with the sinister . . .

Magdalen MacKellar. Some said she dabbled in the black arts, others said she only suffered from a black heart. But in her gnarled hands she held the key to Alyssa's happiness—to her very life.

A tale of breathtaking love as wild and hauntingly romantic as the Scottish Highlands.

HIGHLAND ROSE

Catherine Linden

LEISURE BOOKS ∞ NEW YORK CITY

For
my brother and sister-in-law,
John and Patricia Lynch

A LEISURE BOOK

Published by

Dorchester Publishing Co., Inc.
6 East 39th Street
New York, NY 10016

Copyright © 1988 by Catherine Linden

Printed in the United States of America

HIGHLAND ROSE

She was skilled in music and the dance
And the old arts of love
At the court of the poisoned rose
And the perfumed glove. . . .
Consider the way she had to go
Think of the hungry snare,
The net she herself had woven,
Aware or unaware.
Of the dancing feet grown still,
The blinded eyes—
Queens should be cold and wise.

—Marion Angus

Reprinted by permission of Faber & Faber Ltd.
from *The Turn of the Day* by Marion Angus

Prologue

Cumbray Castle
February 12, 1545

The lying-in chamber at Cumbray Castle was lit by guttering torches placed in iron brackets around the stout granite walls, but even so the vast chamber was shadowy. Animal skins fastened to the slitted windows did little to keep out the icy drafts blowing with ferocious intensity across the bleak and treeless moorland beyond the castle walls. Night and day the howling of the wind merged with the wailing of the women-folk, crying for husbands and lovers off again to yet another war with the English, this time at Ancrum Moor.

Henry VIII's patience with Scotland had come to an end as he saw the arranged marriage between his son Edward and the child queen Mary of Scotland slip farther and farther beyond his grasp. Enraged, he abandoned his attempts to win over his barbarous neighbors with blandishments and promises and decided to subdue them with the sword. The time, as he saw it, was propitious. Scotland in 1545 was in a dangerous state of religious and political unrest, the best and bravest of her nobles decimated by a series of recent wars.

As he prepared to leave with his men, Lord Angus MacKellar of Cumbray had tried to soothe his pregnant young wife. "We'll be back in time for the babe's birth, my lady, and this time triumphant. 'Tis said the English have grown overconfident, their forces made up of a motley crew of mercenaries from abroad, and the Red Douglas and Scott are fired for revenge." Smiling, the forty-five-year-old Earl of Kilgarin laid a gentle hand on Lady Alicia's swollen stomach. "This time we will rout them from the borders and live in peace to enjoy our newborn son."

For her husband's sake the lady had forced a weak and quivering smile. "Aye, if it *be* a lad, my lord."

"Lad or lass, it fain be welcome!" he boomed heartily, adding with confidence, "And the first of a fine, stalwart band."

Alicia prayed it would be so. Her dearest wish was to present her husband with a nursery full of robust children. She knew he was worried about leaving her at such a time, so she tried—in spite of her inner apprehension—to share his optimism as she kissed him deeply and waved him away.

Four days later her pains began.

The atmosphere at Cumbray Castle was dolorous that icy February eve as Lady Alicia labored on the great tester bed under the watchful eyes of her attendants, and she suffered doubly as she struggled to bring forth her first child. Naturally anxious for her husband, no longer a young man, she was also concerned that the only resident of authority left at the castle was an elderly uncle of Lord MacKellar's who the previous day had taken to bed with a severe attack of gout. Every able-bodied man of her own household and of other clans had been called into service to fight for their country. Those left in charge were, of necessity, either very young or advanced in years.

The midwife, Caitlan Weir, laid a hand on her brow. "Are ye cold, lady?" she asked, her experienced eye noting how she shivered and the faint bluish tinge around her mouth. The labor had been long, more than fifteen hours, but now her time was very near.

Lady Alicia glanced up at her anxiously. "Lord Archibald, is he improved?"

Caitlan thought of the gnarled, crotchety nobleman left to run the estate, and shook her head.

"And still no news of the battle?"

"Nay, madam, but for now think of your *own* battle. Ye must save your strength to birth the babe."

The twenty-two-year-old noblewoman sighed and turned her head on the pillow, sinking her teeth into the soft flesh of her lower lip. She was willowy and delicate, with flaxen hair and eyes as blue as the forget-me-nots dotting the moorland in spring, and at that moment was well aware that there were those hereabouts who did not look favorably on her marriage to Lord MacKellar.

Her first marriage at the age of sixteen had been to a man of forty-nine and had produced no issue. A year ago she had wed Lord Angus, himself a divorced man who already *had* an heir. But the state of the country being so uncertain and fraught with endless wars, his lordship was anxious for more children to strengthen the line.

"Oh, why did he have to be gone tonight?" she cried aloud as another pain struck her, made that much more agonizing as she thought of Cumbray Castle left in the ineffectual grasp of old Archibald and a small band of aging men and boys. Was it her imagination, she brooded, that a dour pall hung over the castle that night; a chill aura of foreboding?

Once the pain had passed, the lady tried to raise herself on the pillow, her eyes seeking to pierce the gloom at the back of the chamber. "Who . . . who stands yonder?" she cried in a shrill voice edged with fear. "Let him hasten forward and be identified."

Caitlan Weir pushed her back firmly. "Nay, nay, my lady, dinna tire yourself. The only ones here are me and my twa assistants, Flora and Agnes, and ye've met both o' them before."

"Jesu—" Alicia groaned as another pain built to a grinding crescendo. "Help me!" she moaned. "God help me and my babe!"

Caitlan's lips tightened and she glanced quickly to the back of the room, understanding perfectly the lady's uneasy state of mind. Dangers lurked everywhere for unprotected noblewomen whose husbands had had other wives who had given them an heir. What mother wants her firstborn to be surrounded by other potential claimants to the title, twigs that might cling, even strangle the branch nearest the top of the tree?

When her contraction was over, the midwife examined Alicia and then announced to the room at large, "No' lang now. The bairn's head appears."

At that the two young assistants were galvanized into

action. Sixteen-year-old Flora set an ewer of water on the brazier while Agnes, not quite eighteen, arranged strips of clean linen over the foot of the bed. The movements of both girls were jerky. Their hands shook, and neither dared look over her shoulder. Caitlan wasn't concerned about her assistants. She was confident that both could be trusted. They were frightened, just as she was, but the prospect of gold provided a powerful antidote. Just the same, Caitlan was acutely conscious of the tall, dark figure silently watching the proceedings from the shadows. An image surfaced in her mind of a long, pale face framed by a mass of raven-black hair; of black eyes that seemed fathomless.

The silent witness was Magdalen Hepburn MacKellar, the first wife of Lord Angus and mother of the heir, Robert. Divorced after the birth of her illegitimate daughter Serena two years before, she was still accorded respect because of her former position. As part of the divorce settlement Lady Magdalen had been given the fortress of Thornburn, some three leagues north of Cumbray, and there she had retired with her servants.

To dabble in the Black Arts, or so it was whispered.

The lady's dark eyes never strayed far from Cumbray where she had craftily planted many spies, and with their help industriously watched over the interests of her son, at that time only twelve years old. Young Robert had survived his two older brothers, both of whom had been killed at the battle of Solway Moss three years before. But Robert, much to his father's disappointment, was unlike his older brothers, both in appearance and character. It had been hinted that he was really the issue of Magdalen and a groom, but Lord Angus never succeeded in gaining proof. The boy was spoiled and lazy, and already showed more interest in fleshly pleasures than in deeds that tended to strengthen character.

Magdalen was well aware of her former husband's humor regarding his heir. She knew that if Robert should fall from grace she would tumble with him, and what more likely to nudge him aside than a bright new star in the firmament of Cumbray? So with that in mind she watched the woman writhing on the bed through cold, narrowed eyes, congratulating herself that her spells had succeeded and the English had chosen that particular time to attack.

Lady Alicia's cries were growing weaker. "My babe . . . pray you keep it safe?"

"Aye, lady," Caitlan murmured through clenched teeth as she felt hard eyes boring into her back.

"Swear on it!"

The midwife hesitated. For a second she put herself in Alicia's place and shuddered. Then she heard a faint hiss from the back of the room, a dry, poisonous rustle such as an adder might make. She stammered quickly, "Aye . . . dinna worry, the bairn will be safe."

The moment her enemy sank into a pain-filled haze, Magdalen moved stealthily to an oaken table set under one of the slitted windows and gazed down at a threadbare tapestry covering a small mound. She reached out a white hand and lifted the edge, exposing a tiny naked infant whose waxen flesh gleamed bluish in the cold.

A piercing howl rent the bedchamber, and Caitlan hastily motioned her assistants to Alicia's side. Lady Magdalen whipped the dead infant off the table and totally submerged it in a basin of warm water. It was necessary to warm its frigid flesh before presenting it to Alicia as stillborn. Magdalen had plans of her own for the newborn MacKellar whelp.

With a final anguished moan Alicia pushed her baby into a savage world, and promptly swooned, leaving the infant to the mercy of her attendants and her mortal enemy, Magdalen MacKellar.

2

"A lass!" Caitlan Weir announced, holding the babe up by its feet, and out of long habit smacked it sharply on its tiny rump. Immediately a loud, lusty wail shattered the tension in the chamber, and forgetting the circumstances, Caitlan laughed and said, "A good, healthy lass wi' golden hair like his lordship."

"Silence, imbecile!" Magdalen spat, glaring at her, then cocked an ear to the door where she had posted a sentry to keep the castle servants away.

The midwife blanched. "Pardon, lady," she muttered, then passed the child to Flora and quickly turned her attention back to the newly confined woman. Magdalen glided to the head of the bed and stood gazing down balefully at the young beauty who had supplanted her as Mistress of Cumbray. "How exquisite," she thought gleefully, "to have her so completely in my power."

At that heady moment her usual shrewdness and cunning deserted her. Plucking a satin pillow from the tumble around Alicia's head, she shrilled inwardly, "Die, meaching-mouthed whore! An eternal curse on you and all your kin."

Caitlan had completed an examination of the afterbirth. Glancing up, she was horrified to see Magdalen lowering a pillow over the unconscious woman's face. The midwife sprang up and caught her arm, crying, "Nay, mistress, dinna be daft! Ye have nothing to fear from her. She canna have any more bairns, I promise ye, nor is she like to live."

The frightened voice snapped Magdalen out of the evil trance that had fallen over her and brought her back to her senses. Lord Angus could be expected to accept the death of his child, given the hazardous process of birthing, but might well be moved to investigate if both his wife and babe were to die.

Her attention jumped to where Flora stood in the background with the now-quiet child in her arms. In a soft, deadly voice the noblewoman commanded, "Bring the whelp hither. I have a use for her."

A chill swept over the young attendant and she didn't move. Indeed, couldn't move. It was as if her body had been turned to stone. But her mind was alive and active, sifting through all the gossip she had heard about this imposing woman, among it the ghastly rumor that she kept her skin soft and white by bathing in the blood of kidnapped infants.

Flora glanced down at the tiny babe in her arms who only the moment before, in a reflex action, had curled an incredibly tiny hand around her finger. In the folds of the swaddling clothes she admired the little rosebud perfect face topped by a down of fast-drying gold fuzz. The unseeing blue eyes seemed to be staring up at her in mute appeal.

Suddenly the young girl was overcome with horror at her part in this evil scheme. True, she desperately needed the gold piece she had been promised, but surely God would punish her if she turned this child over to be used in Satanic rites, which was what she suspected Lady Magdalen was planning for the infant.

Flora stood as if paralyzed, clutching the babe to her breast.

"Are ye deaf, ye muckle lump o' a lass!" ranted Magdalen, lapsing into broad Scots in her fury. She stamped a foot impatiently. "Bring the bairn hither or I'll have ye flayed alive!"

Flora backed into the shadows and shook her head.

With a snort of anger, Magdalen started toward her when there was a sharp rap on the chamber door. It flew open and the young sentry, Jock Semple, muttered urgently, "Riders approach the castle, lady. We maun make haste!" His eyes took in the newborn baby, the exhausted mother, and the dead infant lying on a nearby table. He knew well enough what his mistress meant to do, and he had been well paid to help her. Now he was terrified that they would be caught in the act if they didn't leave Cumbray immediately.

Magdalen stopped abruptly, her black eyes betraying a glint of alarm, her mind spinning to cope with this unexpected intrusion. She must not be found here! Nor dare she chance leaving with the child in her possession lest they be apprehended on their way out. For a moment she experienced a vicious stab of disappointment, of having been cheated out of a few hours of sweet revenge using the babe as the tool, but when Semple urged her again to hurry, she had no option but to change her plans.

Wheeling about, she pointed an imperious finger at the midwife. "I command ye, Caitlan Weir, to dispose of the child." Then, allowing her cold eyes to sweep over all of them, she added, "And I warn ye upon pain of death to say naught of this night to anyone. Swear on it!"

They exchanged a terrified look and nodded.

With that the noblewoman unclipped a pouch from the silver belt at her waist and tossed it to the midwife, instructing, "See that everyone gets her share."

Magdalen swept out of the room and moments later vanished from Cumbray Castle under cover of darkness.

When Lady Alicia revived to the news that her child had been born dead she gaped incredulously at her attendants and screamed, "What mischief is this? Ye lie, I tell ye! As I swooned I heard it said my babe was a lass. And I plainly heard the bairn cry—"

"A dream, my lady," Caitlan broke in nervously, motioning Agnes forward with the substitute infant. Before passing it to the sobbing woman she swiftly covered its sex.

But Alicia unwrapped it completely, examining it through mournful, tear-drenched eyes. In the hideous silence the midwife and her assistants scarcely dared to breathe. Alicia gazed down at a puny babe—a male—with a cap of dark hair so unlike her own or her beloved Angus's. With a choked wail she handed the child back, moaning, "Oh, what bitter fate; what evil wind a changeling brings, for mine was sound! I heard her cry—"

Overcome, Alicia slumped back against her pillows and closed her eyes, sinking into a protracted melancholy that was to last for years.

The visitors to the castle that evening came from Jedburgh with a message from Lord Angus to his lady, but because of Alicia's breakdown it could not be delivered. When MacKellar returned from battle, triumphant as he had promised, he found his young wife in another world and his child dead. "It will pass, given time," the physician assured him in discussing his wife's condition.

Angus MacKellar was not destined to live to see his lady recover. He was killed at the battle of Pinkie Cleugh two years later.

When Caitlan Weir returned to her own tiny cot on the night of the MacKellar baby's birth she was horrified at the responsibility thrust upon her so unexpectedly. She felt that Magdalen had tricked her into having to dispose of the child, certainly not part of their original agreement. Mulling it over, Caitlan reminded herself that power shifts inside the great households took place frequently. The mighty today were all too apt to be the meek tomorrow. Why, she asked herself, should she not tread a safe middle ground? She would follow Magdalen's instructions and get rid of the infant—but wouldn't go so far as to kill her.

The midwife searched her mind for a place where the baby could be safely hidden away and finally hit upon the ideal location—right under the nose of a clan who had never had any love for the MacKellars. Aye, she thought, brightening, she would hide the little girl away in the land of the clan Sinclair! Warming to the idea, Caitlan decided that the baby must go to Isa Dunne, an old friend of Caitlan's mother. But how to persuade Isa, who was no longer young, to take the child in and care for her? Pondering a moment, she saw that it must be arranged so that Isa had no knowledge of where the child had come from or who she really was, yet was forced to raise her out of fear.

She pursed her lips as a thought struck her. If the day ever came when Magdalen MacKellar's fortunes were to change, would this baby be recognized for who she really was?

From the large leather satchel that Caitlan carried to all her confinements she removed several objects, among them a thin knife with a slender tip, a healing paste made of herbs, and a sleeping tincture. Rubbing some of the latter over the infant's tiny mouth to induce slumber, the midwife then proceeded to heat the tip of the knife in the candle flame. She closed her eyes and tried to envision the great crest of Cumbray, certainly a most elaborate thing, yet when reduced to the basics it was a thistle within two crescent moons—or the letter C. Caitlan had viewed it so often she could have drawn it by heart.

When the baby was sufficiently drugged, Caitlan painstakingly branded her with the small but important part of her family crest, inside her right thigh. Sitting back to view her handiwork afterwards, Caitlan felt a little less troubled about the gold in her purse. She was a poor widow with two sons to support and a certain amount of ambition for her children, both of whom at that moment were fast asleep in a cupboardlike enclosure in a corner of the room. The gold would buy them a cow or two and perhaps a few acres of land. And if Lady Magdalen were to fall . . . well, anything was possible. One thing Caitlan could rightly claim, she had saved the MacKellar baby's life tonight.

The night was sullen, but no more so than the mood of the masked rider who cast a baleful eye over unfriendly territory and then at the clouds obscuring the face of the moon. He had traveled at a snail's pace due to the snow and the bundle wrapped in a sheepskin and strapped to a padded sling on his back.

As the moon peeped out briefly from the edge of a ragged cloud, like a woman's white breast emerging from the tatters of her gown, the brooding countryside was momentarily touched with silver, lending the wild terrain a haunting, mysterious aura that might have stirred some but left the lone rider singularly unmoved. He cared nothing for the silvered beauty, and was far more in tune to the darkness lurking below. All his senses were acutely alive and suspicious, primed for quick action should the need arise.

He leaned over the flank of his mount and spat in the snow, growling under his breath, "Pagan country. Heathens, the lot o' them! Aye, even the lairds hidden away in their fortresses among yon granite hills. The Sinclairs"—again he spat—"whoresons o' hyenas." Only his love for his sister Caitlan could have persuaded him to venture into this accursed land.

A loch glinted far below, one that he'd heard was bottomless and infested with giant beasts, and on the opposite shore sprawled the dark shape of an ancient monastery. Nudging his horse out onto the lip of the hill, he glanced below and saw the castle. Augusta! "Aye . . ." he muttered with dark significance while unconsciously reaching around to pat the small bundle strapped to his back.

A wave of superstitious dread touched him with a cold finger. Was it right, he fretted, to bring an innocent child into the very maw of her father's enemies, no matter how lofty the reason?

The Earl of Belrose and all the Sinclairs hated the MacKellars because of their kinship to the Protestant clan of Campbell, whose chief they accused of being a traitor due to his suspected dealings with Protestant England. The Sinclairs, on the other hand, were in alliance with the powerful clan Gordon, whose chief, the Earl of Huntly, was the most important Catholic noble in Scotland and violently opposed the new religion that was claiming converts even among the Scottish nobility. Their child queen, he pointed out, was Catholic, and it boded ill for the turncoats when the day came when she was old enough to rule in her own right. She would strike down the heretics, he predicted, for a monarch could not sit easy on a throne within a land torn apart by religious strife.

The masked rider cared little for politics. Religion, however, was another matter. With a scowl at the abbey below, he felt a surge of resentment, thinking that the Catholic clergy had grown rich and lazy while the common man who slaved to provide the wherewithal to help support them grew ever more lean and work-weary. Lately many had been harkening to the passionate preachings of John Knox and were in complete agreement when he accused the priests and friars of the church as being a "grasping crew," not only greedy, but in many cases debauched and exceedingly corrupt.

But for the moment the country was distracted from internal troubles as ancient enemies temporarily banded together to fight a larger one: the English. For that the masked rider was grateful, relieved that the Earl of Belrose's forces were engaged elsewhere. As he moved like a shadow through the frozen countryside, he suddenly spied the village of Lochmore huddled below. At a glance it was a mean, inhospitable place, and by the looks of it there was not much stirring at the late hour of nine of the clock. Picking his way cautiously down the hillside, he remembered Caitlan telling him that Isa Dunne's cottage was at the north end of town, next to the crumbling remains of an old convent.

He found it without trouble, and at the sight of it his heart sank in dismay. A tiny place, it was in little better condition than the nearby ruins. From its tattered thatched roof to the cracked planks of the door, a pall of disinterest and neglect hung over the place. The rider, after a swift glance up and down the street, dismounted and hurried to the door. Assuming an authoritative, intimidating manner, he struck the door a thunderous blow.

"Open up!" he demanded. "Open up in the name . . . of your betters!"

He had to knock twice more before he heard the bolts being scraped back. The door opened a crack and a scrawny chicken darted out from the interior, squawking in relief at encountering fresh air and freedom, and in a flash disappeared into the nearby woods. In the light of the moon the rider glimpsed a dour, hawk-nosed face as the owner peered out at him suspiciously. He saw a wizened countenance as pitted and wrinkled as a fig. At the same time his belly tightened in rebellion at the foul odors wafting out the door.

He sucked in a breath, thinking, Holy Mother, was it to this crone that he must deliver the baby? Surely Caitlan had made some mistake.

"Be ye Mistress Isa Dunne?" he inquired in his most officious tone, half-hoping she would deny it.

She looked him up and down, sly eyes examining him through hooded lids. "And who might you be, sir?"

He saw at once that he must show her who was master.

Raising a booted foot, he kicked open the door, sending the hag reeling into the vile chamber that looked and smelled like a charnel pit. Cowed now, its owner shrank back into the deep shadows against the far wall as a pair of goats rose, bleating piteously at the disturbance.

The rider glanced about in disgust. "Some light, auld woman, then you and I maun speak of weighty matters." And seeing that she was too frightened to move, he added, "Make haste! There be gold in it if you harken to my instructions and follow them to the letter."

The word "gold" galvanized her to action.

When the candle was lit and peat thrown in the fire, sending up a fine blaze that took the chill from the air, the babe was unwrapped. She at first appeared dead, but after a little while was revived by the warmth of the fire. Watching its vigorous struggles for survival, the rider felt a surge of admiration, thinking, Faith, but Lord Angus would be proud of this one, lass or no lass. And after all the wee mite had been through, surely she deserved better than this? His mother and Isa had been ye friends, but that had been long ago, and by the looks of her the intervening years had brought out the worst rather than the best in the woman.

But it was dangerous to dither. Now that his mission had been accomplished, he was eager to be on his way. Like the other nobles, the Earl of Belrose would have left some men behind to guard his interests while he was engaged on the border, and the rider had no desire to tarry and risk being spotted as a stranger and made to account for his business in Sinclair domain. He shuddered to think of it, imagining how they would react if they knew he had brought a despised MacKellar into their midst, even though she was but a babe. It would mean certain death for him and a fate he dreaded to dwell on for the child.

Just the same, he took pains to give Isa Dunne careful

instructions. The babe, he stressed, was to be named Alyssa (for her mother, Alicia) and raised as her grandchild. "And unless ye relish a lang and painful death," he went on darkly, "tell nobody how she came to your door. In due course," he continued vaguely, purposely tantalizing the crone with the promise of future gold, "the bairn will be claimed by her rightful kin, very important people, and you will be most generously rewarded for your service."

When the hag pointed to the inflamed brand on the girl's thigh, he said brusquely, "That be no concern o' yours, mistress. Just make sure it heals proper and treat the child well. If you don't, powerful folks will hold ye responsible."

Isa nodded, her sunken eyes gleaming with avarice. "Faith, but she'll be like ma' ain flesh and blood," she assured him.

The rider winced at the thought, but drew a small pouch of coins from his leather jerkin and tossed them into her lap with the remark, "More will come from time to time," though he was far from certain of this.

He took one last look at the baby. Laying a gentle hand on her head, he whispered, "God keep ye," and left.

The moment he departed, Isa dumped the infant on the hearth and pounced on the purse, her bony fingers trembling as she counted the money, more than she had ever owned at one time in her life. She cackled with anticipation, thinking of how many tankards of ale this small fortune would buy her in Lochmore Inn. Thinking of her best friend, Molly Sampson, she muttered with relish, "Holy Mother, wait till Molly hears aboot this!"

Then her face fell. She could not tell Molly, who usually shared all her secrets. Nay, the masked man had been emphatic. "Unless ye relish a lang and painful death, tell nobody how she came to your door."

Isa clicked her tongue against mostly toothless gums in consternation, longing to share this exciting development but knowing she didn't dare. A small whimper broke into her thoughts, and she glanced at the bundle on the hearth with a jaundiced eye. She had never taken to bairns, not even as a young woman, and had made sure during her brief marriage that she would have few of them clinging around her neck. Her only son had been killed the previous year during a cattle raid on the MacNeith, but they had not been close for years. Isa had no idea if Georgie had had a wife, but no matter. She would invent one for him. Aye, she could say the woman had died recently in childbirth, and this—this whelp had been brought to her to be raised.

Where had the child *really* come from?

Turning a deaf ear to the baby's cries, Isa again disrobed her and in the light from the fire studied her brand for a long time without being able to make sense out of it. A noble's get? she wondered; the bastard offspring of some lord and his favorite mistress?

Isa's thin lips tightened as the infant turned her head about, her tiny puckered mouth searching for nourishment. "My teats are dry, ye greedy wee churl!" she snapped, and instead of stirring herself to locate a wet-nurse she stuck a grimy finger in the child's mouth, hoping fervently that her kin would come to claim her soon. She was not of a temperament to be pestered with the likes of this, and though the money was most welcome, the child was not. And she could tell already by her struggles to find food that this babe was more lively and demanding than most. Aye, she thought irritably, it would be necessary from the start to show her who was boss.

Within two weeks of Alyssa's birth everyone involved in the drama—except the principals—were either dead or had vanished. The masked man was intercepted on his way home to Cumbray by a contingent of the Earl of Belrose's men. When he refused to state the nature of his business in their territory, a fight ensued and his head was struck off.

Two days after the child's birth both the young attendants, Flora and Agnes, died suddenly of a severe belly distemper. The following week Caitlan Weir herself, on her way home from a confinement late one stormy night, "fell" into a swollen river and was drowned. Jock Semple, the strapping young sentry that Lady Magdalen had bribed to guard the chamber door, abruptly disappeared from the area . . . only an hour or two ahead of the men that Magdalen had sent in the night to silence him forever. Semple, with his purse tucked into his boot, did not tarry until he reached the border and quietly slipped over onto English soil.

The midwife left two sons, five-year-old Robin and ten-year-old David. David Weir, young as he was, was in no way deceived as to the cause of his mother's death. After her young attendants had met their untimely end, and fearing for her own life, Caitlan thought it prudent to warn Davie. At the same time she had quietly begun making arrangements to leave Cumbray and follow the baby Alyssa to Lochmore in Inverness-shire.

Davie had been shocked to learn of his mother's crime. The day she died he knew that he and his brother were in terrible danger. Lady Magdalen would find them and kill them too, and it could happen at any moment unless they left at once. Taking the remaining coins from the hiding place his mother had shown him, and with Robin in tow, he begged a ride on the cart of a passing peddler and left the village of Cumbray at dawn one bitterly cold morning. Very gradually the two boys made their way in the direction of Loch Ness and Lochmore.

Once there, Davie felt safe. A MacKellar would think twice before venturing into the stronghold of the Sinclairs, and Lady Magdalen would never dream they had fled in that direction. Aside from that, Davie had a feeling that it might be wise to remain close to the MacKellar baby, though he could not have explained why, except that, other than Magdalen, he was the only one left who knew of the child's existence and her true identity. Mayhap one day when she grew up he would tell her the truth about herself.

The Changeling

1

The dressmaker's gesture was jerky and increasingly impatient each time she motioned for Alyssa to hand her a pin, and it was not difficult to see why. The young woman she was fitting had been transformed into a different person the moment she stood encased in the rudiments of her wedding gown, changing from a rather sullen, bovine creature of little beauty or humor into a coy, giggling mass of quivering flesh, constantly craning her neck around to view herself in the looking glass. "The rose satin becomes me, does it not, Mama?"

Her mother stood to the side watching the proceedings, at first indulgently, uncharacteristic of Mistress Lindsay, but then it was not every day that a girl is fitted for her wedding dress. And the girl was her only daughter, sixteen years old, and all too frequently the butt of her mother's impatience. So under the circumstances the doctor's wife schooled herself to be tolerant, even though with each simper Myrtle put her teeth on edge, reminding herself that soon she would be married and out of the nest, mistress of her own home. And a good marriage it was! Just the kind of union she had planned for Myrtle all along, and by a miracle the silly burde had not managed to sabotage her chances through her own deportment. She might have done too, mused her mother, but for the fact that her betrothed, Charles Newton, was too dim to notice, and his father, Sir Richard, too preoccupied with his older sons to care.

While the dressmaker struggled to get a good fit and Myrtle continued to giggle and preen, Mistress Lindsay glanced sideways at her young housemaid. In the light streaming through the window, Alyssa Dunne's head seemed to be aflame as the sun turned each strand of her long red/gold hair into glistening threads of fire. Alyssa had a pensive expression on her face as she watched the dressmaker intently, and a lovely face it was, thought the older woman with a sigh. She could guess what the girl was thinking. She was wondering, felt the doctor's wife with conviction, when her own wedding day would come. And she was asking herself what chance she had of being married in such a beautiful gown, or to such a well-born bridegroom.

The lady of the house at that moment had an unexpected thought that left her feeling a little guilty: If Alyssa had been *her* daughter, and in Myrtle's place at that moment, it would be to Sir Richard's heir that she would be wed, rather than to his foolish brother. She was sure of it! When Alyssa had been taken into service in her home at the age of twelve, the child had been like a little savage, vile-mannered, her diction deplorable, her knowledge of the world confined to the narrow main street of Lochmore. Through no fault of her own, of course.

Since then there had been a great change in the girl, due entirely to her own determination to take the half-starved little heathen whom her husband had found wandering in a daze through the streets, bleeding from her gums, and make something decent out of the very raw material. It had been surprisingly easy, considering the state Alyssa had been in when she arrived. Mistress Lindsay found that the girl was bright, quick to learn, and almost embarrassingly grateful for the slightest kindness. She strove to please, in sharp contrast to her own daughter, Myrtle, who accepted all the benefits that came to her as her due. Being naturally ambitious for her children and expecting them to do their part by cooperating, Myrtle had been a great trial to her mother. But Alyssa—

Mistress Lindsay, when her new housemaid had been in service only a few weeks, tried to make arrangement for Alyssa to live permanently in her home, but Isa Dunne would not hear of it. No, her granddaughter could work for the doctor's wife, but she must bring her wages home. And nothing could induce her to change her mind.

Now, through local gossip, Mistress Lindsay knew that Isa

Dunne was casting about for a husband for her granddaughter, the only requirement a heavy purse with loose strings of the type liable to spill a few coins the old lady's way. At this, perhaps overstepping her bounds, she had taken it upon herself to warn Alyssa to hold herself dear, angered to think of her beautiful creation being auctioned off like some dumb beast at the county fair, perhaps wed to some lout who would mock and resent the polishing Alyssa had received in her home. Harsh reality dictated that a good marriage was not possible for such a low-born, dowerless girl, but something inside Mistress Lindsay refused to believe it. Had she been *my* daughter, the doctor's wife thought, anything would have been possible.

When Myrtle yelped in pain, crying that the dressmaker had stabbed her with a pin, her mother responded more sharply than she had intended. "And 'tis no wonder! You wriggle and bounce like a great jellyfish in a storm."

Myrtle cast a venomous look at Alyssa, who held a length of satin material against her cheek, liking the feel of it against her skin. Jealous of the housemaid, and certain that Alyssa was hiding a smirk behind the piece of cloth, the bride-to-be said maliciously, "I'll have the last laugh when your old hag of a grandmother weds you to some tinker with a few coins in his purse."

"I was not laughing at you," Alyssa told her with dignity, even as a flush rose in her cheeks when she realized that they knew about Isa's abortive efforts to find her a husband. If Myrtle could but know it, Alyssa was thinking, *she* was the envious one. She envied Myrtle her fine, caring parents, her comfortable home, her part in the big, happy family. Did she also envy her Charles Newton? Alyssa was less sure about that, though she knew that Charles was an excellent match and of a higher station than Myrtle or her parents, therefore a wonderful catch. That he was also skinny as a twig, very near-sighted, and had a huge red nose frequently dripping since he suffered from chronic breathing problems, undoubtedly mattered not at all. Marriage, by and large, was a business arrangement.

All were relieved when the fitting was over. Myrtle stormed from the room and flew upstairs in a huff, refusing to be mollified when the dressmaker assured her with a heartiness that didn't quite ring true, "Why, you'll be as fair as our lovely young Queen herself in that pink satin gown; I swear you will!"

As Alyssa gathered up the pins and snippets of material cut from the dress, delicious smells of roasting meat wafted out from the kitchen. The front door banged open and she heard Dr. Lindsay and two of his four sons enter the house, their voices warm and companionable as they exchanged the day's news, laughing together as they entered the hall where, though it was June and quite warm, a welcoming fire was burning in the hearth.

With the approach of the supper hour it was time for her to leave and make her way back to her grandmother's cot at the other end of the village. She somehow never thought of it as home. As usual she tarried at the Lindsays' as long as she could, reluctant to leave, until the family went in to dinner.

The man was waiting when Alyssa walked into Isa Dunne's dank little cot, a dwelling that had provided scant succor and even less love during the seventeen years she had lived there. Her grandmother had always resented having to care for her, and though Alyssa had been made to work hard for her keep from the time she was eight years old, the old woman's attitude had not softened toward her.

Alyssa had no idea why. She couldn't know that Isa seethed with resentment as she waited in vain for Alyssa's so-called important relatives to come and claim her, and reward Isa handsomely for her services. The old woman had never cared for children. She had no time for them. Yet she had been tricked into raising one, not even her kin, by the promise of recompense. Worse, she had been threatened by the masked rider! She'd had no choice but to obey. Isa had long since managed to convince herself that she had not taken Alyssa in because of the money, but because she had been too frightened to refuse.

Each time the old woman looked at the beautiful young girl, rage surged inside her, and gradually there grew the lust for revenge, or, as Isa saw it, a clamoring for justice. It was not in her nature to be made the fool, the dupe, while those responsible laughed up their sleeves. Nay, she fumed inwardly, a way would be found to settle the debt, to repay her for all she had done for the girl. The obvious way was through marrying Alyssa to a man who would gladly pay to have such a prize in his bed.

So when Alyssa walked into the cottage early that evening and the bowlegged figure of Sanny Taws, a peddler, minced out of the shadows the girl knew immediately what was happening. After all, it had happened before. Many times. From the time she had reached her sixteenth birthday her grandmother had brought one suitor after another to the cot, each applicant for her hand more disgusting and decrepit than the last. At first Alyssa had been deeply hurt that the old woman would think to wed her to such unworthies, men who made her flesh crawl and her stomach churn in revulsion. She had to face the fact that Isa didn't care about her feelings in the slightest, that all she represented to the elderly woman was a pouch of gold.

This hurt Alyssa deeply. At the age of seventeen it *still* had the power to wound her, even though Isa, all the time she was growing up, had never shown her even a hint of love or affection. Why? Over and over the young girl asked herself this same question. She had worked hard to try to win her grandmother's favor. In countless ways she had tried to reach her on an emotional level, starving for a gentle hug or a pat. As a small child she had cried, "Why don't you love me, Grandma?" And Isa had snorted a reply, "Because you're a wee pest, a thorn under ma' hide." Why, why, why? Her questions irritated the old woman and would finally earn her a cuff on the ear that would silence Alyssa for a time.

Hurt turned to resentment, then hostility, never more evident than when a new suitor appeared in the cot. Sanny Taws struck Alyssa as being the worst of the lot. Before she could recover from the surprise of finding him there, Taws slipped behind her and bolted the cottage door, certain she meant to flee. When Alyssa wheeled on him angrily, he held up a hand placatingly. "Now listen to me, lass. I'm here on an honorable mission. I want tae marry ye—"

"Nay!" Alyssa shook her head emphatically.

Undaunted, he continued, "How many men in ma'

position would be willing tae forgo a dowry and wed ye nevertheless?"

Alyssa backed away from him. Her face hardened as she wondered how much money he had promised her grandmother, and a cold light glinted through the tears in her eyes. Long ago she had learned to stand up for herself against the village children who called her a bastard, for all that she was supposed to be the offspring of Isa's son and his wife. They had not believed this story. Isa was a tinker, they had taunted her, and she the tinker's bastard cur. Now she said with biting sarcasm, "You are over generous, Master Taws, but I wouldn't want to put you out of pocket."

The mockery was lost on the peddler. Even in the gloom inside the sour-smelling little cottage, Sanny Taws, staring at her, was overcome by the girl he intended to make his wife. She was as tall as he, sweetly formed, with a mane of red-gold hair rippling down her back to her waist. The eyes that gazed into his were long and uptilted at the outer corners. Taws felt himself mesmerized by those eyes, mist-green rimmed by deepest jade. He stared at her full red mouth, the dusky-rose flush over her high cheekbones, the twin hills of white velvet rising above the too-tight bodice of her shabby grey gown. And like a man in a dream he reached out a dirty hand to touch her; to assure himself that she was real.

Alyssa jumped back, her eyes raking him from top to toe, and a sorry sight he was, she was thinking. Somewhere in his late forties, he had the pinched, sly look of a rodent, and even in the dim light Alyssa could see the dirt embedded into the pores of his skin. Nay, she thought grimly, she could not take pity on Sanny Taws. It was well known that he had worked two wives to the grave and was callous with his brood of ragged children, not to mention cruel to his horse—for all that he was rumored to have a considerable amount of money hoarded away! Straightening her shoulders, Alyssa eyed him disdainfully and, using the precise tones she had learned from Mistress Lindsay, informed him firmly, "I'm sorry, but I cannot wed you, Master Taws."

He gaped at her, his long underlip jutting out in a manner comically reminiscent of his horse. "Whit—?"

"Stand away from the door, sir!"

The peddler blinked, disconcerted by her refined diction, then his face flushed with frustration and anger. Grabbing her arm, he sputtered into her face, "Your grandmother's right. Working for the doctor's wife has gi'n ye fancy ideas, ye ungrateful wee besom. But see here, I'm aboot the only man left hereaboots wi' the wherewithal tae satisfy your granddam, so ye can just set aside yer airs and graces and face the facts."

With that he pushed her up against the wall, his bony frame lewdly rubbing her softness, a feverish gleam in his eyes. Before Alyssa could struggle free, a filthy paw snaked down the bodice of her gown, hot fingers closing over the lush fullness of her breast. With a foot poised to trip her when she jerked away, Taws sent her tumbling onto her own straw pallet. He threw himself down beside her, panting, "So you're still a virgin, are ye? Well, henny, once I've ta'en yer maidenhead ye'll hae no option but tae marry me. Ye'll have nothing left at a' tae offer another."

Recognizing the sense in this, for in truth her virginity *was* all she had to offer a husband, Alyssa panicked. Struggling violently, she brought her right knee up, pistonlike, and rammed it between Taws's legs. Howling with pain and fury, the peddler rolled to the side, clutching himself between the thighs. Alyssa sprang to her feet and glanced about wildly. Spying a bucket of water left down for the goats, she seized it and dumped the contents over Taws's head. Then she ran to the door, calling back over her shoulder, "I wouldn't wed you, sir, if you were the last man left alive in Scotland!"

Isa Dunne was enraged. Spittle flew from her mouth as she berated her granddaughter for spurning yet another suitor. Now, she wondered, who was left? More to the point, who was left willing to pay a stiff price to possess Alyssa's rare beauty? Alyssa's fiery reputation had spread around the area, and lovely or not, Isa fumed, what man wants to have to continually fight for his rights as a husband? It might be fine sport for a day or two, but would quickly grow irksome.

The old woman was beside herself with rage and disappointment. This was the thanks she got for all she had done for the worthless wretch! It was obvious now that Alyssa would continue to defy her, making it impossible to recoup the expense she had incurred in raising the girl. Injustice piled on top of injustice. Beside herself, Isa grabbed a willow switch and brought it down across her granddaughter's shoulders, screaming, "Ye'll do what I say, wench! T'was a mistake letting ye work for the doctor's wife wi' her high-flown ideas. Whit dae ye think ye are; a lady? Pah! T'would take more than fancy talk and manners tae fashion a silk purse oot o' a sow's ear!"

Alyssa suffered the beating with clenched teeth, reminded of so many others through the years. It conjured up painful memories of her childhood, a long, dreary ache of hunger and cold, of frequent thrashings, of never receiving the slightest bit of affection from the woman who was her own flesh and blood. Just the same, she was startled when Isa suddenly shrieked in the height of her fury, "Bastard!" —a name she had never called her before. Alyssa took her arms away from protecting her face and gazed at the old woman in astonishment.

Isa nodded, a malicious glint in her eyes, and the truth burst from her lips like a pent-up dam. Out poured everything she had yearned to tell the girl years ago, things she had held back out of lingering fear of the threats of the masked rider. Now she no longer feared him. It was obvious that he was never coming back. So she spewed her ire down into the innocent, bewildered face of the girl huddled at her feet, beginning by informing her that she was no kin of hers. It all broke over Alyssa's head with the stunning force of a tidal wave, totally engulfing her, rendering her mute. "Bastard, bastard, bastard!" the crone jeered. "Why, even yer ain folks couldna love ye. They got rid o' ye so ye'd never trouble them again."

Finally Alyssa found her voice. "Who . . . who are they?" she asked in a choked whisper.

Isa chortled, enjoying her shock. "Och, mayhap gypsies pretendin' tae be high-born folks so's I'd be tricked into caring for ye." She seized the girl's arm and thrust her face close. "Now that ye ken the truth o' it ye can banish a' the fancy dreams from yer mind and settle down tae wed Sanny Taws. Who else wid have ye?"

Alyssa bolted to her feet, causing the older woman to

stumble back. "Never!" she cried bitterly, tears running down her cheeks. "I'll never marry Taws, or anyone like him, no matter what, and you can't force me!"

"Ye'll be sorry," Isa called after her as she flew for the door. "Ye'll be powerful sorry. Ye'll soon discover, my fine young fool, that worse can befall ye than couplin' with Master Taws."

The ominous warning rang in Alyssa's ears as she raced blindly from the village and down into the misty quiet of the glen, there to throw herself on the grass and sob wretchedly. She believed the old woman's story, simply because it explained her so-called grandmother's coldness through the years. She had been given away at birth, tossed to such a one as Isa Dunne by parents who didn't care what became of her. Discarded. Forgotten. Erased from their lives as if she had never existed at all.

Who were these unfeeling parents? Gypsies as Isa had taunted? Alyssa recalled whispered snippets of conversations she had overheard as a child between her grandmother and her best friend and crony, Molly Sampson. As a small child she remembered Molly examining her strange "birthmark." Afterwards the two women had exchanged a peculiar look. Molly muttered something about the countryside being full of the unwanted "get" of noblemen; that she knew of several in Lochmore and neighboring Blairafton who had been fostered out and forgotten, except for a few coins dispensed for their care—and sometimes nothing at all!

Alyssa sat up, pushed back the skirt of her gown and studied the brand, which had become stretched and greatly distorted by time, and had faded to a pearly hue like a scar left from a burn. She could make nothing out of it, but felt certain that her true parents had put it there. Yet why had they done that if they meant to turn their backs on her forever?

She would never know why, and there was no point in musing. They had cast her aside and that's all that mattered. The reality was Isa Dunne's cot and the bleakness and harshness of her life there, the almost total lack of emotional warmth in her life. Were it not for Mistress Lindsay and the Weir brothers, it would have been complete. They, for some odd reason, seemed to have found *something* in her to like, especially Davie Weir, the one she loved best in all the world. Mistress Lindsay was kind, but strict and demanding and rarely demonstrative, but she had taught Alyssa much, and Alyssa knew deep inside that the doctor's wife truly cared for her.

Lifting her head to the gentle evening breeze, Alyssa stared through the bracken and sniffed the odor of heather, pungent and dry, and the delicate sweetness of honeysuckle. She wished she could hide away in her bower forever and never have to return to Isa Dunne's cot. The old woman's parting remark lingered uneasily in her mind. "Ye'll soon discover, my fine young fool, that worse can befall ye than couplin' with Master Taws."

She knew her erstwhile "grandmother" well. By nature Isa was sly, vindictive, and above all, greedy. Her aim had been to trade Alyssa for gold, and nothing would change that. Alyssa was just as determined not to marry Sanny Taws or any other man who offended her sensibilities. Mistress Lindsay had advised her to hold herself dear, and she intended to do that. To be able to love the man she would one day marry was perhaps asking too much, but at least she could respect him, as she never could Taws.

The grizzled crones huddled around the fire in Molly Sampson's tiny woodland cot sipping from tankards of ale. The night had grown chill and the peat fire drove the stiffness from aging bones. Isa complained, "I'm telling ye, Molly, one o' these days she'll run away and I'll end up wi' nothing for a' my bother. She's willful and disobedient and bound tae have her way."

Molly patted her hand sympathetically. The women had been friends from girlhood and told each other all their secrets, though Isa had held one back for a number of years, until Alyssa was almost eight years old. Molly was the village midwife and unofficial doctor, the person to see when one needed a potion to cure anything from a fever to a broken heart. In her little cottage set away from the village proper and surrounded by Lochmore woods, the midwife was said to keep a familiar who whispered the ancient recipes and spells that made her concoctions so successful. Her reputation had now and then brought a personage of some importance to her door, for the midwife was known to be dependable and discreet. In her modest way she had connections, and through one of them had found a way to help Isa out of her predicament with her granddaughter.

When she had first suggested the solution, Isa had been startled and frightened. Now, Molly sensed, her old friend was in a more receptive frame of mind, requiring only a nudge to get her to agree, and she had to win her over that night. In two days it would be the first day of summer.

The midwife had just the thing to make Isa see things her way. Chanting softly under her breath, she cast a special powder into the fire. The result was dazzling. With a swoosh like a gust of wind howling through the glen, the flames roared and crackled, leaping up in violent hues of orange, purple and yellow. Isa reeled back on her stool, a clawlike hand at her throat. Except for the fire, the chamber was in darkness and was filled with an eerie, preternatural aura that spoke of spirits about. The midwife canted softly, "The blue yonder"—she pointed into the flames—"is the loch, and that spiral o' white a lass in a lang trailing gown; like a bride, ye ken."

"Aye . . ." Isa nodded slowly, eager to see exactly what her cohort was telling her. Molly droned on: "And yon dark puff o' smoke is the abbey and there aboot it the monks." Then, pretending to be startled by the swirling "pictures" in the fire: "Oh my, whit a shame! Did ye see that, Isa? The bonny bride has drappit into the loch, swallit up by the water." Her eyes slid cunningly to the other woman's rapt face and she added eerily, "Poo'd down by the beasties, nae doubt."

"Aye, aye, I can see that plain as day," responded Isa, and such was the state of her mind, conditioned by years of impatience, that she *did* see it exactly as Molly described. And who was she to question the spirits of the loch? Isa asked herself self-righteously. Who was she to gainsay them? They must have their bride or the entire village would suffer, and what was one life against so many? Naturally, the abbot would have to pay for his sacrifice, particularly a beautiful virgin said to have noble blood in her veins, or so Isa had hinted, even though Alyssa's origins were obscure.

The monks were waiting to waylay Alyssa on her way home from work the following evening, appearing suddenly from the woods, robed and hooded figures who formed a tight circle around her. One of them stole up behind her and thrust something wet over her mouth and nose.

2

Alyssa revived in a vile-smelling dungeon with the rhythmic sound of water lapping close by. A squat, heavy-set man in the garb of a monk loomed over her, his fleshy face glistening with sweat in the light of a single candle guttering on a stony ledge. Alyssa blinked up at him, her senses swirling, but as her mind began to clear, terror rushed in. She recalled walking home through the woods, then the snap of a twig behind her, and spinning about to find the hooded black figures rushing at her from the trees, like crows from the fringes of hell. One of them had leaped on her from behind, slapped something wet and pungent over her mouth, and after that—

She screamed, her cry echoing through the underground recesses of the abbey and bouncing back at her from the dripping walls.

"Be silent, girl," ordered the man bending over her, throwing a furtive glance over his shoulder. "You have no reason to fear me."

With a start Alyssa recognized him as the Abbot of Lochmore Abbey. Sudden hope filled her heart. Surely this man of God, she reasoned, had come to make everything right. "Why was I brought here?" she asked him in a whisper.

He straightened up and gazed at her down his long nose, and did not reply right away. Instead, small eyes lost in puffs of flesh crawled over her consideringly. Finally he said, "It seems you have been very disobedient. You have offended God by your defiance and now must make restitution. You wish to do that, do you not, my child?"

"Sir—?"

He ignored the puzzlement in her eyes as he scratched the stubble on his chin and voiced his thoughts aloud. "Can it be true such as this is truly a virgin?"

At these words the hope in Alyssa's heart was blasted away. She shrank back into the sour, vermin-ridden straw, suddenly aware that her own gown had been removed and she was clad in nothing but a thin white shift so threadbare that her flesh showed through.

With another sly glance over his shoulder to ensure that they were alone, Hector Ogden, the abbot, sank to his knees beside the girl's pallet and a hairy paw reached to fondle her arm, quickly creeping upward to her shoulder, then down to her breast. Alyssa gasped in horror and revulsion and jerked away until her back hit the wall. Her eyes were wide with shock and she sobbed, "Dear God . . . nay! You're a—a priest of the church—"

"Quiet, wench!" Ogden broke in as he leaned over her and dragged her protesting form toward him. "Keep silent and do what I say."

As his small, moist eyes slithered over her, hot with desire, moving from the soft fullness of her lips to the inviting peaks teasing the front of the shift, Alyssa's shock gave way to anger and an overwhelming urge to protect herself from the animal panting over her.

She bit his hand, choking, "I—I'd rather die! God will punish you. You . . . you'll roast in hell!"

A warning bell rang in Ogden's mind, even as he rubbed his sweating bulk against her and groped feverishly for her breast. Four things ruled the abbot—gold, power, food and flesh—but above all of them rode superstition. In a rash moment he had decided to take her maidenhead himself. Now he hesitated, thinking that were he to cheat the spirits of the loch, deny them their annual rights, all that he owned would be swept away in the twinkling of an eye. Still . . . while he dare not cheat the spirits, surely he might yet nibble the crumbs from their feast. He might fondle the girl, he assured himself excitedly, but not go so far as to possess her completely.

As he groped and stroked her, Alyssa bit his hands and

clawed at the oily face. "Witch!" he roared in a fury when her nails opened bleeding cuts on his jowls, and he drew back and struck her viciously across the face. Alyssa hardly felt the blow or noticed the warm trickle running from her lip to her chin. All her being was concentrated on fighting him off, even if she must die in the process.

Unable to get her to follow his lewd instructions no matter how he beat her, and afraid of killing her and denying the loch monsters their treat, Ogden finally gave up. But Alyssa's moment of triumph was short-lived when he snarled at her from the door of her cell, "You deserve to die! Tomorrow you will meet those who will make you behave."

The cell door clanged shut behind him and she heard the scrape of a key in the lock. Once he had gone, she sprang up and tried the handle, then rattled the bars while demanding release, but nobody came. Alyssa screamed until she was hoarse. She examined the tiny chamber to see if there might be some way out. There was none. Finally she slumped on the mound of straw and put her head in her hands. Surely he didn't *really* mean to kill her? What reason would he have to do such a thing? He didn't know her, yet he had said, "It seems you have been very disobedient." The only one she had disobeyed had been her "grandmother" when Isa brought would-be husbands to the house.

A chilling suspicion entered Alyssa's mind. Did Isa Dunne have anything to do with this situation she found herself in?

At dawn two burly women entered her cell. The larger of the two smiled at her and held out a cup of ale. "Drink it, dearie, then ye can be on your way."

Alyssa sat up slowly, relief flooding her eyes. "I can leave?"

The woman with the moustache nodded. "To be sure, once ye drain the cup."

Alyssa swallowed it at a gulp, aware of the bitterness only after it was down. She saw the two matrons exchange a look of satisfaction, then the big one turned and motioned a third woman into the cell. The newcomer carried a white silk gown over her arm, and a long gauzy headdress. At Alyssa's look of perplexity, she explained, "'Tis your wedding day, lass. Your grandmother thought ye'd make a bonny bride for the beasties."

Alyssa tried to fight them off as they proceeded to dress her, but her limbs had grown heavy and slow, her eyes misty, a great humming inside her head. She could not stop the women as they dressed her in the white garments, then supported her between them and led her out onto a parapet jutting over one of the deepest holes in Loch Ness. She was immediately surrounded by a host of black-garbed figures, their robes billowing out in the chill morning breeze. Hector Ogden, grave and officious now, stepped forward and with an ebony wand painted a red smear on her left breast.

The voices of the monks rose in an exultant chant, the sound rising, falling, then rising again to a louder pitch, this outburst of religious fervor and joy at variance with the dour grey morning. Alyssa stood in the midst of the circle transfixed, unable to move or speak, yet dimly aware that she was about to die.

They bound her wrists and ankles, then her body was lifted and suspended over the side of the parapet. Below lay black water, still and fathomless. The chanting grew to a frenzy and the hands grasping her by the legs and arms began to swing her back and forth, gently at first, then with more abandon as they put their hearts into it. The very air about them trilled as the male voices rose to a shrill crescendo. Then stopped.

The hands holding her were gone. Alyssa felt herself falling through space, her gauzy headdress swirling around her, black water rushing up to close over her head.

"Done!" said the abbot with an air of great satisfaction, and he hurried into the building to get out of the cloying chill. It was time for breakfast and his appetite was especially mighty that morning.

In the forest to the right of the abbey the sound of chanting shattered the dawn silence, sending a cloud of birds rising indignantly from the treetops and small woodland creatures scurrying for cover. Lord Blake Sinclair and his cousin Edward Grant were furious. They had concealed themselves in the trees near the water's edge in the predawn stillness to wait, bows in hand, for the stags to come down to the water's edge to drink. Off to their right, on a distant hill, rose the stark, fortresslike bulk of Gower Castle, Sir Edward's home, and across the lake loomed Castle Augusta, the stronghold of the clan Sinclair.

Blake Sinclair, the present Earl of Belrose, turned his dark head in the direction of the abbey. "In the name of God, what are they about at this hour?"

Grant, a stocky, normally good-natured man of forty-one, muttered irreverently, "Whatever it is, an infernal curse on the abbot and all his followers. We can abandon all hope of success this morn."

The dolorous mumbo-jumbo rose in intensity instead of abating, ensuring that whatever beasts were in the forest nearby would be well warned away. Swearing, Lord Blake plunged through the underbrush in the direction of the racket with the intention of bellowing his rage at the abbey walls or the abbot himself, were he about. He had no respect for the falsely pious Hector Ogden, an ignoramus much too puffed up with his own importance. Sinclair had heard stories of his greed, his debauchery, the weird rituals he was said to perform in his ignorance and superstition. Nothing could be proved against him. The fellow was nothing if not cunning, and though miserly he was not averse to spreading a little gold around to buy silence when necessary.

"Mangy blackbirds!" spat Edward as he and Blake came out of the trees and spotted the strange tableau on the parapet of the abbey. As they watched in astonishment, the circle of robed figures parted, revealing the girl in their midst. Both men realized at once that it was pointless to try to stop the ceremony, since by then the participants were in a frenzy, shouting at the top of their lungs. Guessing what was about to happen, Blake pulled off his boots and dove into the loch and swam through the reeds to an area just under the parapet of the terrace.

When the unfortunate girl struck the water, he was less than twenty feet away, concealed from those above by a tall bank of reeds. Marking the spot where she had gone under,

Sinclair gulped air, then propelled himself down through the murky depths of the loch, which in spots was over nine hundred feet deep. He found her almost at once, the pressure of the water holding her slim body fairly close to the surface. Slipping an arm under her chin, Blake struck out for the shore where his cousin was pacing anxiously.

Taking turns, they worked to revive the still figure for close to fifteen minutes while the morning mist swirled around them. Over the countryside hung a vast silence, and the grass the girl lay on was glistening with dew. It had soaked her fine white gown so that it clung to her body, well-nigh transparent, but Blake had no eyes for the bewitching form revealed to any who cared to see. Nor did he notice how vividly the long, coppery hair that spread out around her contrasted with the green of the grass. His whole intent was to bring her back to life; to make Hector Ogden pay for his evil; to attend to minor problems on his Highland estates, conclude other business to his satisfaction, and return to Edinburgh and the Queen as soon as possible.

Blake Sinclair, the Earl of Belrose, was twenty-five years old, well-educated, and in the enviable position of being one of Queen Mary's favorite noblemen. He had first met Mary Stuart years before in France, where he received his education, and where, though still a child, Mary had been betrothed to the dauphin, Francis. Since that time Mary had married Francis, become the Queen of France, been widowed, and the previous year at the tender age of eighteen had returned to rule Scotland. She did not forget her early affection for the handsome Earl of Belrose, who had once fought a mock duel in her name. She sent for him to come to court at Edinburgh, anxious for a glimpse of a friendly face and the support of one who was a Catholic, as she was, in a country newly Protestant. He had gone at once, harboring grand ambitions of his own, mainly to unite the various warring clans so that they might form a solid bulwark against the ever-menacing English. The fledgling relationship between the Queen and the Highland lord that had first begun in France when they were both still children—a relationship that defied categorization—had blossomed during the past year he had been in the Scottish capital.

Now, with ominous clouds gathering around the nineteen-year-old Queen's head, Sinclair was anxious to return to Edinburgh. Even as he leaned over Alyssa, his mouth on hers as he breathed life back into the still body, Blake wasn't really seeing her. To the earl she was just an unfortunate victim of the ignorance and superstition that still held Scotland enthralled, the "devil worship" that John Knox decried from the pulpit.

He drew back instantly when he felt a soft sigh whisper over his lips. On his knees, one on either side of her body, Blake sat back and watched as the girl opened her eyes; eyes the crystal green of a sunlit mountain pool, rimmed by long lashes the color of soot.

For a moment their eyes locked, the girl obviously dazed. Under his thighs he felt her body go rigid as she gazed up into his dark face, at his broad shoulders outlined against the sky, powerful arms on either side of her body. Alyssa cried out and tried to twist away.

Sir Edward bent down beside them and hastily assured her, "We won't hurt you, lass. We saw them toss you into the loch and thought to save you. How do you feel?"

Her eyes flickered to his face, then back to Sinclair's. Alyssa's first impression of him was that he looked hard and ruthless with his aquiline nose, thin, cruel-looking mouth, and eyes dark as the devil's. At that moment, fresh from Hector Ogden's attack, the man bending over her seemed the very embodiment of everything threatening and predatory, the impact of his masculine virility so close to her overwhelming.

Sensing it, Blake immediately rose and moved off a few paces. Edward continued to soothe her, even as her eyes followed the younger man. "I am Sir Edward Grant, my dear," he said, "and the gentleman yonder is Lord Blake Sinclair. We deeply regret the ordeal you've just been through—"

He was interrupted when Alyssa was seized by a violent fit of coughing, and he quickly drew a clean square of linen from his pocket and pressed it into her hand. Her flesh was icy cold, he noted, and tremors shook her body. With a glance back at the abbey, Blake said gruffly, " 'Tis unwise to tarry here. There are many of them"—with a nod to the building—"and few of us, and Ogden, were he to discover the girl still lives, has much to lose."

"Can you rise, maiden?" asked Edward gently. He slipped an arm under her shoulders and raised her into a sitting position, whereupon she was overcome by another coughing spell. Sinclair strode back and stood staring down at her, and in a detached way became aware of her beauty. "Where do you live, lass?" he inquired, speaking to her for the first time. "Sir Edward and I will escort you safely home."

The long, uptilted eyes rose to his face and they were filled with dread. "I—I have no home," she told him huskily.

Blake exchanged a look with his cousin, then gestured at the abbey. "We must get her safely away from here and Gower Castle is closer. I will deal with Ogden," he added grimly, "once you are gone."

Before Alyssa could guess what he intended, he swept her up into his arms and deposited her in the saddle of Edward's horse, then removed his doeskin jerkin and draped it around her shoulders, the heat of his body still clinging to the garment and transferring itself to her chilled flesh.

"Thank you, sir," she whispered, holding it tightly around her, flushing when she realized how revealing her sodden gown had been.

He nodded, his eyes on the rose bringing a vibrant radiance into her white face and a soft brilliance to the clear green of her eyes. For a second, struck more forcefully by her beauty, he gave her a bold, appraising stare and wondered who she was and where she had come from. Then, as Edward mounted behind her, the curiosity ebbed from Blake's mind. Directing his attention to Grant, he said, "Farewell. I will meet with you tomorrow afternoon as planned." And to Alyssa, who was watching him intently: "Sir Edward will see that no harm comes to you."

As they rode away, Alyssa closed her eyes and wondered if she was dreaming. A multitude of conflicting emotions churned about inside her. First had come the terror of her abduction by the monks, then her disgusting struggles with the abbot, and finally the horror of being thrown into the loch. That she had been rescued by the lord of Castle Augusta seemed nothing short of a dream. The castle had dominated her all through her life, looming over the village as it did, but the occupants of the fortress had always seemed as remote to her as a distant star. She knew about Blake Sinclair, of course. As clan Chief, his various exploits were of avid interest to everyone in the area. He was a brave soldier, his expertise with the sword something the common people bragged about in Lochmore Inn to whatever stranger happened to pass through the territory. Further, they boasted, he was a real gentleman and well-schooled in book learning, not like some of the other lords who could neither read nor write and had manners little better than those of the peasants who worked their fields. He had been married once as a youth, but his young wife had died soon afterwards. Now, they said with great pride, he sat at the right hand of the Queen herself in Edinburgh.

While all this raced through her mind, Alyssa was compelled to glance back, just to make certain she was not living a fantasy. Sinclair was on the point of mounting his horse but at that moment raised his head, as if drawn by some magnetism flowing between them. They looked at each other through the mist, neither acknowledging the moment in any way. Then the earl sprang into the saddle and turned his horse in the direction of the abbey.

3

When they arrived at Gower Castle, Sir Edward placed Alyssa in the capable hands of Allan, the housekeeper, a plump, brisk little woman who moved about with the bouncy gait that Alyssa had observed before in some rotund people. Under her dark blue cap a cluster of salt-and-pepper curls framed a pleasant face brightened by curious brown eyes; eyes that swept over the girl before her and seemed to understand her plight instantly. "Leave her to me, sir," Allan told her master. "I'll have her hale and hearty again in no time."

Still Edward lingered, a worried frown between his brows, not a little intrigued about this beautiful girl they had fished out of the loch. His curiosity would have to wait. The lass looked about ready to swoon. "Be most gentle with her," he instructed his housekeeper, even while aware that Allan, soft-hearted despite her briskness, *would* be gentle. "She has just lived through a hideous experience. Thank God we reached her in time."

Allan took the girl under her wing. Alyssa was put to bed in a tiny chamber that was spare but pristine clean, but first she was bathed in a wooden tub of warm water, then clad in a white bedgown, and finally helped between smooth sheets that had been warmed by the chambermaid, Polly.

It was evening when Alyssa awoke to find Polly again by her bed, a steaming bowl of beef broth in her hands. The chambermaid was a strapping lass with a nut-brown look of glowing health about her, and eyes that fairly crackled with inquisitiveness. "What befell ye, lass?" were her first words to the lovely girl lying on the bed.

Dark memories rushed in on Alyssa, memories she

struggled to push back for she was not ready to deal with them yet. "I . . . I know not," she replied, pretending loss of memory.

"Then sup," said Polly, handing her the bowl. "T'will a' come back once ye feel stronger."

When the chambermaid returned to the kitchen to announce that their patient's mind had gone blank, Allan warned her to ask no more questions, explaining, "We would not want to vex her and set back her recovery."

Alyssa, as the days passed, was relieved that they didn't try to probe. Instead, the chatty chambermaid kept her amused by telling her all about Gower Castle and its owner, of whom she was obviously very fond. Sir Edward, she informed Alyssa, was a childless widower and soon to remarry, and this was the reason for all the work going on around the castle. He wanted everything to be just perfect for his young bride, or soon-to-be bride, a lass little older than themselves. "Ye've no doubt heard o' the MacKellars?"

Alyssa nodded. At one time the MacKellars and Sinclairs had been enemies, but over the past few years hostilities between the two clans had died down, and by way of strengthening the new alliance a rash of marriages had taken place. She listened with interest as Polly said that her master was to wed the Lady Serena, Magdalen MacKellar's bastard daughter and the cause of Magdalen's divorce from Lord Angus.

Seating herself comfortably on the edge of the bed, Polly settled down to relate all the gossip she had heard about the family from Cumbray Castle. When Lord Angus had been killed, his young wife, childless, had been dispatched to a convent and Magdalen and Angus's son, Robert, had inherited. But Robert had expired in his teens, whereupon Angus's younger brother, Thomas MacKellar, had become the new Earl of Kilgarin. Thomas, who had always harbored an attraction for his brother's first wife, had applied for special permission to marry Magdalen soon afterwards, and for the second time she became Countess of Kilgarin.

Polly's round face tightened. "They say she's no' liked by the family, but she wasted nae time in punishing those who rose up tae oppose her. And 'tis known that she rules the feckless Lord Thomas and governs Cumbray like a queen."

"And 'tis her daughter who will wed Sir Edward?"

The chambermaid nodded grimly. "Her *bastard* daughter, Serena," she stressed, making a face. "Soon they will come here tae visit, more's the pity, and if ye ken what's good for ye ye'll keep clear o' them."

"Why?" Alyssa asked uneasily, not liking this picture that Polly had painted of the Countess of Kilgarin.

But Polly only replied darkly, "You'll see soon enough," and with a nervous glance at the door, aware that she had tattled too much, as usual, she hastily rose to leave.

That night Alyssa had a hideous dream about Hector Ogden and woke up thrashing about on the bed in the early hours of the morning. Pulling the covers up about her chin and glancing about in the darkness, she was vastly relieved to find herself behind the stout walls of Gower Castle, rather than in Isa Dunne's dingy little cot in Lochmore. Tears flowed when she thought of how her grandmother had sold her to the abbot, but behind the tears was anger. Never would she go back to Lochmore! The thought of having to live there made her ill, though she supposed that Mistress Lindsay would take her in if she knew the circumstances. There was a problem about living at the Lindsays': Myrtle! Myrtle was extremely jealous of her and would be bound to make trouble, and the entire household would consequently be upset. Alyssa hated the thought of causing strife in the family.

Beyond the window she heard the dawn wind rustle in the branches of the trees and snuggled deeper under the covers and for a moment put herself in Polly's place. She envied the chambermaid her position at Gower Castle. Polly was so obviously happy here, as were the other servants. Sir Edward was kind and fair, they said, and Alyssa believed them. Several times he had popped his head into her room to see how she was faring, and once brought her a small pot of chocolate, a treat Alyssa had never tasted before. During that visit he told her that Hector Ogden had been arrested. In answer to his gentle questions, Alyssa told him her name and that of Isa Dunne, and how she had come to fall into the abbot's hands.

By the time she finished, Grant's good-natured face was grim.

"Isa Dunne will pay for this," he promised.

She was too ashamed to admit to being a bastard; to confess that Isa wasn't her true kin.

Now, watching the dawn light creep into her room, Alyssa longed with all her heart to stay on at Gower Castle. She felt safe here and greatly admired Sir Edward. For a second or two a dark face flickered into her mind, that of the man who had actually rescued her from the loch, and though she was infinitely grateful to him too, he aroused very different feelings in her than she felt for Edward Grant.

In truth Alyssa wasn't sure exactly how she *did* feel about Sinclair. He was so different from Sir Edward. Though she had much to thank him for, the Chief made her . . . uneasy. She supposed it was because she—and everyone else in the area—was somewhat in awe of him. In their eyes he was akin to a god, endowed with special qualities far above mere mortal men.

Alyssa shivered, recalling how she'd felt when his bold dark eyes looked her over so thoroughly, almost as if he meant to impress her image on his mind for future reference. Mayhap, she mused, he was annoyed at her for being the means of spoiling his stag hunt. After all, what could the life of a penniless orphan girl mean to the Chief of the clan Sinclair?

Would it be possible for her to stay on at Gower Castle? Alyssa made up her mind to ask Allan the following day.

Alyssa took her place among the chambermaids at Gower Castle the very next day, and the weeks that followed were the happiest of her life. The training she had received under the demanding Mistress Lindsay now stood her in good stead. Alyssa sent her former employer a message by one of the stable lads. He returned to say, "The lady wishes ye well. She said tae tell ye tae mind everything she taught ye; that she's proud o' ye for trying tae better yourself." Then he thrust a small package into her hands. In it was a delicate silver locket and a shining gold coin. Watching her face, the boy smiled. "The locket is tae remember her by and the coin is tae wish ye good fortune."

Alyssa was stunned at such generosity. Tears flooded her eyes. She vowed to make Mistress Lindsay *very* proud! She would work her fingers to the bone, never complain or cut corners, and try to be pleasant and well-mannered at all times, no matter how sorely provoked. The doctor's wife had had faith in her abilities. She had said, "You must always hold yourself dear and never give anyone the impression that you can be bought cheaply. You must be proud of yourself, Alyssa, because you have accomplished much in the time I have known you. Aye, and can accomplish much more."

Almost without realizing it, Mistress Lindsay had instilled confidence in her, or as Isa Dunne might have put it, given her grand ideas. As yet these ideas were sketchy, hazy, lacking a specific goal, other than the drive to improve her lot in life, though how she would go about doing that was still unclear.

The stable lad coughed for her attention. He had also brought her a message from her old friends the Weirs. Davie and Robin would visit her on Sunday, he said. They had been desperately worried about her after she disappeared from Lochmore.

As a band of riders clattered into the courtyard of the castle, Alyssa hurried back to her room in a happy, optimistic frame of mind, certain that her life was taking a definite turn for the better. In a few days she would have the pleasure of seeing Davie and Robin, and with the gift of the gold coin she had suddenly become a rich woman!

In her room she tried on the silver necklace, then, longing to see how it looked on her, ran down the hall to one of the guest bedchambers where there was a looking glass that Sir Edward had imported from Italy, among all the other rich furniture he had bought to please his betrothed. Alyssa stopped in front of the mirror, her eyes on the locket that lay like a caress against the milky-white column of her throat, the only thing of its kind she had ever owned. The gleam of silver made her feel prosperous; grand, regardless of her plain blue cambric gown. Slowly her eyes rose to her face, to the coppery mane of hair surrounding the pale oval; hair that tumbled like molten gold over her shoulders and down her back to her waist. For a second or two her mind played a trick on her. She saw herself clad in an emerald silk gown—her favorite color—and imagined a rope of seed pearls entwined in her hair. She was at a court ball, surrounded by gorgeously attired people, and a handsome gentleman had just asked her for a dance. Carried away, Alyssa curtsied gracefully before the mirror, first in one direction, then another. "Charmed, my lord," she murmured to her phantom admirer. "Charmed—"

A sound at the door behind her shattered the dream. Whirling around, Alyssa saw a tall, dark figure framed in the doorway. At sight of him she froze, hot color flooding her chest and face, and her indrawn breath strangled in her throat as she almost swooned in embarrassment.

Blake Sinclair made her a sweeping bow, his thin, sensuous mouth curved in a mocking smile at her antics. He stepped into the room and nudged the door closed with the heel of his boot. Leaning against it with his arms folded across his chest, one dark brow raised quizzically, he asked, "What are you about, Mistress Dunne?"

Alyssa dropped him a stiff curtsy. When she looked up, her face was stinging red. "I . . . you startled me, my lord."

"Obviously." He glanced about the room and, finding it empty, said, "Do you frequently talk to yourself, or was it my imagination that I heard you address some gentleman?"

Alyssa was mortified. In the wicked dark eyes she spied a teasing glint and knew he was making sport of her, aware that he had surprised her in some foolish game. Well, she thought, straightening her shoulders, she would not make matters worse by lying. "I was pretending, sir."

He stepped closer and stared down into her face, his own face deeply tanned and just as disquieting and ruthless as when last she had seen him. More so! Now they were alone together without the comforting aura of Sir Edward's presence. Hastily she dropped her eyes from his and fixed them on a spot where his broad chest strained a seam of his wine-colored Cramersy doublet. Then, annoyed at her lack of courage, she raised her eyes again to his.

Sinclair was amused by her defiance, because that quality

stood out in her sea-green eyes, perhaps the most beautiful eyes he had ever seen. He felt the pull of them; the magnetism, even as he admired the flawless features of her upturned face. There were many comely women at court, the Queen herself among the best of them, but this girl, a common village wench, could have challenged them all and stood an excellent chance of winning. But that was not all. Nay, he thought as they stood in awkward silence, there was an odd pride about the lass; a certain dignity that complemented her beauty and added to it. He felt a stirring of interest. "And what were you pretending?" he asked her quietly.

The rose deepened over her cheekbones, but she answered truthfully enough, "I was trying to imagine how I would look in an emerald silk gown."

There was a long pause. He was struck by how well she spoke, in contrast to the other villagers who gabbled away in a broad Scots tongue that defied outsiders to decipher it.

"How would you like to have such a gown?" he asked, startling himself, and suddenly wondering at the urge that had prompted him to come upstairs and inquire about her health. He had thought of it as an act of human kindness, a gesture he might have extended to anyone in similar circumstances. Before they could arrest her, the girl's grandmother had fled. Now Alyssa Dunne had no one. He pitied her, he told himself. Further, he admired her courage, and it was obvious that the lass had many worthwhile qualities. As he eyed her speculatively, Blake had a sudden mental picture of how she might look in an emerald silk gown.

The room crackled with tension as Sinclair awaited her response to his casual offer. He saw her eyes narrow slightly and had the impression that she was about to take flight. He smiled, hoping to put her at ease, and, to dispel any misconceptions his offer might have given her, smoothly changed the subject. "So you are happy working at Gower Castle?"

Alyssa nodded warily. "Aye, my lord, very happy. And . . ." she swallowed, "I haven't yet thanked you for saving my life. I'm most deeply grateful."

Now, he thought, he ought to leave her to her game.

Instead, he stepped around her and stopped to gaze out of the window, his back to her. "You should know," he went on, "that Hector Ogden has been arrested and removed from his post. Also that your grandmother has vanished from Lochmore."

"I hope I shall never see her again."

Blake looked back at her over his shoulder. "You speak well for a village lass."

Alyssa told him about her job at Mistress Lindsay's.

Sinclair turned all the way around and, smiling, said, "Then I applaud you, Alyssa Dunne. You have learned your lessons well, and I'm glad to find you recovered and content at Gower Castle."

He left without mentioning the emerald silk dress again.

Alyssa sat down on the nearby bed and stared at her fingers, her shoulders relaxing as the tension ebbed out of the room, but with it went the strange aura of excitement she felt whenever Sinclair was near. It came from the fact that he rubbed shoulders with the Queen, she reasoned; that much of his life was spent in the royal city of Edinburgh where all the great people of the land congregated, and where he had a hand in making the rules that governed the country.

No wonder he engendered excitement in her! When he was near it seemed that some of the sparkle of the capital radiated onto her, that the very air around him dazzled her, causing her to be dazed and light-headed. He was the Chief of the clan Sinclair. He was one of Mary Stuart's favorite courtiers. And he was also, in a rather unsettling way, the most attractive man she had ever known.

Their paths crossed again much sooner than Alyssa had expected, when Allan announced that Sir Edward was holding a political dinner the following Saturday night. Alyssa, who knew very little about politics, was surprised to learn that all was not well in Scotland.

"Oh my yes!" said the housekeeper. "There's great unrest ever since the Protestants came into power two years ago."

They were in the kitchen with some of the other servants making preparations for the coming dinner. Temple, the steward, said, "'Tis a thorn in their flesh that our Queen is a

Catholic, while her ain bastard half-brother, Lord James Stewart, and most o' the other lords in power are Protestant." An officious man in his late sixties who prided himself on having an astute grasp of the political situation in the country, Temple cocked his head at Alyssa and asked, "Why do you think Stewart and the Protestant crew invited Mary back from France to rule here in person?" And when the girl shrugged, he said, "Because she was still a green girl and biddable, and Stewart saw his chance to rule Scotland through her!"

Allan remarked, "Mary was only a bairn o' five when she left Scotland to be raised at the court o' France as the betrothed o' the dauphin, yet even then she was already Queen o' Scotland. Why shouldn't she come back to rule her own country? Did she need an invitation frae Lord James?" she snapped irritably.

Temple responded condescendingly, "Ye forget how long she was away. The Scottish people almost forget she *was* their Queen. When she returned last year at the age o' eighteen she was a stranger, and"—he grinned ruefully— "ye ken how ill our countrymen take to outsiders. Forbye that, she was a Catholic, and now, by all accounts, we are a' Protestant, or supposed to be. Then as if that isn't bad enough, she's a woman! Mercy sakes, is it any *wonder* the country is in a turmoil!"

"She's a good Queen," Nancy, one of the maids put in staunchly. "The common people love her already."

"The common people!" sneered Temple. "What do they ken about what goes on at court? And if John Knox has his way he'll soon enough poison their minds agin her—"

"Knox!" roared Barkley, the cook, raising his massive head from the bake oven. "Now there's a heretic if ever a' saw yin! The turdyguts should be flayed alive for darin' to raise his voice agin his betters, aye, even the Queen herself. To think that he, a common man like any other, would have the gall tae stand up in the pulpit and accuse our Queen o' consortin' with the Pope tae establish the Catholic religion back in Scotland, why, he should be hung at the market cross!"

Alyssa listened with great interest as she stuffed tarts with fruit and custard, thinking of the large portrait that hung in the Hall of Gower Castle in its place of honor over the mantelpiece. When she had first seen it she had been awed, for looking down upon her was a lovely girl about her own age, but dressed in a magnificent white satin gown and with the glitter of diamonds about her throat, ears and wrist. Alyssa had learned to read a little at Mistress Lindsay's, and slowly picked out the legend on the small brass plaque beneath the painting: "Mary Stuart, Queen of Scotland."

Alyssa had always been interested in anything she heard about the Queen, since Mary was only two years her senior, but somehow, as she gazed at her portrait and admired the topaz eyes and humorously curved lips, the young Queen had seemed that much more real. From then on Alyssa became avidly interested in everything she could learn about her. Adding to that interest was Blake Sinclair, a man known to be one of Mary's favorites. The pair—a magical pair—were connected in Alyssa's mind.

The political machinations going on in the capital mystified her. She began to be embarrassed by her own ignorance. But with Sir Edward Grant being related to Sinclair, even the servants at Gower were well informed as to the state of the country and soon provided Alyssa, who kept her ears open continuously, with more than a smattering of knowledge. She laughed when Polly remarked, "Lord James Stewart sounds like a scurvy louse, nor any tae loyal tae his sister."

"Maybe so," Temple replied, "but he's no dolt for a' his other failings, and he has the weight o' the Scottish Parliament behind him, and, so some believe, the favor o' the English Queen herself. Elizabeth, ye can be sure, has no desire to see Catholicism reinstated in Scotland, given that it might give their compatriots in England dangerous ideas. Dinna forget, Mary Stuart has a solid claim to the English throne through her father, James V, and there are many across the border ready to put her there, since in the eyes o' the Catholics Elizabeth is a bastard and Henry VIII's marriage to Anne Boleyn illegal."

Barkley laughed shortly. "Aye, and they'd get plenty o' help from some hereaboots. Who kens what might happen when Queen Mary makes her northern progress," he added enigmatically, "regardless o' the fact that Jamie Stewart and many other Protestant lords will accompany her. If a' were Stewart I'd come north at my peril."

"Then there might be a battle?" Alyssa burst out, chilled to think of the rivers running once more with the blood of the clansmen, as had so often happened in the past. She thought of the mighty Gordons. Catholics. She thought of the Frasers, Grants—and Sinclairs. None of them, she had gleaned, had any love for the Queen's half-brother, Stewart.

Might they seize the opportunity to rid themselves of him during the Queen's northern progress? Stewart and his cohorts were certainly all-powerful in Edinburgh, but in the Highlands, surrounded by mighty Catholic clans, they would be as helpless as newborn babes to defend themselves. Alyssa wondered why a man as seemingly astute as James Stewart would expose himself to such a risk.

Seeing her anxiety, Allan patted her arm soothingly. "The Earl o' Huntly, George Gordon, could well be reckless enough to plunge the country into rebellion, but Sinclair is no' so foolish. He has a better grasp of things in Edinburgh—"

"And the country as a whole," put in Temple sententiously, not to be outdone by a mere woman.

Allan ignored the interruption. "As I was saying, we can count on the Chief tae keep a cool head. He kens that nae good can come o' rebellion. That's yin o' the main reasons he returned tae Augusta, tae try tae calm the Earl o' Huntly and stave off a war."

Alyssa's secret admiration for Sinclair grew, and she prayed fervently that he would be successful. The night before the dinner the housekeeper took her aside and gave her some sage advice. Alyssa would be waiting at table during the dinner. She was to be polite and obliging to their guests, though not *too* obliging, "if ye take ma' meaning, lass." Once in their cups, she continued, some of the noble lords could be a wee mite forward, and since they were well used to having their way . . .

Alyssa smiled thinly. "I'll be careful," she promised, thinking that she was not quite so untutored in such matters as the housekeeper seemed to imagine. She'd had plenty of experience in fighting men off, and her mind went back to Sanny Taws and Ogden and others. She was still a virgin, which was significant, and would remain one until *she* chose to give it up, and it wouldn't happen during a careless tumble with anyone, lord or no lord. There were enough bastards fostered out over the countryside.

4

At eight o'clock on Saturday evening the hall of Gower Castle bustled with Highland chieftains and their men, some of whom wore the short, colorful attire of the area that left their legs bare from mid-thigh to just below the knees. Their footwear varied greatly, ranging from rough boots made from the hide of animals and laced to the knees, to handcrafted leather imported from Italy.

These were rugged, often uncouth men by the standards of those at court in Edinburgh, and the tongue that echoed from the massive stone walls was predominantly Gaelic. Few among these nobles could read or write and many had received no formal education. They were wild, often undisciplined, and when measured against the rest of Europe, sometimes primitive. Cut off from the main body of Scotland by the mountainous terrain, these chiefs did more or less as they desired and thumbed their noses at the official government in faraway Edinburgh.

At the head of the board, as was his due, sat the powerful Earl of Huntly, George Gordon, first cousin to the Queen though almost thirty years her senior. Gordon, who had been raised with Mary Stuart's father, James V, managed his vast empire as he saw fit. Naturally, lesser lords in the Highlands were inclined to look to *him* for direction rather than to the capital, and viewed with extreme suspicion everyone below the Grampian Mountains. Secure in his domain, the bull-like Huntly sat at the head of the board and gazed benignly at his family and followers ranged around him. As one remove, or course, followed another, his rumbling voice and booming laugh could be heard above all the rest. Between each remove was an interlude of entertainment—fiddlers, singers, a couple of fools—and of course the ever-present piper, for no feast in the Highlands could be properly digested without the sound of bagpipes to get the juices flowing smoothly.

Four serving wenches moved continuously up and down the board and back and forth from hall to kitchen. The guests dined on venison, suckling pig, fresh loch salmon and jellied eels. Alyssa, her cheeks flushed a bright pink from the heat engendered from the steaming platters of food and all the bodies in the room, tried hard to keep her eyes from constantly straying in the Earl of Belrose's direction. He was by far the most strikingly handsome man in the hall, where there were many comely men, particularly the young John Gordon. There was another quality about Sinclair that stood out above all the rest, the unmistakable force of a vibrant personality and air of command no less than that of Huntly himself. Dressed soberly in a dark green doublet with very little ornamentation, he still cut a debonair figure because of his broad shoulders and his height.

When Alyssa had first come into the room to help serve the meal, Sinclair had given her one of his wicked white smiles, but since then he seemed to have forgotten her. And why should he remember, Alyssa asked herself as she moved about the board attending to the needs of the guests, many of whom tried to grope her thigh beneath the table. He had important matters to discuss this night, and each time she glanced at him he was deep in conversation with the Earl of Huntly. Had he not come back from the Queen's side on a crucial mission, to try to dissuade Huntly from any plans he might be nourishing to seize Stewart and the other Protestant nobles during the Queen's progress and try to reinstate the Catholic religion in Scotland?

It struck Alyssa that Sinclair was in an awkward position. The Gordons and Sinclairs had long been allies. Gordon might expect Blake to side with them during a confrontation with Stewart and his supporters, regardless of the fact that it would lead to rebellion. How could Sinclair refuse and still remain friends with Huntly? And it was obvious from watching the pair that they *were* friends. At that very moment Gordon had an arm draped affectionately around the younger man's shoulders as he rose to signal the end of the meal.

With dinner over, the table was cleared of food and a fresh hogshead of Gower's best ale was brought in to appease the guests' thirst while they settled down for their meeting. At that point the servants left the hall—all except Temple—and the great double doors were closed. Alyssa returned to the kitchen with the other serving wenches.

"How many sons does my lord Gordon have?" she asked Allan curiously.

"Nine," replied the housekeeper, overseeing the preparation of the sweet which the guests would partake of after their meeting. "Nine braw laddies and three lassies! And the countess, God bless her, is just as strong and doughty as ever. She has tae be," Allan chuckled, "wed tae a firebrand like George Gordon."

"Young George, the heir, seems much quieter and more serious than his father," Alyssa commented as she arranged strawberry tarts on a silver tray. "But the third son, John, strikes me as being a merry, devil-may-care lad—"

"And bonny," interjected Polly with a little giggle.

Allan pursed her lips and gave her a disapproving look. "He's a wild young rover, so just you bide clear o' him, my lass! Ye ken what he's like once he gets a dram or two under his belt."

Nancy sighed, a dreamy look in her eyes. "Ye might have Johnny if ye will, but I'll take Sinclair. Now there is a man who fain stirs ma' blood!"

"Wheest!" Barkley thundered. "By God's bones, how can ye babble so when there's such serious business goin' on in the hall?"

Chastened, the girls bent their heads over their work.

As she filled the platters, Alyssa wondered if Sinclair would have any success with George Gordon. Gordon, she had heard, had incurred the anger of the Queen for openly criticizing her for failing to support the Catholic cause in Scotland. Temple had explained that Mary Stuart was in a difficult position, particularly since Scotland was now officially

Protestant. Privately she might wish to support the Catholics, and probably did, but if she were to rule the country successfully she could not risk opposing her Protestant ministers led by her half-brother. "She's damned if she does, and damned if she doesn't," was the way the steward put it, adding, "I'd defy Solomon himself to find an equitable solution, so what chance for a young lass o' nineteen?"

Shortly after eleven o'clock the great double doors to the hall were again thrown open and a piper was brought in to lighten the mood of the assembly, many of whom looked grim. John Gordon entertained them by singing some of the old songs in his fine baritone voice. When the serving girls entered bearing platters of sweetmeats, it was to find the great table pushed against the wall and the clansmen milling about in groups, brawny, hard-muscled men, arrogant and proud, virtual autonomous rulers of the lands passed down to them from generation to generation.

The noise in the hall was deafening. Some of the men were arguing loudly, others—those less politically inclined— laughing uproariously as they exchanged the latest bawdy jokes. With the coming of night, cool in these northern climes even in summer, the massive fire had been lit and Alyssa saw everything through a smoky blue haze.

Setting a serving dish on the table, she heard someone say, "You're all forgetting something important. Mary Stuart is a widow and must soon find herself another husband, and you ken well the mad scheming and conniving *that* will bring about, not just in Scotland but throughout all of Europe. Now"—and a lilt of mischief entered the voice—"would it not cure all the ills in one fell swoop if we kidnapped the Queen during her progress, spirited her north—and wed her to me!"

Shocked, Alyssa turned her head slightly and saw that this treasonable suggestion had come from the lips of none other than John Gordon. He was standing in a group that included his father, Huntly, and several other lords. The little gathering fell silent, most of them as stunned as Alyssa. Lord Rankin was the first to break the tension. He guffawed, and after a moment the others broke in, but with a tone of uncertainty in their mirth. Rankin teased, "Right bonny that roguish face o' yours would look wearing the crown matrimonial. And what exactly would Her Majesty call ye—cousin?"

A tall, elderly knight stroked his grizzled beard thoughtfully. "Well now, permission can be got for kin to wed, and second cousins are not overclose."

Alyssa caught the look that flashed between Huntly and his son, a quick glint of triumph.

"You jest, of course?" queried a Fraser.

Huntly's booming laugh rang out, but the glittering brightness of his eyes in the red, heavily jowled face put his response in doubt. "A lad can always dream. And never forget, though we might jest, that Her Grace has always been most affectionately disposed toward my Johnny. Who at court can stir her merry mood better than he, or take her mind off more troubling matters? Faith, she loves ma' laddie dearly, and a man must always be ready to move with the turn o' the tide," he finished enigmatically.

From the hearth Alyssa saw Sir Edward looking at her. Flushing, she hastily bowed her head, pretending to fuss with the food. A moment later she started out of the hall. Near the door she was startled to spy Polly locked in an embrace with a stout clansman who at that moment thrust his hand down the bodice of her gown. Polly's ready giggle pealed out, even as she pretended to push him away.

In the kitchen Alyssa poured herself a cup of water, sipping it slowly while she waited for the racing of her heart to slow. She was afraid to return to the hall, where most of the guests were now drunk and in a mood to dally, and was surprised that Polly would allow one of them to make free with her. Even more troubling was the conversation she had overheard, John Gordon's teasing suggestion about kidnapping the Queen. He had been only half joking, Alyssa was sure of it. And she was just as certain that his father, Huntly, was not exactly averse to the idea. Could this mean that Sinclair had failed in his mission?

Alyssa tarried in the kitchen as long as she could, then was ordered by Barkley to take a bowl of fruit into the hall. Walking down the corridor, she spotted John Gordon and two other men chatting by the stairs. As she made to go past them, Gordon reached out and clamped a hand on her shoulder, turning her about. "By the rood," he cried, "what have we here? What's your name, bonny lass?" He took the bowl from her and set it on the stairs.

Alyssa looked up into a handsome, weatherbeaten face topped by a head of chestnut curls; a face made sensual by a full, voluptuous mouth and lazy, caressing eyes that both appraised and approved at once. They seemed to swallow her at a gulp.

"I'm Alyssa Dunne, if it please you, my lord."

His brows shot up and he laughed, casting a quick look at his companions. "Forsooth, it *does* please me, darling!" For a moment his bleary eyes looked perplexed. "Are you a servant in this house?"

"Aye, sir."

He looked her up and down through wine-hazed eyes. "Are you, now? You deport yourself well for a serving wench."

Gordon slipped an arm around her waist and drew her closer. She tried to resist, but his grip was like iron, his intention obvious now that he knew she was merely a servant. "I won't hurt you, lass," he cajoled. "Just . . . just a bit of sport to lighten a sober evening."

He bent his curly head and nibbled the soft, silken flesh above the bodice of her gown. As Alyssa fought to release herself, a hand came down on Gordon's shoulder. Startled that anyone should interfere, the nobleman let her go and swung around to encounter Blake Sinclair. Realizing he was drunk, for John was generally good-natured and not a man to force a wench, Sinclair remarked lightly, "It seems the lass mislikes the way you go about things, Johnny. Now it's *my* turn to try my luck."

In a flash Alyssa found herself in Sinclair's arms, his dark head bending over hers, and while the other men laughed in amusement as she tried to pull back, Blake whispered, "Don't fight me, or don't you want him to leave you alone?"

The Chief kissed her slowly, teasingly, on the lips, his mouth warm and tasting pleasantly of wine. As he drew her closer and the kiss deepened, Alyssa felt the hard strength of his body press firmly against her own, and at that moment the strange excitement she always felt in his presense took on a new dimension, one that robbed her of her will to resist. Sensing the change in her, Sinclair turned so that his broad back blocked the view of the others. With a few lewd remarks they wandered off, and Alyssa and Sinclair were temporarily alone.

Alyssa thought he would release her. She felt his arm slacken—then suddenly tighten to draw her closer still. Now his mouth moved on hers hungrily until her lips parted and she felt the probing thrust of his tongue. At the same instant the hard heat of his body, fierce and demanding, kindled in her blood a new and frightening surge of fire, a whole spectrum of sensations that she had never known before.

Blake took his arms away and stepped back, laughing softly at the dazed expression in her eyes and the bright pink flush on her cheeks, even as he found himself grappling with an unexpected reaction of his own. He concealed it by teasing, "Your lips are much warmer this night than the day I pulled you from the loch, and sweeter too, like clover honey. Do you sup on clover honey, Alyssa Dunne, like the Glaistig I thought you were when we fished you out of the loch?"

Flustered, and still deeply confused by the emotions he had stirred, she pushed the long strands of hair from her eyes and replied unsteadily, "You . . . you mock me, sir."

He shook his head, the glint still in his eyes. "Allow me to escort you safely to your chamber." And when she started to shake her head, he added, "One cannot tell who might be lurking above stairs just waiting to waylay a comely lass such as yourself."

"I still have work to do in the kitchen."

He studied her for a moment. "Ah . . . such a conscientious girl you are, even though there are many in the kitchen and you would not be missed." He watched her closely, and when she said nothing, he said, "It was wise of Sir Edward to take you into his house, and foolish of me to let such a hard worker slip through my fingers." He smiled slightly. "At Augusta I would not have you labor so long into the night."

Alyssa couldn't take her eyes from his face. He fascinated

her, even as he made her uneasy. His deep brown eyes had hidden fire; they blazed down at her, and the thin, mobile mouth—the lips that could kiss so fiercely and draw forth from her feelings that made her shiver—filled her with a hunger she hadn't known existed. He made her breathless, looming over her with a hand casually propped against the wall. At any moment she expected him to seize her and sweep her up the stairs.

But gradually her pounding heart slowed and she was able to respond more normally, "I do not mind working so late because I am happy here and Sir Edward is good to us."

"I too would be good to you, Alyssa Dunne."

Loud voices coming out of the hall shattered the strained silence that fell between them. When one of the men hailed Sinclair, Alyssa expelled a long breath of relief.

That night, late as it was by the time she crawled into bed, Alyssa couldn't get the Chief out of her mind. Even to think of him filled her with a feverish excitement that set her blood racing and turned her flesh hot and dry. He was different from other men. When he was close to her he had the power to make the very air crackle and her nerves threaten to snap. At such times she tasted danger, yet a thrilling kind of danger. He was fire and she a helpless moth, unable to bring herself to fly away.

She knew the ways of men, but could not be sure about Sinclair. His wicked brown eyes were so often, when they looked at her, full of mischief. They seemed to say, "'Tis only harmless sport and you must not take it seriously," even as his kiss said something quite different.

Before she went to sleep, Alyssa decided to be on guard should they meet again before he returned to Edinburgh.

Sinclair rode back to Castle Augusta with his uncle and cousin and a small group of his men. He rode in silence, mulling over the outcome of the evening. As usual, he had found it impossible to get a definite answer out of Huntly as to his intentions when the Queen came north. Though they had long been friends and he personally liked the bluff, hearty

Gordon and had no great fondness for James Stewart, Sinclair was not ready to throw in his clan with Huntly for a cause that he knew was doomed to fail.

The situation brewing in Edinburgh was much more serious than Huntly realized. James Stewart had long cast a covetous eye to the north and had made no secret of the fact that he felt that certain Highland chieftains, particularly Gordon, had far too much power. He resented Gordon's arrogance, his outspokenness, and above all, his manner of doing exactly what he pleased, regardless of the dictates from the capital. Gordon, he grumbled, was a bad example for the other nobles and was likely to communicate to them grandiose ideas, such as that they too should conduct themselves as they saw fit, and worship as they desired. How long, Stewart had once asked the Queen in Blake's presence, could they tolerate this thorn in their flesh?

George Gordon was not afraid of Stewart or, indeed, anyone in Edinburgh. To his way of thinking, he was The Gordon, and invincible. Further, he had a mighty ambition, to restore the old religion, and had imagined, when the Queen returned to Scotland, that she would be in complete agreement. A man of action rather than contemplation, Huntly could not appreciate Mary Stuart's awkward position. For her people to accept her, she must play down her religion. Scotland was now a Protestant country, and to try to change that would bring about her demise. So she had tried to steer a middle course, hoping to keep everyone happy. That no one was happy was a source of confusion to the nineteen-year-old monarch.

His cousin Jason rode up beside Sinclair and broke the long silence. "Do you think Gordon will make trouble during the Queen's progress? Forsooth, I could not get a clear picture of his intent."

Blake laughed grimly. Gordon was not called the Fox of Strathbogie for nothing. He had a habit of talking in riddles, as well as changing his plans at the last minute, so that even those closest to him were frequently left in doubt as to his intentions until he was ready to act. Sinclair shrugged. "I warned him that Stewart is waiting for an excuse to cut him down, and that this is not the moment to flaunt his will. I also warned him that he might get less support than he imagines if it comes down to a confrontation. Now the rest is up to him."

"Stewart might think you are secretly in league with Gordon."

Blake snorted. "Stewart may think what he likes. The day he questions my loyalty, Her Grace will have one less half-brother."

"And well he knows it, cousin," said Jason with relish. A year younger than Blake, Jason Sinclair had been raised with him and also had received his education at the Marquis d'Este's estate in France. D'Este had been a venerable old soldier and statesman, second cousin to Diane de Poitiers, the favorite mistress of Henry II of France. Blake and Jason had enjoyed a wonderful boyhood together, more like brothers than cousins. Not quite so tall, and of a slighter frame, Jason too had the Sinclair dark eyes and hair and his share of the family magnetism. Though they were close in age, there had been little rivalry between them. Blake had always so clearly taken the lead and, out of long habit, Jason still looked up to him.

Now their uncle, Harry Sinclair, reined in his horse beside them. Big and bluff, he spoke his mind, as was his habit. "Huntly has a trick or two up his sleeve. If Jamie Stewart expects him to lay down his arms and let them walk all over him, then he is not the man I think he is."

Blake's jaw tightened. "For all his talk of peace, Stewart expects him to do nothing of the kind. He's spoiling for a fight, and, lofty sentiments aside, knows there's an excellent chance that Gordon will give him one."

"Ah, the poor Queen!" sighed Jason. "Little does she understand her brother's true nature, that while he talks of peace he incites strife behind her back—and manages to make Gordon look the bogey."

And there, thought Blake, lies the crux of the problem. Not only did Mary fail to grasp the character of her brother, but that of her Scottish nobles as a whole. Having spent many years in France himself, Sinclair knew there was a world of difference between the French aristocracy and the Scottish. Though many of the former were no less depraved, they concealed it under a veneer of exquisite courtly ritual, refinement and culture. In Scotland, with some exceptions, the majority of the nobles were less learned and more primitive, some of them wild, tractless, and arrogant enough to put their own interests well ahead of the crown's. Their boldness, even with herself, startled Mary. She had been shocked and profoundly disturbed when, the week after she arrived in Scotland, Lord Lindsay tried to break up the Mass in her own private chapel at Holyrood.

Such was the brazenness of some of her nobles, men like Morton, Lindsay and Ruthven, and though she tried to conceal it, Blake sensed that they secretly frightened her. He knew also that it helped strengthen James Stewart's hold on his sister. *He* could control such men; he was the buffer between them and the Queen.

Sinclair's mind returned to Huntly, in his own way every bit as wily as Jamie Stewart. As a show of good faith, Huntly had ordered his son John to return to Edinburgh with Sinclair the following day, there to use his considerable charm to set royal fears at rest.

They were to leave after the morning meal.

The party rode downhill, following a track along the bands of the loch, the black surface silvered with moonlight. Scanning the territory moodily, Blake's eye touched on the abbey. Into his mind flashed a pair of crystal-green eyes, and the memory of soft, yielding lips under his. He recalled the feel of masses of tumbled red/gold hair slipping through his fingers and the pleasant sensation of her warm breasts pressed against his chest. He smiled slightly when he thought of her quaint dignity, her pertness, the other unusual qualities he sensed in the girl, and thought with regret that it might have been most pleasant to stay on in the Highlands for another week or two. He also wondered, with a lessening of amusement, if Alyssa Dunne had a suitor.

5

On Sunday afternoon the Weir brothers paid Alyssa a visit. Both embraced her and seemed much relieved to find her not only in good health, but very bright and happy.

As they carried their picnic—leftover food from the political dinner—to a hill behind the castle, Alyssa assured them enthusiastically that she liked working at Gower better than at Mistress Lindsay's. "Here I don't have to contend with Myrtle."

Davie, the older of the brothers and just about to celebrate his twenty-seventh birthday, gave her a penetrating sidelong glance. Indeed she seemed contented. She appeared to have blossomed in some way since moving to the other side of Loch Ness. Her eyes twinkled and her cheeks were rosy and her willowy frame had filled out, undoubtedly due to comfortable lodgings and three good meals a day.

Robin Weir was saying, "I kenned the day would come when that auld tink o' a grandmother would de ye ill. She's unnatural, I tell ye. Why, even a miserable cur takes better care o' its young than Isa took o' you, lass."

It was the moment for Alyssa to make her startling announcement. "Mayhap because Isa wasn't my true kin at all."

Pulling the brothers down beside her in a sunlit bower sheltered from the wind by a ring of larch and bramble, Alyssa told them everything that had happened from the day she spurned Sanny Taws, or almost everything. Her subsequent encounters with Blake Sinclair she kept to herself. The brothers were shocked, indignant and angry. Robin especially displayed amazement to discover she was a bastard. "And she had no idea who your real parents were?" he queried, selecting the plumpest chicken leg from the picnic basket.

Alyssa shook her head. "Nay." She sighed. "Mayhap some genteel family in the area, or a shiftless couple pretending to be so to get her to take me in."

Davie Weir frowned and looked away, his eyes roaming the countryside as if admiring the scenery. The air was sweet and clean, scented with honeysuckle and thyme, and the lonely cry of a whaup on the wing drifted back from the crest of the mountains. Wild, rugged, hauntingly beautiful countryside lay all about them, territory that had come to the Grants and Sinclairs directly from the crown. The rivers and lochs teemed with fish—salmon, pike and eel—and roebuck and stag roamed the glens.

But Davie was blind to the landscape about them. His eye was turned inward, reaching back through time. He was of medium height and rather stocky, with powerful shoulders and large, work-roughened hands. He had a broad, serious face, shy blue eyes and a thatch of unruly brown hair. He had come a long way from the time he had been a frightened ten-year-old boy arriving in Lochmore in the dead of night, solely responsible for his little brother.

Because of the war with the English, Castle Augusta had been short-handed and Davie had been taken on as a stable boy. Now he was the head groom under the stable steward. He thought of the village of Lochmore as his home, the people as his friends, and the Earl of Belrose as his master. Castle Augusta had been kind to him, rewarding him for his hard work and loyalty, but Davie Weir never forgot his reason for being there.

Quiet and sensible, he had kept his wits about him and his ears open, for the servants in the great households knew everything, and now and then gossip trickled back from Cumbray Castle. All of it was bad. Lady Magdalen, through guile, cunning and violence, had once more managed to establish herself as Countess of Kilgarin through marriage to her former husband's brother.

Davie was glad that miles of desolate countryside, mountains and moorland, separated them from Cumbray. His mother's pouch of evil money had been used up long ago, a coin slipped under Isa Dunne's door from time to time, as if deposited there by the mysterious masked rider, who in fact had been his uncle. Davie had never told the truth of things to Robin, who had been much too young at the time they left Cumbray to remember much about it, least of all the reason for their flight. Robin, five years his junior, was impulsive and flighty and there was no saying how he would have taken the news.

Davie had been terrified when Alyssa disappeared from Lochmore, wondering if in some way Lady Magdalen had tracked her down. He had been vastly relieved to discover she was safely installed at Gower Castle, though shocked and angry at Isa Dunne's treachery. Luck had been with the lass when she had been rescued by none other than the Chief himself, and his cousin Edward Grant. Why did he still feel uneasy?

Alyssa, noticing his preoccupation and solemn face, teased, "Cat got your tongue, Davie? Why so sober on such a glorious summer day?"

Before he could reply, Robin scolded, "Aye, Davie, for the love o' God, cheer up! I swear ye'd cast a pall ower heaven itself, for a' that ye can see Alyssa is doin' famously."

Davie ignored his brother. His eyes were on the girl, and a winsome sight she was, he was thinking, with the warm breeze making her long hair billow up around her head like a flame. He blurted out his thoughts: "Alyssa, what happened to ye just goes to show how badly ye need protection, the strong arm o' a husband. I think the time has come for ye to be wed."

Both Alyssa and Robin stopped eating abruptly. Robin choked on a mouthful of beef and coughed until he was red in the face. By nature the younger Weir was easygoing and merry, the delight of all the unattached wenches in Lochmore. There was a resemblance between the brothers, but very slight. Robin, with his mop of chestnut curls and shining hazel eyes, was leaner, quicker, and impetuous where the older Weir was serious and conscientious. It had not been an easy task for Davie to act the part of mother and father to the lad, who'd been in and out of minor mischief all his life. Davie had never told Robin about his mother's blood money, aware that the younger man's most cherished dream was to get his hands on a little coin, buy himself a good horse, and set off to earn his fame and fortune in Edinburgh. Robin was a randy lad, and over the past two years his former jealousy of Alyssa had changed to a lusty interest. But still Davie knew that Robin was in no hurry to put a ring through his nose.

Well, Davie mused, Robin needn't have worried. Davie had other plans for Alyssa, and prayed she would agree with them. Watching his brother wipe his streaming eyes, he said, his eyes resting tenderly on the girl, "Aye, henny, ye must have a strong man to stand up for ye." At the same time he was thinking that he was not good enough for Alyssa, even though he loved her dearly and would devote his life to making her happy. True, they would be far from rich, but his hard work had paid off and now he had a neat little cot of his own, and two mules, and earned enough to keep their stomachs satisfied and their feet well shod.

So nervous and excited was he that it took several moments for him to notice Alyssa's expression. The rosy color had vanished from her cheeks and her eyes were fixed on his as a rabbit might stare at a weasel. "Robin," she breathed.

Davie was taken aback. He was crushed. Robin! Why, the idea that Alyssa might choose Robin over him had never crossed his mind. Robin was . . . unsuitable. She would never be able to depend on him, even though it was high time the lad settled down and faced up to responsibility.

Davie swallowed, his beautiful plans lying in waste about him. The younger pair were closer in age, he reflected unhappily. Robin was a comely man and far more exciting to women. He owed Alyssa so much, because of his mother's crime, and if it was his brother she wanted, well . . . so be it.

"Hold on a wee!" the younger Weir burst out nervously, looking from his brother's determined face to Alyssa's pale one. "I—I think we could be rushing things a bit." His nimble mind groped for a good reason to delay an event that went against the grain of his happy-go-lucky way of life. Alyssa, he said gravely, was just recovering from a hideous experience and should have time to recover completely before being asked to make an important decision. For the moment she was perfectly safe at

Gower Castle. They could discuss this again, he hurried on at his most convincing, when she had fully recovered in body and mind.

Davie gave him a baleful glance, not taken in by this show of consideration, but Alyssa blurted out, her eyes awash with relief, "Aye, we can think of it later. I . . . I still feel too upset to think of the future at all."

The Weir brothers had a violent quarrel on the ride back to Lochmore. Robin announced angrily that he was not ready to take a wife, and Davie pointed out that he couldn't be feckless forever, that he was tired of constantly having to bale him out of trouble and make excuses for his failure to shape up and start behaving like a real man. It was time, he went on firmly, to establish his own home and stand on his own two feet, shiftless though they were, and set aside his daft dreams of adventure and glory. "Lucky you are that she would have ye!" Davie said bitterly. "And I'll break your foolish neck if ye ever let her down."

They would wait a few weeks, he went on determinedly, and approach Alyssa again, and this time Robin had better show some enthusiasm. Privately he was soothing himself by reflecting that after they were wed he would be close by to keep an eye on them, and see that Robin treated her right.

Alyssa was deeply disturbed when she returned to Gower. Marry Robin? Oh, dear God, how could she? She had never thought of the Weirs as other than friends. Yet . . . she supposed Davie was right. A girl in her position must marry and establish her own family. What else was open to her? And it wasn't necessary that she love Robin. Love, as she well knew, took a back seat to other, more important considerations, and it was only in tales, such as the kind Allan sometimes related, that romance was the basis for a man and woman to unite.

How she loved listening to such stories after the day's work was done, with Allan and the other girls clustered comfortably around the kitchen fire while the housekeeper was prevailed upon—usually by Polly—to entertain them with a love story. "Tell us the one aboot the Lord o' Cannondale and the miller's daughter, or the tale aboot the laird and the wee lass from Fife." After a little coaxing, Allan would always begin,

"Now mind ye, this is a true story. Think what ye will, but the nobility sometimes *does* wed out of rank."

Alyssa had been highly skeptical, even while enjoying the idea of simple girls being swept up in romance with men far above their station, and through the magical power of great love ending up as their brides. It was so exciting! So stirring. But . . . so unlikely.

"Don't be so sure," said the housekeeper when Alyssa voiced her doubts. "The wee lass from Fife in my story is now Lady Kennedy, and the other the Earl of Cannondale's countess."

Often Alyssa thought about those fortunate girls, wondering what they were like and how they had managed to attract the eye, and even more important, the lasting devotion, of such high-born men. Love, Allan assured her, sometimes transcended all barriers.

Well, Alyssa thought in disgruntlement when she returned from seeing the Weirs off, she certainly did not love Robin. Until lately, he had been jealous of the attention Davie paid her. There had been a time when he slyly pinched and pushed her behind his brother's back, and made it plain that she was a nuisance. Now, though his pinches had changed to furtive caresses, Robin was not of a mind to wed. As for herself, she supposed she must resign herself to marriage in the near future since there was nothing else for a girl to do, and an aging spinster quickly found herself to be in a dreary position—but she could not bear the thought of being wed to Robin!

Alyssa forced it out of her mind, refusing to let it dampen her happiness at working at Gower Castle, where already she had good friends, a tiny clean room of her own, and all the good food she cared to eat. Best of all, she had a wonderful master.

For a moment, as she stood mulling things over in front of her window, Blake Sinclair leaped back into her mind. Her face grew hot and flushed when she thought of the way he had kissed her and held her body so close to his. That kiss . . . it had melted her very bones. It had aroused the desire in her for more, hinting as it did that it was only the beginning of countless mysterious delights he could bring to her.

Sinclair spelled danger. She was not herself at all when he was near. He was too commanding, too persuasive, somehow making her do things and behave in a manner completely unlike herself. He sapped her will, made her weak, left her ready to follow wherever he might lead. Sinclair seemed to enjoy kissing her, but then a virile man such as he was might enjoying kissing any pretty girl—and just as quickly forget her.

And there lay the danger. As a bastard herself, cast off to the likes of Isa Dunne, she had no intention of bringing another such hapless babe into the world. *Her* future children would stand proud behind their father's name. No one would jeer at them or point a condemning finger. In Allan's romantic stories, true as she vowed them to be, all turned out well for the poor girl and her high-born lover, but in truth how often did that happen? One could not forget all the fatherless children fostered out across the countryside. Did they not attest to the rarity of such unions enduring?

Alyssa thought of this often in the following days. The romantic stories and harsh reality clashed in her mind. At such times she seemed to see, in her mind's eye, a mocking smile and a deep voice murmuring persuasively, "I too would be good to you, Alyssa Dunne."

6

The Earl of Belrose had been in Edinburgh less than a week when a messenger arrived at Clairmont to tell him that John Gordon had been arrested. He had wounded one of the Queen's men in a fight and was now imprisoned in Edinburgh Castle.

Blake groaned and struck his fist against the wall. So much for young Gordon's mission to charm the Queen and set her fears to rest! Worse, at that very moment, Sinclair learned, one of John's men was riding hard for Aberdeen to apprise the Earl of Huntly of his son's plight. Blake dreaded to think what would come of it.

When he arrived at Holyrood, the Queen had anticipated his visit. The audience chamber, as usual, was filled with white roses, Mary Stuart's favorite flower. She sat among them, no less a flower herself, her skin almost as white and her amber eyes flashing with anger. "What now, Sinclair?" she greeted him, her voice prettily accented, yet foreign to the Scottish ear. "Is this how the Gordons would show me their good will—by striking down one of my household?"

"They say, Your Grace, that it was a private quarrel, one that flared out of control because of strong drink," Sinclair replied calmly, "and had naught to do with political matters."

"Indeed?" The girl-queen studied him closely, then said, "And how did you find my cousin Huntly while you were in the Highlands?"

Blake eyed her sharply. The day after he had returned to Edinburgh he had had a meeting with Stewart and the Earl of Morton to report the situation in Aberdeen. And they in turn would have reported to Mary.

"From your own lips, my lord," she said. "I want your true feelings on this."

It was a tricky question. The intentions of a man as changeable as the Earl of Huntly was difficult to assess. But in essence Blake told the Queen much as he had told James Stewart, that the Gordons would never be first to draw their swords against the crown—and this he firmly believed—and would fight only if provoked.

The Queen's face immediately brightened. "Then we have nothing to worry about, since we too want peace with the Gordons, nor would we have reason to provoke them in any way. Are they not my kin? 'Tis natural I would crave good relations."

And what of Stewart? Blake wondered. Did he too crave good relations? Aloud, he asked, "And John?"

Mary's face softened and for a moment she seemed lost in thought. She was remembering the gay, handsome knight and how he amused her while at court. Aye, and oft moved her to tears when he sang the old ballads and love songs in his rich baritone voice. That he also flirted with her outrageously had both excited and exasperated her—but never made her angry. Why should it, when all men, young and old, looked at her with admiration and yearning in their eyes? John had even been suggested as a possible husband for her by the Catholic faction—something that caused her brother and other ministers to howl in protest. But even more importantly, Queen Elizabeth, her dear cousin, was adamantly opposed to a Catholic union, pointing out acidly that Sir John Gordon met none of the requirements.

Indeed, thought Mary ruefully, who did?

But her vivacious nature reasserted itself because she could never be grumpy for long. Laughing softly, she reached for Sinclair's hand and confessed, "In truth, you know how John pleases me." And lest Sinclair be jealous: "Almost as much as you do, my lord."

The flirtatious gleam was back in her eyes as they moved over the darkly handsome face beside her. "Ah, 'tis so difficult to harden my heart against him, or think of him languishing in the castle. But I think," she went on with a wicked grin, "that I may leave him there for a week or two until that hot Gordon blood cools. Then, when he is properly repentant for injuring one of my own household, I may release him."

Blake felt vastly relieved. A possible confrontation with the Gordons, once John's father got wind of his son being in prison, was averted. The moment he left Holyrood, Sinclair intended to send Huntly a message.

But the Queen refused to let him take his leave of her just yet. All during their conversation a musician had been strumming a lute in the window embrasure, for Mary must always have music about her. Still holding Blake's hand, she would have him tarry a little while and give her his opinion of some pieces the musician had composed. As they listened, smiling at each other, her foot tapped in time to the music. At any second Blake expected her to leap up and dance.

Such a girl to be Queen of Scotland! he thought with a touch of pity. Lovely she was, mercurial and passionate, quick to laugh and just as quick to flare into sudden eruptions of anger, though it quickly passed. How difficult it must be to curb that vibrant blood surging through her veins, Sinclair found himself thinking, but curb it she must, as best she could, with the watchful eyes of the world upon her, ever ready to point a critical finger. Mary had never given them cause. In spite of her warm, flirtatious ways, her virtue had never been questioned. Under her gaiety there was a serious streak in her nature. She took her religion seriously. And she had a horror of the depravity that lurked under the glitter at court. From infancy she had been Queen of Scotland, and at a tender age Queen of France. Mary, he knew, was well aware of her position, and the responsibility that went with it, and would never do anything to tarnish her crown.

Now, when their gaze locked, Sinclair saw a yearning in her eyes. He knew it would never be transferred into action. Political considerations would govern her choice of a second husband. Once, long ago in France, he had made her a promise that one day his sword would do her honor, but deep inside—even were it possible—he had no wish to become consort to a Queen and live his life in her shadow.

The Chief left Holyrood thinking that a crisis had been

averted, but a few days later received word that Sir John Gordon had escaped from Edinburgh Castle, tired of waiting for the Queen to set him free. The escaped fugitive had vanished, but no one had any doubt as to his destination or that his father, Huntly, would provide sanctuary.

This changed everything. James Stewart had the excuse he needed.

Alyssa was troubled. More than two weeks had gone by and she had not seen Sinclair again. In an offhand way, growing weary of waiting and wondering, she queried Allan, "Has our Chief returned to Edinburgh, then?"

When the housekeeper nodded, Alyssa felt a sharp disappointment. More than that, she was alarmed. So distracted had she been by Sinclair's kiss the last time they met that she had completely forgotten to tell him about the conversation she had overheard in the hall the night of the political meeting. Of course, Sir John Gordon could have been joking when he talked about kidnapping the Queen, but Alyssa couldn't forget the smug look that had passed between John and his father. On reflection, it struck her as being ominous.

It had been her duty to report it to the Chief. And she would have, too, she thought irritably, if he hadn't amused himself by dallying with her in the corridor, driving everything else from her head, then leaving the area without a backward glance. It will serve him right, she fumed, if Gordon *does* kidnap Her Majesty during her Highland sojourn. Since they were friends, any mischief the Gordons became embroiled in would be bound to besmirch Sinclair as well.

Her self-righteous indignation evaporated abruptly. She had a vivid mental picture of the Chief being captured, taken to Edinburgh and charged with treason—and hanged.

And now it was too late to warn him. Or was it? Sunday afternoon was her day off. Tad, the stable lad, was smitten with her. He might be persuaded to lend her a mule so that she could ride to Castle Augusta and leave her information with one of Sinclair's kinsmen, who he in turn could carry a message to the Chief in Edinburgh.

On the Sunday everything went as planned. Tad turned

his back and allowed her to take one of the mules. Aware that she could be dismissed from Gower Castle by her actions, Alyssa nevertheless had to go. On the outskirts of Lochmore she came upon a hunting party and saw by their badges that they were from the castle. "I have an important message for the Chief!" Alyssa hailed them boldly.

Much amused, young Robert Sinclair rode up to her, his eyes brightening with interest as they moved over her face and hair. "You may speak, lass," he said, at the same time wondering what this village girl could possibly have to say that would be of importance to his cousin.

The tale she related did not surprise him unduly. John Gordon was forever making grandiose announcements calculated to shock them. Just the same, they had just received word at the castle that Johnny had escaped from justice, and that the Queen and her ministers were enraged by his defiance.

"The Chief shall hear of this," Robert assured her, and not in such a hurry to let her go. "Pray return with us to Augusta for a refreshing cup of ale. By the flush on your cheeks, you must have ridden hard and must be thirsty."

Alyssa shook her head. She thanked him, saying she couldn't tarry. As she turned to go, Sinclair called after her, asking her name.

"Mistress Dunne," she called back, and turned her mount in the direction of the valley.

She was relieved. There was still time to warn Sinclair before the Queen began her progress. Now she had done her duty and could put the whole business out of her mind, or try to.

Mary Stuart began her northern progress on August eleventh. The ostensible reason was to give her the opportunity to get to know her more distant subjects. With this in mind she stopped to speak at universities, village squares and market places along the way. The common people were enchanted by their vivacious young Queen, and the Queen was filled with a lively interest about her Highland subjects and their rugged mode of living. Mary's fondness for outdoor sports and recreation now came into play. Halting at various castles en route, the party enjoyed hawking, hunting, balls and masks, the Queen dancing until the wee hours of the morning and then rising at dawn to hunt stag as they came down to the rivers to drink.

If only grave matters of state could be forgotten, she grumbled to her brother, Lord James, who was almost twelve years her senior. Sober, shrewd and self-seeking, he reminded her of her position and that she must ever concern herself with such things, even on holiday. Also, he added pointedly, a monarch must be strong and not seem to rule with a woman's faint heart, since the eyes of the world were watching her. Look what had happened with John Gordon! "See the mischief that leniency breeds? You were oversoft with him. Now he defies you, putting himself above your royal command."

Mary frowned and turned away to admire the scenery they were riding through, reminding herself that James knew these people much better than she did. Her eyes swept the high moorland where the heather was in full bloom, shimmering in undulating waves of pink and mauve to the foothills of the mountains, deep purple giants tipped with snow, rose-tinted in the afterglow of the sunset.

In the morning the royal train began encountering small hunting parties moving silently through the glens. James assured his sister that they were Huntly's scouts, not surprising since they were now inside Gordon territory, but Stewart frightened the Queen by imbuing them with sinister motive. The morose Earl of Morton increased her alarm by advising eerily, "Your Grace, I strongly urge ye to bypass Strathbogie, for once inside Huntly's stronghold there's no saying what might happen. Evil rumors have come to our ears. I wouldn't want to be responsible for your safety were ye to go there."

Mary hesitated. Huntly was her cousin. He had been raised in the royal nursery with her father. To pass by his castle would be an unforgivable slight. Yet . . . if he were planning some mischief once he had them in his power . . .

"Oh, how I wish that Sinclair was here!" the distracted young woman cried. "He knows Gordon much better than we do."

Morton and Stewart exchanged a smug look. At that

moment the Sinclairs were on the border, ostensibly keeping the English at bay, for with the Queen and her most important ministers occupied far from the capital, they might well seize the opportunity to attack, as James had explained to his sister. Now he said somewhat impatiently, "Even King Solomon himself could not anticipate George Gordon, and while Sinclair has, er . . . remarkable qualities, he's no Solomon. We cannot afford to take the risk."

Mary was torn two ways. Typically, her uneasiness turned to hurt and fury that she should be placed in such an awkward position—and by her kin! James was right, she thought, these arrogant Gordons needed to be put in their place, taught a stern lesson as to whom they owed their allegiance to. So the royal train journeyed on to Darnaway Castle, and once there, egged on by her brother and his cohorts, Mary had James Stewart officially proclaimed Earl of Moray, a rich earldom long in the hands of the Gordons.

In London Cecil brought the news to Queen Elizabeth, saying, "I fear the Queen of Scots has just made a fatal mistake. By alienating the most powerful Catholic noble in Scotland, and potentially her greatest ally, she has unwittingly cleared the path for the Protestants, headed by Stewart, to dominate the government."

Elizabeth, then approaching thirty, was astounded at such a tactical blunder, one such as she would never have been guilty of. She remarked dryly to her secretary, "My good cousin has much to learn, methinks, and may suffer much in the learning."

"Aye, Your Grace." He added slyly, "Now more than ever she must pray that her brother, the new Earl of Moray, will not fail her."

Elizabeth chuckled, her heavy lids drooping, but she made no response.

Huntly, when he got wind of it, was not so reticent about expressing his opinion, and the remarks he made were not fit to be committed to a history book. At length he cried passionately, "Mary must be gotten loose of that pack of swine who seek to bring her low, and who but me has the might to accomplish it?"

At that juncture George Gordon felt he had no option but to stand and fight.

Far off on the border, Sinclair and his men were engaged in a few skirmishes with the English, but none as serious as Morton had led him to expect. As he patrolled the wasteland that separated the two countries, his squire Wyatt and cousin Jason at his side, his troops following behind, Blake's brooding mood lingered. The Queen had at first requested that he join the progress, but Morton and Stewart had persuaded her that Sinclair's strong arm was needed to keep the savages ever active on the border at bay. Blake had to concede that there was some wisdom in this. It was always possible that the wily English would choose this time to launch a full-fledged attack.

Nothing of the kind had happened. The intelligence supposedly brought back to Morton by his spies had as yet not been transformed into action. Gradually Sinclair began to suspect that he had been sent south on a wild goose chase, to ensure that he was well away from the Highlands by the time the royal entourage reached Aberdeen, therefore not around to support his ally, Gordon, should trouble develop.

The following morning he sent a scout north to find out what was happening. The message sent by Alyssa had not reached him.

7

The ever capricious Earl of Huntly fought his last battle on the field of Corrichie on a misty autumn day in October 1562, surrounded by his sons and over a thousand Gordons. He faced the royalists with his usual reckless confidence and bravado, certain that before the day was out many of the Queen's soldiers would defect to his side.

The reverse proved to be the case, just as Sinclair had predicted. Huntly completely underestimated the almost mystical hold that Mary Stuart was beginning to exert over her people and, indeed, over all who knew her. Tall, stately, and in her tender youth charmingly vulnerable, only the most hardhearted of clansmen could bring himself to take arms against her.

Just before the battle, Sir John Gordon challenged the new Earl of Moray to a duel, a common occurrence at the time. John's confidence was no match for Stewart's prudence. The latter declined.

Huntly heaved his massive bulk off his horse and prostrated himself on the crest of the hill to pray. The Gordon piper blasted a ferocious tune and the soldiers made their final preparations. When their Chief remounted, breathless and red in the face, every eye was upon him. A huge fist shot into the air and the men heard the signal they were waiting for. "A Gordon forever! God light the way."

Then putting spurs to his horse, he led his followers in a sweeping rush down the hillside to clash with the royalists racing across the moor. They met in a thunderous shock of steel and bloodcurdling war cries, the tranquility that Mary Stuart had so admired in the Highlands, shattered in her name.

The Gordons fought with their usual ferocity, but even the wind was against them, blowing the smoke from the royal arquebusiers back into their faces until all about them swirled in a pall of grey.

Gradually they were driven back up the hill and over the top, then down into a bog below where, as they floundered in a seething morass of muck, the royal troops mercilessly cut them down. Huntly, Sir John and a younger son were taken alive, spared to face the ultimate ignominy—forced to fall on their knees before the new Earl of Moray.

But in the end Huntly cheated his enemy out of his moment of triumph. As Stewart hurried forward to meet the prisoners, Huntly pressed a fist to his heart and sprawled dead on the ground.

John Gordon's end was neither as quick or merciful. Though Mary tearfully pleaded for his life, her advisers were adamant that he must die. "To show mercy to a traitor would be insanity," said Lord Lindsay.

Then Moray, her brother, made a chilling announcement. To still the wagging tongues, the whispers that hinted that the Queen might have secretly acquiesced in John's plot to kidnap her, she must attend his execution. "Since all know how much you favored him, we must take care to put vile speculation at rest."

When the appointed day came, handsome Sir John stepped up to the block with something of his old swagger. He spoke passionately to the white-faced Queen. "Madam, if I must die for love of you, then I take comfort that you are here in person to see the proof of it."

The first blow of the ax sheared off the top of his head but did not kill him. Mary screamed and broke into hysterical weeping as the blundering executioner hacked at the bloodied figure, cursing loudly that he refused to die. Finally the Queen fainted, and John Gordon's irrepressible spirit departed his mutilated corpse.

Moray and Morton exchanged a look of supreme satisfaction.

Young George Gordon, the heir, had also been condemned to death though he had been away and had not taken part in the rebellion, but in her first show of defiance against her brother, Mary cried, "Nay, he will be allowed to live! 'Tis enough that his father and brothers are dead and everything they had taken away. I command that clemency be shown to him, and my will be obeyed."

Edward Grant returned from Aberdeen a sad man, his voice breaking as he told his household of what had taken place. He added, "I quail to think how Sinclair will react when he hears of it, but in many ways it's fortunate he was not involved."

Blake returned to Inverness-shire in a black rage. His anger covered an aching heart that grieved to think that his boyhood friend was no more. Though his uncles and cousins echoed Sir Edward's advice that it was just as well he was not involved, Blake was determined to have it out with Moray and the Queen. When he stormed into Her Majesty's audience chamber at Aberdeen Castle, he found that the Queen was not alone. Ranged about her were a group of lords including Morton, more notable for soldiering than the social graces, and his close associate Lindsay, a brutish type with an explosive temper who, together with Morton, had been responsible for some of the worst atrocities against the Catholic clergy. William Maitland, the Queen's secretary, sat at the other side of the room, as if too fastidious to share space with the pair. Silent and watchful, Blake could almost hear the well-oiled wheels spinning inside the intelligent head. A capable man, and more learned and cultured than most, it was Maitland's chief task at that time to treat with Elizabeth of England and try to convince her to name Mary Stuart as her heir.

With a scathing eye Sinclair swept the others. Lord Seton, refined and intellectual and at that moment very ill at ease, and the sickly Thomas MacKellar, attired like the most showy court dandy in contrast to the sober garb of the other lords.

Beside the Queen sat Moray, the title he wished to be addressed by from now on. When Sinclair's hand dropped to his sword, Moray said hastily, craftily, "You look out of patience with us, my lord, but I cannot believe you have come here to berate us for punishing traitors."

"I came to see justice done!"

"And it *has* been done. Need I list Huntly's crimes against our party—"

"I would know them," Blake broke in coldly, still standing in the center of the room, a tall, proud figure with restrained violence in every line of his body. As Moray explained that Huntly and his son John had harassed the royal train even before it reached their territory, the others were remembering Sinclair's skill with the sword and the fact that Augusta Castle, with all its men and power, was not very far away. They were thinking apprehensively of his allies in the area, the rumblings rolling through the glens like muted thunder against their treatment of the Gordons. Most of all, they were reminded that Edinburgh was a long way away.

Moray, perhaps even more conscious of their vulnerability than the others, was at his persuasive best. Crime after crime he heaped upon the Gordon name. Their flagrant disregard of the Queen's commands. Their arrogance, placing themselves above the crown. The fact that Alexander Gordon, one of Huntly's sons, had treasonably refused to admit Her Majesty to Inverness Castle, even though it was a royal stronghold. On and on he hurried, beads of sweat bursting forth on his brow, and Blake could not refute any of the charges since he had been absent at the time.

Sinclair wheeled on Morton. "It seems, sir, that your border spies have turned into fanciful old women, conjuring up trouble where it doesn't exist," he sneered. "A band of callow youths could have kept the English in abeyance, so I must wonder why I was sent south at just this time."

Lindsay lumbered to his feet, his fleshy face quivering with rage. "By Christ's blood, must we defend our actions against one who was known to be allied with Gordon!"

Blake's sword was in his hand. "You doubt my loyalty, Lindsay?" he roared, murder in his eyes as he advanced on the heavy-set nobleman. The others reared back in their chairs. Mary screamed, then burst into tears. It was Maitland who alone had the courage to act to avert the crisis, springing to his feet and rushing across the room to catch Sinclair's sword arm, crying, "My lord, my lord! Not in the Queen's presence.

Lindsay spoke hastily. No one in this room questions your loyalty, least of all Her Majesty."

"'Tis so," sobbed Mary. She ran to place herself between Sinclair and Lindsay, who had turned the color of old cheese, his face streaming sweat. The Queen's amber eyes pleaded as she looked up into the dark face, tight with fury. "Ah, Sinclair, don't do this thing! Must treachery breed more evil? My lord Lindsay did not mean—"

"Lindsay must speak for himself, madam," he interrupted curtly.

Moray thought quickly. He had achieved what he came for and had no wish to provoke more strife among the Highland clans, many of whom were now openly speaking against him. And Sinclair was no Huntly. He was of a new breed of Highland lord, well-educated, logical and far-sighted. Greatly respected both here and in Edinburgh, Moray knew it would be most imprudent to make an outright enemy of such a man. With Huntly gone, Sinclair had it in his power to incite the clans to fresh and even more dangerous hostilities or, if he so desired, to calm them down. Most important of all, the Queen put great stock in his abilities and liked him personally. Moray could not forget that Mary had countermanded his order to have young George Gordon put to death, standing up to him for the first time. What, he asked himself worriedly, might she do if he were to alienate Sinclair?

With this in mind, Moray nodded brusquely to Lord Lindsay, leaving him in no doubt as to what he wished him to do. Lindsay, visibly relieved, stammered, "Faith, Sinclair, but . . . in truth we are a' a bit overwrought and vexed unto death at what has happened." He steeled himself to look the Chief in the eye; eyes now black as pitch and singularly soulless. "Maitland is right, I spoke hastily and without thought and meant no offense, my lord."

There was a moment of high tension as everyone in the room waited to see how Sinclair would react. Blake's mind had turned back to Huntly, the wily Fox of Strathbogie, who might or might not have been guilty of the crimes Moray had outlined. Yet, knowing the man as he had, he had to face the fact that the reckless Gordon had been quite capable of committing each and every one of them if he saw fit. John had been much like his father, both of them volatile and rash, the types to act first and think later. Blake considered this against the good of his own clan. At this moment the future of the Sinclairs was hanging in the balance, depending on the outcome of this meeting. He, as their Chief, had to set personal feelings aside and now make the wise decision . . . or turn them into outlaws.

At the scrape of Sinclair's sword being returned to its scabbard—loud in the quiet room—everyone present breathed a vast sigh of relief. Blake nodded curtly to Lindsay, bowed to the Queen and the room at large and, turning on his heel, strode from the chamber.

When he rejoined his men in the courtyard and mounted his horse he did not for a moment imagine that Morton or the hot-headed Lindsay would forget that he had made them look like cowards, and in such an illustrious gathering. If the day should come when Moray lost favor, or if events should ever turn against the Queen herself, Blake knew that both these men would be ready to pounce and, if they could, take a vicious revenge. Pah! he thought scornfully, let them dare try! The day he would quail before such as Morton or Lindsay would be the day he turned over Augusta to Jason and entered a monastery.

Yet he started for home in a somber mood. His boyhood friend John Gordon was no more. The Queen, by allowing Moray to so thoroughly decimate the Gordons, had made a disastrous mistake, both at home and abroad. She had now placed the security of her throne entirely in Protestant hands. She might well have alienated her powerful Catholic friends abroad, both in France and Spain. How Queen Elizabeth in England must be rubbing her hands in glee, he brooded.

Soon after Sinclair's return to Augusta, his young cousin Robert gave him the message from Alyssa, which events had now rendered worthless; a message he had never received while far away on the border. But it brought the girl vividly back to mind, distracting him from the morbid mood that had settled about his shoulders. On a whim Blake decided to see her.

* * *

On Sunday afternoon, which she usually had off, Alyssa stood at her window gazing out at the dripping countryside. The latter part of October had been dreary, almost as if the very elements were in mourning for the fallen Gordons. Daily the skies had wept and the wind howled through the glens, and all the trails to and from the castle had been rendered all but impassable. Twice Sir Edward's betrothed had had to postpone her visit. Alyssa had not seen much of the Weirs either, but though she missed them she was almost relieved, dreading the subject of her marriage to Robin being raised afresh.

She was desperately restless, weary of remaining indoors, her healthy young body craving fresh air and exercise, anything to lift the depression that had settled over her like a shroud since she had heard of the Gordons' death. Sinclair, it was said, had not been involved. When she heard this piece of news, Alyssa had almost wept with relief. Yet her feelings about the Chief were ambivalent. Why, she pondered, did he persist in lingering in her mind? Had he not demonstrated long since that he was quite capable of taking care of himself, regardless of the adversity—and had long since forgotten her?

Impatient with herself, Alyssa threw a shawl over her head and ran down the back stairs and out into the rear courtyard by the stables. She had hardly poked her nose outside for a week and stood for a moment breathing deeply of the fresh, moistly pungent air that smelled richly of peat moss, herbs from the nearby garden, and horseflesh wafting from the stables. It was not really cold, and for the moment the rain had stopped. Moisture hung in the air like minute beads of crystal, and as far as the eye could see everything was a rich and vibrant green.

The castle was looking its best. Everything was now in readiness for the MacKellars' visit. Lady Magdalen, Alyssa had heard, would chaperone her daughter while she was at Gower, and the servants muttered darkly that they would just as soon suffer a visit from "auld Nick" himself.

As Alyssa wandered off in the direction of the gardens, she heard the clatter of riders coming into the other end of the yard. Glancing back, she saw a small group of men all wearing cloaks to protect them from the uncertain weather. Visitors were common and she paid little attention, intent on enjoying a walk before the late afternoon faded into twilight, early at that time of year.

The newly constructed summer house on the banks of the stream attracted her like a magnet. Each time she viewed the little pavilion it charmed her. Craftsmen had been brought over from Italy to do the work and make of it a miniature dream house. The granite stones had been polished to a glassy sheen and clearly reflected her image as she stood before the structure admiringly. The roof was a graceful pink-tiled dome in perfect scale to the size of the building; the doll-size lattice windows twinkled with glass imported from Florence, and the delicately carved oak door sported cherubs and flowers entwined with garlands. Even the door knocker delighted Alyssa. It was in the shape of a swan, its long, curved neck the handle, all of a highly polished brass.

That handle seemed to beckon her. It seemed to whisper, "Lift me and walk inside."

Suddenly Alyssa couldn't resist, though none of the servants had thought of venturing into this entrancing place that Sir Edward had fashioned for the pleasure of his beloved. Thinking that a quick and satisfying look around could hurt no one, Alyssa furtively glanced about, lifted the flowing neck of the swan and stepped gingerly inside.

Drifting from one small room to another, she was overcome with a pang of envy for Serena, who would soon be Sir Edward's bride. How he must love her! Not only a vast amount of money had gone into the refurbishing of Gower for her pleasure, but a great deal of thought too. What woman could fail to be entranced with the final result, Alyssa thought with a sigh, taking in the beautiful, pastel-tinted tapestries, the dainty, finely crafted furniture, the velvet and satin pillows scattered about the canopied bed.

Standing in the idyllic bedchamber where, if the mood struck them, Sir Edward and Serena might spend a night or two, Alyssa felt suddenly disgruntled. Would *she* ever be lucky enough to have a man build such a monument to signify his love for *her*?

She laughed softly, bitterly, well aware that the type of man she would some day marry would be hard-pressed to provide *any* kind of roof over her head. She was foolish indeed to dream, aye, in spite of Allan's fanciful tales of noblemen galloping out of the mist to sweep simple girls off their feet. In truth, she mused with a sigh, just to have someone love her would be grand. Her parents hadn't, nor had Isa Dunne. Davie Weir obviously cared for her deeply, but could never be more to her than a friend, and there was that in her that yearned desperately for so much more; for arms to hold her close, warm lips to kiss away her hurts and fears, for a strong shoulder to shield her from the harshness of the world. To be close, really close, to another human being was surely worth all the gold in the world and a dozen dream-houses, such as the one she was in. Hard work and ambition were fine, yet in the end empty if one had no one to share the little failures and triumphs one encountered in life.

Alyssa slumped down on the edge of the satin bedcover and watched the room fill with twilight. There was an urge in her to get ahead, to rise out of her lowly station . . . but how? Other than being a servant, there was nothing open to a girl of her class except marriage, but marriage to the likes of Robin Weir, whom she not only couldn't love but couldn't quite respect, was not the answer.

Her thoughts skittered away as Alyssa imagined she heard the crunch of a footfall on the gravel path outside the door. She turned her head to the window and listened, her heart jumping with alarm in her chest. She had trespassed, invading the privacy of a place meant for Serena's eyes alone—and before the young noblewoman had even seen it yet.

Again she heard the footsteps and sat very still, hoping the person would think the house empty and go away. The interior was almost dark now, and her eyes, huge and frightened, caught and reflected the last of the light. Helplessly Alyssa heard the latch being lifted, then stealthy footsteps moving through the rooms, to pause at last in the door of the bedchamber.

A tall, dark figure stood there shrouded in a cloak.

8

For several suffocating moments they stared at each other in silence, then his deep-timbred voice echoed in the empty rooms. "What are you doing here?"

He sounded almost grim to the girl who watched him nervously from her perch on the edge of the bed. His face too, made harsh in the semidarkness, displayed none of the lighthearted mischief she had grown to expect from him. As Alyssa frantically searched her mind to think up a good excuse for being in the summer house, a fresh spatter of rain pelted the window at her back, yet within the small building all was eerily silent, shot through with a sudden tension that caused her nerves to scream.

Sinclair was beside her, gazing down into her upturned face. He saw that her eyes were luminous in the shadows, her soft lips slightly parted, like crushed rose petals. Above the square neck of her gown her breasts rose and fell with her quickening breath, and a change came over him that brought a smoldering hunger leaping into his dark eyes.

Alyssa was hardly aware of him pulling her up into his arms. Her head reeled alarmingly until she felt her mouth crushed fiercely under a burning kiss, one that made her knees buckle so that she sagged against the hardness of his body. The contact inflamed both of them. She felt his long fingers moving through her hair, his free hand gliding down her back to her hips to weld her tight against him.

Then she was in a trancelike state where nothing mattered except the exciting new sensations he was bringing her, his tongue teasing the sweet interior of her mouth, his fingers at the bodice of her gown, then closing over one quivering breast, the throbbing heat of his loins now clearly demanding, stirring an answering need deep within herself.

He overwhelmed her. Skilled and experienced as he was, Alyssa was no match for him. Until that moment she had not dreamed that a man's lips and fingers could arouse such ecstasy inside her and make her starved flesh crave more, or that his whispered endearments could so easily still the warning voice clamoring to be heard inside her swirling head.

Sinclair swept all other considerations away, making them seem meaningless. Suddenly Alyssa found herself naked on the bed and him beside her, the devouring magic of his lips claiming a nipple, his fingers and tongue slowly, maddeningly seeking and finding the secret, sensitive places to her body and stroking them into a blaze of tingling fire. She ceased to think at all, giving herself wholly up to sensation, her trance shattered only at the moment when Blake bore down against her and she felt, with a shock, his manhood penetrate her body.

"Jesu!" was all she could gasp before his lips again claimed hers in a savage kiss, silencing her as his hard strength rose and plunged above her, again and again until, oddly, the first pain ebbed and another, altogether different feeling took its place. It came in a rush, rapture such as Alyssa had never known existed. She strained against him, her lips parting, each nerve in her body aching for it to last . . . and last.

Blake drew her very close, her head against his chest. Pushing aside her tumbled mass of red/gold hair, he put his lips to her ear and murmured, "How fair you are, Alyssa, and sweet and heady as rare wine." His hand, warm and deeply tanned against her own white skin, stroked her hip lightly as he added, "And I must drink more of it; much more."

Alyssa felt too dazed to respond. He had swept her along so swiftly. Now, as Blake rubbed his cheek against hers and drew away slightly to smile down into her eyes, she felt hot shame burn like fire in her cheeks. He was the Chief of the clan Sinclair and she but a girl of the village below his castle. He had taken her as his due, and she . . . she had given in so easily. She was not yet sure how it could have happened, only that she had never intended such a thing and already regretted it bitterly.

Blake gazed into her face, then down at her body stretched out rather stiffly now beside his own, and marveled at her beauty. Delighting in such a marvelous discovery, he announced, "I shall buy you a gown such as the one you described at Gower—and a dozen more."

Alyssa burst into tears. The impact of what she had had to give in exchange for his offer struck her forcefully. She felt sick with resentment and shame.

With a choked cry she tried to rise, but Sinclair's arm came down about her shoulders and barred escape. "What ails you, darling?" The satisfied smile had left his face.

"I—I must go. They will wonder—"

His arm tightened. "Nay, bide awhile." He glanced with a nod to the window, which had darkened to a smoky grey. "Harken to how it rains. Were we to leave here now we'd be soaked to the skin. No one will miss you. Here"—still holding her firmly with one arm, he reached with the other toward the small carved chest beside the bed—"I shall light the candle—"

"Nay!" It was a cry of horror. Better the near-darkness than for them to see each other, naked and guilty, in the bright golden flame of candlelight. He, of course, did not feel in the least guilty, Alyssa thought angrily. Why should he? He was used to taking what he wanted and discarding it when he lost interest. With that in mind she pushed with both hands against his chest, lying, "They will expect me to help serve the evening meal."

He let her go, lying back casually as he watched her scramble into her clothes, her cheeks stinging hot as she felt him studying her. But as she made to hurry away without a word, Sinclair sprang to his feet and caught her by the shoulder, spinning her around. Laughing huskily, he bent his head and kissed her lips and, ignoring her resistance, said, "We must meet again soon, my sweet. I will let you know when and where."

And I, of course, must await your pleasure, she bristled, staring at him out of eyes glinting with defiance. "I cannot, sir."

"You can!" His own eyes burned down into hers, seeking to exert his will. "We both wish it, regardless of how you try to deny it, Alyssa, so I will contact you again very soon."

Not trusting herself to speak, and reminding herself that he was still the Chief and therefore had every right to make demands of her, Alyssa threw off his arm and almost ran from the summer house.

That night she beat clenched fists into her pillow and soaked the bedcovers with remorseful tears, yet what good was weeping? What had been done couldn't be undone. She had treasured her virtue, the gift she would one day bring to her husband, and Sinclair . . . Sinclair . . .

He fascinated her! Proud, arrogant and supremely confident as he was, sure she would fall in with his wishes, Alyssa knew she should hate him. But she didn't hate him. What she felt for him was a complex mixture of emotions that included an overwhelming sexual attraction, vast uncertainty and something like fear. Fear because her very personality seemed to change whenever he was near, so that she behaved in a way entirely foreign to her nature. Mayhap, she mused, lying dry-eyed now as she gazed up at the ceiling, mayhap he had cast some sort of spell over her, such as Isa Dunne used to mutter about with her friend Molly Sampson.

One thing was certain, she would not risk being alone with him again.

Alyssa awoke from a restless sleep to brilliant sunshine. After weeks of rain the weather, as it was wont to do in turbulent Scotland, took a turn for the better. Sir Edward announced that if the fine weather continued, as predicted, the MacKellars would visit that coming weekend. Immediately the household plunged into a flurry of activity. Under the directions of Temple and Allan the servants were set to scrubbing, sweeping and polishing with a vengeance. The banquet-sized board in the hall was scraped and sanded, ridding it of the slightest vestige of past meals, then it was rubbed with Allan's secret polish to a high, mirrorlike gloss. The new tapestries were hung and the wainscotting wiped with a cloth dipped in linseed oil, until all that remained was for the hall to be strewn with fresh rushes mixed with scented herbs and flowers.

Cooking and baking went on for the entire week under the inflamed little eyes of Barkley, the cook. Huge and red-faced, he rode the kitchen staff mercilessly, lashing out with a raw, meaty fist when a scullion was too slow to do his bidding or botched up a sauce or pudding. The aromas wafting through the castle were delicious. Thick salmon steaks straight from the loch were marinated in a concoction of wine, herbs and cream to mouth-watering succulence. Partridge, grouse and venison were gently roasted to a turn, the faces and arms of the spit-boys with them. Barkley himself prepared his famous specialties, gingered peacock and swan slowly simmered in clotted cream and seasoned with his unique combination of spices.

From the great ovens came hot mutton pies, strawberry and custard pasties, marzipan comfits and various types of bread, from white manchet, deemed most in keeping with the elevated tastes of the high-born, to barley, wheaten and rye.

When a young servitor nervously dropped a case of Sir Edward's best claret, Barkley turned purple in the face and roared, "Ye'll get a good sousing for that, ye clumsy wee scunner!" And grabbing a meat mallet, he advanced on the unfortunate lad, who promptly took refuge under the long kitchen work table. He whimpered, pointing to a smirking page, the son of a minor nobleman taken into Gower for his education. "Yon sleekit whelp tripped me. Ye ken how he craves tae see me thrashed?"

The smirk vanished from the page's face when Barkley fumed, "Then ye'll both catch it, for n'ere have a' suffered such a feckless pair o' bumblin' curs in a' my years at the castle!"

And so the preparations for the MacKellars' visit continued.

The party from Cumbray Castle arrived shortly after three o'clock on Friday afternoon. Alyssa and Polly watched their retinue ride into the courtyard from an upstairs window. Alyssa's eyes were immediately drawn to the Lady Serena, who sat her roan with the proud hauteur of a princess, her peacock-blue velvet riding habit spread out gracefully over her hips and legs, a matching hat perched jauntily on her waist-long black hair. Though too high up to be able to see her features clearly, Alyssa glimpsed a pale, heart-shaped face and dark eyes that stood out strikingly against her white skin.

Beside Serena, just as tall and proud, rode her lady mother, Magdalen MacKellar, and even from where Alyssa watched, her resemblance to her daughter was startling. The older woman's blue-black hair was done up in twin coils under a forest-green riding hat that matched her habit exactly.

"Oh, are they not grand!" breathed Alyssa admiringly.

But Polly snorted, "And who wouldna be grand, clad in a' that finery? If we had a' the wealth o' Cumbray at our disposal we'd look just as fine." Then with a sideways glance at Alyssa's excited face, she amended honestly, "And you, lass, would be twice as comely as the Lady Serena."

Alyssa gave her a quick hug. "Allan said I might not wait on them just yet, since I'm still inexperienced—"

"And lucky ye are that it is so!" Polly made a face. "This pair likes nothing better than to keep ye hopping like a hen on a hot griddle."

Within hours of the MacKellars' arrival Alyssa understood what Polly meant and could see why they were so unpopular with the staff. Both women were extremely demanding and brusque, impatient and thankless with the servants who did their best to please them. Serena would have a large tub of lilac-scented water sent up to her bedchamber, then when it arrived the temperature of the water was not to her liking and the perfume oversweet. A fresh tub had to be carted up the narrow stairs, this time scented with essence-of-roses. Magdalen craved sweetmeats and a scribe to dispatch a letter back to Cumbray. She ordered up a lute player to soothe her jangled nerves after her long journey across the mountains, then sneered at his music, muttering disparaging remarks about him to her daughter which the poor fellow couldn't help but overhear.

Grumbling under their breaths, the beleaguered servants trudged up and down the stairs and suffered verbal abuse until everything was exactly to the MacKellars' liking. One hapless soul who spilled a cup of wine received a swift cuff on the ear and the promise of a beating should he bungle again.

By this time Alyssa was glad to stay out of their way. When she heard that Blake Sinclair was to be a guest at the banquet to be given for their guests the following night— Saturday—she made up her mind that somehow she would avoid being present. Like the other girls, she would be expected to serve their guests, and she couldn't bear the thought of encountering those smoldering dark eyes again and all the tumult they stirred up inside her.

Late the following afternoon she pretended to be sick from a stomach upset. Barkley snapped, "Aye, and it's no wonder, what wi' a' the rich stuff ye've been sampling this past week."

Allan allowed her to go to her room after dosing her with a heaping tablespoonful of treacle mixed with baking soda. Gulping the sticky mess, Alyssa gagged, her stomach heaving in protest. But it was worth it, she reasoned, to escape the knowing eyes of Sinclair.

In the evening, torches were lit around the courtyard and an air of excitement gripped Gower Castle and all within it. There had been few great social affairs since Sir Edward's first wife had died in childbirth, and now even the servants were making the most of it. With her nose to the window, Alyssa watched the lords and ladies arrive from her upstairs bedchamber. She glimpsed gorgeous attire made of satin, velvet and brocade in jewel-like shades of blue, scarlet and gold. Distantly she heard the musicians tune their instruments, and delicious scents from the coming feast wafted up from below. She could imagine Polly, Nancy and the other girls skipping about in their freshly starched gowns, their cheeks glowing pink from the heat of the kitchen, their eyes enormous as they carried stuff to the board in the hall and, close up, could inspect their illustrious guests.

What, Alyssa mused, would the Lady Serena be wearing? And Magdalen MacKellar herself? Gradually Alyssa began to resent being shut away from all the excitement—and all because of Blake Sinclair. At the same time she stayed by the window anxious for a glimpse of his arrival, until she heard footsteps hurrying to her door and Polly burst in to see how she felt. By the time she left and Alyssa flew back to the window, it was crowded down below in the courtyard. Just the same, Sinclair's height would have made him stand out and she saw he wasn't among them. Certain she had missed him while Polly was in the room, and curious to see how he might look dressed grandly for such an affair—not to mention who he might have brought with him!—Alyssa quietly left her room and slipped along to the minstrels' gallery that ran around three sides of the vaulted area above the hall.

The scene below blazed in the light of hundreds of candles. The hard fire from precious gems flashed from throats, ears and wrists. A veritable garden of colors moved about below, like blooms swayed gently in the breeze, radiant hues that took Alyssa's breath away. And the fabrics! The delicate mauve watered silk, the tissue-thin rose-tinted gauze, the sea-green satin shot through with threads of gold! Hiding behind the big oaken kist near the balcony rail, Alyssa drank it in with yearning eyes, the most dazzling assembly she had ever seen gathered together in her life, even more spectacular than her most romantic dreams.

Serena was stunning in cream-colored Florentine lace over crimson taffeta, her ebony hair dressed becomingly in one of the latest court fashions and offset by an exquisite little cap made of cobweb-fine lace. Even from where she was, Alyssa noted how her black eyes glittered like large jet beads and her full lips glowed red as dew-laden cherries.

Lady Magdalen too, she saw, looked very elegant in a gown of peach-colored silk that emphasized her exotic coloring. Had she been less gaunt she would still have been a strikingly attractive woman, thought Alyssa, though there was something about the older woman's appearance that put one off and made Alyssa think of the dark hole she had almost sunk into on the morning Ogden had tossed her into the loch.

There was no sign of Blake Sinclair among the other richly garbed gentlemen, but about fifteen minutes after she had concealed herself by the kist, he strode into the hall with his cousin Jason, and after that Alyssa had eyes for no one else. Her heart swelled, then constricted painfully at the sight of him, so darkly handsome and standing head and shoulders above all the rest. How wondrous he looked in his wine-brocade doublet! she thought with a sigh, the froth of lace at his neck emphasizing his dark skin and the gleam of his raven-black hair. Unconsciously Alyssa moved closer to the rail, her eyes following him about. She saw him kiss Serena's hand and bow low to Lady

Magdalen, his strong white teeth flashing in one of his melting smiles.

The company sat down to an elaborate feast with many interludes between the courses during which entertainment was provided for the enjoyment of the guests. Dancing followed, and Alyssa watched with a fierce pang of jealousy as the ladies flirted and preened before the appreciative eyes of Sinclair, easily the most attractive man in the room. A savage twist wrung her heart when he danced with the Lady Serena who, for all that she was betrothed to Sir Edward, struck Alyssa as showing unseemly interest in the Chief. Nor did he seem immune to the charms of the woman he held rather too close in his arms. She recalled Polly remarking that Lady Magdalen had had her sights on Sinclair for her daughter's husband, but of course it was out of the question considering Serena's birth. Good! thought Alyssa in a rare fit of malice as she watched the young woman smile beguilingly up into the eyes of her dancing partner; at least in *that* way she's no better than me!

But Alyssa could not bear to torture herself further. With a deep sigh she turned away and grumpily returned to her room to throw herself across the bed and grind her forehead into the bedcover, thankful that she'd pretended to be sick. At least she had spared herself the ignominy of having to serve them, bowing and scraping before them, jumping to obey the MacKellars' many commands while Lord Sinclair watched her humble herself.

Of course she *was* a servant. It was her place to be humble, to obey, and it was ridiculous to envy Serena and all the other fine ladies in the hall when she would never be one of them. She supposed she would eventually have to marry Robin Weir, like it or not. At least he was a vast improvement over the likes of Sanny Taws!

Disgruntled, and seething with an intense restlessness and unnamed yearning, Alyssa removed her plain blue cambric gown—while trying not to think of the gorgeous ones she had seen in the hall. She washed her face and hands, dutifully brushed out her hair, and climbed into bed. Faintly she could still hear the revelry from below, the music and the occasional peal of laughter louder than the rest, and tried to hold back the sense of dissatisfaction that took hold of her. Irritably she blamed it on Allan's romantic stories, wherein anything seemed possible, even for lowly girls such as herself. Would that she had never listened to such tales! They had awakened a wild and foolish hope inside her, that she too might be as lucky, that she would win the love of a man who would adore and respect her enough to fight the convention of the times and carry her over the gaping chasm into a richer, more interesting life.

After a long time she fell asleep, only to be swallowed up in another nightmare where she found herself on the parapet of the abbey about to be thrown like a piece of worthless refuse into Loch Ness, fit only to be a "bride" to the monsters. In this dream, as in countless others, Alyssa felt herself being lifted by the monks, swung to and fro, then tossed over the side while the black water rushed up to meet her.

She screamed. As she jolted bolt upright in bed, sweat drenching her thin white bedgown, she heard pounding on her chamber door. Then hard arms closed about her, and in the darkness a deep voice spoke close to her ear. "Wake up, Alyssa! T'was only an evil dream. You have nothing to fear . . . nothing to fear . . ."

In the pitch darkness her senses gradually registered the warmth of his hand at her back, the special woodsy scent that she identified with him alone, the special timbre of his voice. She wanted to believe him, that she had nothing to fear; wanted to desperately. Yet how, with such a man, could she be sure?

9

Sinclair lit the candle by her bed, and in the soft golden glow his strong face seemed to be cast in bronze. Deep brown eyes smiled soothingly into hers as he took both her hands—icy cold—and carried them to his lips. In his rich doublet embroidered with gold thread, the buttons fashioned from diamonds and pearls, it struck Alyssa as incongruous that he should be sitting here beside her, rather than down below making merry with all the high-born ladies who vied with each other for his company. Mayhap she was still dreaming, she mused.

Suddenly aware of the delicacy of her position, seated in bed and with her damp gown clinging in an unseemly manner to her skin, she drew back and tried to free her hands to pull up the covers. A hot flush crawled up her flesh, and embarrassment vied with mounting anger that he should have barged into her room. "Why . . . why are you here, my lord?" she finally stammered, wishing that he would move back so that she could breathe more easily. "I—'tis not meet that you should come here."

"I heard from one of the serving girls that you were ill."

She stared at him in surprise, amazed that he would have made inquiries about her; even more amazed that he would have left the ball to look into the state of her health. Or . . . was it not far more likely that he had seized the opportunity to come to her room, to be alone with her as he had been in the summer house?

Watching her closely, her beautiful face naked of guile or subterfuge, Sinclair easily read what was going through her mind. Shrewdly he moved back a little and released her hands, allowing her to draw up the covers about her. "Tell me of this dream?" he asked softly.

Alyssa looked away, her long lashes casting a curved shadow onto the smooth skin of her cheek, the tumbled mass of her hair falling about her in burnished waves, her firm breasts peaking the thin white sheet. She was more beautiful, more alluring in her simplicity, to the man watching her so intently than any of the sumptuously clad women below in the hall.

Haltingly, Alyssa told him about the dream.

"And it returns often to haunt you?"

"Aye," she nodded, "much too often."

"That part of your life is behind you. Now you must fill your life with pleasant things so that *they* will reflect in your dreams and drive out the other."

She gave him a quick sidelong glance, wondering if he was laughing at her, but found him to be quite serious. "Mayhap in time I'll forget."

"We must *make* you forget!"

Alyssa fixed her eyes on a spot just over his left shoulder.

"And you were sick today?"

"I'm much improved."

"Now that the ball will soon be over."

Her eyes jumped back to his face, startled and guilty.

He nodded, smiling mischievously. "You wished to avoid me, is that not so? You despise both of us because of what happened a few days ago and think that by hiding away it will be forgotten?"

Alyssa's cheeks burned. It was exactly what she had been thinking.

"Well," he continued in the same quiet tone, "I for one have no wish to forget. I think of that pleasant afternoon often, and the lovely girl who made it so pleasant—"

"Please go away!" she choked.

But he continued as if she hadn't interrupted, his face filling her vision, his eyes burning into hers, making it impossible to turn away. "I treasure that day, Alyssa, and the gift you made to me, the sweet gift of yourself."

She closed her eyes and raised both hands to her ears, but he took them away and leaned forward to kiss her lightly, tenderly, on the forehead. Her senses reeled at his closeness, at the remembered touch of his mouth against her flesh, and suddenly, unexpectedly, her body betrayed her, straining against him instead of moving away. His hands came up to her shoulders as his mouth moved slowly, hungrily, over her face—her eyelids, cheeks, the curve of her chin—lingering for a moment at the pulse beating excitedly in the hollow of her throat.

Then, restraining the hunger that flared inside him, Sinclair forced himself to move back. "We cannot run from this, Alyssa," he vowed huskily. "We cannot! But . . . I will not force you." He smiled slightly, thinking that it wouldn't be force at all. "I think your life has been hard until recently and I have it in my power to wipe those harsh memories away, but only if you desire it as I do."

He rose and stood for a moment gazing down at her. "Now you must ponder whether or not you would like to belong to Sinclair who can drive all the bad dreams away and bring happy ones in their place."

He moved back into the shadows near the door as he added in a low, persuasive tone, "We both know what that answer must be."

The questions bubbling on her lips evaporated with the soft closing of the door. The room was empty, and only the footsteps fading away down the corridor testified to the fact that he had been there at all.

Alyssa sagged back against the pillow and closed her eyes. It took several minutes for the thudding of her heart to slow to normal; before she could think clearly at all. It was amazing that Sinclair would have torn himself away from the many enticements in the hall just to see her, and that he had not tried to take advantage of the moments they had been alone together. He had spoken to her gravely, seriously, almost with . . . respect, and somehow managed to turn those shameful moments in the summer house into something precious and beautiful. "I treasure that day, Alyssa . . ."

Nay, nay, she caught herself quickly, it was *still* shameful. And what did it cost Sinclair to whisper pretty words, especially when those words might quickly lead to a gratification of his desires, which at the moment meant her? He wanted her. At least he had not lied. And he would not force her, but leave her to reach her own decision.

He had come to the banquet alone. For all the women linked to his name over the years, Sinclair was still a single man.

As Alyssa's distracted mind carried her in one direction after another, as memory of him turned her warm, then cold, some of the housekeeper's romantic tales stole back into her mind. What if—

Hastily she stopped the thought before it could take root, calling forth the hard, inescapable fact that a great chasm lay between her world and his, a chasm that could never be bridged except in fairy tales.

Still, Alyssa fell asleep thinking of him, remembering his touch, the warm, tender light in his eyes when he spoke to her—and most of all the fact that from all the beautiful women at Gower Castle he had singled her out when he discovered her missing.

She liked and admired him. Nay . . . it was more than that, she admitted finally with a sigh. The truth was that she was afraid of the attraction between them; deeply afraid.

Much cleaning up had to be done the day after the ball, and no one was allowed any time off. Alyssa worked willingly, the chatter of the other servants leaving her less time to brood. Unfortunately, Sinclair and Grant were the chief topics of conversation, particularly Sinclair's exciting position at court. The pompous Temple never missed a chance to air his views on the political situation, and Allan, naturally, must have her say, unwilling to give the steward—her competitor at Gower— the slightest edge. As they argued back and forth, Alyssa could not avoid listening. She learned much, including the fact that many of the Highland lords now looked to the Earl of Belrose for leadership, with Huntly cut down so suddenly. He had already demonstrated his power to unify some of the warring clans, the MacKellars and others, and only by unification could the Scottish Highlands expect to be a force to be reckoned with in Edinburgh, said Temple unctuously.

By the time evening came, Gower Castle was once more in order, everything shining and in its place.

At ten o'clock, since the MacKellars had announced their intention of retiring early that evening, the housekeeper sent Alyssa upstairs with a warming pan for the Lady Serena's chamber and Polly with one for Magdalen MacKellar's bedroom down the hall. Afterwards Alyssa was to rue the impulse that possessed her to tarry in Serena's room for so long—moments, as it turned out, that were to change her life.

10

Once the warming pan was in Serena's bed, Alyssa should have immediately left the room. Instead, she lingered to sniff the delicate scents wafting in the air—the perfumes, oils and lotions used in the young noblewoman's toilet. And since the kist was standing partially open, she could not resist running her work-reddened hands over the satins and velvets or to finger the incredibly fine laces, fragile as a spider's web.

Suddenly Alyssa heard footsteps and voices, and they were unmistakable. Serena and her mother were on their way to their chambers. Alyssa tensed, her eyes darting to the door, but it was too late now to leave without being seen. Quickly she crossed to the bed and, turning her back to the door, pretended to fuss with the warming pan.

The voices were very close now.

"Good eve to you, my lady Mother," said Serena. "I pray your slumber be serene."

"Thank ye, my angel." Lady Magdalen still frequently lapsed into the broad Scots when alone with her family and no impression need be made. "God grant ye good night." Her footsteps drifted off along the corridor to her own room farther down the hall.

Serena stepped into the room. Alyssa could feel the young woman staring at her but she didn't turn around, busying herself by moving the warming pan around the huge bed.

Serena's first glimpse of the chamber wench was a rear view, and the first thing to catch her interest was the red/gold hair spilling from the string where Alyssa had fastened it at the nape of her neck. Serena rarely wasted time by really looking at servants, but now her curiosity was piqued and her dark eyes raked Alyssa closely from head to toe. She saw a fairly tall girl with a slender, shapely figure, clad in a plain blue cambric gown with a dust cap covering most of her hair except for the long burnished tail that rippled down her back to her waist. That hair . . .

The young noblewoman snapped her fingers imperiously. "You, wench!"

Slowly Alyssa turned around and bobbed a curtsy. Before lowering her eyes, as was seemly when in the presense of the high-born, she surprised a look of astonishment on the other girl's face.

Indeed, Serena caught her breath. The wench's beauty was startling. Moreover, she looked familiar, bearing as she did a strong resemblance to her cousin Fiona MacKellar. Yet this lass was far comelier than her Aunt Lydia's oldest daughter. More than that, she was the fairest creature that Serena had ever seen.

Soundlessly she moved closer until no more than a few feet separated them. Alyssa, sensing the sudden tension in the room, held herself very still, puzzled as to why Serena should be paying her so much attention.

"Your name, wench?" the other spoke at last.

"I'm Alyssa Dunne, if it please your ladyship."

"You have lived long in these parts?"

"Aye, lady, all my life."

"Hummm . . ."

Serena walked around her slowly, examining her as if she were a beast up for auction at the county fair, then returned to face her once more. The intense silence became excruciating, and by now Alyssa's heart was thudding painfully in alarm. Could she guess, Alyssa wondered, that she had touched her clothes and the crystal bottles and jars set out on the washstand? Mayhap her ladyship imagined that she had stolen something!

At last Serena broke the awful silence. "Wait here. I must have a word with my lady mother."

She turned and swept from the room.

Alyssa had an impulse to bolt. She tasted danger all about

her—and all because she had been foolish enough to linger to admire the other girl's fine possessions, a crime in itself, she supposed.

She heard footsteps returning and the low murmur of voices, and a tremor went through her as she recalled all the gossip about the Countess of Kilgarin, none of it good.

Magdalen MacKellar preceded her daughter into the room, and up close she was forbidding. Once upon a time a great beauty, her face had grown lean and pinched with age, her high cheekbones more pronounced, lending her gaunt face a disquieting appearance. Wings of grey-streaked black hair rose in swirls from a wide, snowy forehead, and her aquiline nose seemed sharp and predatory. But it was her eyes, deep-set and pit-dark, that struck sudden fear into the heart of the girl who stood rigidly awaiting her fate with as much dignity and courage as she could muster.

At her first glimpse of Alyssa the older woman's mouth fell open in shock. A curious hoarse sound choked off in her throat, and unconsciously a hand rose to her mouth. But Magdalen recovered herself almost instantly, so swiftly that Alyssa wondered afterwards if she had imagined that first reaction of astonishment and dismay.

The countess was in an awkward position with both the serving wench and Serena staring at her curiously. Naturally, she had never told her daughter of that long-ago night at Cumbray. A parent must sometimes do harsh things that her child might find difficult to understand, let alone forgive. But thank God, she thought, that Serena had noticed the girl and brought her to her attention, for indeed she bore a startling— and ominous—resemblance to the MacKellars.

"Mother . . . ?" Serena prodded, alarmed by the look on the older woman's face.

Magdalen shook her head for her to be silent. She looked Alyssa up and down, totally immune to the girl's discomfort. "Your name is Alyssa Dunne?" And when she nodded: "How long have you worked at Gower Castle?"

Alyssa swallowed anxiously, her mind reeling, wondering what this line of questioning had to do with her touching

Serena's things. But she answered truthfully, "A—a few months, my lady."

"And before that?"

"I worked for Mistress Lindsay of Lochmore."

"Indeed . . ." Magdalen took stock of the girl. She noted her refined manner of speech, surely odd in a lowly serving wench. Her mind made rapid calculations. The lass appeared to be about seventeen or eighteen, and at the time she was born the MacKellars and Sinclairs had been bitter enemies. Nay, nay, she soothed herself, it could not be. Assuming that Caitlan Weir had disobeyed her orders, a possibility that had haunted her ever since, there was no chance that the babe would have been sent into the territory of their enemies, none bold enough to transport her there.

Just the same . . .

"Your father's name, girl?" she inquired briskly.

Now Alyssa was truly frightened. Further, she was confused. What did all this mean? Why were they questioning her thus? Could it matter to them who her father was or where she had come from, given their vastly different station in life. She didn't understand.

Magdalen stepped closer, her eyes narrowing. "Speak up, wench! I warn you, do not try my patience at this late hour."

"My sire was George Dunne," Alyssa replied automatically, though of course it wasn't so. "He . . . he died before I was born."

Serena tugged at her mother's sleeve, perplexed and eager to know what was going through the older woman's mind. She could feel something like fear emanating from the countess. Sensing her daughter's unease, Magdalen checked her fierce urge to investigate further. For the moment. Her thin shoulders relaxed and a faint smile touched her lips, one that never reached her eyes. "We wish ye no harm, lass," she told Alyssa. "'Tis just that ye remind me of a tiring woman who used to work . . . on one of our estates, and the likeness startled me for a moment. But now, on closer inspection, I see that I erred in fancying a connection. You may go."

Alyssa hardly slept that night. The chill she had sensed in

Serena's bedchamber lingered on. Why, she asked herself, were the noble MacKellars so interested in her background? What could she mean to the likes of them?

Instinctively she disliked them intensely. In spite of Sinclair's grand scheme to unite the clans, Alyssa almost wished that they were still enemies and that the MacKellars had never come to Gower Castle. She could not forget that soon Sir Edward would marry Serena and she would live here always. Undoubtedly, Lady Magdalen would visit her only daughter frequently, a thought that Alyssa found even more disturbing.

Temple had said only that day, "Sinclair has the right idea in trying to patch up old feuds. Only by banding together can the clans enforce their rights in Edinburgh. But from what I ken about our Chief, far-sighted as he is, he has a larger plan, to unite all of Scotland in a solid flank against the greater enemy—England."

For once Allan had agreed with him. "Och aye," she smiled proudly, "our Chief is a man o' grand ambitions and the drive and intelligence to see them through. Look how he won over the MacKellars! Now *there* was a feat many swore could never be done."

"A triumph!" Temple had nodded. "Only one o' many, and all for the greater good of Scotland. Neither Jamie Stewart nor any o' the other mincing court dandies in Edinburgh can take that away from him."

Alyssa lay brooding in the darkness of her room. She understood and applauded Sinclair's ambitions, and she tried to be far-sighted as he was said to be, and not allow herself to be bowed down with pettiness. She disliked these MacKellars, but since she knew how important they were to Sinclair's plan, she would keep her feelings to herself. By tomorrow, like as not, the haughty pair would have forgotten her very existence.

Serena had followed her mother back to her room bubbling over with questions. The countess forestalled her by sighing, "For a moment or two methought she had a look of a MacKellar bastard, but obviously I was wrong. Her father was George . . . George Dunne, no connection to us."

The dark-eyed young beauty studied her mother anxiously. "You seemed upset upon meeting the wench. 'Twas one moment when I thought you might swoon."

"Nay, nay," the other chuckled with a negligent wave of the hand, "'tis only that I'm wearied from the revelry last eve and, aside from that, the girl's beauty startled me."

"Aye . . ." Serena pouted. "I like not the thought of such a one being under this roof, so close to my beloved. I wonder if Edward might be bedding the wench. Mayhap she's his mistress!"

Magdalen soothed her, seizing the opportunity to make good use of her daughter's jealousy. Patting her hand, she promised, "We will feel him out in the morning and try to find out more about this wench. You are right, my pet, 'tis never wise to have anyone so fair about one's husband. Men"—she shrugged—"are ever weak in matters of the flesh, and this creature would be a powerful temptation."

From an early age Magdalen had held the male sex in low esteem. It was a man's world and a woman had to be ruthless to survive, and even more ruthless to prosper. At the tender age of eleven she had become orphaned and sent to live with an aunt and uncle. Tall and exotic even then and already budding, she had fallen victim to her uncle's lust. Lord Greer had been a man infamous for his lasciviousness and cruelty and quickly saw in his helpless niece a target on which to vent his baser instincts. His little mouse of a wife lived in terror of her husband and made no protest when he removed Magdalen to one of his more remote hunting lodges, and there he proceeded to subject the girl to all manner of depravity, beating her savagely when at first she resisted, thinking to break her spirit.

The reverse proved to be the case. With each thrashing, each new indignity thrust upon her, Magdalen hardened and a fierce hatred grew and festered inside her and with it the lust for revenge. She loathed her spineless aunt almost more than her uncle. One day, she vowed, both would suffer even more than she had, and at her hand.

She bided her time, learning to be cunning, manipulative, deceitful. She carefully cultivated the affections of the old crone who tended to her needs in the lodge. This hag, she had heard, was wont to dabble in the black arts. By showing an interest in this little "hobby," Magdalen in time snared the woman over to her side. Through her she procured certain plants that could be made into a posset that when mixed with wine was undetectable. When Lord Greer died suddenly of a violent stomach upset, Magdalen was taken back into the home of his lady, who expired in her sleep less than a year later after imbibing too heartily at table.

It was then that Magdalen discovered that the money left to her by her father had been squandered. Once more, at the age of fifteen, she was dependent on the charity of relatives, though not for long. Pouncing on the first opportunity that came her way, she set about charming an elderly knight, a friend of the family, and married him a week before her sixteenth birthday. The union to what she thought of as the "dribbling old fool" was short-lived. By seventeen she was a widow, some unnamed internal ailment having struck her husband down.

This time there was an important difference. Though not wealthy, the old man had left her with a stout and comfortable manor house and enough money to enjoy a few luxuries. The only drawback came from certain disgruntled members of his family who muttered darkly about the somewhat mysterious manner of his death. Magdalen had no intention of allowing them to upset her—or the next stage of her plan, to find a new husband who would elevate her to a position of prestige and power, where no one would be able to touch her.

That man was Lord Angus MacKellar, a far cry from her doddering, easily hoodwinked old knight, and with a large clan around him ever vigilant to guard his interests, including a cousin who had heard veiled rumors regarding the spate of sudden deaths in Magdalen's background. But Angus was completely smitten with the bewitching young beauty and at first paid these gossips no heed. When Magdalen gave him three sons one after another, he was ready to strike down anyone who spoke against her.

Gradually, as the years passed, disillusionment set in. Angus received a message, unsigned, that his wife was consorting with low-born young men, one of whom accused her of keeping him a prisoner in one of their lodges and there subjecting him to hideous abuse while the countess gratified her unholy lust at his expense. Her tiring woman was said to be in reality a tame witch, a woman wise in the ways of mixing evil potions and casting spells. Finally, and most damaging of all, his youngest son, Robert—so ran the letter—was really the result of a liaison between Magdalen and one of their grooms.

Angus took to examining Robert more closely. He watched his wife and had her followed when she went abroad, especially when on occasion she retired to one of their hunting lodges for a "rest." The ax fell when he caught her with a lusty young house carl at one of their remote manor houses in the far north of Scotland. This resulted in the birth of her daughter, Serena, whereupon Lord Angus divorced her and the MacKellar family breathed a sigh of relief—all except Thomas, who had long been intrigued by his mysterious former sister-in-law and, against the violent objections of the rest of the clan, married her after Angus's death.

The MacKellars, by and large, hated her, Magdalen brooded after Serena left her room. They despised Thomas for marrying her, calling him a weakling and a spineless puppet behind his back. Though they could prove nothing against her about the night Lady Alicia had given birth to her dead babe, there had been evil whispers that had taken some time to die down. Ever since, Magdalen had judiciously tried to live circumspectly and to deny them fuel for their fire, but she knew there were many in the family just waiting for her to make a mistake.

Had she come face to face with that mistake tonight? Had her past come back to taunt her? It struck her as being too improbable, yet she was in no position to be careless with a noose hanging over her head. Caitlan Weir had been given the task of disposing of the child, but had she? As far as Magdalen knew, all concerned with that distant night at Cumbray were dead except for Jock Semple, the youth she had deployed to guard the chamber door, and he had vanished in the direction of England soon afterwards, never to be heard of again.

Yet . . . Semple was another loose thread, she fretted, drumming her long nails on the window ledge. And assuming he were still alive, Semple could be a damning witness to the affair if he ever decided to return to Scotland.

Jock Semple, now thirty-five years old and a prosperous farmer outside the town of Carlisle, had no intention of returning to Scotland. By careful conditioning through the years he had almost managed to banish that night at Cumbray Castle from his mind. He had a thriving farm, a comfortable wife and two fine sons. Though Scottish, he had gradually become accepted and even respected in his adopted country and generally tried to avoid contact with travelers from north of the border whenever they passed through the area.

Semple, his strapping youthful frame grown heavier and somewhat flaccid with the passage of time, wanted no reminders of an event he now felt deeply ashamed of. When first married he lived in dread of his good wife ever finding out about his part in the crime, then of his sons learning the grim truth about their father. In the past he suffered from hideous nightmares. There had been a time when even the sound of a Scottish voice caused him to break out in a cold sweat.

Eventually he succeeded in pushing it all into the past. He meant to bury it there. Satan himself could not have prevailed upon him to return to the country of his birth regardless of the means used to lure him. If left to Jock Semple, Magdalen, Countess of Kilgarin, was perfectly safe.

The following morning at the breakfast board Magdalen skillfully manipulated the conversation around to Alyssa. She warmed Sir Edward's unsuspecting heart by praising his well-organized household, then added with a smile, "Your servants are so willing to please, particularly the bonny serving wench with the beautiful flaming hair. Where on earth did you find such a jewel?"

Edward beamed, waxing expansive under their approval, and launched into the story of how he and the Earl of Belrose had rescued Alyssa from the loch.

"You say her own granddam sold her to the knave, Ogden?" Magdalen lifted her brows in pretended horror. "God's feet, what kind of creature would sell her own flesh and blood?"

"One who has small regard for kinship, obviously," Grant replied grimly. "Not to mention the instincts of a beast."

"And the lass has no other relatives or friends in Lochmore?"

Grant hesitated, stroking his chin thoughtfully for a moment. He knew that Alyssa had no other kin, but it seemed to him that Allan had mentioned two brothers who came now and then to visit her, one of whom the housekeeper suspected of being her sweetheart.

"Ah, 'tis good she has someone," sighed Serena with relief, sure now that she had been mistaken in thinking the girl to be Edward's mistress. But her mother leaned forward inquiringly. "These fellows, the . . . the . . . ?"

Edward shrugged. "Their names, I fear, have slipped my mind, but when the weather is fine they usually visit the lass on Sundays."

Later, behind the closed door of her chamber, Magdalen and her daughter conferred. "It would still be best if a way was found to oust such a tempting wench from under Edward's nose," cautioned the countess when Serena allowed that she was no longer quite so worried. "A juicy plum," she went on, watching her daughter closely, "just asks to be tumbled from the tree."

Serena's quick jealousy flared. "I would that she could be gone from Gower Castle before we return to Cumbray!"

Her mother hid a smile. Squeezing the girl's hand, she purred, "You must trust me to handle it, precious. When the rest go off on the hunt I will pretend to be indisposed. Nay!" she hurried on when Serena opened her mouth, "you must not badger me with silly questions. Has your mother ever failed you in the past?"

Magdalen made her plans. It was imperative that she learn all she could about this Alyssa Dunne, and how better than through her friends? Edward had mentioned two brothers who came to visit her on Sundays. With the help of her squire, Bruno, she would intercept them when they left Gower and make some excuse to satisfy her driving curiosity. Only then could she rest at ease.

On Sunday morning Blake had a heated argument with his uncle Harry Sinclair when he returned from an all-night battle with the local outlaws, the MacNeith, a band who had plagued the territory for years. Riding into the courtyard of Augusta at dawn with six captives in tow, including MacNeith himself, Blake had good reason to expect applause rather than glowering disapproval from his uncle.

The moment they were alone the older man turned on him. "You dare to risk your life in fighting a pack of common brigands!" he fumed. "You should know that a Chief lacking an heir does not expose himself to needless danger. What will the Lady Elizabeth think when she learns of this folly? She must wonder about a man who endangers himself so recklessly on the eve of signing the marriage contract."

Sinclair shrugged and gazed into the blazing fire, his mind conjuring up a mental picture of Elizabeth Bancroft, fair as a lily and of a dreamy, idealistic disposition. Had it not been for the recent death of her mother, he and Elizabeth would have been officially betrothed by now. It would be a propitious union and greatly desired by both families, and while she stirred no great passion within him, a man in his position did not take a wife merely to gratify the clamoring of the flesh. It was accepted that that could come from quite another direction.

The direction of Gower Castle!

Sinclair knew well the cause of his recent restlessness, the pent-up energy that had driven him to seek release in hunting down the MacNeith. He had forced himself to hold back and give Alyssa time to think over his proposition, an arrangement commonplace for a man of his rank, and one that need not conflict in the least with his formal life. He would set Alyssa up as his mistress and take pleasure in indulging her with many costly gifts. And she would have many! The girl had had a hard life and he was in a position to make it up to her.

The lass had captivated him totally, so much so that it was

perhaps unseemly in a man about to be wed. She was different from others in a way he couldn't quite define. There was a cool pride about her, a dignity, and a quick intelligence that set her apart from other village wenches. Blake made up his mind to wait a day or so longer, then seek her out again, never doubting that she would agree to his plans for them.

11

On Sunday afternoon Robin Weir set out to visit Alyssa with the stern pep talk from his older brother still ringing in his ears. He was shiftless and unreliable, Davie told him bluntly, and the time had come to mend his ways. Alyssa was just the girl to help him accomplish that mammoth task. Thinking that giving the young couple more time alone together would stimulate their ardor, Davie waved his brother off with the warning, "Now dinna dither. Press her to settle on a date. The sooner ye're wed the less worry for a' of us."

Robin disagreed but thought it most unwise to gainsay him, especially as Davie had threatened to throw him out of the house to fend for himself unless he corrected his many deficiencies. Resentful as he was, the younger man was well aware of his own limitations. He needed his brother—at least until he managed to get his hands on a little coin, at which point he would be off to seek his fame and fortune in Edinburgh. A life of high adventure was much more to his taste than being tied down with a wife and children, regardless of how attractive that wife might be.

Once away from Lochmore Robin slackened his pace, reasoning that a man shouldn't be so quick to put a ring through his nose. He nudged his mule onto a path cutting through the Great Glen, a gigantic chasm in the earth's surface that ran in a straight line for more than sixty miles through bottomless lochs and deep glens, overlooked by snow-capped mountains. Brooding over his own predicament, he at length started uphill through the bracken and heather to the high, wild moorland. For a moment or two he paused on the rim of the glen to give his mount time to catch breath. Below lay the mysterious deep blue waters of Loch Ness, while over his shoulder, the haunting solitude of the moor stretched to the misty horizon. The air he breathed was filled with mingled scents of peat and gorse and the dry, earthy tang of the heather, and over all hung an awesome silence.

Robin followed the lip of the hillside for half a league before turning right in the direction of Gower Castle. Passing through a wooded gully, he came out of the trees to see a lone rider sitting motionless on the ridge directly ahead of him, the fellow's massive bulk outlined against the sky. Naturally outgoing and friendly, Weir raised a hand in greeting as he rode up the slope toward the stranger. "God give ye good day, sir," he greeted him pleasantly.

The other looked him over well. He was dressed in a well-worn leather jerkin, a round, wide-brimmed hat pulled well down over his face. He nodded in response to Robin's greeting and waited for him to draw abreast. Robin's eyes flicked over him—then suddenly he looked again, this time more closely. The man was no less awesome than the rugged scenery, though considerably less beauteous. Huge and bull-like, his broad face was exceedingly ugly, made more so by a jagged scar slashing from his right cheekbone to the corner of his mouth. A pair of small, curiously dull eyes examined Weir impassively while Robin automatically noted that he was well armed. An unexpected tingle of uneasiness stole over him.

The stranger spoke at last, the words rumbling up from the great chest that swelled the front of his jerkin. "Sir, from whence come you?" he queried.

The younger man was a little taken aback by the bluntness of the question, one that struck him as being presumptuous. Without committing himself too much he gestured vaguely to the south.

The merest smile touched the big man's lips, as if he sensed Robin's apprehension and was amused by it. He introduced himself, appearing a little more affable. "The name's Bruno, lad, and I'm in want o' a dog; a wolfhound." He waved down the hill into the trees. "I made camp there last eve and awoke to find the animal missing. I spied gypsies here-abouts yesterday and fear they might ha' made off wi' him. The dog is very valuable and I'd like him back."

Weir relaxed. He scratched his head dubiously. He knew all about gypsies and their thieving ways, and a good hunting dog meant meat in the pot to them. But he shook his head. "I saw none o' the mangy crew between here and Lochmore. Could be they ranged over by Blairafton way."

He gave the stranger directions to the neighboring village.

"Much obliged," said Bruno, and held out his hand with a grin, displaying a wide gap where his two front teeth should have been, "er . . . er . . . "

"Weir's the name, sir. And guid luck in finding that dog."

They shook hands, Robin wincing to find his own crushed in a beefy fist. Then the stranger touched a finger to his hat and started on down into the wooded ravine.

Robin continued on thoughtfully. The more he considered it, the more convinced he became that the man had lied. The tale about the missing dog just didn't ring true. For one thing, he asked himself, why had Bruno waited so late in the day to search for his "valuable" companion? It was now well past two o'clock in the afternoon.

He glanced back over his shoulder, relieved to find that the fellow had disappeared. There had been something distinctly menacing about the man—and he flexed his bruised fingers gingerly—the type you wouldn't relish meeting in the dark.

Robin made up his mind to start the return journey to Lochmore well before sunset.

Alyssa walked with Robin along the banks of Loch Ness. Both were uncomfortable and trying hard not to show it. Alyssa's heart had dropped sickeningly when the younger man arrived at Gower Castle alone and she immediately knew the reason for it. What would she do, she fretted, if he chose this time to ask her to marry him? Blessed Virgin, she thought, spare me from having to hurt him with a refusal!

Somewhat stiltedly, Weir brought her up to date on all the latest gossip from Lochmore. Now and then he cast a furtive glance at her face, though taking care not to meet her eye. In the bright sunshine the breeze lifted her hair like a shimmering golden halo around her head and her eyes were so intensely green that he felt himself drowning in their sparkling tropical depths. She had borrowed a pink-and-white sprigged muslin dress from Polly, and the creamy tops of her breasts rose from the scooped neckline like pale, succulent fruit awaiting the hunger of a man's mouth. He swallowed, imagining the feel of that velvety flesh against his lips, and found himself reasoning that if he had to wed anyone Alyssa would at least make it bearable.

He wheeled on her suddenly and blurted, "We'd best set a day for our wedding."

The sparkle went out of her eyes and they filled with dismay.

Robin laughed and took her hand. "Dinna be bashful, lass. Ye ken that's why I'm here this day."

Alyssa took a step back. "Robin . . . I—I . . ."

He pulled her into his arms, her hesitancy stimulating his desire, and kissed her eagerly on the mouth. Alyssa wrenched free and rubbed the back of her hand over her lips. "Nay, Robin, I beg of you! I—I can't . . ."

Now he saw the revulsion on her face. It was as if someone had slammed a clenched fist into his stomach. Nothing in his success with the village girls had prepared him for this. "What?" he cried, his fingers tightening on her wrist. "What are ye saying, lass?"

Miserably, Alyssa turned her head away. "I cannot marry you, Robin," she whispered. "I—there's someone else," she lied.

His neck and face flamed beet-red. "Who?" he shouted, his pride cut to the quick. When she shook her head, he grabbed her by the shoulders and glared down into her face. He was breathing hard, his eyes glittering like slivered glass. And perversely, at that moment he wanted nothing more in the world than to have Alyssa for his wife, unable to tolerate the notion that any woman would reject him. "Who?" he roared. "Must I beat it out o' ye?"

With a flaring of anger Alyssa pushed him away from her,

crying, "You don't truly love me, Robin Weir! And I don't love you, not as a husband. So—"

"I want ye! And I mean to have ye!"

With that he seized her roughly and bore her down on the grass. They struggled for a few minutes, Alyssa biting the hand that tried to force its way down the front of her gown. Robin howled and reared back, lost his balance and tumbled backwards onto the grass. By the time he righted himself, Alyssa was running back to the castle.

Once in her chamber she was so winded she could hardly breathe. She was furious at Robin, yet sorry too. Not only would they never be husband and wife, but undoubtedly no longer friends. Sighing, Alyssa went to the window and leaned her burning face against the cool stone and let the breeze wafting in ease the tumult inside her and dry the sweat on her brow. Marry Robin?

Never!

Suddenly she found herself comparing him to Blake Sinclair, which, of course, was ridiculous. Yet even had Sinclair been but an ordinary man, still Robin would have come off a poor second. There was none of the spark with Weir that she had felt with Sinclair, nor the respect and admiration. If only the Chief *were* an ordinary man! If only—

Alyssa heard the voices in the courtyard, deserted only a little while before with all the guests gone to the hunt. Looking down, she was startled to see Robin and Lady Magdalen strolling across the yard from the direction of the stables where Weir had left his mule. "Holy Mother!" Alyssa breathed, the sight of this pair together so incongruous, so startling, that Alyssa was bemused, then apprehensive. First the MacKellars had questioned *her*, now Lady Magdalen appeared to be questioning Robin. Why? What did it mean?

As they passed below her line of vision and entered the castle, Alyssa ran from her room and hid behind the huge oaken kist at the top of the stairs and saw the Countess of Kilgarin lead Robin into a small antechamber off the hall. The moment they were inside, Alyssa slipped down the stairs, glanced swiftly around to make certain she was not being observed, then crept up to the chamber door. With everyone away, many of the servants had been given the afternoon off and with the weather being so fine most of them had taken themselves out of doors.

The murmur of Magdalen's voice was quiet, but clear.

". . . quite concerned about the lass," she was saying. "Naturally, her experience at the abbey shocked us greatly. So if you would not mind answering a few questions it would set our minds at rest."

Robin, seated in the brocade chair opposite her ladyship, was too overwhelmed by this unexpected turn of events to answer. He had been about to lead his mule out of the stables when Lady Magdalen herself had appeared in the building, crooking a finger at him imperiously. "I would have a word with you, lad," she had said. "It concerns your friend Alyssa Dunne."

So he had followed her numbly into the castle, seating himself after she gave him permission to do so, his mind groping to understand why this woman—not even from the area—should be so interested in a simple girl from Lochmore. Then too, he recalled snippets of gossip he had heard about the countess, and though it was vague now, it seemed to Robin that little of it had been good. Holding a rag to the bleeding scratch where Alyssa had nipped him on the hand, he tried to hide his curiosity as he waited for the lady to speak.

The black eyes raked him over well. Magdalen was an excellent judge of character and felt she had sized him up correctly. From her chamber window she had watched him arrive to visit his sweetheart, swaggering across the courtyard from the stables whistling jauntily between his teeth. Though he was supposedly committed, he had paused to joke and flirt with a couple of wenches sweeping the cobbles. A randy bantam cock! she had thought immediately. A preening young rooster who thought much of himself, and an unlikely candidate for matrimony, surely. Further, from the cut on his hand and the sullen expression on his face when she had surprised him in the stables, it appeared that his tryst with his beloved had not gone well.

Hiding her smile, she decided to flatter him.

"Well, lad," she began, infusing her eyes with warm appreciation, "I would say that your young lady is fortunate indeed to have the attention of a worthy such as yourself. Yes indeed," she went on, stroking his vanity, "and I'll wager you have a good head on your shoulders too."

Robin gaped at her. It was one thing for the village wenches to find him pleasing, but a woman such as this . . . ! "Your ladyship is most generous," he managed, and as an afterthought flashed her one of his devastating smiles, thinking that it was not out of the realm of possibility that a high-born woman should look with favor upon a common lad, particularly if that lad was irresistible.

"Tell me," Magdalen continued, "when is the wedding to take place?"

Robin's mind ticked rapidly. And his ego being what it was, he convinced himself that the Lady Magdalen, though much older, lusted for him. Aye, aye, his mind raced on, feverish with excitement, he had heard how such ladies were prone to dally with comely lackeys in their households, often rewarding them handsomely for their, er, services. His face flushed as glorious possibilities swept through his mind, but first it was necessary to set her mind at ease where Alyssa was concerned.

Looking falsely downcast, he murmured, "I fear, my lady, that there will be no wedding. Ye see, we thought it better to break it off now than rue it later, being unsuited as we are."

Magdalen feigned surprise. "A pity, a pity. I trust you are not too cast down?"

"Oh . . . nay!" he hastily assured her. "'Tis of course disappointing, but mayhap fate has something better in store for me." And he eyed her hopefully.

Ha! she thought in satisfaction, a prideful fool is quick to fall. She smiled at him sweetly while thinking, enough of this tedious prattling! "Well, we must take pity on the girl, what with all her troubles, and would know if she has any other relatives she can turn to?"

Robin shook his head.

"None at all?" she pressed. "Even outside Lochmore?"

Eager to turn the conversation back to himself, Robin replied quickly, "Narry a soul, lady."

Magdalen felt a stab of irritation, aware that he hadn't stopped to think. "Was the lass born in Lochmore?"

Robin stared at her, surprising a peevish frown between her brows. He noted that her eyes had a piercing intensity now and, confused, he sensed her impatience. "Aye," he replied slowly, "she was born in Lochmore . . . as far as I ken."

The countess laughed softly, a sound like the empty clicking of dry bones in an Arctic wind. "Ye don't sound oversure, lad."

Weir felt the first touch of uneasiness. Of course he couldn't be sure! Had not Isa Dunne blurted to Alyssa that she was a bastard, brought to her by a masked rider late one winter's night? Even Isa hadn't known anything about her background, let alone where she had been born. Besides, why was this noblewoman so interested in a girl like Alyssa, who was not from her own territory at all?

"She's from Lochmore," he assured her with a positive nod, impatient to dispense with the question and return to more personal considerations, such as what the lady had in mind for him.

"And you?" she persisted softly. "Are you originally from Lochmore?"

It was as if a cold finger had touched the back of his neck, and he looked at her sharply. He saw that she was bristling with impatience barely held in check under a honeyed veneer of solicitude. With a sick lurch in his gut Robin realized that this interrogation concerned the time before he and Davie had moved to Lochmore—and was the real reason she wanted to talk to him. Infinitely wary now, Weir cursed himself for a fool for allowing himself to be so easily taken in. He began to sweat under his clothes.

Robin knew very well that he and Davie were not originally from the area; knew that there was something mysterious, even shameful about their past; something that didn't bear talking about. At least, Davie refused to discuss it, nor had ever divulged the location of their former home. It was in the past, he said, and best forgotten. Now Robin found himself wondering if Alyssa was somehow connected to their past; if that explained the reason for Davie's long interest in the girl.

Magdalen's strained affability cracked and she spoke sharply, "Come, lad, I asked you a question! Where is your true home?"

Robin gulped. "Lochmore."

"Nay, I think not. But here's a question any lad can easily answer—what was your mother's name?"

It seemed to Robin that all the air had been sucked out of the room and his lungs about to collapse in the vacuum. Lady Magdalen was so still, he thought, so terribly, frighteningly still . . . like an adder the moment before it strikes. Robin felt the salty trickle of sweat moisten his dry lips. There was a sloshing in his ears, his own blood clamoring wildly through his veins. He had a sudden impulse to jump up and flee, to keep running until he was far away from Gower Castle, and Scotland itself if necessary. The shame he sensed in his past was in some way bound up with his mother. Davie refused to talk about it, a measure of how serious it was. What had she done? Did it . . . was it possible that it had something to do with Lady Magdalen?

She leaned forward and rapped him on the knee. "Answer me! Do you not realize that I have ways of loosening your tongue, methods that might curb any pleasure you might take in the wenches hereabouts?" She unclipped a small doeskin pouch from the gilt belt at her waist and tossed it lightly in her hand so that the coins rattled together, many of them, her black eyes never leaving his face. "Gold," she breathed, "Much gold. Enough for a lad such as yourself to live like a prince. All you need do to earn this small fortune is to answer a simple question."

And with that she tilted the pouch and dumped a small pile of glittering coins in her lap.

Robin's mouth fell open as he gazed at the money as if in a trance; more money than he had ever seen in his life. There was more than enough to buy . . . to buy anything his heart desired! Enough to make a man's most cherished dreams come true. No more would Davie dictate to him! There would be no fear of him being forced into marriage. Besides, Alyssa had insulted him—

"What do you say, lad?"

"My mother's name was Caitlan Weir," Robin blurted. "We were no' originally from Lochmore, though where we hailed from a' canny say, since I was but a wee bairn at the time. I—"

"And Alyssa Dunne?" Magdalen broke in impatiently.

Regretfully, Robin shrugged. "All a' can tell ye is that she's a bastard, brought to Isa Dunne's door late one night by a masked man. Davie, my brother, has long taken an interest in the lass, though I don't rightly ken why."

Magdalen looked deep in his face. She believed he was telling the truth, that he would gladly spill more if known to him, anything to get his hands on the gold. Well pleased, she returned the coins to the pouch and tossed it carelessly into his lap. "Well, bonny Robin," she said with a faint sneer, "I wish ye much luck in spending this coin, but if you wish to live to enjoy it tell no one of our conversation this day. Now you may go."

Alyssa backed away from the door, then turned and flew up the stairs and down the corridor to her own chamber where she had felt so secure until the MacKellars came to visit. But she could not stay at Gower Castle now! Confused as she was by the conversation that had taken place between Lady Magdalen and Robin, she knew she was in danger. And Davie Weir was in danger. She sensed that the countess's next step would be to contact him. Frightened, Alyssa knew she must warn Davie in advance, and there was no time to lose. As for Robin . . . well, there was no time to think of him now.

She left her room and ran through a twisting maze of corridors and down several flights of stairs to the back entrance of the castle and peered out cautiously. Two grooms were chatting near the stables, and she waited impatiently, her heart pounding in terror and frustration, until they concluded their conversation and went their separate ways. She was on the point of stepping out when Robin Weir came into view, his head down as he started for the stables where he had left his mule. For all his newfound wealth she saw that he looked far from happy. Traitor! she wanted to scream, how could you sell your brother who has cared for you all your miserable life . . . and all for a little pouch of gold!

Presently Robin left the stables, mounted the mule and rode off at a gallop. Alyssa watched him bitterly, shuddering to think that this was the man she might have married, but for Lord Sinclair coming on the scene. Had she not met and fallen in love with Blake she would have been under considerable pressure to marry Robin, since life had little more to offer a girl in her lowly position.

The instant the courtyard was empty Alyssa darted across to the alley that ran down the side of the building to a field where a dozen mules were grazing. She knew it would be difficult to control an animal without saddle and bridle, but didn't dare risk going into the tackroom in the stables. After looking the mules over she spotted one that seemed likely, but the creature refused to let her mount. As she coaxed the animal to willingness, Alyssa cast an apprehensive glance over her shoulder to the castle windows, sick with terror lest she be seen. By now, she reasoned, Lady Magdalen would be searching for her, and once in that dark lady's grasp—

Sweat trickled in icy rivulets down her back as the mule continued to back away. Her heart swelled to bursting in her chest. At any moment Alyssa expected to hear a shrill outcry of, "Thief, thief!" and the strident blast of a horn.

Finally she was able to mount. Gripping the mule by the short tufts at her neck, Alyssa turned her head around and pointed it to the opposite side of the field, and dug her heels into her side.

The mule refused to budge.

Bruno, Magdalen MacKellar's squire, waited with grim patience on the moorland between Gower Castle and Lochmore. He had his instructions, orders to apprehend anyone by the name of Semple or Weir. He had allowed Weir to pass on by for a reason. His mistress had made it clear that she wished to interrogate the lad first; to extract certain information from him before turning him over to Bruno.

The squire smiled with anticipation. No matter where Weir was headed when he left Gower Castle, he had to come through the ravine to pick up the road leading either north or south, since behind the stronghold loomed a solid mass of mountains where only the foolhardy dared venture.

Bruno was hunched over the bank of a stream paring his nails with his dagger when he heard a rider approach at a gallop. Lumbering to his feet, he scrambled up the bank to where he had concealed his horse among the trees, a bag over his head. The squire's broad face was flushed with excitement, delighting in the fine sport ahead of him; a task at which he was so skilled. Then, when it was over, Lady Magdalen had promised him the girl.

12

Alyssa prodded the mule frantically, hideously conscious of the precious minutes ticking away. As desperation grew, her patience with the balky creature snapped. Digging her heels into its side, she fumed, "Hasten, you scunnersome beast!" and smacked her smartly on the flank.

Nanny tossed her head and brayed her indignation to the sky, highly affronted at this rude handling. But she still didn't move.

"Oh, dear God, be silent!"

Alyssa threw a terrified look over her shoulder at the castle and stables, hastily stroking the animal's neck to calm her down. Nanny's annoyance attracted the attention of the other mules and they ambled over to see what was amiss. One of them, a bay-brown creature with gentle eyes, came to within a few feet of them, not in the least nervous or shy. Alyssa looked her over swiftly and came to a decision. In a second she was mounted on the newcomer's back and on her way to the far side of the field. From there she cut down a tree-shaded lane that led down into the glen.

Once out of sight of Gower Castle, Alyssa grabbed the mule firmly by her short mane and urged her to a gallop, her breath whistling out in relief when the obliging creature was soon flying along like the wind, her rider clinging desperately, fearing to be thrown off at any moment. Bending low over the mule's neck, Alyssa paid little attention to the passing scenery as they pounded through the late-afternoon sunshine, heather and gorse bending before her and now and then a rabbit darting away. The thundering hoofbeats disturbed a flock of waterfowl which rose from the loch below in a silvery shower of spray, the honking of the geese echoing through the primeval stillness of the glen.

At a ford over a fast-flowing river the track split in two, leaving Alyssa with a choice as to which road to take. The shorter route was more direct and led through the moor to join the main road leading to points north and south. She decided on the longer way, reasoning that those who pursued her would be bound to think she would take the swiftest road in her haste to warn Davie, and might well overtake her if mounted on good horseflesh.

After a few miles the violent thumping of her heart slowed a little, yet the terror remained lodged in her chest like a lump of ice. Why had Lady Magdalen questioned Robin about her background? Why was this woman so interested in *her*! Another surprise had been to learn that the Weirs were not originally from Lochmore. It astounded her that Davie had never mentioned this fact. Had he kept silent for a reason; a dark reason? Holy Mother, she thought agitatedly, what could it all be about?

When she burst into Weir's humble cot in Lochmore village it was to find Davie enjoying a solitary supper of mutton and barley bread. Her sudden appearance and the expression on her white face startled him and he sprang up, overturning the stool, his first thought being that his brother had gotten himself into mischief.

Words tumbled out of Alyssa so quickly he could scarcely make sense of them—until she mentioned Magdalen MacKellar. Upon hearing the dread name, terror like liquid fire flashed through his veins, his mind conjuring up an image of the specter who had haunted his darkest dreams. And after that he needed no urging.

He packed rapidly, pausing only long enough to toss items they would really need into the bedrolls, then picked up his purse from its hiding place under a loose hearth stone. At the door he turned for one last look at the cozy little home where he had been so happy, yet all along sensing that he would have to leave it all behind one day.

Strapping the gear to his mule, he swung Alyssa up behind him, spurning her suggestion that they retrieve the other mule from where she had left it grazing placidly in a nearby meadow. "Nay," he said, "we have trouble enough without the risk of hanging for theft. Someone will find her and take her home."

"Where are we going?" Alyssa queried, her eyes drawn to the castle high above, her thoughts on the one person who was strong enough, powerful enough, to vanquish a MacKellar.

"First we find Robin, then leave the territory immediately."

Alyssa bit her lip. How could she tell Davie that his own brother had betrayed them; that even now Robin was undoubtedly far away from the area, flying to freedom and adventure with the satisfying jingle of gold in his purse? She caught his arm. "Robin got away. I saw him leave—"

"Then where is he?" Davie asked worriedly.

"Mayhap . . . mayhap he thought it best to flee."

Weir twisted around and frowned at her. "Never! Robbie might be feckless but he's no' a coward. Nay, he would hasten back to warn me. How can ye think he would leave me in the lurch?"

They turned down a side road that wound around close to Castle Augusta. As they neared the massive stronghold, Alyssa blurted, "Davie, Lord Blake might help us! Please—"

"What!" he all but shouted, this time turning to glower at her in exasperation. "The Sinclairs and MacKellars are allies and the Chief right proud o' bringing it about. Why would he jeopardize the likes o' that to help *us*? Great galloping centipedes, lass, use your head!"

But Alyssa persisted stubbornly, not quite able to divulge the true reason why she had so much faith in Sinclair. "Lord Blake saved my life, Davie, and—"

"What matters one life when compared to those o' both clans? A man in the Chief's position must ever put that first, ahead o' aught else, if he wishes to remain at the head o' his clan, and Sinclair is nothing if no' ambitious. We mean next to nothing to him in the larger scheme o' things. Why, the auld earl let his ain brother be hanged to settle a score wi' another clan, just to prevent warfare."

This sobered Alyssa, and they continued on in silence for

a while. *Would* Sinclair be willing to help her if it meant a breakdown of the long truce between them and the MacKellars? He did like her; he had made that clear, but as Davie had rightly pointed out, many a Chief had to set his own private feelings aside for the good of his clan.

Her heart sank as they left Castle Augusta behind. They circled the village without meeting a soul, since it was the supper hour, and started down into the glen. The great chasm was filled with purple shadows and a melancholy silence, a faint silvery mist rising from the ground. They had only gone a short distance when they turned north, Davie steering the mule onto the narrow trail that rose steadily to join the high moorland road, the shortest route between Lochmore and Gower Castle. As she stared out at the bleak landscape before them, Alyssa's fear got the best of her and again she grabbed Weir's arm, crying, "Nay, we must not go there! Robin ran away! He—"

With a heavy sigh Davie dismounted and lifted her from the saddle. He gazed steadily into her eyes and said quietly, "You gan back to the village and we'll come by for ye later, but now I must find ma' brother. I *must*, Alyssa. I've cared for him a' his life and now . . . now a' have a great feeling that he needs me more than he ever did afore."

She read the terrible concern in his eyes. She remembered all that Davie had done for her through the years, making her life in Lochmore bearable with his warmth and understanding. "Mayhap," she ventured, "we can go partway?"

He nodded. "If we dinna come upon him by the time we reach the ravine, then I'll be inclined to believe you that he ran away."

They continued on.

When Bruno returned to Gower Castle he found Magdalen pacing her chamber. He stood in the doorway with his hat in his hand. She wheeled on him impatiently and snapped, "Well? And I warn you, if you tell me you've failed I'll have your tongue fed to the hounds."

After questioning young Weir and sending him on his way, she had immediately hastened to the girl's room, only to find it empty. A frantic search of the castle and grounds proved equally fruitless. Then a stable lad had come running to report that one of the mules was missing, and Magdalen knew what had happened.

Now she listened to what Bruno had to say, thinking that at least he hadn't failed. When he finished she said, "Your day's work is not over. Young Weir, I have learned, has an older brother in Lochmore. Davie. The girl has fled too and gone to warn him, methinks. Mayhap they'll come here looking for the young lad when he fails to return, but regardless, this pair must be found and silenced."

Bruno bowed and backed out of the room.

Davie and Alyssa rode in silence through the countryside. When the sun dipped behind the mountains, dusk descended on the moor and a damp, peaty mist rose in a cloud from the moist earth. As they approached the wooded ravine, a flock of crows fluttered up from the gully, startling them with their sudden, raucous cries.

Davie halted the mule. "There's something doon there," he said in an eerie whisper that made the fine hair spring erect at the nape of Alyssa's neck. He dismounted and led the mule behind a rock outcropping, drew his dirk and muttered, "You bide here, and dinna make a sound."

Alyssa watched him disappear into the ravine.

The silence was oppressive after he left. As she sat astride the mule in the shadow of the rock, Alyssa hugged herself against the chill in the air, for evenings were usually cool in Scotland even in summer, and now autumn was approaching.

She glanced over her shoulder across the moor, straining to probe the spiraling vapor rising from the boggy ground, and the widening dark pools forming around the base of the few trees scattered here and there over the wilderness. In the thickening fog, familiar shapes became distorted and somehow menacing. She started violently at the cry of a whaup echoing through the glen to die away in the distance, a shiver passing over her cold flesh.

The mule, sensing her apprehension, stamped her feet restlessly. Alyssa stroked her neck with a trembling hand, afraid she might bray and reveal her hiding place. It was so still. And Davie was taking so long. If he didn't return in a minute—

A wrenching wail, anguished and lingering, drifted back to her from the gully. Alyssa was off the mule in a flash and running into the ravine, her heart pounding as she darted between the trees. Bursting into a small clearing, she found a ghastly tableau awaiting her. Some kind of animal carcass was strung up to a stout branch of a tree, swinging slowly back and forth in the breeze, partially blocked from view by Davie. He stood gazing at it as if petrified, his arms raised to the sky. Then, with a choked sob, he threw himself face down on the grass—and she saw it.

Alyssa's eyes widened in shock. It was red and glistening, a froth of blood and spilled entrails, no longer recognizable as a man. Her mind recoiled from acceptance. Nay, nay, she thought, it *wasn't* a man! How could it be? He had no eyes, nose, and his body . . .

Gagging, she reeled away and vomited on the grass, falling on all fours to grind her forehead into the turf in an unconscious attempt to erase the carnage from her mind, telling herself that some hunter had killed a beast and strung it up to drain.

Davie dragged himself to his feet and with tears streaming down his face cut what was left of his brother down. Even then, he realized, he had no time to mourn him; aye, nor give him a decent Christian burial either. There was a savage aura hanging in the air all about them, a malevolent pulse beating just below the silence. He hurried to Alyssa and pulled her to her feet. "We'll take him to the loch. 'Tis all we can do for now. Where did ye leave the mule, lass?"

She swallowed, trying to avoid looking at Robin. "I—I left her where she was hid, by the crag."

"Ye tethered her?"

Alyssa shook her head. "I heard you cry out and came running."

Davie frowned, but he took her hand and they hurried back through the gully, their eyes combing the gloom, every nerve in their bodies alert to pick up the slightest sound or movement. Where the trees thinned out, Davie stopped and gazed out onto the moor, now a sea of slate-grey mist, the rock where they had concealed the mule seeming to float in space.

But there was no sign of Peggy.

Alyssa's heart jumped when Davie's fingers tightened painfully on her hand. "If ye left her untied, Peggy would ha' followed ye into the ravine," he said very low. "But as ye can see, there's no sign o' her."

At that Weir wrenched her back into the protection of the trees, the whites of his eyes shining in the dusk. As he opened his mouth to speak, a twig snapped loudly on the other side of the clearing.

At that Davie propelled her deeper into the woods where darkness would afford them better cover. Terror streaked through Alyssa's limbs, and she would have broken into a run if Davie hadn't whispered fiercely, "Hush! Quiet or ye'll betray our position. Move at a swift, steady pace without making too much racket."

Restraining a natural urge to flee, to race for their lives, they glided from tree to tree and paused for a moment to listen, making their way downhill in the direction of the loch. Now and then they heard the crunch of a fallen branch behind them and a stealthy rustling, as of a large animal moving through the bracken. Sweat streamed down both of them. Alyssa felt faint from the wild drumming of the blood in her head, and each time she detected sly evidence of the beast following them she would have made a dash for it, but always Weir held her back.

When he thought of what the fiend had done to Robin, a taste like rusted iron filled Davie's mouth. He glanced at Alyssa in the thickening darkness and inwardly quailed, thinking that he would kill her himself rather than allow her to fall into the hands of the one who stalked them so relentlessly.

If they could only reach the loch in time!

They broke out of the woods less than fifty feet from the water's edge to find a pearly haze hanging over the surface. Davie paused only long enough to yank off his boots, reasoning that if they could only swim out a little way they could lose themselves in the fog—provided the hunter couldn't swim.

They dashed down the beach and plunged in, fighting the

numbing coldness of the water as they swam desperately into the cloying vapor that thickened farther out. Alyssa glanced back only once to spy a hunched shape watching them from just inside the treeline, but at least he didn't try to follow them into the loch.

One of her few pleasures in life had been swimming, and she had been able to swim like a seal from a very young age, though mostly she had stuck to the rivers because of the dark legends about the supposed beasts in Loch Ness. Now she was prepared to risk the loch monsters rather than the one left behind on the beach. She had never seen a one of *them*, while the other . . .

The first arrow flew past Davie's head. The second struck him on the upper arm, the shock driving him below the surface. Alyssa glanced around to find that he had disappeared.

13

Just after the noon meal that Sunday, Blake received a messenger who brought him a letter from Elizabeth Bancroft in Edinburgh. She wrote to remind him that the long mourning period for her mother had now ended and that she would enjoy a visit from him whenever convenient.

"I fear for you, my dear," she wrote, "given the uncertain state of affairs in the North, and pray you are not drawn into something I know you do not believe in your heart." She went on to describe an impassioned sermon she had heard delivered by John Knox in which the preacher had railed against the Gordons, calling them heathenish puppets of the Pope who deserved to be massacred for their crimes. "One must marvel at his courage," she continued, "considering the fact that our Queen is one of that ilk. Truly, when Knox speaks the entire congregation falls under a spell, with no one, from the highest to the low, daring to raise a voice in disagreement. I must confess that the fellow intrigues me . . ."

Blake raised his eyes from the parchment and gazed moodily out of the window, a spark of irritation inside him. In her recent letters Elizabeth never failed to mention the preacher, speaking of him in glowing terms, likening him to a saint sent to earth to deliver them from paganism.

He chuckled grimly. From everything he knew about Knox, and he had run into him often at court, the man struck him as being bigoted, judgmental and more interested in inciting his followers to strife than to encouraging a peaceful resolution of differences. And for a self-proclaimed man of God, the preacher dabbled his lean fingers in politics much more than was seemly, going so far as to upbraid the Queen

herself and preach to her as to how she should handle her
affairs. The fellow was nothing if not bold, and filled with an
inflexible fanaticism and a rigid determination to have his own
way—using God as the tool when all else failed. Few other
monarchs would have tolerated him. Most would have had his
head long since. Though he grieved her almost continuously,
Mary Stuart tried to placate the fellow in the hope of avoiding
more religious conflict.

As for Elizabeth, she completely misunderstood the
character of the man she so admired, thought Blake grimly. She
seemed to have forgotten that he had been among the
murderers of Cardinal Beaton, a fact that hardly made him a
good candidate for sainthood, as she appeared to view him.
After she had embraced Protestantism, her quiet, dreamy
personality had undergone a great change. It was almost as if
she had been waiting for a catalyst to come along and breathe
fire into her blood.

Blake dropped the parchment on his desk, thinking that
once they were wed things would be different. She would have
enough to occupy her attention as his wife and the mother of
his children to have time to brood over the fiery sermons of
John Knox. His own family were pushing hard for an early
wedding, it being imperative that he beget himself an heir—a
legitimate son who could be groomed from an early age to
follow in his footsteps.

Aye, he mused, he could not tarry much longer in the
North. He had a duty to his clan, and in that Elizabeth
Bancroft figured prominently, but before going South there
was something he must do for himself, for a man must have a
private life to his liking. And that too was perfectly acceptable
—even expected—provided he was discreet.

He had given the little Dunne ample time now to make
up her mind, or more to the point, the illusion of making up
her mind. He wanted her, would be good for her, and
he meant to have her regardless of what her answer might
be!

When Davie battled his way back to the surface, Alyssa
saw the arrow protruding from his arm. "Let it be," he gasped,

tossing water from his eyes. "It will bleed less if it remains undisturbed."

The next hour was a nightmare. They were in deep water about a hundred yards from the shore, mercifully enveloped by the fog and swimming in the general direction of Lochmore. Alyssa could tell that every movement of his left arm and shoulder was agony for Davie, nor could he swim very well. Floating and floundering, they slowly made their way south.

The long Northern dusk sank into darkness. Now Alyssa had a new fear. She could no longer see Davie but she could hear his harried breathing as he struggled to keep up, and the sounds terrified her. At length he cried hopelessly, "Go, lass! Swim for it. I . . . I'll catch up wi' ye later."

But nothing could have induced her to leave him. In spite of the risk, she knew there was only one thing to do. They must take their chances on shore.

They crawled onto the bank of the loch at a spot known locally as Tinker's Lair, a place favored by gypsies because of the caves dotting the hillside that afforded them protection from the elements when the weather was foul. But there was no sign of the wandering folk that night; no blazing campfires or music or yipping dogs to cheer them, nothing but darkness and silence.

Davie groaned aloud in pain and exhaustion. They shivered violently in the cold autumn wind sweeping down from the mountains. When she had recovered her breath, Alyssa cautiously scouted the cliff face until she found a shallow cave that might shelter them for the night and from the man who stalked them. Until Davie was made as comfortable as possible she could not stop to think of what they were going to do.

They huddled together in their wet garments, starting up at the slightest sound outside the cave, never for a moment forgetting the horrible mutilation done to Robin. Davie muttered his name many times as he drifted off to sleep. Alyssa lay awake with his dirk in her hand, not daring to close her eyes, a burning hatred blazing in her heart when she thought of Lady Magdalen. She was certain that it had been the countess who had had Robin killed, or almost certain. It *might* have been a highwayman, she supposed, for the countryside abounded with them. Robin had been mounted on a good mule and he had had gold in his purse, and many an unwary traveler had been slain for far less. Yet . . . in light of all that had happened, she was sure that Magdalen MacKellar was responsible. Why remained a mystery. She glanced at Davie in the darkness, remembering Robin telling the countess that they were not originally from Lochmore, a fact Alyssa had known nothing about. Why had Davie never mentioned it? He had been frank about all other aspects of his life. There was something strange, even sinister, about his keeping such a thing a secret, and in Lady Magdalen being so interested in them; all three of them! Could this mean, Alyssa brooded, that Davie might know much more about her own background than he had ever revealed?

In a way it was exciting. She was impatient to question him, desperate to find out more about herself. But first things first! Straining to hear into the silence, she had more immediate concerns. With the mule gone and Davie wounded, all hope of fleeing Lochmore was gone, at least for a while. Now they needed a safe place to hide; a place where Davie could have his wound tended properly and rest until he was strong again.

Alyssa thought of Blake Sinclair, powerful enough to protect them from the MacKellars of Cumbray. She would go to him, swallow her pride, and beg his help for Davie's sake.

In the morning Weir was delirious. Tearing away the sleeve of his shirt, Alyssa exposed the damage, and a spurt of nausea rose up in her throat. The head of the arrow had cut deep, and now the blood-encrusted wound had swollen in livid puffs of inflamed flesh around the offending metal. Streaks of red, akin to lightning, snaked across Weir's shoulder in the direction of his neck.

Clenching her teeth, Alyssa took a firm grip of the shaft and pulled. Davie howled in agony, semiconscious as he was.

Alyssa's hand froze and the color ebbed from her face. She saw that the arrow had barely moved. Even worse, the wound appeared to be poisoned and Davie's life in jeopardy. She must go to Augusta alone and bring men back with a pallet, and as soon as possible.

Kissing the wounded man and making him as comfortable as possible, Alyssa cautiously ventured outside the cave and paused for a few moments to look and listen. As she gazed at Loch Ness an idea came into her mind, a way she might reach the castle safely. She would swim most of the way! Robin's killer had stalked them right to the bank of the loch but had stopped short of venturing into the water. Either he couldn't swim or he believed the legend about the dark waters being populated by giant beasts. But at that moment Alyssa was prepared to take her chances with the latter in the hopes of evading the former.

By alternately swimming and floating she arrived at the outskirts of Lochmore without mishap, though when she stepped out of the water she was exhausted and somewhat resembled a water rat. From the position of the sun Alyssa judged it to be about seven of the clock, which meant that the villagers had been up and about for more than an hour. She cut through the woods and climbed a steep hill to the castle.

A young, rosy-cheeked guard stopped her at the gate. "Your business here, mistress?" he asked officiously, looking her up and down as she stood shivering in the cold and dripping water all over the flags.

"I would have speech with the Chief," responded Alyssa with as much dignity as she could muster.

The guard threw back his head and roared with laughter.

Alyssa thought of Davie, sick and in great danger at the cave, and her patience snapped. "Let me pass, churl!" she snapped, "or you'll find yourself laughing on the other side of your face."

He waved her away, still chuckling. "Be gone, wench, afore I have ye tossed in the dungeons. Holy Mother, what would the Chief want wi' a tink like you?"

Jason Sinclair and a dozen clansmen left the stables and clattered across the courtyard to the portcullis. As they drew up before the gate they noticed some sort of fracas going on. Jason hailed the guard. "What now, Dunsmore?"

"The gypsy yonder demands to see the Chief."

The men around Jason tittered. Jason himself was about to wave her away when he looked closer. He took in her shabby, dripping gown, her bare feet and the muddy smudges on her face . . . then the dark-lashed green eyes, the long, burnished hair, and the firm white breasts rising from the square neck of her gown. Intrigued, he asked, "Why should my cousin the Chief, who is a very busy man, take the time to see a gypsy?"

Alyssa lifted her head and stared him in the eye. "Give him my name and he will see me, and I'm not a gypsy, my lord."

Gypsy or not, Jason thought, she is wondrous fair. And she stood gazing back at him with none of the humility he had come to expect from lesser folk. Amused and inquisitive, he motioned for her to follow him and led her to a side entrance into the castle, then along a twisting corridor into a very grand room filled with fresh flowers from the garden. Bowing to her, he murmured, "Wait here, Mistress Dunne."

When Blake Sinclair strode into the room a few moments later he was momentarily flabbergasted to see Alyssa standing there. All Jason had said to him, with a mischievous wink, was, "A lady awaits you in the blue lounge."

Sinclair took in her bedraggled appearance and the terror in her eyes and crossed the room and put his arms about her. "What happened?"

Alyssa collapsed against him and closed her eyes, the steely grip she had kept on her frayed nerves finally snapping. "We were attacked," she sobbed, "on the road from Gower to Lochmore. Davie lies in a cave now dreadfully wounded. Oh, my lord"—she lifted drowned eyes to his—"please help him! I—"

"Just tell me where he can be found."

Within the hour Davie Weir was safe behind the towering walls of Castle Augusta, installed in one of the guest bedchambers rather than in the servants' quarters. Lord Blake's own physician was sent for, and Weir was made as comfortable as possible until he arrived. After a brief examination Dr. Gilespie set about extracting the head of the arrow, then applied a poultice to the poisoned wound and was about to call for a maid to sponge the feverish man down when Alyssa interrupted to say she would do it herself.

Cool water was brought to the room, and they were left alone for a while. As she gently bathed his flushed face, Davie opened his eyes. "We are safe now, sweeting," Alyssa told him with a smile. "Lord Blake has given us sanctuary."

But his look of alarm did not go away. With his good hand he fumbled for hers and pulled her closer. "Dinna tell him . . . dinna mention Lady Magdalen," he said hoarsely. "Remember . . . they are allies."

Alyssa nodded. "He thinks we were waylaid by highway-men—"

"'Tis good," he broke in, and heaved a sigh of relief. "He must not ken the truth o' it."

All her curiosity rushed back. "Davie, there is so much I don't understand. Why is Lady Magdalen so interested in us?"

But he had closed his eyes and drifted off to sleep.

For four days Davie Weir trembled on the brink of death, the poisoning caused by the arrow bloating his body up beyond recognition. Dr. Gilespie tried every remedy at his disposal with increasing frustration. Finally he confessed to Sinclair, "Only his basically strong constitution and the Almighty can save him now." Then as an afterthought: "And methinks his sweetheart will soon sicken too if she does not rest from tending him."

Blake frowned. The good doctor had unwittingly planted a doubt in his mind, one that swelled up out of proportion in a matter of minutes. Alyssa had steadfastly refused to have anyone else care for Weir since the day he entered the castle. She had remained by his bedside night and day, turning down all his inducements calculated to pry her from the room. Sweethearts! Was it possible? Nay! he all but cried aloud, it couldn't be.

Sinclair barged into the sickroom to find Alyssa slumped wearily in a chair by the bed. Ignoring her protests, he lifted her bodily to her feet and half-carried her out of the room, rushing her down the corridor to another small chamber in the west tower. Once there he firmly pushed her down on the bed and wagged an admonishing finger in her angry little face. "Doctor's orders must be obeyed and Gilespie insists you must rest."

"But . . . Davie?"

He gestured impatiently, his dark face hardening. "Weir has nurses aplenty to care for him. Now it's your turn to be the patient and my responsibility to ensure you receive the proper attention."

Alyssa could see he was adamant, and she was too exhausted to make a scene. In sharp contrast to how she looked and felt, Sinclair was tanned and vigorous, the fine white lawn of his shirt emphasizing his dark hair and skin. There was a lithe animal grace about him as he leaned over the bed frowning down into her eyes, as if challenging her to gainsay him. Alyssa lacked the energy. She nodded, "I will rest here for an hour or two."

Immediately his expression softened. "You look much like a wee bedraggled spaniel at this moment," he said, unaware of the tenderness in his voice, "one that could fain use a bath and combing. Wait here, lass, and we'll soon remedy the situation."

A tub of perfumed water was brought to her room. She was bathed in the foaming soapsuds and her long hair washed and brushed until it glistened like a shawl of cloth-of-gold. Then Beth, the tiring woman, reached for a delicate cream silk bedgown edged with lace and slipped it over her head. Alyssa shivered deliciously, amazed at the sensuous feeling of the whispery material against her skin, clinging to cunningly outline all her firm young curves most shamelessly. Blushing, she thought of Sinclair who had made all this possible, treating her and Davie like honored guests rather than the servants they really were. They were safe now. The Chief would protect them. He had placed his physician at Davie's disposal, a man who had trained under the barber-surgeon to King James V. Nothing, it seemed, was too good for them in the eyes of Blake Sinclair.

When Beth helped her into bed, Alyssa sank down gratefully into the cool clean sheets, a great excitement lurking under her exhaustion. Here was proof that Sinclair truly cared for her! How could she dispute the facts when they stared her in the face? Wary and suspicious as she was, it impressed her that the earl had not sought to hide their presence at Augusta. She was happy, then ashamed of it whenever she thought of poor, foolish Robin. He too had had his dreams, and they had ended in disaster. She had dispatched friends of Davie's to find Robin's body so that it might be properly buried, but all they had found were bones—the only parts that the wolves hadn't eaten. How, she wondered, could she tell Davie?

Alyssa slept for almost twelve hours and awoke to the scent of flowers. Blinking, she turned her head slowly and for a moment or two, still dazed, imagined she was in a garden. Enormous bouquets of roses were everywhere, in entrancing shades of cream, ice-pink and deepest red—oceans of them! Servants were trouping into her room and an ornate silver bedtray was placed across her lap. Back and forth marched the servants with steaming dishes in their hands, and while Alyssa watched, wide-eyed, they filled the tray with a miniature banquet—salmon, gingered grouse, and strawberry tarts daubed with cream. There were tiny rolls and small wedges of cheese, and a dish of sugared bonbons.

"And wine for m'lady!" laughed the motherly Beth. With a flourish she handed Alyssa a goblet of malmsey bearing the Sinclair crest, thinking that this was all so unexpected and romantic, a wee liaison that had even caught the castle servants by surprise. The astonishing thing was that the Chief had brought this young woman into the castle itself, something that had never happened before. The staff were fairly buzzing about that—and what it could mean—below stairs.

Alyssa glanced about and laughed with delight. "Thank you," she said, raising shining eyes to Beth's face.

"Thank the Chief, lass. 'Twas he would have everything just perfect for ye when ye awoke."

Coming to the door, Blake overheard this exchange. He glowed at the sound of Alyssa's enchanted laughter. His eyes gleamed when he heard her say, in the soft tones she had used when tending Davie Weir, "Oh . . . how sweet and kind he is!"

The servants discreetly melted away when Sinclair stepped into the room. He was amazed at the transformation in the girl. She sat up alertly in bed, her skin glowing, the smooth satin bedgown outlining her full, high breasts. Masses of silky hair poured over her shoulders and down her back like a cape of dark gold; never had he seen such glorious hair, except perhaps on a MacKellar.

Alyssa smiled at him shyly, her long, uptilted eyes innocently provocative, kindling in him a smoldering desire, an anticipation of the delights soon to be his. Preoccupied with the stirring of his own senses, he couldn't know how his sudden appearance in the room disconcerted the girl on the bed. Against the pastel tints of the flowers he loomed big, dark, and handsome enough in his gold doublet to take her breath away. When she quickly pulled the sheet up to her chin, Sinclair snapped out of his pleasurable trance and set about putting her at ease.

"Eat, lass," he urged heartily, pulling a chair up to the bed. He teased her, his eyes twinkling. "A little while gone you were as pale as the underside of a puddock. Gilespie said you must have rich food to put the bloom back in your cheeks."

Alyssa pretended affront. "You would compare me to a frog, sir? Faith, 'tis most ungallant!"

He laughed, enjoying her pertness. "Well," he said, "you leap about faster than I can keep track of you and you *do* seem to have an odd penchant for water."

Remembering how she must have looked when she arrived to seek his help, she chuckled, but with a touch of grimness in her eyes.

Blake selected a plump strawberry from the tray and told her to open her mouth, and kept feeding her succulent tidbits from the various dishes until finally she held up her hand. He handed her the goblet of wine and bade her drink, and when she asked about Davie he assured her that he was improving at last. He inquired casually, "Have you known Weir long?"

She nodded, explaining that they had been lifelong friends.

"You seem very close to him." He watched her from under his brows.

"Davie has been like a brother to me."

Sinclair sat back in the chair, relaxing as his doubts were laid to rest where the groom was concerned. "And Robin Weir?"

Her face fell. "Also like a brother, though we were never truly close."

With all potential obstacles swept away, and relieved that she lacked the coyness and guile of so many women he had known who would undoubtedly have kept him guessing about these other men, he next would know all about the circumstances surrounding the attack. Remembering Davie's warning, Alyssa shrugged. "I—I know not who he was. When we came upon Robin he was already dead and his mule gone. Then . . . then we were hunted through the woods to the loch, and managed to escape in the fog."

Blake took her hand, his strong, tanned fingers closing over hers, and assured her that his men would find the knave if he was still in the area. Raising her fingers to his lips, he murmured, "And now, my sweet, you are under the protection of Sinclair and no harm will come to you."

Alyssa nodded in the candid way that delighted him so much and set her apart from the other women who had passed through his life. "Aye," she said, "'tis the reason I came to you."

Blake melted. "Ah . . . darling, you did well to come to me." Then he made an admission of his own: "I adore you." And as her eyes searched his face, Alyssa saw nothing there but genuine tenderness, and she too melted and finally allowed herself to hope. She ached to be loved, even as she was afraid to reach out lest she find rejection, but nothing in Sinclair's face gave her reason to doubt. He was as delighted as she was—and it showed. He was thinking that she had come to him of her own free will, aware of all he could do for her—and what he *couldn't*—so that they understood each other perfectly and were of one accord.

The time of waiting had inflamed his desire for her, yet mixed in with the desire was an unexpected urge to cherish. This lovely girl had had a hard life, but it was all in the past. He thrilled to all the countless good things he could do for her . . . and she for him.

Blake moved to the bed and took her in his arms and kissed her gently, then after a moment with more passion. He pushed the gown from her shoulders and kissed them too, his mouth moving to each breast in turn, his tongue lingering on the nipples. A great weakness sapped Alyssa's strength and she closed her eyes and allowed him to undress her, murmuring, "God meant this to happen, my love. Did He not lead us to each other?"

Naked, they lay locked together, Alyssa helpless in the onslaught of ecstatic sensations that only he could kindle, and this time it was different. Gone was the uncertainty, the fear, even the shame. They loved each other and hurt no one by this love. Sinclair whispered that they would be together from then on, that she was his and let no one dare try to come between them.

"Nay," Alyssa breathed, thrilling to the way his strong, muscular body burned against her own, "no one ever could."

He was a skilled lover and taught her the exquisite art of waiting, so that the supreme moment would be that much more intense. He taught her the secrets of her own body, then of his, delighting that he had such an eager student, one that promised and quickly revealed a passion to match his own; one who held nothing back now that he had gained her trust. And she was right to trust him, thought Sinclair the lover, a man quite different from Sinclair the Chief, given that he never made a promise he could not keep.

When he finally left her, Alyssa fell into a drugged, rapturous sleep, overwhelmed with happiness and—for the first time in her life—feeling truly secure.

14

For the next few days as Davie Weir slowly mended, Sinclair managed to pry Alyssa more and more from the sickroom. Weir, he assured her, had the finest of nurses and one of the best doctors in Scotland, so there was no need for her to spend so much time hovering over him and getting in the way.

Alyssa, once certain that her old friend was indeed recovering, allowed herself to be lured away. Blake had much to show her; to teach her. He took her on a tour of Castle Augusta, and in a forgotten little turret chamber they succumbed to the passions flaring between them and made fierce, heart-stopping love on the bed, more fiery this time than tender. That afternoon she discovered the driving nature of the man she had linked her life with, but she found it exciting rather than frightening since her own blood burned as needfully as his.

Blake showed her the library and was surprised to discover she could read a little, thanks to Mistress Lindsay's insistence that she sit in on Myrtle's lessons. "I think mayhap she did that to shame her daughter into learning," Alyssa told her lover with a grin. "Poor Myrtle, she could do naught right to please her mother, and kept protesting that a lass need not concern herself with such foolishness, since once she was wed she would have others to handle the cumbersome chore for her."

"And I'll warrant this did not endear you to the young lady?"

Alyssa laughed ruefully. "Nay, she hated me."

Blake slipped his fingers through her long, silky hair and brought her face close to his. "Unfortunately, there will always be women to hate you, Alyssa, even were you never to open your pretty mouth—a mouth I must drink from deeply at this very moment."

She drew back, flushing, aware of servants hovering in the background. "Here . . . ?"

He took her hand and hurried her back to the tower room.

It was the same when they went to the stables and he proudly pointed out the merits of his fine horseflesh. Very shortly they forgot about the horses as flesh of another kind clamored for attention and appeasement. They laughed together when he taught her bowls and golf, and stood close behind her as they stationed themselves in front of the blinds, Alyssa with a bow in her hand, struggling to fix her attention on archery rather than the hard body brushing hers.

Those were idyllic days when they plumbed the depths of love and drank to their fill, oblivious to the whispers of the castle servants or the curiosity of Lord Jason Sinclair, who was surprised that Blake would keep his paramour right there in the castle. Though Jason was tactful and restrained the impulse to pry, his uncle Lord Harry, a bluff, forthright man, exercised no such restraint. Harry finally succeeded in gaining the Chief's attention one evening before supper. "What means this?" he demanded, his disapproval obvious. "Must you install your mistress right in the castle itself, feeding fuel for the servants to gossip about? Take care, nephew, that word of this does not find its way to Edinburgh and come to the ears of your future wife. How will she feel, think you, to learn that her betrothed thinks so much of his paramour that he would keep her by him in Augusta?"

Blake, made careless by the force of his passion, growled a curt reply that temporarily silenced his uncle, but privately he saw the wisdom in his warning. Calling his squire to him, he instructed him to make certain arrangements, adding impatiently, "See that all this is accomplished in the next few hours."

Alyssa had been called to Davie's room. He had recovered consciousness and would now, Gilespie assured her, quickly regain his strength. "The crisis has passed," said the doctor, "and since he's basically in excellent health he will mend rapidly."

The moment they were alone, Davie motioned her over to the bed. "Robin . . . ?"

Alyssa had the painful task of relating what had happened to his brother's body, slipping an arm about him comfortingly when his eyes filled with tears. He was silent for a few moments, struggling to contain his emotion, then as a thought occurred to him he asked abruptly, "How much ha' ye told Sinclair?"

Again Alyssa felt a twinge of pain. Though she had not actually lied to her beloved—since she could not be absolutely sure who the killer had been—yet she had not been as open with Blake as she would have liked to be.

"You did right," Davie said in relief when she explained the story she had given the Chief. "The less he kens o' this, the better for both o' us."

"Davie . . ." Alyssa leaned forward and searched his face, "why did you not tell me you were not truly from Lochmore?"

He glanced away evasively, avoiding her eyes, and shrugged. "I oft forget myself, Alyssa, since we were very young when . . . when my uncle brought us here. I've always thought o' Lochmore as ma' hame. 'Tis the only one a' rightly recall."

"Where *are* you from?"

He hesitated, then lied, "Stirling."

She was puzzled. Cumbray Castle was nowhere near Stirling. "Then why is Lady Magdalen so interested in us, Davie? What can we mean to her?"

Again he shrugged. He had awakened at dawn that morning clear-headed for the first time in days and had done some serious thinking, deciding that the time had come to tell Alyssa the truth about herself—even if she would hate him afterwards. But as the day wore on, his courage ebbed. He dreaded to see the loathing in her eyes when she discovered his mother's part in Magdalen MacKellar's crime; to watch all the trust and respect she felt for him being destroyed before his very eyes. Dear Lord, he just couldn't bring himself to do it! He wanted Alyssa to go on thinking well of him, to love him, if that were possible, even a tiny fraction as much as he loved her.

"'Tis plain that Lady Magdalen mistakenly connects us to some others she knew in the past. I canna fathom any other reason for her interest," he murmured, the lies coming so easily they sickened him.

"Mayhap," Alyssa replied thoughtfully, and after a moment with a shrug: "How else to explain it?"

"Robin paid for her mistake, and dinna forget that *we* are still in danger." He nodded to where his belt with its coin purse hung over a chair. "Thank Christ a' still have ma' money. Lass"—he looked into her eyes intently—"we must leave the area just as soon as I'm able, mayhap in a day or two—"

"Leave!" Her expression was a study in dismay. "B-but . . . why, Davie? We are safe enough here. The Chief will protect us."

Weir brushed this off impatiently. "Did a' no' explain afore that clan unity comes well ahead o' the likes o' us humble folk? Nay, henny," he shook his head firmly, "we must be off afore the countess gets wind o' who is sheltering us."

Alyssa rose and went to the window, her back to him, wondering how to break the news to Davie that she and Sinclair were in love and intended always to remain together. It would undoubtedly be a shock to him, and he'd had enough shocks of late. Buried deep inside her was the feeling that her friend might view her relationship with the Chief quite differently than she did. Davie was sober, straight forward, without a romantic bone in his body, and she sensed that he would have great trouble recognizing the fact that love had the power to sweep all obstacles away.

She was right. In the sudden silence that fell between them, Weir examined her set profile and the rigid cast of her shoulders, and read in them resistance to his plan to leave. For the first time since Alyssa entered his room he noticed her gown, a pretty thing of blue silk with a froth of lace at the neck and cuffs. He had been amazed to awaken from delirium to find himself inside Castle Augusta, not in the servants' quarters, but in a guest bedchamber, then more amazed still to be attended by the Chief's own physician. In his lucid state he had wondered at this royal treatment from his master, surely not the sort of care normally accorded an ailing groom. A dark suspicion entered his mind, and he asked harshly, "How came ye by such a gown?"

"When my own gown was ruined, a servant brought this for me to wear. 'Tis just on loan," Alyssa added hastily—but her blush gave her away.

Davie started up from the pillows. "By Christ's blood, was this the price he made ye pay for helpin' us?"

"Nay, Davie! You—you don't understand. We love each other—"

"Love!" he howled, the veins bulging in his forehead. "And where, think ye, that this fine love will get ye?" Before she could say a word, he sneered, "I'll tell ye, ma lass! Nowhere! Unless it's your ambition in life to be a nobleman's whore."

"Davie!"

"Aye, and one day ye'll have nothing to show for a' this great passion but a crew o' bastards. I can promise ye this, ye daft wee fool, Sinclair will never marry ye!"

Alyssa ran out of the room and slammed the door. She was furious. And but for the fact that he was still weak and mourning Robin, she would have set him right in no uncertain terms. Oh, she had known Davie would never understand! And she had no intention of staying in his room to listen to his cruel words sully their love. Davie's trouble was that he had no imagination, and he automatically thought the worst of any man who looked at her twice. In his simple way he was unable to visualize anyone managing to rise out of their station in life. Well, Myrtle Lindsay had done it, not to mention all the others Allan had told her about, so why couldn't she? Simple she might be in terms of rank and worldly goods, but she wasn't uncouth. Had not Blake told her more than once that she had great potential?

Angry and hurt, Alyssa stayed away from Weir's room all the next day. Sinclair kept her fully occupied, at one point confessing that he would have a special surprise for her the following afternoon. On the appointed day Beth came to her chamber with a forest-green riding habit, beaming. "Ye are to ride abroad wi' the Chief, so bathe and make ready at once."

He was waiting in the hall when she slowly descended the stairs, the rich dark velvet material emphasizing her radiant coloring to perfection. To the man standing before the hearth she looked beautiful, elegant, more exquisite than any of the women who clamored for his attention at court. That she lacked their coquettish ploys only increased her charm. Though vastly alluring in her vibrant beauty—and one day, he thought with a sigh, she would be well aware of the weapons at her disposal over the opposite sex—at this moment she retained an innocence that was sweetly appealing.

Blake was waiting when she reached the bottom step. Smiling up into his eyes, her cheeks pink with excitement, she thought he looked every inch the handsome country gentleman in a kidskin jerkin and tan riding breeches that hugged his muscular hips and thighs. He exuded rugged strength and vigor; aye, and a certain ruthlessness too, yet now that touch of restrained violence that always clung to him merely added an extra thrill to their relationship, since she had learned it would never be directed at her.

"Green becomes you," he told her softly, his eyes saying much more as they moved over the close-fitting bodice of her riding habit that so snugly outlined the fullness of her breasts. He was thinking that beside this girl Elizabeth would look colorless and tepid. Aloud he said, " 'Tis a bonny autumn day and I thought a ride over to Blairafton would be a pleasant diversion." At her inquisitive look he grinned and tickled her under the chin, adding, "Besides, I have something to show you."

With Alyssa mounted on a dappled palfrey and Blake on the spirited Fleet, they made the journey to the neighboring village in just under an hour. Both were in high spirits and chatted lightly the entire way. Alyssa could hardly contain her curiosity about the surprise he had in store for her, though she suspected what it might be. Today, she felt certain, he wished to be alone with her away from the constant claims on his time at the castle so that they could plan their future together! And oh, how grand it would be to go to Davie and tell him he had been wrong.

Cresting a ridge, rolling countryside sweeping away

before them in all directions to the granite mountains, Alyssa looked down and saw a beautiful manor house in the valley below. Cradled in a lush green hollow, the house was the most graceful she had ever seen and was surrounded by colorful gardens. Perfectly proportioned and built of mellow cream-colored stone, the building had crenelated turrets on either end. A meandering river wound close by and disappeared into the deep green of pine woods.

"Oh, what a bonny place!" Alyssa cried out in delight. "I wonder who lives there?"

"I own Lynnwood House, Alyssa," Blake replied as they sat their horses admiring the view—or at least Alyssa did. Sinclair was watching her face closely, gratified by her response. He explained that it had come to the Sinclairs as part of his mother's dowry, and to the end of her days it had been Anne Sinclair's favorite residence. "Come," he invited eagerly, putting spurs to his horse, "I can see you are anxious to see if the inside is as fair as without."

The house enchanted Alyssa. Though much smaller than Augusta, it was charming where the castle was grand. The beautifully handcrafted and inlaid furniture had been imported from France, Blake told her, the walls of each chamber tinted in the delicate pastel shades his mother had loved so much. Each room was filled with fresh flowers from the bountiful gardens; some said the finest gardens in all of Scotland. "Much of my mother lives on here," Blake told her quietly, "so for me too this place is very special."

Alyssa reached for his hand. "You were close to your mother?"

He sighed somewhat regretfully. "Aye, as close as a lad of my rank can ever be, considering that I was a page in other households in my early years and was sent to France at the age of fourteen."

Alyssa frowned. "If I had a child I would want him by me always. I think it would be unbearable to be separated all these years."

He slipped an arm around her and drew her close, smiling tenderly into her eyes. "I can see you will make a fine mother when the time comes, but, alas, children who must take on great responsibility in the future must be trained well in advance."

With Blake following along indulgently, Alyssa moved from room to room examining everything with a childlike wonder—from the lilac silk walls of an upstairs bedchamber to a tiny satinwood music box inlaid with jade and mother-of-pearl. Her eyes rose to his, enraptured. "Oh, 'tis no wonder your lady mother loved it so! I love it already!"

Relieved and happy, he took her hand and led her back downstairs and into the hall. "We'll partake of a little wine to refresh us, then I must show you the gardens."

The servants trooped out, as if at a signal, to be presented to her. Keane, the housekeeper, was a small, wiry woman in her late fifties. She had a brisk manner and small, alert eyes; eyes that studied the young beauty with great curiosity and a certain condescension, though Alyssa was too excited to notice. The steward was gravely polite and the lesser servants agape. Lacking the subtlety of the older, more experienced servants, they ogled Alyssa with avid interest, mindful—so they had heard—that not so long ago she had been no better than them and now was to be elevated to such a high position. Grudgingly they could see why. The lass was exquisite, had a proud bearing, and could easily have passed for a lady had they not known the truth.

Alyssa was too distracted to notice the sly glances that passed between the staff. All her attention was on her host, and soon she discovered that Blake had intended for it to be a day to remember. They strolled the lovely gardens, wandered hand in hand by the river, and partook of fruit and wine at a little ornate table under the trees.

Since she was interested in life at court, Sinclair answered all her questions in great detail, trying to paint a vivid picture with words. Aye, he told her, the Queen was vivacious and fair. She adored music and loved to dance the night away. She had a sparkling wit and admired a sense of humor in others, yet there was a serious side to her nature too. And during this exchange both were acutely aware of the physical hunger flowing between them, lending an intense excitement to every second of that special day, and the anticipation of the night to come—a night they would finally spend together.

They dined by scented candlelight in the green-and-gold hall where a great fire crackled to ward off the evening chill. After the meal they relaxed before the blaze, and Blake set about trying to teach her the rudiments of playing the lute, at which he was quite accomplished, much to Alyssa's surprise. "Think you that I'm good for nothing but wielding a sword?" he said, pretending affront, and when she abandoned her clumsy attempts to follow his instructions he suggested she sing instead, adding, "In that department you cannot possibly be worse than me."

Between bursts of laughter Alyssa tried to follow the tune, her naturally husky voice cracking on the high notes until finally he clapped a hand over her mouth to silence her. "A singer you will never be, my sweet, but then a lass cannot expect to have *all* the talents."

Firelight smoldered in his dark eyes. Her heart beat as impatiently as his. She could see that he was anticipating the taste and feel of her body under his hands and lips, that he was growing tired of waiting—though the evening was still early.

Finally he drew her to her feet. It was the moment they both had longed for through the pleasant hours of teasing their senses to fever pitch, the better to sharpen their desire. In the lilac chamber he closed the door firmly and swept her into his arms, lifting her clear of the floor as he crashed her against his hard, urgent body, his mouth devouring the soft lips that parted eagerly under his. Her gown fell before the onslaught of his passion, thrown carelessly to the floor, and they collapsed naked on the bed together. His lips burned like moist fire upon her breast, his hands seeking and arousing her willing flesh, and Alyssa gave herself up to a wild abandon she had never dared at Augusta, matching the fierceness of her love to his. At Lynnwood there was a heady sense of being alone, something never quite possible at Castle Augusta, and she reveled in it, much to her lover's surprise and delight.

That night Blake discovered her brand, and Alyssa confessed that she was a bastard, something she had been too ashamed to tell him before. He listened to the story with interest, then sighed. "Aye, it happens often enough. And you have no idea of who your parents were?"

Alyssa shook her head.

He kissed her, promising, "I shall make it all up to you, my darling. You'll have everything you can possibly desire."

"I desire only you, my lord," she replied softly.

He drew her close, frowning above her head, made uneasy by something he heard in her voice, a possessiveness that vaguely alarmed him, yet stated so sweetly, even innocently, that he could not take offense. She understood the situation well, Blake assured himself. How could she not understand it? Aloud, he said, "I must return to Edinburgh soon. Mayhap arrangements can be made for you to join me."

Alyssa was content, or almost so. They would never be parted. Blake had sworn that often enough, and now—now he proposed to have her join him at court!

The blissful hours slipped away and, without either of them noticing, the first grey streaks of dawn rose in the eastern sky.

It was to be the last night of happiness for Alyssa for a very long time.

15

The moment breakfast was over, things began to go wrong. The steward appeared with an important message for Blake. Will MacNeith and what was left of his band of cutthroats were to be hung in Aberdeen the following morning and Sinclair, as chief justice of the Highland Tribunal, was required to be present.

Alyssa shuddered. "Oh, I would that we didn't have to leave here," she sighed. "How grand if we could forget aught else and stay on here forever."

It was the perfect opening, one he couldn't have contrived better himself, and when the door closed behind the departing steward Sinclair turned to her eagerly. "Then you find Lynnwood pleasing and would be happy to stay here?" he asked her softly.

"Aye, who would not?"

"Well," he said, "Keane is getting on in years and requires assistance to manage the place. Would you like that responsibility, Alyssa?"

She was seated before the looking glass brushing her hair. Raising her eyes questioningly until they met his in the mirror, she noted that his expression was suddenly intense, as if her answer were of prime importance to him. "But . . . Keane seems hale and hearty enough to me," she replied in confusion. "She strikes me as being most capable."

Blake lifted her from the stool and turned her to face him. "Alyssa, my sweet, I intend that *you* be in charge here. I want you to think of Lynnwood as your home."

Her eyes roamed his face and she said faintly, "My lord . . . I fail to understand . . ."

Blake groaned inwardly, wondering why it had to be more difficult than necessary, and as he studied her he saw that it was going to be very difficult indeed. "At Lynnwood we can be together, my darling, with no interference from others. I know you want that as much as I do."

Alyssa felt something dark and chilling rush toward her. As a vicious band tightened about her chest, squeezing the breath from her lungs, Blake's face went out of focus behind a rush of tears. Understanding came in great, agonizing surges of pain. He loved her—but only enough to make her his mistress! To observe a semblance of propriety he would make her the bogus manager of this estate; then, when his busy schedule permitted, he would visit her from time to time—and as Davie had warned—just often enough to father a brood of bastard children. And when she grew older, sadder, and undoubtedly embittered, he would cease to visit her at all and would shunt her off to one of his more remote establishments and there quickly forget her.

She reeled in the circle of his arms as all her dreams came crashing down about her head. Her mouth opened but no sound came. Watching her, Sinclair winced to see her face crumble before his eyes and realized that Alyssa had never understood the situation at all. Huge tears trembled on the tips of her lashes and splashed down her face, and her lips, soft and wounded, trembled wordlessly.

Sinclair crushed her against him fiercely, unable to stand the sight of the havoc he had unwittingly caused in the false assumption that they understood each other perfectly. Burying his face in the silky mass of dark gold hair, he said huskily, "Don't, my love; please don't. I want you desperately! And I know you want me. This can be our home together, Alyssa," he rushed on, "and I swear to you on my mother's grave that I will always take care of you."

"Oh, God!" she choked, shaking violently in his arms. "Dear God in heaven . . . no! Tell me you don't mean this thing?"

Fearing the wild look in her eyes and the hysteria building inside her, he grasped her shoulders firmly and said harshly, "I meant every word of it. What more would you wish me to say?

I want you more than I have ever wanted another woman in my life. God's blood, lass, is that not enough for you?"

"Nay! To be your mistress is *not* enough."

Sinclair stared at her incredulously. There was no escaping her meaning. But what she proposed was unthinkable; that she would hint at such a thing at all, preposterous. Her failure to grasp that fact only demonstrated the yawning chasm between her world and his. But for all that, he wanted her and meant to have her. "Be reasonable, Alyssa—"

"Reasonable!" she cried. "We love and want each other. Is that not reason enough?"

He steeled himself to be bluntly honest with her. "I'm betrothed to a lady in Edinburgh." And at the shock in her eyes: "It was arranged long since, before I met you." Not, he was thinking, that it would have changed anything as far as they were concerned. He could imagine how his family would react if he called a meeting to announce that he, the Earl of Belrose and head of his clan, proposed to wed one of their village women who lacked property, rank, powerful connections of any kind. His uncle would have a stroke; Jason would assume that he had lost his reason, and the others that he had grown weak and self-indulgent to the detriment of his house. All the respect they felt for him would vanish in an instant. All the good he could bring to them through an advantageous marriage, swept away. A man in his position simply did not marry for personal reasons, and this Blake took pains to try to explain to the weeping girl in his arms.

But she struggled violently, closing her ears to what she took to be excuses, and sobbed, "At this moment you are free. Betrothals can be set aside if—if you want to enough. So now you must choose." And raising her eyes to his, she added, "I will not be your mistress."

For a moment his face darkened with anger and frustration. To him it was simple, easily arranged, the separation of his formal and private life. Why, he raged inwardly, must she make it so difficult? Had he not sworn on his mother's grave to care for her always? Had he not been prepared to give her Lynnwood, his favorite house, the place that held such tender memories for him of another dear lady in his life? There was nothing he wouldn't do for her, a fact he had made plain—nothing except wed her, and that was impossible.

Alyssa had stopped crying. Her face, he saw, had grown stiff and cold and there was a stubborn glint in her eyes as she awaited his answer.

"Dear love, though it pains me more than I can tell you, I cannot marry you, Alyssa."

The ride back to Castle Augusta was a nightmare of tension. Blake tried to talk to her, to reason with her, but Alyssa turned a deaf ear. She felt as if she had been turned to stone. Something warm, sweet and vital inside her had been viciously crushed, her pride broken along with her heart. Davie, she thought grimly, had been right. Dear Lord, why hadn't she listened? What a simpleminded, trusting little fool she had been to weave her silly romantic dreams! Harsh reality was all she had left now.

The courtyard was full of clansmen when they rode into Augusta. All of them seemed impatient, anxious to be off to Aberdeen. Blake dismounted and swung Alyssa from the saddle and spoke urgently to her cold, averted face. "You will tarry here until I return two days from now," he commanded. "This thing between us is not finished." And angrily: "Mayhap in the interval you will mature a little so that we may settle things to the satisfaction of both of us."

Then he was gone.

Alyssa flew to her own small chamber inside the castle and bolted the door. She threw herself across the bed and let her anguished tears flow. He loved her, but not enough to make her his wife, and she would never settle for the backwater of his life as his mistress, mother of a brood of bastard children like herself. Never! she felt like screaming aloud as she beat the pillows until she thought she would go mad with grief. He was still free. He could have chosen her, the one he professed to adore. That he hadn't was like a sharp, cruel knife savagely shredding her heart and pride.

The following morning, drained of all emotion and white at the lips, Alyssa went to Weir's room and announced that she was ready to leave Lochmore; that she wished to go as far away as possible. "Edinburgh," she said woodenly, thinking to lose herself in the crowded city.

For once Davie was tactful. He asked no questions. Nor did he have to, since the grim truth was written on her face. That afternoon Weir went out and purchased two mules and enough supplies to last them for the trip south, and at dawn the next day—without seeing Sinclair again—they left the village.

Magdalen MacKellar bristled with frustration. She didn't dare question Sir Edward further about the girl lest it arouse his suspicions, but she made discreet inquiries among the servants. None had seen Alyssa again.

The countess vented her wrath on her squire, Bruno. How could he be sure they had drowned in the loch? She dispatched him to prowl the countryside, to comb each hill and glen and village in search of them, and each evening he returned shaking his head. "They are out of your life forever, lady."

Magdalen's tame witch said otherwise. The crone announced darkly, "There's a black aura around my lady's head, and this morn at sunrise a golden hind appeared in the garden beneath your window. 'Twas standing amid tongues of fire."

Finally, throwing caution to the winds the countess ordered Bruno to go into Lochmore itself and make subtle inquiries at the inn. This time when he returned he had news for her. "The Earl of Belrose has given them sanctuary. 'Tis rumored that he lusts after the wench."

"God's feet!"

She considered the import of this most carefully before making a move. Robin Weir, even under rigorous questioning, had not known the exact circumstances of the girl's birth. Was it possible, she pondered, that his older brother was equally ignorant? Mayhap, out of guilt and shame, Caitlan Weir had concealed the truth from her sons. It made sense. A mother, at least outwardly, tried to set a good example for her young.

A great weight fell from her shoulders, with the conviction that she had been worrying for naught. She could still find a way to get at the wench, perhaps through bribing a servant at Augusta, but . . . it might be wiser to let sleeping dogs lie, at least for now. She had no desire to tangle with Sinclair, to stir up strife between the clans, particularly since there were those among the MacKellars who were waiting for an excuse to oust her. Inevitably the time would come when Blake Sinclair tired of the girl; when he would withdraw his protection. When that time came she would be ready.

Magdalen lay down on her bed and tried to relax, telling herself that she had nothing to fear. The only person alive who could stand up and accuse her was the long-absent Jock Semple, her sometime groom. It was Semple, more than Alyssa Dunne, who rose like a specter to haunt her dreams and bring visions of a noose being lowered over her head. He had been with her that night at Cumbray. And he had witnessed everything.

But perhaps there too she was fretting for naught. He might have expired long since, or upon learning from some traveler that she was again the Countess of Kilgarin, was too afraid to think of ever returning to Scotland.

As they rode through the wilderness of Badenoch, Alyssa gazed about bleakly, only half-listening as Davie talked about how fortunate it was that the weather remained mild, at least during the day, and game was plentiful. Inwardly, Alyssa shrugged. What did she care about game when she could hardly force a morsel of food past the hard lump in her throat? And mild weather or not, she felt chilled all the time; a coldness that came from deep inside her and left her feeling numb.

"Wolves and wildcats might well be a problem were game scarce," Weir went on doggedly, trying to catch her interest. "I mind the time we had a battle wi' the wily buggers on our way back from a border fray . . ."

He launched into another story while Alyssa nodded vaguely from time to time, thinking that with every league they journeyed the dank misery of rejection only hurt the more. Damn his clan! she raged. And damn *him* for putting them first! Jealousy churned inside her when she thought of the woman he was to marry—and marry only because of the benefits she could bring to his house! In exchange for that, this high-born lady would become the Countess of Belrose, the mother of his heir, but he would never, never, *never*, love her!

She turned her face away hastily and wept acid tears.

For a time they rode on in total silence, Weir having run out of things to say. Finally his forthright manner reasserted itself and he asked bluntly, "Can ye no' talk about it, lass? Mayhap it would help."

Alyssa shook her head, at the same time swallowing down a hot spurt of anger. Why couldn't Davie leave her alone with her grief? Could he not see how much she was suffering? Every pitying glance he sent her way was like a fresh slap to her pride, reminding her over and over that she was a fool, especially after he had tried to warn her.

Davie was troubled. He was asking himself what might have happened if Sinclair had known who she really was. Guilt ate into him savagely, and he groped for a reason to appease his conscience and quickly found one. Even had he told Alyssa the truth about her background and she had gone to the Chief with the story, he would never have believed her. He would have demanded proof, and all they had was hearsay, since he— Davie—had not actually been present at her birth. Worse, the earl might have suspected a trap, that she had concocted the wild tale to try to lure him into marriage. And to dig into the past with Lady Magdalen hovering about would have been to invite disaster.

She would get over this grand passion, Weir managed to convince himself. Alyssa was young and healthy and not of a nature to brood for very long. Once in Edinburgh, with all its many distractions, Sinclair would soon fade from her mind. At this moment they had something more immediate to worry about.

As they rode along, Davie continuously scanned the hills and glens, and whenever he could he tried to bypass the forests they encountered along the way. Their vulnerability, now that they had left the protection of Augusta, was something he never forgot for an instant. If only they knew the identity of Robin's killer. Because he remained a mystery, Davie's hand was never far from his dirk when they met up with the occasional traveler along the way, any of whom might have been the one.

At night they slept in the open, huddled up in blankets around a blazing campfire to frighten off the wolves, both too preoccupied to talk, their thoughts too dark to share. The weather was mild and sunny during the day but cold in the evening, the sky awash with stars. Alyssa lay awake for hours listening to the mournful howling of the wolves echoing through the glens, a cold, lonely sound that found an answering echo in her heart.

One afternoon, her thoughts far away, Alyssa carelessly stumbled into a bog, and both she and the mule promptly began to sink. The more they struggled, the deeper they sank in the mire. Alyssa screamed in terror. Confronted with the specter of a gruesome death, she suddenly wanted to live again.

It took Weir a desperate half-hour to haul both girl and mule clear of the muck. Alyssa hugged him desperately in relief, transferring some of the mess onto him. When they broke apart, black from head to toe, they looked at each other, then at the mule, and burst out laughing. The poor animal looked as if she had been dipped in chocolate and promptly rolled in the grass in a frantic attempt to clean herself.

"It was worth the fright to hear ye laugh," said Davie softly.

Contrite, and ashamed of the long hours when she had ridden along steeped in self-pity, forgetting that Davie had heartache of his own, Alyssa put her arms around him and kissed his cheek. "I'm sorry. I promise not to be such a—a dour creature from now on."

After that, things were better. The ache was still there, but she valiantly tried to ignore it and be cheerful for her friend's sake. They passed through towns and villages and met up with other travelers—peddlers, journeymen, and near Dalwhinnie a group of mummers on their way to a county fair. Alyssa had always loved fairs and they decided to go, and enjoyed a few hours wandering about the booths and trying their hands at the various games, ogling a woman with two heads, and sampling new-mulled cider and treacle dumpling studded with fruit.

For a whole hour Alyssa forgot about Sinclair. She didn't

know whether to feel guilty or relieved. Davie noticed with relief that the color had returned to her cheeks and a brightness to her eyes, at least when something caught her interest. The days had all been crisp and sunny, spiked with an invigorating hint of frost, and since they traveled through breathtaking scenery and passed so many pretty little villages and hamlets, it was hard to remain completely depressed.

The day they left Dalwhinnie the fine weather broke. By evening, clouds draped the crests of the hills and the lochs were shrouded in mist. That night as they curled up to sleep it began to rain, a fine smirr at first, then heavier toward dawn. Rising stiff and cold from the damp blankets and unable to get a fire going at first, they had to settle for a chilly drink of water from the loch and a breakfast of soggy oat cakes.

Again Alyssa's mood took a darker turn. The pain came back fiercer than ever. Riding through the dripping country-side, gazing dolefully at the sullen, rain-swollen clouds obscuring the crests of the mountains, she loved and hated Sinclair by turns and became ill at the thought of another woman in his arms, one he deemed grand enough to be his wife. She tortured herself by recalling their most intimate moments and then imagining another woman taking her place. Her nails sank into the palms of her hands and she bit her lip to keep from wailing aloud.

Outside the little town of Crosshouse they met the Corrigans, a young couple fleeing from a cruel master. Sara Corrigan, a dark-haired girl with a sharp face and nervous manner, was pregnant with her master's child. The pair had run away with nothing but the clothes on their backs. They too hoped to lose themselves in Edinburgh.

Davie and Alyssa took pity on them and allowed them to ride pillion. At night they shared their simple meal around the campfire. Bill Corrigan lacked most of his front teeth, knocked out by his employer. His nose too was broken and had mended in a crooked fashion. But in spite of his problems he ate heartily and between mouthfuls painted a grim picture of the life they had left behind until Alyssa almost wept with pity for them. Davie too was moved. He offered, "Ye can bide wi' us until we reach the city. We have more than enough to share."

They journeyed on together. Davie estimated that they would reach the capital sometime the following afternoon at their present pace. Before going to sleep he took a few coins from his purse and pressed them into Corrigan's hand, muttering, "It's no' very much but it will buy ye a bite to eat and a night's lodgings in Edinburgh."

Settled around the fire, Alyssa felt the first stirrings of excitement at the thought of living in the royal city. She could hear the other couple whispering together too, undoubtedly making their own plans for the coming day, she supposed. Lord love them, she thought with a sigh, she wished them well. But for the grace of God she too might have been pregnant by her overlord. Thankfully that was not the case, since her monthly flow had begun the previous day.

Alyssa and Davie awoke at dawn—but the Corrigans had arisen earlier. Gazing around the campsite in shock, they saw that it had been stripped of all their possessions. Both mules, Davie's purse and Alyssa's tiny leather pouch holding her gold coin and the silver necklace from Mistress Lindsay were all gone. So was their camping gear. All that remained was the one blanket they had shared and the clothes on their backs.

Alyssa burst into tears, wondering how they would be able to go on. Davie shouted his rage and disappointment to the dripping sky. "Without the mules we canna expect to reach Edinburgh for days! And how can a' hunt without my bow? Suffering cats, what a mangy pair!" He shook his fist in a southerly direction. "And to think a' felt sorry for the likes o' them!"

Suffering from exposure and near starving, they limped into Edinburgh three days later—and were promptly arrested for vagrancy.

Revelation

16

Edinburgh
1562–1567

Unfortunately for Alyssa and Davie, the citizens of Edinburgh had been complaining bitterly about the beggars and riffraff who had flocked into the city for the Queen's homecoming the previous year and remained to prey off honest townspeople ever since. Constables had been hired to report on all "foreigners" who entered the city and arrest those with no visible means of support.

It was the last straw for Alyssa. The moment three burly constables converged on them wielding their clubs, something exploded inside her head and she screamed in pent-up frustration and outrage, "We are not beggars! We are honest people and—and we *had* money until it was stolen off us a few days agone."

One of the men grabbed her and twisted her flailing arms behind her back while the other two seized Davie, stunning him with a blow to the head. The one gripping Alyssa laughed at her story, liking the way she twisted and struggled in his arms in a flurry of cascading golden hair and blazing green eyes. When her gown ripped to expose one creamy shoulder and the upper swell of a moon-white breast, he muttered thickly, "Aye, that's whit they all say, lass," while hot little eyes crawled over her and the hardness of his body ground suggestively against hers. "However," he continued, remembering his official responsibility as people began to gather, "it don't alter the fact that ye are paupers, wi' no coin or possessions between the two o' ye." Pressing greasy lips to her ear, he whispered, "Come quiet-like, henny, and I'll show ye a way to make a fine living." Under the pretense of restraining her he clamped a sweating hand over her breast.

"Whoremonger!" she spat, and kicked him in the shins, even as the other men were dragging Davie away. She bit, slapped and clawed at her captor until he finally caught her in a bearhug, pinning her arms to her sides and grinding his loins against the soft curve of her buttocks. "I like a fighter, sweetheart," he panted. "Come away now and we can ha' some grand sport in private."

A tittering crowd had gathered to watch. Shopkeepers whose premises faced the Lawnmarket ran out of their doors to see what was happening. Mistress Livingstone, wife of J. Livingstone and Son, Cordwainer, flew out with one of her customers, a young dandy in a peacock-blue velvet doublet richly embroidered with silver thread. He was Sir Simon Ogilvy and he arrogantly pushed his way to the front of the crowd, the wife of the cordwainer hot on his heels. She was a stocky little woman of fifty-eight with a determined chin and a no-nonsense manner. Elbowing Ogilvy aside, she stepped up to the constable and rapped him smartly on the shoulder. "Here, you! Afore ye can arrest the lass ye must ask her if she has anybody who might take her in."

The constable smirked down into Alyssa's flushed face. "Well? Do ye have somebody who might give ye shelter?" he demanded, certain she did not.

Goodwife Livingstone glared at him. She had no love for these law officers, most of whom were corrupt. Late one night less than a year before her only son had come home slightly the worse for drink but otherwise harmless, only to be set upon by two of these so-called peace officers and beaten unconscious when he refused to hand over an on-the-spot fine levied for public intoxication. The following day her dear Bart had died, leaving them heartbroken, with only their daughter, a lazy, sullen girl of twenty, to provide comfort in their old age.

Now, with a sympathetic glance at the captured girl, a strikingly fair creature who would be bound to be subjected to all manner of lewd antics by these ruffians, she snapped, "*I* will vouch for this bairn! Aye, and the lad too"—with a wave toward Davie. "Release them, ye bugger. I demand ye leave them in peace."

The constable flushed angrily, loath to be denied his fun.

Ever since her son had died, this woman had done her best to obstruct justice in whatever way she could. "If ye take them now ye must swear to keep them under your roof and provide succor," he warned darkly. "Dinna think ye can let them loose the moment ma' back is turned."

A silver-headed cane prodded the officer in the stomach, and Sir Simon Ogilvy—who had been astounded once he got a close-up look at the wench—barked authoritatively, "Unhand the girl at once!" And more ominously, "What right have you to call this good woman," with a nod to Mistress Livingstone, "a liar in my presence?"

The constable eyed the knight appraisingly, noting the elegant clothes, the sword at his side, and the cold arrogance in the slate-grey eyes regarding him so haughtily, and thought better of arguing with one who undoubtedly had influence in high places.

Alyssa and Davie were released.

Smiling down at Alyssa, the knight gallantly extended his arm, murmuring with a slight bow, "Sir Simon Ogilvy at your service, mistress. Allow me the honor of escorting you safely indoors."

Bemused, and with her heart still thumping madly in a mixture of fear and anger, Alyssa took his arm, stammering, "I—thank you, sir. You are very kind."

As they crossed the square to the cordwainer's establishment with Mistress Livingstone and a still dazed Weir following along behind, Alyssa stole a side long glance at her rescuer. Except for Sinclair, she had never laid eyes on such a handsome man. Tall and lean as a racehorse, the knight had fine chiseled features, long-lashed grey eyes and a mane of waving blond hair the color of wheat.

He grinned down at her, well used to feminine admiration, and found himself wholeheartedly reciprocating as his eyes moved over the lass, his first interest in her sharpening. Fishing, he drawled, "Such a comely girl must surely have a bonny name?" His gaze rested on the torn bodice of her gown.

Alyssa introduced herself and explained that they had just now arrived in the city, after having been robbed along the way. The knight murmured regret about this sorry situation while thinking that he, lucky fellow, would have the pleasure of initiating the sweet little innocent into the varied inducements the capital had to offer. Such was his confidence with the opposite sex that Ogilvy did not question success for an instant. The man Weir, he quickly discovered, was merely a friend— not that Sir Simon even remotely considered the rustic to be competition.

At the door of the shop he bowed low, savoring the delights soon to come. "I bid you a hearty welcome to Edinburgh, and I trust we shall meet again soon."

Alyssa was not nearly so innocent as he supposed, nor as receptive to his charm. She recognized that special look in his eyes, a slumberous, heavy-lidded look that bespoke a feverish desire. Fresh from her bitter rejection at Lynnwood, it chilled her, caused something to harden to steel within her, the determination not to be taken in again. She returned his interest with a cool, knowing smile that took him aback, thinking that whether in Lochmore or Edinburgh, certain things never changed.

But she had.

17

In November of 1563, a year after they had arrived in the city, Sir Simon had still not abandoned his attempts to win Alyssa over and make her his mistress. Alyssa was equally determined to resist.

"You need someone to care for and protect you," the knight had burst out in growing exasperation the last time he had been in the shop.

"Nay," she had responded confidently, "I can care for and protect myself well enough, sir!"

She had changed. And J. Livingstone and Son, Cordwainers, had changed with her. At the time she had been taken on to serve in the store, the business had been floundering. "Forsooth, it's gone downhill ever since oor dear son died," confided the lady of the house sadly. It hadn't taken Alyssa very long to see why. From what she had heard of young Bart, he had been a cheerful, affable type who loved people, therefore the store had done well with him behind the counter. At his death they had tried his sister for a short time, but Helen was unable to read or write and was scatterbrained and forgetful, not to mention far from willing to work.

Since then Mistress Livingstone herself had tended the customers. Unfortunately, the goodwife's blunt, no-nonsense manner was not appreciated by their clientele, and more and more of them began to take their patronage elsewhere, even though Livingstone's was generally known to be one of the finest shoemaking establishments in the city. Yet it was failing, threatened with bankruptcy at the time Alyssa and Davie arrived.

Upon learning that she could read and write a little, and had no objections to long hours and hard work, the Livingstones offered Alyssa the chance to try her hand in the shop. She seized the opportunity enthusiastically and ever since had slaved to make the business prosper. First she reorganized the premises, since when she came it was in chaos. Their ready-to-wear stock was neatly rearranged according to line and size and the entire store scrubbed spotless and given a fresh coat of whitewash. Plants were brought in to add interest and color, and more candles so that the customers need not walk to the door to closely inspect the merchandise. But most of all it was the new serving girl herself who won back their old customers and attracted new ones. Bright, beautiful and friendly, with the patience to tolerate those who dithered and had a difficult time making up their minds on what to purchase, and the tact to make the right suggestions without seeming to push, Alyssa rapidly put the business on the road to recovery.

Grateful and delighted with their new salesgirl, the Livingstones made Alyssa shop manager, the only woman to hold such a responsible position in any business throughout the city.

Davie Weir too was satisfied enough, at least for the moment. Though he would have preferred a post as a groom, which he had been trained for, he was happy enough to learn all he could about the leather business from Master Livingstone, who had three journeymen and several apprentices working busily in the back of the store. At the outset Davie didn't know the difference between kidskin, pig hide and fine Spanish leather, but after several trips to the tanners he gradually came to know the difference. Livingstone was a gruff man who spoke little, but it didn't take Weir long to discover that a kindly heart lurked beneath his somewhat crusty exterior. With there being so many people out of work in the city, Davie considered them most fortunate to have been taken in.

The shop was in one of the busiest parts of Edinburgh, with the store in front and quarters for the male help behind. The family lived on the second floor, and Alyssa had a tiny room on the third under the peaked gables. The food was plain but nourishing. They were up at dawn and usually in bed by nine at night. The challenge of handling the store combined with the hard work and unwavering routine had been good for Alyssa, Weir felt. She had matured, become much more realistic and less inclined to lose herself in dreams. With improvement in the business, her ambitions soared. Nothing would do but for J. Livingstone's to grow into the finest establishment of its kind in Edinburgh. Every day more and more customers were flocking to the shop. Their employers were overjoyed, so thrilled that, not long after she arrived they began to pay the girl a small salary, a fact that did not go down well with their feckless daughter, Helen.

And that's where potential trouble lay! thought Davie privately. It was almost like Mistress Lindsay's all over again. Helen was stout and ill-favored physically. That alone gave room for jealousy. The fact that her parents quickly began to sing Alyssa's praises while continuing to point out *her* shortcomings only added more fuel to the simmering fire. Aye, mused Weir, there would be problems from that quarter eventually. Already the young woman of the house was building up a fine head of steam, and sooner or later it would explode.

But no matter, he thought complacently. When that time came, he would be there to take over. The moment he located a secure position as a groom in one of the grand households around the city, he intended to ask Alyssa to marry him. She must be made to face the fact that she needed a husband's protection. A woman on her own was a danger to herself and a temptation to others, all the more so if that woman happened to be young and beautiful. They never discussed the past. As far as Weir was concerned, it was dead and buried, and he hoped that Alyssa felt the same and in due time would be ready to embrace the future as his wife. Until then he made no attempt to push himself on her, since at present he had nothing to offer, and it wasn't his nature to ask favors of a woman when he had nothing substantial to give in return.

Alyssa's mind could not have been further removed from love and romance. She was thoroughly enjoying her new career and the challenge of building up the business while at the same time learning all she could. By the time she fell into bed at night she was too tired to think, and that was exactly how she liked it. Many of their customers had connections at court, and through a certain Lady Brodie, a gossipy dowager in her sixties, Alyssa learned that Blake had been married to Elizabeth Bancroft in February of that year. She had felt a wave of such intense pain that she felt physically ill, and for days she could think of nothing else, unable to keep her mind on the business. Then she made a serious mistake in an important order that lost them one of their best customers.

Disgusted with herself, Alyssa viewed her position squarely and soberly. Even had she lowered herself and fallen in with Blake's wishes, she could never have played an important part in his life. By the very nature of the relationship, she would have had to hover in the shadows, snatching what crumbs of his time he could spare. And, regardless of how much he denied it, he might have grown tired of her in time. Nay, nay, her mind rushed on before the ache became too unbearable, she had done the right thing to leave. Now, after talking to Lady Brodie, came the final proof that he was lost to her forever— even had she needed proof—and it was imperitive that she get on with her own life and make as much of it as she could.

Edinburgh had much to offer, many things to claim her interest and preclude the tendency to brood. Sunday was their day off and a time to explore the city. Its size, magnificence, the sheer press of the never-ending crowds of people who flocked through the gates daily for one reason or another, lent a constant panoply of changing colors.

Sometimes they joined the throngs strolling along the High Street to the Canongate in the direction of Holyrood Palace, or to Edinburgh Castle high on the hill known as the Seat of Arthur. They listened to impromptu speeches at the Tolbooth, watched jugglers perform at the Cross, and often took simple picnics of bread and cheese to one of the beautiful parks dotting the city.

Weekdays were even livelier, with stalls set up near Greyfriars Church where peddlers could be heard shrilling, "Boxwood and ivory combs, cobweb-fine lace, and braw satin ribbons to adorn m'lady's bonnet!" Others beckoned, "Hot mince pies! Live eels and winkles. Salve for sore feet and tinctures for any distemper!"

Over all this din, carts, litters and mules clattered by and now and then a Highlander in plaids flung rakishly over a brawny shoulder. Great lords and ladies in silks and satins were carried in covered litters, their squires and retainers bellowing and waving to make passage, "Give way! Make room for your betters!"

In spite of dour Knox preaching abstinence and moderation, few paid heed during fete days and holidays. They drank, they reveled; they enjoyed the pagan skirl of the pipes, or devil's sticks, as the preacher named them. They danced with abandon. They fought and loved with equal verve. Though such activities were declared illegal, the people found ways to indulge their taste for cockfights and bear-baiting, and seized on any excuse to light great bonfires on the hills surrounding the city or to organize torchlight parades.

Edinburgh seethed with vibrant life. Death too was never very far away. Once, out on an errand for Mistress Livingstone, Alyssa happened on a public execution at the Tolbooth. She would have turned and fled, but the press of crowds closed in about her and she couldn't escape. "Traitor!" the people screamed, thirsting for blood as one of the unfortunates tried to make his final speech, a customary procedure when one's last hour had come, but no one would listen. Blood flowed in rivers from the platform as ten men—six of them aristocrats—lost their heads that day. The watchers jeered and hooted, damning the traitors and praising the man who had caught them and brought them to their just deserts.

It was the first time Alyssa had heard the dreaded name of the Earl of Morton. And there he sat gloating on the platform with the other officials, the blood of the condemned almost soiling his fine Spanish leather shoes. Heavy-set and with a florid complexion, he had sandy hair and a straw-colored beard and pale eyes that struck Alyssa as being hard and merciless.

"Swine!" sobbed a woman close to Alyssa, her gaze fixed balefully on this high-born member of the Queen's court. "There sits a man wi' the blood o' innocent women and children on his conscience, let alone that o' these poor wretches, maist o' whom be innocent."

One of Morton's henchmen barreled through the crowd and hauled her away.

Edinburgh was never dull. The pulse of the city throbbed in tune to every snippet of gossip that filtered down from the castle on its rocky crag high above. The Queen did this. Her brother, Moray, said that. And more and more in that year of 1563, "Why should our Queen think to please Elizabeth of England in her choice of a husband, especially when Elizabeth refuses to name a candidate to Mary's liking?"

True to form, Queen Elizabeth refused to commit herself on that touchy score, though she was less loath to imperiously reject those others suggested as a husband for the very marriageable Mary Stuart.

"Why cannot the Queen wed without her consent?" Alyssa inquired of Mistress Livingstone.

"Och, ye ken she must please the English Queen if she hopes to be named as her heir," the good wife responded somewhat impatiently.

"Is it so important to be named as her heir when there is not such a great difference between them in age? Surely 'tis far more important to choose the man who will be one's husband; aye, and the King of Scotland too!"

The older woman chuckled wryly. "Henny, 'tis not so simple wi' Queens. When the high-born wed 'tis for business reasons or to make advantageous connections between countries, and our Queen's advisers think it would be *maist* advantageous if she were to be officially declared the heir to the English throne, and that's where Elizabeth's goodwill comes in! Ye see, m'dear, love has very little to do wi' it and quite often nothing at all."

How well she knew that! Alyssa felt almost sorry for Mary Stuart.

Early in 1564 Sir Simon Ogilvy swaggered determinedly into the shop. He waited until Alyssa was alone, then approached the counter and whispered in her ear, "Heartless witch. How cruelly you tease me, Alyssa. For more than a year you have turned all my invitations down, but this one you cannot refuse." Reaching for her hand, he startled her by asking, "Will you do me the honor of accompanying me to the Winter Ball at court?"

Alyssa was dumbstruck. This was his most dazzling invitation to date. She had never been to a ball in her life, and to attend one at court, escorted by the dashing Sir Simon, to rub shoulders with some of the most important people in Scotland and perhaps see the Queen herself, was a prospect that took her breath away.

"Say yea and I will buy you the finest gown in all of Edinburgh," he rushed on when she hesitated, that hesitancy giving him hope. This time, he thought triumphantly, she could not possibly turn him down. The temptation was too great for one in her lowly position in life.

His long pursuit of the heartless little wench truly astounded him, he who could have his choice of any woman in the city, even any woman at court. It had stung his pride to the quick to be rejected by such a one, far below him in social status, actually with no status at all. How could she? It perplexed him, enraged him, drove him to the edge of distraction. He longed to flaunt her incredible beauty before the envious eyes of his friends, confident that the girl would not let him down by her deportment. She was well-spoken, quick-witted, and for all her low birth, had the delicate manners of a lady. How came she by all this, Simon had often asked himself—and gone so far in his frustration as to ask her. But she would reveal little about her background except for a vague reference to her "home in the North."

Alyssa remained a mystery, and this accounted for some of her allure. But not all. She was ravishing, he thought as his hungry eyes dropped to the neckline of her gown where he glimpsed a tantalizing view of the velvety chasm between the creamy swells of her breasts. He would win her yet. And soon! Ah, how he yearned for the moment when he would finally crush that sweet form in his arms; when she would yield herself to him.

"Thank you, Sir Simon, but I cannot accept."

Ogilvy stared at her in amazement, at first doubting that he had heard aright. Then his handsome face flushed with anger. "And why, pray, can you not accept?" he demanded stiffly.

In a vain attempt to soothe his pride, yet with an edge to her voice, she replied, "Because I would be out of place at court, not having a title or a grand family name."

He brushed this aside. "What nonsense! You will be *my* partner, and the Ogilvy name is grand enough for both of us. Alyssa . . ." his tone softened and turned on a pleading note, such was the force of his desire for her, ". . . you weave excuses to torture me." She could feel his hot breath on her throat as he leaned yet closer, saying thickly, passionately, "You will be the loveliest woman at the ball and I proud to be your escort, so tell me you will come. I—I entreat you," he heard himself beg in astonishment.

And what of *after* the ball, Alyssa asked herself soberly. What would happen once she had accepted his gift of the beautiful gown? She would have taken a step from which she could not easily retreat; a step she had refused to take for a man she had loved with all her heart and soul; aye, and still loved. Against Sinclair, Sir Simon Ogilvy meant nothing to her.

"I'm sorry, but I cannot."

He drew back abruptly, straightening to his full height, his posture stiff and haughty as he gazed at her coldly. That coldness masked an inner fury that he could barely contain. He had lowered himself to her, pleaded with her, *begged* her—and still she had callously rejected him! At that moment he ached to put his slim white hands around the lovely throat and squeeze until all the breath vanished from the body that she continued to deny him. He knew he must leave at once before he lost his head.

"Damn you!" he grated, then turned on his heel and strode out.

Alyssa slumped against the counter and closed her eyes, then started violently when Mistress Livingstone came up quietly behind her. "I couldna help but overhearing, lass," she apologized, "since I was on ma' way into the shop, but . . . ye did right to refuse him."

He was a charming rake, the goodwife told her bluntly, and not the sort a girl could rely on at all. Though Ogilvy was from a good family, he himself was penniless and had run up a large account at the store. "There's only one thing men o' his rank want from a lass like you," she went on grimly. "Aye, ye did right fine to turn him down."

As she well knew!

But the scene upset Alyssa more than she cared to admit. It left her wondering what Sinclair had done or felt on the day he returned to Castle Augusta only to find her gone. Sir Simon, faced with rejection, had looked furious enough to kill, and Ogilvy had only a fraction of the drive and determination —and the pride—of the Chief of the clan Sinclair.

Never again, Alyssa vowed, would she involve herself, even remotely, with men above her own station in life. By "holding herself dear," as Mistress Lindsay had once advised, she had only subjected herself to disillusionment and pain. The barrier of rank was unbridgeable, insurmountable, rising above all other considerations, even love.

Thankfully, she had much to be grateful for. She had a wonderful friend in Davie, kind employers and a job she excelled at. That she had met no one of her own kind who interested her enough to form a romantic relationship with troubled her not at all. For the moment she was content. She had come to think of the Livingstones' home as her own, their business of vital concern to her, and the older couple as her dear friends. She managed to convince herself that she was happy with her life as it was.

A year went by without Alyssa seeing Simon Ogilvy again. Then that winter something happened to give her wheel of fortune yet another vicious turn, and once more her life took a new direction.

18

The winter of 1564 was the coldest in living memory. Edinburgh was smitten with a strange sneezing sickness said to have been introduced into Scotland by a foreign visitor. One after another each member of the Livingstone household fell ill. By December half the city had taken to bed, and hundreds, then thousands, died. Mistress Livingstone ailed for only three days before she expired. Her husband too was gravely ill. After a few weeks he partially recovered, but both his robust good health and his spirit were broken, the latter by the loss of his wife.

A pall of gloom hung over the city and in the cordwainer's shop. Alyssa cried for her mistress as she might have done for a mother. She had been sick herself, but forced herself out of bed before she felt really well because the household had quite fallen apart, and Helen whined that she was much too poorly to be able to care for her father.

On her feet and busy from dawn to dusk, Alyssa collapsed into bed each night exhausted, and this exhaustion, hard on the heels of her own illness, led to an uncharacteristic depression. How she missed the kindly Mistress Livingstone! Even Davie was gone most of the time, trying to shoulder much of his master's work. Helen was even more nasty when under the weather and rarely spoke to her except to give orders. "Remember," she said, "*I* am the lady of the house now. You will harken to *me* and do my bidding."

The moment that Davie had anticipated had come. Helen quickly found ways to make Alyssa's life miserable, and there was nothing Alyssa could do about it if she wanted to hold onto her job. It was pointless to appeal to Master Livingstone since he had retreated into a world of his own, and there was rampant unemployment in the city and no hope of finding another job.

By late February when most of Scotland was beginning to recover a little, conditions at the cordwainer's shop were very different. With her father broken, his daughter had free rein. Helen finally managed to win over one of the journeymen and quietly married him at the end of the month, and together these two took over everything.

One day Helen came to Alyssa and accused her of stealing money from the till.

"'Tis a lie!" Alyssa gasped. "I would never do such a thing."

The young matron brought a handful of coins out of her pocket. "I found these in your room."

Alyssa's face reddened with anger. She stared at the hand holding her savings, money she had carefully set aside from the wages the Livingstones had paid her—the only security in the world she had.

But Helen refused to listen when she tried to explain. Holding up a hand imperiously, she snapped, "If it happens again you will be dismissed!"

Alyssa had to choke back a feeling of outrage as she saw the older woman slip the money back into her pocket, neatly snatching her small savings away. It was useless to protest. To do so would be to furnish Helen with the excuse to let her go. And Alyssa didn't doubt that that time would come soon, the moment the business recovered from the slump brought on by the epidemic.

One of the first "economy" steps the new mistress had taken upon assuming control was to cut back on the expenses for the servants, so that night Alyssa huddled in an unheated room wondering what she would do. Beyond the tiny window, thick snow lay on the ground and an icy wind swept down from the castle high overhead and moaned through the deserted streets of Edinburgh. Here and there a lantern reflected a tepid pool of light on a sea of ice. The bleakness was complete, the city steeped in mourning for the thousands who had died.

Curling into a ball, with only her nose peeping out over

the covers, Alyssa lay awake in a room made frigid by drafts whistling in under the eaves. She had to face the fact that she could be dismissed at any time, and Davie with her. Helen Livingstone's moment of triumph had come and she would make the most of it, nor give a thought to how it might affect business at the shop.

What would they do? Where would they live and how would they survive? There were no jobs to be had, and beggars were to be seen on every street corner and roaming in desperate bands through the narrow wynds and closes, ready to kill for a crust of bread.

Helen had confiscated her savings. Davie too had next to nothing. To be tossed into the street now in the midst of winter meant almost certain death. Had she not heard the carts rumble past the shop every morning just after dawn, picking up those who had frozen during the night?

The hopelessness of her situation was borne home to Alyssa, and once again she bitterly realized that she had made a serious miscalculation, deluding herself into thinking she was secure, in a position to take care of herself. The grim truth was that she was no different from what she had ever been, a woman alone with neither husband nor family to turn to at a time of crisis. Except for Davie. And Davie was little better off than she, his only advantage the fact that he was a man and less likely to be taken advantage of or exploited.

Exhausted, still not quite well, and suddenly desperately lonely, Alyssa buried her head in the pillow and wept. All she had worked for at Livingstones' had been swept away — because it had never been hers to begin with. In truth she had nothing. And she was deeply afraid, the rumbling of the death carts echoing in her ears, and no one she could turn to for help; no one her pride would allow her to turn to.

Sinclair was in residence at his Edinburgh mansion on Abbey Hill, within walking distance of the store, but she had never given in to the impulse to walk that way. Alyssa had heard through one of their titled customers that the important lords of the realm had been gathered in town for the better part of the year haggling over the weighty question of the Queen's choice of a husband.

A sudden fierce longing took hold of her, one she was too weak and dispirited to resist: an intense desire to see him. Into her mind flooded all the memories she had struggled to hold back, the sweet, passionate hours they had shared, the way his sometimes hard face had softened when he looked at her. Every touch, every whispered endearment, rose in her mind to torture her, and she sobbed into the pillow, thinking of all the happiness they might have shared had he made a different choice that day at Lynnwood.

The pain of remembered rejection drove everything else out of her mind, and it hurt as fiercely now, two years later, as it had then. Nay, she thought bitterly, she would not try to see him, for she would rather die in the streets than crawl to him for help, nor would she resign herself to a secondary place in his life for all the gold in Scotland.

The biting cold hung on, and at the end of that week Helen sent Alyssa on an errand that should have been handled by one of the young apprentices, to deliver a pair of boots to a house off the Canongate. An early dusk had fallen when Helen put the package in her hand with the remark, "And see to it that this"—with a nod to the order—"is not seized by footpads. If it is, don't bother to come back."

With starving mobs roving the city, it was unsafe for even a man to go abroad late in the day without a weapon or strong companion, yet mercifully, Alyssa managed to deliver the parcel without mishap. Almost running, she started back to the shop through the twilight. As she passed a rowdy tavern, a whipcord pair of arms suddenly grabbed her from behind.

Alyssa screamed and fought to free herself. Instead she was spun around and found herself looking up into the handsome face of Sir Simon Ogilvy. In the light of the tavern lantern his grey eyes were very bright as they swept over her, and—to her surprise—his smile was very warm. "Alyssa Dunne! For a moment I was unsure." He studied her thin white face keenly, his eyes dropping to her flimsy shawl. "Have you had the sickness?" he asked softly. "Faith, but you seem a mere shadow of the bonny lass I knew a year ago."

Shivering violently in the cold wind, her heart still thumping madly from the fright he had given her, Alyssa was horrified to feel tears welling into her eyes. Ogilvy sized up the situation at once. Slipping a firm arm around her shoulders, he steered her into the tavern and found them a table near the back of the room. Over steaming tankards of spiced ale he soon had the full story out of her of the changes that had taken place at J. Livingstone and Son, Cordwainer.

"So now Helen is in charge," he said grimly, "and if I know that wench, the shop will not be long in business."

"Nor will I have a job for long," laughed Alyssa shakily.

But already she felt a little better, the heat in the tavern and the hot drink kindling a pleasant fire in her numb body. And in contrast to the dolorous atmosphere in the city and the drab attire worn by most of the customers, Sir Simon was, as usual, elegantly attired in a burgundy velvet cloak lined with fur, his golden coloring and air of command and prosperity very attractive to Alyssa at that moment.

He seemed to have forgotten the circumstances of their last meeting, or more likely, she thought, had chosen to ignore it. Steering the conversation away from her own troubles, Alyssa asked how things had been with him. He was a witty conversationalist and soon made her laugh, something she hadn't been able to do since the day Mistress Livingstone died. He confided an exciting piece of court news, something that had Holyrood Palace all atwitter. "My Lord Darnley is expected from England shortly. They say he's the latest candidate for the Queen's hand, though, being a Catholic, the Protestant faction don't think overhighly of him."

"Then Queen Elizabeth has made her wishes on the subject of a husband clear at last?"

Ogilvy smiled cynically. "Nay, not exactly. 'Tis not the English Queen's way to commit herself so irrevocably. With that one 'tis always necessary to read betwixt the lines, but it would seem—since she has given her permission for Darnley to travel to Scotland—that she's not averse to such a match."

With her eyes on the ornate gold ring on his finger, Alyssa asked with a smile, "And you, Sir Simon, do you have some important position at court?"

He picked up his tankard and took a sip, his eyes finally leaving her to casually scan the smoky room. "Aye . . ." he replied somewhat cautiously, "I work with the Earl of Moray and travel frequently on the Queen's business."

Her interest sharpened and she studied him curiously, thinking that this position explained his new prosperity. Until now she had viewed him as a charming rogue. Now, at mention of his association with the Queen's half-brother and chief adviser, she found herself wondering if she had misjudged him after all. "I'm happy for you," she told him honestly. "I—I had no idea that you were so well situated at court."

Ogilvy was quick to seize this unexpected advantage. He invited her to dine with him at Bell's Tavern the following Saturday night, adding by way of persuasion, "Everyone of importance in the city eventually ends up at Bell's. Why, even Her Majesty herself has supped there on occasion."

Alyssa hesitated and turned away from the coaxing look in the warm grey eyes—and it was then she noticed the man staring at them from a nearby table. He was a hulking, ugly creature with flat features and a peculiar stony expression in his eyes. The flaring torchlight on the wall fell harshly across the livid scar running down his face.

Simon tugged on her hand to regain her attention. "Tell me that I may call for you on Saturday eve. Say you will come, lass, and Simon Ogilvy will be the happiest man in Edinburgh."

"Aye," she heard herself say, "I will be happy to accept."

He raised her hand to his lips and kissed it. As he bent his head, Alyssa gazed at the waving gold hair, the expensive ring on the hand holding hers, and told herself that here was someone who might well help them out of their difficulties, and when one was desperate it was necessary to seize any opportunity that happened by. Besides, Sir Simon appeared to have matured. He had gained a certain stature, possibly because he had conducted himself like the gentleman he professed to be and had refrained from making love to her with his eyes.

He escorted her safely back to the house in the darkness, chuckling complacently when at one point Alyssa was certain they were being followed. Dropping a hand to the sword at his side, he said, "This has never failed me yet. It once belonged to my grandfather and was blessed by Cardinal Beaton himself."

It wasn't until after she was in bed that Alyssa remembered the ugly lout who had watched them so closely in the tavern. Could he have stalked them home with a mind to rob Sir Simon?

Elizabeth Sinclair watched her husband dancing with the Queen, and amid the glittering throng filling the enormous ornate ballroom Mary Stuart stood out from all the rest. There was never a Queen as fair, as witty, as skilled in music and dancing and all the social graces as Mary, and it seemed to the Countess of Belrose as she watched them glide around the ballroom chatting and laughing together—in a way that Blake never thought to amuse himself with her—that this Queen had everything, including the adulation of every man in Scotland.

She hated Mary Stuart! And she raged inwardly at her lord's attachment to a papist, a wicked tool sent from Rome to bedevil them and drive men mad with her wanton charms, Blake among them. So Elizabeth was delighted when later in the evening, within hearing of everyone around the high table, the Queen and her brother Moray had a spat. It concerned the fact that Mary had given permission for the exiled Earl of Lennox to return to Scotland over Moray's vehement objections. Now Lennox's son, Lord Darnley, was to be allowed to join his father. Blake had explained that Mary had done this at the express request of her cousin, Queen Elizabeth. Mary, it seemed, was loath to deny her English relative any request within reason.

After the ball the Earl and Countess of Belrose had a spat of their own. As they were preparing to retire at Clairmont, their Edinburgh mansion, Elizabeth waspishly commented, "Is it any wonder that Moray lost his head at table, forced to welcome his old enemy Lennox back to Scotland? You would think, would you not, that Her Grace would be more careful of her brother's feelings, considering the time and effort he has expended helping her these past few years."

Blake laughed thinly, "And helping himself!"

"Ha! As ever you defend her."

Blake glanced at her in the mirror. She was seated on a cushioned bench before her dressing table while her maid stood behind her taking the pins out of her hair. The rich burgundy color of her gown suited her well, since she was very fair, but the hard gleam in her eyes and her pinched mouth detracted from her appeal.

He gave her a warning look in the glass, his eyes moving from hers to the tiring woman who at that moment unfastened her low-cut gown. Even as it slid from her shoulders to expose her white breasts, Sinclair casually turned away and walked into his dressing room. Elizabeth bit her lip. "Be quick!" she snapped at her maid. "God's blood, I swear you are all thumbs this night."

Even the sight of her half-naked body failed to hold his interest, the countess fumed. Even that left him remote and indifferent! Nothing about her truly interested him, not her beauty, her conversation, her deep involvement in the Church. Though in all honesty she could never accuse him of being unkind, anything other than an attentive husband as far as her needs were concerned, Elizabeth was well aware that she had never had his love.

When the tiring woman left, Sinclair returned to their chamber and climbed into bed without a word, turning his back to her. He was in no mood for an argument, most of which came back to the question of religion. In the space of two years his wife had become almost as fanatical as her mentor, John Knox.

After a moment he felt her climbing into bed, but didn't turn around.

"You danced much with the Queen this night," Elizabeth said petulantly, her eyes on his back.

"Her Grace dances well, and makes a lively partner," the earl replied smoothly.

"And I do not?"

"My dear Elizabeth, I danced more frequently with you than the Queen—"

"But enjoyed it less, I vow."

With a sigh, Blake finally turned around. "Enough, Elizabeth. Come"—he drew her down beside him—"and let us kiss and retire. I must be at Holyrood early on the morn."

"Holyrood! Always Holyrood!" she exploded in a jealous

rage. "So you would persist in serving the Catholic Queen even though the Lord has seen fit to punish you because of it. He made our babes stillborn, did He not?"

"We will get more children, my lady."

"Nay!" And aware of how much he wanted a son and thinking to frighten him into changing his attitude, she burst out incautiously, "Nay, husband, for I cannot, in all good conscience, lie with you again until you see the error of your ways. So if you would have your heir you must repent. It is God's will."

At that moment the last of the affection Blake had felt for her died and black fury exploded inside his head that she would dare to try to blackmail him into bending to her will. "Madam," he said tightly, "You have just handed me grounds to set you aside."

19

Alyssa glanced around the dining room of Bell's Tavern with great interest. A landmark in Edinburgh, it had a dark beamed ceiling and creamy walls broken by half-timbering, softly glowing wainscotting and a sturdy flagstone floor. Tiny latticed windows and a massive open hearth, the whole place blazing with candlelight, lent the atmosphere a warm, convivial aura that delighted her.

Sir Simon Ogilvy chuckled, "Many a plot has been hatched in this room. 'Tis said that eventually everyone of importance in Europe comes to Bell's." He nodded to a roistering group of men seated to the left of the fireplace. "The tall, handsome fellow yonder is Henry Stewart, Lord Darnley, but lately arrived from England and soon to join the Queen at Fife. The wee fellow on his left is David Riccio, a musician seen much about court, and the man to Darnley's right is one of the Queen's bastard half-brothers, Lord Robert, a rascal of a lad . . ."

Alyssa listened avidly, and by the time supper arrived it seemed to her that half the illustrious figures in the city were seated right there in the room. She was particularly interested in Lord Darnley, who struck her as being quite drunk, though for all his great height seemed scarcely older than a boy. He turned flirtatious eyes to their table often, nor was he the only one in the tavern who gazed admiringly at the beautiful girl with the flaming gold hair.

Sir Simon was gratified by all the attention directed at their table. He enjoyed being the envy of other men, and basked in the thought that he had run the little vixen to ground at last. From across the table his eyes devoured her with a hunger that had grown greater with each rejection. Now here she was, her long green eyes sparkling, ravishing for all that she was dressed in a simple blue cambric gown. She had the richness of gold in her hair, emeralds in her eyes, her teeth like small neat pearls in a row. The demure hint of bosom above the neck of her gown inflamed his long-frustrated desire. For two long years he had tortured himself with the image of her lying naked and submissive in his arms, and tonight, he thought with satisfaction, he had persuaded her at last to take the first step in that direction.

A servitor arrived staggering under a tray loaded with many dishes. Alyssa laughed softly. "Surely this cannot all be for us?"

Nodding to one of the plates, Simon advised, "If you will eat good meat, try some of this larded venison. Or mayhap you'd prefer the carp with the piquant Dutch sauce?"

He would have her eat heartily and, reaching for a capon, pulled it apart and set it on her plate, saying, "See if this does not provoke your appetite."

Between courses he kept refilling her glass with wine.

The food was delicious, the wine smooth and heady, and the handsome Sir Simon an engaging companion. Conversation flowed easily between them. Alyssa laughed merrily as he kept her amused with tales about some of the people in the room, most of whom he seemed to know. After a while she gave him a mischievous smile from the corners of her eyes. "And what of you, sir? What exactly is your office at court?"

Smiling, he tickled her under the chin. "'Tis highly confidential, my sweet. All I can say is that I work for Lord James Stewart, the Earl of Moray, as I told you before."

She studied him quizzically. "Methinks, sir, that you deliberately pique my interest by being evasive," she teased. "Or . . . mayhap you have something to hide?"

Something to hide! Ogilvy leaned back in his chair away from her, and for a moment the lids lowered over his eyes. As the fifth son of Hugo Ogilvy, Lord Stratton, whose estates had been plundered, rebuilt, and plundered yet again in endless border warfare, Simon had inherited precious little when his father died. To his lot had fallen crumbling Mordrun Hall, a dreary, antiquated manor several leagues outside the city, and so little money that Ogilvy had had to borrow funds from an uncle to finance several abortive business ventures. So for the past few years, perforce, he had had to live by his wits—until James Stewart had taken note of his unique talents and thought to make use of them, but he was engaged in the type of work it was unhealthy to boast about in a crowded room.

With a negligent flick of his hand, Simon smiled across the table. "Nay, nay, sweetheart, though 'twould be exciting to say I had some great secret, I fear, alas, that the actual truth makes dull relating. When not on court business I'm much occupied with the running of my estates." He thought of Mordrun Hall and winced. Set on a stony hillside of sullen soil, the village itself tiny and moldering and populated by a band of morose and wretched serfs, all of whom despised their overlord, he rarely went near the place.

But Alyssa was impressed. He had an important job at court, owned property that required much of his time, and undoubtedly had many connections, one of whom might well require the services of a man and woman who at any moment might desperately need a job. This was her chief reason for agreeing to dine with him, though in truth she was enjoying it immensely. The warm, charming room, the delicious food, and Simon's stimulating company had been pleasant, a tonic to the depression that had plagued her of late.

She could not deny that Simon Ogilvy was attractive, especially when he set himself out to be charming. He made her laugh. He was witty and knowledgeable. Simon could make the very air sparkle when he set his mind to it. Now he was looking at her appraisingly, a gleam in his eyes. Leaning forward, he said, "Now 'tis your turn to confess all the secrets you've been hiding from me. I would know everything about you from before you came to Edinburgh."

For an instant her face sobered as Blake Sinclair's dark face sprang up in her mind, but she quickly thrust it away. "I was born in Inverness-shire, raised by my . . . ah, grandmother, and I came to Edinburgh with much the same idea as everyone else, to seek fame and fortune," she finished on a light note.

Ogilvy's brows rose and he laughed heartily. "Seek your fame and fortune! God's blood, sweeting, you talk more like a lad than a lass. Seek fame and fortune, indeed. Methinks managing Livingstone's has given you peculiar ideas, my lass." And reprovingly, "What of marriage, Mistress Alyssa Dunne? A comely wench like you should have been wed long since. Aye, and had a cottage full of tumbling babes too."

"Ha! And what of you, sir?" she shot back with asperity. "You don't seem overquick to take that step."

He leaned closer, the sleepy look she had come to know in his smoky grey eyes, visualizing as he did so the night he would take masterful possession of her. "I have yet to find one willing to share my lot in life, fair Alyssa."

Her long lashes swept down over her eyes, and, thinking it prudent to change the subject, she grew serious. "Simon, I must find another job. Do you know of anyone who might have need of my services?"

Could she but know it, he thought feverishly, she was looking at one who needed certain services of her desperately. But, experienced as he was, Ogilvy sensed that it would be disastrous to his plans to push her. Aloud, he promised to look into the matter. Alyssa thanked him warmly. "And now," she said, "I must be getting home. Already I'm in the bad books with Helen."

He nodded, continuing to play the perfect gentleman. Patience, he told himself. Before long she will be mine. When they walked out into the foyer, Ogilvy was hailed by a friend, one he wasn't anxious to present to Alyssa. Seating her on one of the benches circling the room, he excused himself for a moment and drew his friend into the corridor so that they might talk in private.

Alyssa glanced around. Through an archway she could see into the common room of the tavern, smoke-filled and noisy. Suddenly, she felt that she was being stared at, and her eyes were drawn to a table near the door. Gazing at her fixedly as he sat hunched over his tankard was a huge brute of a fellow with a disfiguring scar running down his face. Her heart jumped as she recognized him as the one who had watched them so closely the last time she had run into Simon; the one she suspected might have followed them home.

Ogilvy returned and helped her to her feet. Nodding in the direction of the common room, Alyssa whispered, "He chills me to the bone."

Simon peered through the smoke and chuckled gruffly, "Aye, 'tis a face that would curdle milk. I know him; his name is Bruno. He's one of the MacKellar squires."

At mention of the MacKellars he frowned. He was distantly related to Lady Magdalen; their mothers, both Hepburns, had been cousins. But his relationship to the haughty countess had brought no benefits Simon's way. On the contrary, Magdalen disliked him heartily and rarely bothered to conceal it, a situation that rankled a man of Ogilvy's egotistical turn of mind. Consequently, he pointedly ignored the lady and, to salve his pride at being slighted, never mentioned their connection.

"Bruno . . .?" Alyssa had turned pale, all the horror of that misty evening on the moor surging back into her mind. At that moment she was convinced that it had been Bruno who killed Robin. Now this same Bruno, for a reason she still couldn't comprehend, was after her!

Pulling away from Ogilvy, she bolted out the door. He caught up with her on the pavement and spun her around to face him. "Holy Mother, what now?"

With a great effort she tried to pull herself together, even as she ached to run away, but Simon was holding her firmly by the arm, his expression mirroring his astonishment. Alyssa was in no mood to go into a lengthy explanation. Besides, Davie had warned her not to think of speaking out against Lady Magdalen since they could prove nothing against her.

Shuddering, she replied, "'Tis that fellow in the tavern. Bruno. He—he frightens me."

Simon laughed. "Darling, he cannot help his ugly face."

Alyssa took his arm and tugged him on. "It grows late and I must get home at once."

* * *

Davie too was afraid, far more alarmed than he cared to show. Lady Magdalen's squire knew where they lived, so it was more imperative than ever that they find work elsewhere. It was pointless to go to the authorities, for would they be likely to take Alyssa's and Davie's word over that of the Countess of Kilgarin?

The moment he was free midway through Sunday afternoon, Davie set off to search for a job with Alyssa perched on the mule behind him. This animal, all he could afford, was elderly and not about to be hurried. Weir had heard of an opening through Lady Brodie, one of their customers. Her son, she said, was looking for an experienced groom on his estate at Craigmiller several leagues outside town. Further, the dowager promised to vouch for Davie.

He set off with high hopes, wishing they could have left earlier. The weather was still cold and there was a few inches of snow on the ground, but at least the afternoon was sunny. As he said to Alyssa, "Mayhap if I'm taken on they will find a place for you," while knowing that it wouldn't matter. If he landed the job he intended to ask her to marry him.

As he had anticipated, things went well at Craigmiller. The earl's head groom, Breskin, questioned him closely for a long time, then took him on a leisurely tour of the stables and a ride around the estate. Alyssa waited in the huge kitchen with its enormous crackling fire, but her attempts to find work there met with no success. The housekeeper took one look at the young beauty and thought of her prim mistress—then her master—and mentally crossed the girl off the list. The earl had a roving eye, and his wife was insanely jealous. Not about to risk her own job, the middle-aged woman tried to let Alyssa down easily. "There's naught for now, lass, but I'll keep ye in mind if something opens later."

It was dusk when they left Craigmiller. Davie was in fine fettle and Alyssa happy for him, though desperately worried about her own future. Weir chattered away cheerily as they rode along through the winter twilight while privately he made glowing plans. The very next day he intended to take his remaining coins and buy something pretty for Alyssa. Presenting it to her, he would say, "This is only a wee token of the good things in store for ma' wife."

Darkness closed around them swiftly, and they passed few travelers on the road. Preoccupied with his own exciting thoughts, Weir was not as alert as he normally was. As they rode along the bank of Duddingston Loch, their shadow cast on the water by the moonlight, he felt Alyssa's arms suddenly tighten about him. "Davie, we're being followed!" she whispered. "I—I saw something back there in the trees."

His own blood jumped like mercury in his veins even as he replied gruffly, "Mayhap a deer."

Alyssa glanced back. Light and shadow moved languorously in the moonlight, shifting with the swaying branches of the trees hanging over the path. One minute that path was empty, then a black-cloaked rider burst out of the trees. She went weak with terror, all the vile things done to Robin looming dark in her mind. "Hurry!" she screamed. "Oh please, please hurry!"

Davie managed to whip the mule into a clumsy gallop, even as he reached for his dirk, and they belted along the banks of the loch toward the distant lights of Edinburgh less than half a league away. Then with a cry of relief he shouted, "Riders!" Alyssa saw them too, a small group of men on horseback cantering in their direction from the city.

She buried her head into his back and closed her eyes, and felt the jolting impact of the arrow in her own body as Davie sagged against her, a gurgling sound bubbling up from his throat. Alyssa raised her head and gaped stupidly at the quivering shaft of the weapon protruding from his neck. It had missed her head by inches as she laid it against Davie's back.

He toppled from the saddle and fell on the ground, taking her with him. By the time the other riders reached them, the road behind them was empty, their attacker vanished. While one man rode off in search of him, another started back to the city in hopes of finding a leech. Two others stood around awkwardly, gazing down at the sobbing girl bent over the dying man.

Taking her hand, Davie bid her come closer. "I must talk

to ye," he whispered, a trickle of blood running from the side of his mouth.

"Nay, nay, don't try to speak!" Alyssa begged him, tears spattering from her face onto his. "They've gone for a doctor. You must rest until he arrives."

"Listen to me, lass!" His eyes were suddenly fierce, his voice strong. "This I must tell ye for your own protection. I was wrong, Alyssa, to keep it hid from you for so long." He paused for breath then continued, "I ken who ye really are."

"Davie . . . ?" She stared at him, wondering if he could be delirious, then was sure of it as he told her an incredible story, finishing with the words, "You, lass, are the true Countess of Kilgarin. Now ye ken why Lady Magdalen wants ye dead."

She shook her head and covered his cold face with kisses. It was preposterous, the ramblings of a semi-dazed mind.

"Don't . . . don't think o' trying to prove your claim." Another long pause wherein they heard the rattling in his throat. "It would be impossible . . . and dangerous." His voice faded and a film formed over his eyes, but the hand holding hers still gripped fiercely, as if struggling to cling to life until he made her understand. "Go far away from here, Alyssa. Go now!" Finally his hand loosened. "I love ye, lass. And I'm sorry . . . sorry for what ma' mother done."

"Davie!" she screamed as he closed his eyes. "Nay, nay, don't leave me!"

One of the onlookers put a hand on her shoulder. "He's gone, lass. Poor lad, he rambled deliriously there at the end."

Stunned—for Davie had been a comforting fixture in her life for as long as she could remember—Alyssa buried her face in her friend's shoulder and wept as if her heart would break, unable to imagine life without him. Others arrived, and numbly she watched them lift Davie onto a litter and carry him toward the lights of Edinburgh. Somebody took her arm, spoke soothing words she didn't hear. Alyssa walked behind the litter like a wraith, her eyes fixed on the body, and it came to her that she was truly alone now.

Master Livingstone roused himself out of his apathy to

insist they pay for Davie's burial, brushing aside Helen's objections that he should be interred in a pauper's grave. After he was laid to rest, Helen took Alyssa aside and informed her that she had two weeks to find another job.

Alone in her tiny chamber under the eaves, Alyssa cried herself sick, recalling in wrenching detail countless sweet moments that had gone to making up her long friendship with Davie. He had been like a brother, at times a fond father, and when she needed it, sometimes a mother too, as he had been with Robin. Oh, dear God, she sobbed, how dreary and empty her life would be now! How fiercely she would miss him.

Exhausted with weeping, she slumped back against the pillow and fixed dismal eyes on the wall. Slowly a vicious hatred kindled inside her, pushing back the grief. Magdalen MacKellar had done this! And one day, she vowed, Magdalen MacKellar would pay. She thought of Davie's wild rambling at the end and recalled him saying, "Now ye ken why Lady Magdalen wants ye dead."

If she could believe Davie's incredible story she could understand why the countess would go to such great lengths to be rid of her. Aye, and anyone connected to that long-ago night at Cumbray Castle. Robin was dead. Davie too. The only one remaining to threaten the lady was Alyssa herself.

And Bruno knew where she lived! Sooner or later he would get to her and finally wipe out everyone connected with that night. How, Alyssa wondered, could she save herself? What hope did she have of surviving to one day avenge the wrongs that had been done to her and her friends?

Quite suddenly Alyssa believed Weir's story. It explained so much that had puzzled her, mainly the reason why Lady Magdalen should show so much interest in her. At that dark moment she was much too depressed to take any delight at being the true Countess of Kilgarin, the real head of the clan MacKellar. It could never be proved. Who would take *her* word over that of the earl and countess? "Go far away," Davie had warned. "Go now!"

Alyssa pushed back the covers and gazed at her odd "birthmark." Very faintly, helped along by everything she now knew, she thought she discerned the letter C. Cumbray! But even that hardly constituted proof. Any cunning lass might have had it done to her.

Rising, she padded to the window and anxiously peered out. The streets were empty, but that didn't mean that Bruno might not be lying in wait. She would be unable to leave the premises without the fear of having a dagger plunged into her back, yet soon she would be forced to leave, like it or not. If she hoped to survive, she needed help and could think of only one person to turn to, and she must see him at once. Tomorrow!

Simon was flabbergasted and infinitely skeptical, ready to laugh, but as he gazed at her in astonishment he saw her resemblance to the MacKellars. She had the coppery hair, green eyes, their above-average height. Ogilvy sucked in a breath, his heart racing as a dozen glowing possibilities opened up in his mind. In a flash Alyssa went from being a potentially desirable mistress to a very desirable wife. *If* this were true.

At last, he sensed, his luck was about to change.

Simon questioned her closely to try to gauge whether her claim to Cumbray could be proved. It didn't take more than a few moments for him to realize that it was most unlikely. Except for herself and Lady Magdalen, there was no one now alive—at least that Alyssa knew of—who could substantiate her story.

Alyssa watched his face anxiously. "Do you believe me, Simon?"

He leaned forward and kissed her on the tip of her nose. "Aye, sweet, I believe you." And he did, possibly because he wanted to so much. But he took pains to caution, "It will be the very devil to prove, assuming it *can* be proved."

But no matter, he was thinking privately. Gain could be gotten another way were he to handle things skillfully. How gratifying, his mind raced on, to be able to go to Magdalen and wipe the smirk off her face at last, the patronizing disdain that never allowed him to forget for an instant that he was the "poor relation." If all went well, he would be poor no longer. His cousin would be the one to find herself with a much lighter purse!

Aloud he soothed, "You have nothing more to fear and

must leave this business to me." And grimly, "I know how to handle Lady Magdalen."

The MacKellar town house made up in size what it lacked in good taste and elegance. Typically, Magdalen made her second cousin cool his heels for an hour before she would condescend to see him. When Simon was shown into her garish upstairs solar, he found her with some of her women. "Dismiss them!" he ordered, having decided that with such a woman it was necessary to take a bold stand from the first. "We must talk privily."

Once they were alone, the woman heard him out in silence, none of her inward dismay showing on her face. She watched him from under hooded lids, a grim smile touching her lips. So the wench knew the truth! It mattered little, since she had no way of proving it. Because of all the names Ogilvy hurled into her face he left out the most important—Jock Semple! Of Semple, obviously, they knew nothing. And without this vital witness they had no case.

When Simon finished, she chuckled. "A ridiculous fairy tale! Along with your other questionable attributes, Sir Simon, it seems we must add a wild and dangerous imagination."

He was not intimidated by this veiled threat. Too much was at stake. "Madam, either we talk plain here and now or I shall discuss this matter with those who will be only too happy to listen. Aye, and to act upon the information too!"

She glowered at him from under her brows, thinking that even though it was true they had no real witness, could she afford to have questions raised in the MacKellars' minds, questions that might lead them to investigate on their own? Aloud she snapped, "What do you want of me, knave?"

Ogilvy announced the price of his silence, adding, "You should know that by way of insurance, I've written the whole story into a letter and deposited it with someone of great authority at court. The letter is sealed. But should anything happen to me—or to Alyssa Dunne—instructions have been given for it to be opened."

Magdalen hid her alarm, and shrugged.

But Simon sensed the state of her mind. "Lady, rest

assured that neither of us will have reason to be anxious . . . provided you keep to our bargain."

Magdalen's mind ticked furiously. In a milder tone she inquired, "And what of this girl, Alyssa? What means she to you?"

Without the slightest hesitation he replied confidently, "I intend to make her my wife."

She gave a sneering laugh. "Then I suppose I must pity her, knowing you as I do. But what assurance do I have that she will not try to make trouble for me?"

"Once Alyssa becomes my wife I have ways of making her obey."

"Aye, doubtlessly. . . ."

Magdalen chuckled, feeling slightly better; more hopeful. She reminded herself of the type of man she was dealing with, one she knew for his extravagance, depravity and unreliability. Ogilvy, she assured herself, could be managed as long as his appetites were appeased. Not only could he be managed, but mayhap in time brought around to her way of thinking—and acting.

Sir Simon left the house in an expansive frame of mind, everything having gone his way. Now all that remained was for him to persuade Alyssa to marry him, thereby making certain that Magdalen would continue to dole out the money. But Alyssa, he thought with a slight frown, had a mind of her own and could be most stubborn. Ah, but he had just the way to win her over! By using fear, fear for her very life. He could say that without his protection—his powerful friends at court, and the Ogilvy name behind her—she was doomed.

Stopping at a goldsmith's, he bought Alyssa a pretty necklace of rubies and pearls—not too expensive—then treated himself to a new diamond ring. The first installment of the blackmail money was already being frittered away. Inwardly Ogilvy shrugged, thinking that the pot of MacKellar gold was bottomless. Whistling, he turned the corner and hurried to J. Livingstone's, Cordwainers.

20

Blake Sinclair was in a disgruntled mood when he and his men returned to Edinburgh after escorting Lord Darnley to join the Queen at Wemyss Castle. Darnley during the ride had deported himself like a spoiled young fool, complaining about his mount and the inferior hospitality along the way, so that by the time they reached Wemyss the entire party were heartily disgusted with him.

Though he would never have admitted it to his wife, Blake felt privately that Queen Mary had made a mistake in allowing the Lennox Stewarts to return to Scotland, where they had many enemies. Why had they come? Even more to the point, why had Queen Elizabeth so obligingly allowed them to come? Now this feckless youth Darnley had suddenly been catapulted above all others as a contender for Mary's hand—and he a Catholic! He had been charm itself when presented to his cousin Mary Stuart, his moroseness on the ride forgotten. The English ambassador, Randolph, had smiled benignly on the tall couple with the remark to Blake, "Like a pair of young gods, are they not, Sinclair?" his crafty eyes concealing something, or so Blake imagined.

Riding through the city gates, he thrust his misgivings aside, having plenty of his own to worry him. Elizabeth had returned to her uncle's house, and before Blake had left Edinburgh, he had set in force the dissolution of his marriage. His family, naturally, were up in arms, but he had bowed to their wishes regarding Elizabeth before and had suffered through two years of misery in consequence. Now he would please himself and he wanted nothing more than to be free.

Heir or no heir, he would embark on no more loveless marriages!

He found Jason waiting for him at Clairmont, a foolish grin on his face. The younger man was excited. He had a piece of news that he felt confident would bring the Chief out of his black mood, a frame of mind that had plagued the clan leader for the better part of two years.

Drawing him into the study, Jason poured two goblets of wine. Accepting one, Blake eyed his cousin quizzically. "Out with it, lad. You look much like the cat who stole the cream."

"I saw an old friend of yours two days gone in the Lawnmarket."

Sinclair stared at him. "Must we play riddles?" he asked in exasperation, wanting nothing more than to bathe, dine, and collapse into bed and put everything else out of his mind. Tossing back the wine, he unbuckled his sword belt and only half-listened as Jason started to speak, then raised his head abruptly at mention of a name he never thought to hear again.

"Aye," Jason laughed, "I was not mistaken. 'Tis she, by the rood, working in a shoemaker's in the Lawnmarket. 'Twas the hair that drew my attention at first, but once I saw her face—"

"We will speak while we ride," said Blake, rebuckling his belt. The weariness had vanished from his face, impatience in every line of his body as he strode past the younger man to the door.

"You wish to go there now?" Jason was taken aback. "The hour is late, cousin—" but Blake was already in the hall.

Helen and her husband faced them at the door. At the sight of the tall, dark nobleman, his followers waiting on the street behind him, Helen experienced a pang of alarm.

"Alyssa Dunne no longer works here," she told him nervously. "She departed yesterday. Nay, I know not where."

"Think, mistress!" urged Sinclair. "She must have had friends. Mayhap you remember their names, and where they live?"

Frightened by the intense gleam in the dark eyes, the young matron shook her head. "She kept much to herself, my lord, nor did she confide in us at all."

He wanted to seize her by the shoulders and shake every morsel she knew about Alyssa from her reluctant lips. He wanted to ask her a hundred questions, all to do with the beautiful girl who had disappeared from his life so abruptly two years ago, taking all the joy from his existence with her. But he could see that his forcefulness had upset her. She was quaking with fear, her thin sapling of a husband with her. Blake could expect no information from this pair.

Riding back to Clairmont, a sympathetic Jason at his side, Sinclair felt disappointed but not dispirited. She was in Edinburgh, and large as it was, he would find her. And when he did, God help her, she would not escape him again!

Alyssa had spent her wedding night alone, a fact that didn't entirely displease her. Poor Simon, she thought as she rose from her bed the following morning in his apartments in St. Giles Wynd, to be sent off on a mission for the Earl of Moray on his wedding day! He had been beside himself with frustration, a condition that didn't matter to his employer at all. "Postpone the nuptials and wed the girl when you return," had been Stewart's answer.

But Simon had gone through with the ceremony anyway. "We cannot delay," he told her, "with Lady Magdalen and her squire hovering about us."

Now she was Lady Ogilvy and soon to have her own maid when Simon's housekeeper arrived in a day or two from Mordrun Hall. His squire Calvin, a hulking youth of eighteen, had gone away with him. She would be safe enough at the apartment, her new lord assured her, now that she had the protection of the Ogilvy name.

Alyssa, as she dressed for the day in one of the new gowns her husband had given her, did not feel in the least like a wife. She felt . . . in a peculiar state of limbo, neither one nor the other. It troubled her that she didn't know exactly where Simon had gone, nor exactly what sort of work he was engaged in for Stewart, the Earl of Moray. Even though she was now his wife, Simon still had not been "at liberty" to tell her. "'Tis secret business and more than that I dare not divulge."

Now that she thought of it, there was much she didn't

know—had still to learn—about her husband. When he asked her to marry him, Alyssa had confessed honestly that she was not in love with him, feeling that he deserved nothing short of the truth. Ogilvy had laughed, that lazy, hot look in his eyes, and assured her, "I will soon enough change all that, my sweet. You will see when I return."

Alyssa frowned at her reflection in the small looking glass by the window, though in fact she looked very lovely in the gold camlet gown Simon had given her, with a warm cloak to match and more clothes being made for her at that moment. Behind her the apartment, though far from grand by the standards of others of Ogilvy's rank, struck Alyssa as being very fine indeed. Ah, she was fortunate, she told herself over and over. Very fortunate. Her husband was good to her and she fond of him, which put her ahead of many another who had married out of expediency.

On that positive note Alyssa busied herself cleaning their quarters until everything shone, too busy during the day to have time to brood. In the early evening, with the apartment spotless, she sat by the window facing the street watching the activity below, idly wondering about the lives of all the people hurrying by. When she saw a beggar woman shuffling along, her eyes on the gutter as she searched for anything she might use, Alyssa's heart went out to her. There, she thought, but for God's mercy, go I.

On an impulse she ran for her purse and threw down a coin. The woman scrambled for it, stared at it for a moment as if astounded, since it would buy her enough food for at least a week, then raised brimming eyes to the window. "God bless ye, lass!" she cried. "Ye're a gem, yin o' Christ's angels!"

Alyssa drew back quickly. She wanted no thanks. It embarrassed and troubled her, since only the gold ring on her middle finger separated her from that woman; and the ring—and all it signified—bothered her too.

When darkness fell she again climbed into bed alone.

She thought of Davie and a vicious pain smote her heart. She mused over the amazing fact of her birth, the heritage that had been stolen from her and one she might never be able to claim. Simon had promised to try to set things right, but warned that it would take time and must be done cautiously. Somehow—and he had not gone into detail—he had put the fear of God into Lady Magdalen. "I've arranged things so she dare not harm you now that you are Simon Ogilvy's wife, a man with powerful connections at court, including the Earl of Moray."

With great curiosity Alyssa wondered what her parents had been like. Her father was dead, but there was a slim possibility that her mother might still be alive. That filled her with great excitement. She ached to meet the lady who had given her birth, but there too Simon had warned, "It was so long ago, my sweet, and she was told her babe had died. Even were we to find her, if you were to go to her now, a total stranger, she might take you for a charlatan, so we must proceed with great care."

Alyssa lay for a long time thinking of her background and suddenly realized that in point of fact she was as high-born as Blake Sinclair. By rights she was his equal! If only she had known this two years ago! Would he have believed her? Would he have demanded proof, proof she didn't have?

A guilty yearning took hold of her. She still loved him. She would always love him. And knowing it, how, when the time came, could she possibly give herself to Simon? The thought of their physical union filled her with such distaste that it made her ill. Simon was eager for the moment. Somehow she would have to fake pleasure for his sake. With Sinclair, there had been no need to pretend. Even now, as memories of their intimacy came back to her, her famished senses burned with a fierce hunger, one she had struggled to ignore from the day they left Lochmore.

Now she was wed to Simon Ogilvy, a man she didn't love, and doubtlessly Lord Blake had long since forgotten her—as she should him! Lady Magdalen had, in effect, taken away everything of worth to Alyssa—the love of her true parents, her heritage, her friends—and thus had made it impossible for her to go to Sinclair as an equal.

How she hated her! And how she burned for revenge. Regardless of the danger, Alyssa vowed, she would find some way, with Simon's help, to seize back all that had been taken away. It might be too late with Sinclair, and somehow she had to find the strength to put him forever out of her mind, but it was not too late to claim her true identity. She would fight for that to her dying day!

For three days Alyssa did not leave the apartment. On the fourth, a sunny March day with mildness in the air and the new leaves beginning to unfurl, her restlessness got the better of her. Indoors she had too much time to brood, to succumb to a wrenching loneliness, to consider the fact that she was a wife who didn't feel like a wife, married to a man she didn't love and yearning over one she did.

In mid-afternoon, when the very walls began to crowd in on her and the mocking face of Sinclair seemed to stare at her accusingly from the shadows, Alyssa grabbed her cloak and rushed out into the street. The warm sunshine had brought everyone out of doors, and color and activity chased away the winter drabness. On every corner hawkers called out their wares. Riders and carts rumbled by, and now and then a litter holding some important personage grandly attired. In Lady Wynd a curious crowd clustered around a vehicle new to Edinburgh—a horsedrawn carriage! It was a most elaborate thing much decorated and gilded, the crest of the mighty House of Hamilton emblazoned on its side. The carriage was a recent innovation to Scotland, said to have been introduced from France by the Queen herself. Simon, and many others, scoffed at the contraption, saying it would never catch on. "A fad!" laughed Ogilvy. "It's sure to fall from favor in a year or two. God's blood, how could it do otherwise considering the vile roads in Scotland? Much improvement would have to be made to make the carriage feasible."

Alyssa wandered into the park and for half an hour sat on a bench watching young mothers and their children happily taking the air. Soon, she found herself thinking, *she* might be a mother. Then, finally, she would surely reconcile herself to being Lady Ogilvy, wife of Sir Simon.

She rose and hastily left the park and wandered along the Cannongate in the direction of Holyrood Palace, now and then stopping to examine the goods displayed in the shops. She stayed out for hours, reluctant to return to the silence of the apartment. As suppertime approached and the streets emptied, Alyssa knew she should go back. Now she was very conspicuous, and though Simon had assured her she need no longer fear Bruno, still she was nervous. And aside from Bruno, a lone woman richly clad was a prime target for footpads. She should hurry home and lock herself safely inside the house as any sensible young matron should do, except that she dreaded the silence—and the ghosts that gazed at her from the silence— almost as much as she did the brigands roaming the streets.

Alyssa paused for a moment and glanced around. She was at the far end of the Cannongate near Horse Wynd. Before her stood the grandeur of Holyrood Palace in its fine park where deer and wild game roamed, and on her left Abbey Hill where many of the aristocrats had their homes—including Blake Sinclair.

A tremor passed through her. She was seized with a reckless excitement that swept more sober considerations away. For two years she had lived in Edinburgh and never once allowed herself to tread that road or give in to the urge that drove her there. Now, her legs suddenly weak and quaking beneath her, her heart swelling with defiance against the fates that propelled her one way while her desires tugged her another, she took the decisive step and turned into Abbey Hill. She would see where he lived with the wife he had chosen over her. Aye, she thought ruefully, she would torture herself like a fool, for what else could such madness accomplish than to increase her futile longing?

The winter sun had dipped below the tall gables of Edinburgh and a cool wind whispered in off the sea, blowing her gold cloak about her as she slowly made her way uphill. The first of the great mansions appeared on either side of the broad street, each with its proud name on a plaque to the side of the door or on the ornate fence that shut the estates off from the road. With the coming of an early twilight, shadows pooled beneath neatly clipped bushes and trees. Feeling uncomfortably visible, yet unable to make herself turn back, Alyssa drew up her hood to cover her hair and continued on until she was standing opposite the fine edifice that was Clairmont.

At the side of the house a lane led back to the stables. It

was lined with trees, thick enough to provide excellent cover for anyone who might want to tarry there. Knowing full well that she was insane and should leave the place at once, Alyssa crossed the street and, with a quick glance about, ducked into the lane. Now she could watch the house without being detected. Within, she saw, candles had been lit and from all the downstairs windows a warm glow issued forth. As she shivered in the cold wind, that golden glow somehow warmed her. Why had she come here? She had come, she realized, for the simple reason that she had no choice, because her stoic fortitude of the past two years had deserted her and a mindless obsession had taken over.

Alyssa had no idea of how long she stood there in the grip of her memories before she heard the clatter of riders turning into the street. Inhaling sharply, she drew back deeper into the trees.

21

Sinclair and his men rode back from Holyrood in the dusk, his squire and outrider Wyatt in the lead. Wyatt was a seasoned warrior, and as the horses hoofs rang out on the cobbles, his small, alert eyes probed the shadows. A brawny fellow with close-cropped grey hair and a grizzled beard, Wyatt kept a hand near his dagger, well aware that trouble could erupt suddenly and when one least expected it. He considered the new developments stirring with the advent of Darnley in Scotland. Though the court was away, Holyrood seethed with rumors concerning Henry Stewart and the Queen. The increasingly impatient and very marriageable Mary Stuart was said to have taken a great liking to her tall, handsome cousin. He enjoyed the music and dancing that she loved, wrote pretty verses to amuse and titillate her, and was all in all an exceedingly charming lad, one who shared her great exuberance and love of life and took her mind off dull affairs of state.

Wyatt knew that his master, the Chief, was watching this rapidly developing relationship closely. He knew that Sinclair, like many another of her nobles, was made uneasy by the fact that Queen Elizabeth had dispatched Darnley to Scotland at just this time, when Queen Mary was growing weary and exasperated over all the dissension revolving around the question of her second husband. The French, Austrian and Spanish candidates had all been vetoed for one reason or another. Mary declared that he couldn't be Protestant, her queenly cousin in England that he couldn't be a Catholic. It had reached the point, thought the squire in amusement, when the poor Queen doubted that there was a prince in all the world who would make everyone happy. He had heard from the

Chief that she had recently cried aloud in annoyance, "Forsooth, at this rate I will *never* be wed! Mayhap my cousin in England would like to see me as single as herself."

Then out of the blue Queen Elizabeth had allowed Henry Stewart—a Catholic—to come to the Scottish court, and Darnley had the royal blood of both England and Scotland running through his veins. Further, he was a dazzling young man, elegant and cultured, carefully trained to assume a high office by his ambitious parents. He was the type—at least outwardly—glorious enough to turn the head of any woman, and Mary Stuart, so Wyatt had heard, was very susceptible to beauty, from the white roses she loved to surround herself with to fine paintings, music . . . and comely young men.

Wyatt mulled over all these things as he rode along, even as his master too considered them, while recalling the smug look on the English ambassador's face as he watched the couple dancing together. Something in Randolph's eyes had disturbed Sinclair. The very fact that Queen Elizabeth had given permission for Darnley and his father to come to Scotland made him uneasy. Many of the Protestant faction were violently against this visit, including John Knox, and, ever outspoken, the preacher had bellowed rabidly on the subject from the pulpit, laying the blame for this obnoxious development on the ministers surrounding Elizabeth.

Now, as they rode back to Clairmont in the dusk, Wyatt's sharp eyes darted everywhere and his hand hovered over the hilt of his dagger. As the party turned into the lane at the side of the mansion, he caught a movement in the bushes. Immediately he drew up and raised a hand, halting those behind him. Sliding from the saddle, the squire disappeared into the bushes with weapon in hand. In moments he was back dragging a hooded figure out into the open. Blake and his cousin Jason exchanged a look and shrugged, at first taking the poor wretch for a beggar, until they got a better look at her clothes. She was sprawled on the ground by Wyatt's feet, desperately trying to cover her face by holding the hood tight under her chin. "How now?" the squire shouted. "Speak up, wench! Why are ye loitering here?"

With that he seized the hood and wrenched it back from her face. The party clustered around, astounded to gaze down upon a tumbling mass of dark gold hair. Blake recognized her instantly. It was as if an iron band that had constricted his heart for the past two years had suddenly been cut, allowing the blood to surge wildly through his veins in great pulsing leaps that almost jolted him from the saddle. "Stand aside!" he ordered Wyatt hoarsely.

His squire hesitated, stern disapproval in his eyes. "This could well be a ploy, my lord; a trap. She could be carrying a weapon."

Indeed, thought Sinclair dryly, she possessed many weapons, but not of the type Wyatt had in mind. "Ride ahead to the house." And he waved an arm to indicate the entire party. "I will take care of the girl."

Grudgingly, Wyatt and the others rode ahead to the stables, but Jason Sinclair hung back. He too had recognized the lass, and a huge grin spread across his face. Slapping his cousin heartily on the back, he remarked under his breath, "Then I take leave of you, wishing you a most pleasant good night."

When they were finally alone, Alyssa stood up and threw back the shimmering curtain of hair that had partially obscured her face and turned it up to the man who still sat astride the big grey stallion, his tall, broad-shouldered figure black against the faint glow in the sky. Let all my feelings for him have died, she prayed inwardly. Let it be over.

Blake saw her soft lips part in something like anguish, even as he felt himself drowning in the luminous brilliance of her eyes. God help me, he sighed. God help both of us.

He leaned down wordlessly and held out his hand to her. There was a moment when he hesitated, not sure of her or even of himself. But then Alyssa felt the wonderful strength of his arm encircling her body, and try as she might she had no strength to push it away. He swung her up into the saddle in front of him.

The Hare and Hound was a quaint little inn at the corner of Bruce's Wynd and High Street with clean, attractive lodgings above. Blake had never used the premises himself but had heard John Gordon sing its praises more than once. He made a quick decision and turned south.

With Alyssa's warm body on the saddle in front of him, her silken head tucked under his chin, Sinclair started off through the dark streets that such a short time before had seemed dank and cold, echoing the dark depression inside himself. It was an emotional state that had plagued him for some time, and no matter how he railed at himself, seemed unable to shake it off. As he had had ample time to discover, a man needed more than a sword, more than the responsibility attendant on serving the Queen, and more than dutiful attention to a wife and the continuation of his line. Now he *had* no wife, at least in his own mind, with only the long legal process to be waited through until he was free.

When Alyssa and Davie Weir had suddenly vanished from Augusta, Blake had spent weeks searching for them before resigning himself to his loss. First, he reasoned, even had he found her it would have meant bringing her back by force and keeping her more or less as his prisoner, a situation that would have been abhorrent to him. Second, in his heart he knew it was for the best, particularly as he was well aware that his feelings for Alyssa went far beyond the margin of safety. And third, she deserved so much more than he was able to offer her then.

So . . . he had let her go, and with her went the sweet joy and passion from his life. And he had resigned himself to that too, or thought he had.

Blake's arm tightened about her. For a moment he buried his face in the fragrant mass of burnished hair, and it seemed to him, as he hungrily drank in the scent of her, that the essence of the girl was the essence of life itself, as God meant it to be. Not the harsh, punitive, judgmental God of whom Knox preached with so much fanatical relish, but He who had shown mercy to the maimed, the lost and the doubtful. As I am, thought Blake, and sighed deeply. As I am without her.

They rode along without speaking, rendered mute at the bittersweet joy of finding themselves together. In Alyssa's heart a great and silent battle was taking place, one between her mind and her emotions. The first dictated that she order him to take her home immediately—even as her body snuggled against the hard warmth of his chest. Her common sense screamed that she was a fool—while her emotions soared with an unbridled happiness so intense that tears ran down her cheeks. From the moment their eyes met in the lane, locking together in a silent bonding, all the old passion, the hunger, the tender yearning, had overwhelmed her once more. And now? Now she was a married woman! It mattered not that the union hadn't been consummated; that she didn't love Simon nor could resign herself to being his wife. She *was* his wife; aye, even though she had taken that step with the greatest reluctance and mostly out of fear of Magdalen MacKellar, it was still a fact. Fate, ever capricious where she was concerned, had given her fortunes yet another excruciating turn.

Alyssa felt a surge of defiance. All her senses rebelled. It was Sinclair she loved, and nothing mattered but her dear love's warm breath caressing her cheek, his arm holding her tight to his breast where she could feel his heart pounding as rapturously as her own. Had she not learned that happiness came in fleeting moments, misery in boundless stretches of time? Who was *she* to question such joy, when its appearance was so rare?

Alyssa did not protest when Blake quickly rented a private chamber on the second floor of the inn, nor did she notice—or care—that the room was clean, if spare, with a huge bowl of early daffodils on a low oak table under the window. Alyssa saw none of this as she stood in the center of the room while the innkeeper's lanky son lit the candles, drew back the covers on the bed, then conversed softly with Sinclair at the door before placing a large key in his hand. She stood with her hands clasped tightly together, her heart in her eyes, her blood slow and singing, and watched Blake slide the bolt home.

He turned and their eyes met and in that one deep look all reserve was swept away, all impediments inconsequential, all others forgotten. Blake came to her and put his hands on her shoulders and drew her slowly toward him as if wishing to savor the moment, the bliss of having her once more in his arms. As her breasts touched the hardness of his chest, Alyssa raised her mouth to his in willing surrender.

"My love . . . my love," he whispered, and kissed her deeply. And so tender was that kiss, yet so passionate, his heart speaking through his lips, then moving over her face and throat, flowing through her blood like warm dark wine to set her aglow with an unquenchable fire, that to draw back was unthinkable.

Gently he picked her up and carried her to the bed. She watched his face as he undressed her, the gravity of his expression contrasting with the blazing light in his eyes, and when they were both naked he lay down beside her and took her in his arms. For a few moments he held her close without speaking.

From the street below the window, Alyssa heard the clop-clop of hoofbeats on the cobbles and the distant hum of conversation from the inn, interspersed with frequent bursts of laughter. The dim, hushed quality of their own chamber, scented with the earthy aroma of the daffodils, was like a world within a world, their love a barrier against any aliens who would intrude. Those on the outside might dent the barrier but they could never pierce it, she thought wonderingly, knowing she would treasure this time forever no matter what might happen afterwards.

Blake turned his head and looked at her as a parched man gazes upon clear water, almost afraid of the fierce passion, the tenderness, the wild hunger to possess that rose up like a geyser inside him. His hand trembled slightly as he cupped her face. "I love you, dear heart," he confessed huskily. "We won't be parted again."

Before she could speak, his lips moved on hers and his body covered her. His burning hands caressed her breasts, hips and thighs, each sweet, well-remembered inch of her until they were both in a rapture of desire. In her turn, Alyssa explored him blindly, hungrily—his taut muscled back, lean hips, the hard strength of the thighs that moved with sudden impatience between her legs. "I love you," he repeated as he entered her in a driving surge of fire, "and I need you, sweet love . . ."

Afterwards Blake covered her with kisses, starting at her brow and teasingly working his way to her toes. Finally Alyssa pushed him away, laughing softly as she remembered how playful he could be when all was right with his world, as he seemed to imagine was the case now. He scooped her up and rolled her on top of him and they smiled in total happiness into each other's eyes. "My dearest love," he told her, his voice a low caress.

"Am I?" she asked somewhat sadly. She would have him repeat it a thousand times, then a thousand times more.

"Aye," he readily admitted, "and you know it well."

"How long . . . how long have you felt thus?" She ached to plumb the depths of his feelings for her.

He sobered. "From even before you left Lochmore."

A wrenching pain sliced through her. "Oh, why did you not tell me!"

Sinclair, sensing the deep emotion in that cry, tried to hold the lightness of a moment before. "Admit that you cast a spell on me, you alluring little witch! Nay, a man should not so quickly hand a lady a weapon to wield over him." He pulled her head down to his and nipped the velvety lobe of her ear, whispering, "I think you are a heartless lass who from the first set out to enslave me, then made me suffer by running away."

"Then you missed me?"

Blake threw her back against the pillows and pinned her there with his chest, nuzzling her soft neck until she finally giggled and tried to slap his face. He caught her flailing hand and pressed his lips to the palm, then tickled it lightly with the tip of his tongue, all the time studying her from under his brows.

She had changed, he was thinking, grown from a lovely young girl into a ravishingly beautiful woman in the space of two years. Where had she been in all that time? What had she done? He begrudged every hour he had missed from her life.

Leaning over, Blake tugged on the rope connected to the service bell and when the maid arrived asked that a flagon of wine and a dish of fresh prawns be delivered to their room. "How came you to be in Edinburgh?" he asked Alyssa while they waited. "I would know everything that has happened to you from the time you left Augusta."

She had been dreading this moment, knowing it would come. Yet as they shared the wine and prawns and she thought of Simon, it all seemed so unreal. In truth Simon was like a stranger to her, since she knew almost nothing about his background, nor did he seem inclined to discuss it. Even his occupation was a mystery to her. Now, as she thought back, the marriage ceremony they had gone through seemed equally unreal, rather like two children playing a part. Except in name, she was not really his wife, nor felt like his wife . . . especially now.

Feeling Sinclair looking at her, Alyssa took a deep breath and tried to amuse him by relating how she and Davie had been arrested the day they entered the city, an experience that had not been at all funny at the time. Cautiously she told him about the Livingstones and her enjoyable position in the shop. When she reached the part where Davie had been murdered, Alyssa felt her throat tighten and tears flood into her eyes. Again she hesitated. How much should she divulge? Should she reveal her astounding discovery about her true parentage? Would he believe her, or more likely think her sly and conniving, thinking to trap him—

"My love . . . you weep!"

Then she told him of Davie. Nay, she said, she could not be sure who had murdered him, and in a way it was true, since she had never actually seen Bruno's face that night. She longed to tell her beloved the truth, but something held her back. She was no longer the innocent, trusting girl she had been at Augusta.

Sinclair soothed her. As he caressed her, his lips on hers, his fingers in her hair, the length of her slim, sweetly curved form held tight against his hard body, the soothing soon gave way to passion. When it was over, Alyssa wept again, suddenly remembering his wife, Elizabeth.

"That is over!" he assured her firmly.

"Over . . . ?" she repeated faintly, her head reeling.

"The marriage will be dissolved." And at the look on her face, he added, "Nay, nay, do not weep. It had naught to do with you—"

"Why did you marry her?" Alyssa cried in bitter frustration. Now he would be free, and she—she was married to Simon Ogilvy! She couldn't bear it. She wanted to scream.

Sinclair eyed her flushed face, the angry glitter in her

eyes, appraisingly. He was taken aback by her response to the news, thinking she would have been glad. "The marriage is over so 'tis pointless to discuss it. Now we must talk of us." And more softly, "'Tis you I love; *you*, my dear one. Now we will be together, Alyssa. Does that not make you happy?" And when she didn't reply, more determinedly: "You will not run away from me again!"

She shook her head, unable to speak.

He reached out a bronzed hand to cup her breast, then bent his dark head and caressed a nipple with his lips. When she turned away her head, he caught her chin and crushed his mouth to hers, forcing her lips to part, a warm and knowing hand leisurely roaming her body, pausing at the tiny "birthmark" inside her right thigh. He had remarked on it before. Now he leaned down to kiss the spot, lightly stroking with the tip of his tongue. Alyssa tried to resist as he slowly engulfed her with the moist heat of his mouth. Instead, with a soft moan of ecstasy, she plunged her fingers into the crisp black hair and gave herself up to mindless rapture.

When they drew apart, Blake's deep brown eyes smiled triumphantly into hers. "You are mine and well you know it," he said possessively, hugging her fiercely. "Now we must make our plans."

Alyssa felt the first stirring of resentment. He was so sure of her, taking it for granted that she would fall in with his plans, ready to pick up where they had left off two years before. All he need do, or so he seemed to feel, was to make love to her to sweep all barriers away. It irked Alyssa to admit that in this he was partially right. He still had that power over her, the ability to melt her resistance—her very bones—with one smoldering look from those wicked dark eyes. He had accepted her story of the intervening years readily; too readily, without probing to find out if another man might have entered her life. Either he was so supremely egotistical that he rejected such a possibility, or he mentally brushed competition aside as being inconsequential. Had he forgotten the reason why she had left Augusta? she wondered irritably. By finding her at Clairmont tonight, did he imagine she had changed her mind and was now ready to fall in with his wishes?

Suddenly the old conflicts crept back into her mind to disrupt their newly forged closeness. Alyssa recalled in vivid detail that last devastating day at Lynnwood and the pain she had suffered ever since. So when Blake shook her and remarked with a laugh, "Harken to me, Alyssa. I would talk of our future," she felt a white-hot spurt of anger and jumped out of bed, startling herself almost as much as she did him, her emotions suddenly in chaos.

"Our—our future?" she asked breathlessly, staring down to where he lay casually back against the pillows, one tanned, muscular arm behind his head, relaxed and complacent and maddeningly certain of her. "Nay! 'Tis too late for that now." And before she could stop herself, "You were given a choice that day at Lynnwood and you chose Elizabeth as your wife." Thrusting the plain gold ring down into his face, she went on, tears pouring down her cheeks, "Do you not know what this ring means, my lord? It means I am committed to another." She rushed on without a pause. "I'm married, Sinclair! 'Tis a sin that we are even together now!"

All the joy instantly vanished from his face. The brown eyes turned almost black, his mouth a harsh line of dismay. Recalling her own savage hurt that day at Lynnwood when he had allowed rank and the wishes of his clan to come between them; when he had blithely assumed she would be willing to settle for another role in his life, Alyssa tasted a bittersweet revenge.

He sprang up and seized her cruelly by the arms. "You lie!" he ground out through his teeth.

"I speak the truth!"

"Who is he?" Blake demanded, his face a ruthless mask, nothing of the tender lover in his manner now. "Name this man who labors under the false impression that you belong to him!"

"I *do* belong to him—"

"Never!" he thundered, frightening her. "Never!"

Alyssa tried to pull away, but his fingers were like bands of steel bruising her flesh. "You have no right to make demands of me! You gave up any right you had the last time we met." She laughed hysterically, her eyes flashing through her tears. "I should have been honored, I doubt not, to be the mistress of the mighty Chief, the mother of his bastards, content to lap up the dregs from his life—while another woman became the Lady of Augusta! As for me, I was not good enough to occupy that lofty position—"

"You know my reasons for marrying Elizabeth."

"And I care not!" Alyssa shot back, trembling with emotion as all the anguish and crushing sense of rejection she had felt at Lynnwood came surging back. "You, sir, intended to have it all while I—I must be content with the leftovers. Nay!" She shook her head wildly. "In that you made a great mistake, one you must learn to live with as I had to with the other."

Sinclair stared at her grimly while a pulse ticked at the side of his jaw. And in her determination, the hard gleam in her eyes, the set line of her delicate chin as she raised it defiantly, he saw very little of the innocent young beauty he had known at Augusta. She had changed, or, more to the point, life had changed her, and in his heart Blake recognized that he was partly responsible.

His hands threatened to crush her shoulders. "You cannot mean this, Alyssa. Things can be different for us now. Like you, I have learned much since we last saw each other." His face softened and a coaxing light came into his eyes. "Surely you would not sacrifice our love in exchange for a—a name!"

"A man will honor a woman with his name if he loves and respects her enough," she replied crushingly.

He flinched inwardly. Outwardly he was as determined as she was. "Then why did you come to Clairmont tonight?" The softness had disappeared and his eyes brimmed with mockery.

Alyssa shrugged. "I was curious to see where you lived with this great lady you chose in my place."

She turned and picked up her clothes and dressed rapidly. For a few minutes Blake watched her, and for the first time in his life was uncertain as to how to proceed. She had become, quite suddenly, a stranger. That she wanted to wound him, to retaliate, was obvious. And understandable. But he also understood—or thought he did—that she loved him. Mayhap, he mused grimly, in that he had also erred. A fierce anger took hold of him, the growing suspicion that she had come to him tonight for the sole purpose of luring him into betraying his feelings for her—only to laugh in his face!

His eyes, grown very cold, raked her from the top of her mussed golden head to the small dainty feet she was even now thrusting into slippers, and it maddened him that as a mature woman she was even more stunning than before; even more desirable. The fact that she was married was beside the point. Marriages were not done for love, a fact accepted by those of his rank, and by tacit agreement either party to such a union could take lovers, provided they were discreet. He had been raised to accept this situation, that a man could have a private life aside from the formal one he presented to the outside world, and he still found it difficult to understand that Alyssa could not accept such an arrangement.

As he watched her button up her cloak, a savage frustration boiled inside him, the growing certainty that she had come back just to avenge herself against what she imagined to be his slighting behavior toward her. Yet he had been prepared to place her above all others in his life, to satisfy her every wish, and to love and cherish her for as long as he lived.

It was not enough. She had made that abundantly clear. Blake's pride clashed with his need, rage with the urge to crush her in his arms. If she thought to trick him into an admission of devotion only to spurn him, then she was indeed ignorant of the nature of the man she was dealing with.

"I will escort you safely home," he said aloud, his dark face haughty as he caught her arm and spun her around as Alyssa made for the door, seizing the excuse to find out where she lived and the name of the man she was married to.

Alyssa faced him fully dressed, and for the first time Blake noticed her clothes, that the material and cut set them above the ordinary. He felt an unexpected pang of jealousy for the man who apparently could provide her with such fine attire, and was more curious than ever to find out who he was.

As she met his eyes, already Alyssa could feel her strengthening anger evaporating and knew she had to leave at once.

"Thank you," she replied stiltedly, "but I'd prefer one of the inn grooms to see me home."

Blake nodded curtly. "As you wish."

She turned and hurriedly left the room, scalding tears running down her cheeks, the sweet taste of revenge like acid on her tongue. She had salved her wounded pride, paid him back for his earlier rejection of her, and should now feel completely satisfied and vindicated. But in truth she had never felt so miserable in her life.

22

Three days later Simon Ogilvy's housekeeper, newly arrived from Mordrun Hall, prepared Alyssa for the marriage bed. Simon had returned to Edinburgh that morning, not tired as Alyssa had expected, but charged with impatience and eager to waste no time in truly making her his wife.

The preparations were supervised by Megan, lean, sallow and of indeterminate age, a woman of few words and with a face that betrayed no emotion. Simon, it seemed, would make the occasion one to remember. First Alyssa must bathe in a tub of warm water into which special oils had been poured, while her bridegroom did likewise in another room. The ingredients of the bath left Alyssa's tender flesh flushed and tingling, particularly the delicate tissues around her breasts and between her thighs. Next a perfumed salve was massaged into her skin, her hair brushed until it glistened, and a gossamer white bedgown dropped over her head.

"Come . . ." Megan took her arm and led her down the hall into the bridal chamber. It blazed with light, illuminated by what seemed to be a thousand candles, the mingled scents of cloves, woodbine and honeysuckle in the air. Alyssa turned startled eyes on the housekeeper. "What . . . what means all this?"

Pointing to an open space circled by banked candlelight, Megan purred, "You must stand yonder and await your husband's pleasure."

Alyssa's eyes swung back to the room and she laughed uncertainly, though she had already observed that Simon was fond of ceremony, the unusual, the dramatic. Strange people too intrigued him. "Life would be dull indeed were we all of the same ilk," he had commented once.

Deciding to humor him, Alyssa walked into the shrinelike circle, feeling foolish as Megan stepped back and cocked her head to the side as she studied the effect. Ah, thought the housekeeper in satisfaction, the girl's beauty was truly spellbinding, vibrant enough to satisfy the wildest desires simmering in the heart of any man, and as she well knew, Sir Simon's were wilder than most.

"May your marriage be fruitful," she murmured, and with a quick curtsy left the room.

Left alone, Alyssa's amusement fled and nervousness took its place. How could she bring herself to go through with this? How could she bear to have another man's hands touch her so intimately? A panicky feeling gathered inside her. Dear Lord, she thought, why had she not stopped to consider this part of it when she agreed to be Simon's wife?

The candlelight dazzled her eyes, the heat acting as a stimulant to the oils she had recently bathed in. Her flesh tingled with a prickly sensation that made her want to squirm, and tiny droplets of sweat, glistening like crystal, burst out on her forehead and between her breasts. She blinked, straining to see beyond the blinding radiance. With a start of surprise she saw that her husband was already inside the room. He stood silently just inside the door watching her.

"Simon!" she whispered, wondering how long he had been there, but as she made to leave the circle he held up a hand. "Be still," he told her, his voice low and strained. "I would feast my eyes upon my bride for a moment."

Embarrassed, she saw his lust-darkened eyes move over her and heard his sharp, indrawn breath. Ogilvy, as he gazed at her boldly in a way he had never dared to before, felt his blood vault and his heart begin to pound. Never had he looked upon a more exquisite woman, or one who awakened in him such unholy desire. Standing there amid the flames, with her golden hair spilling to her waist and her lush young untouched body beckoning to him as through a teasing veil, she exuded a tantalizing aura of innocence and allure, a combination he found irresistible.

As in most flawed personalities, there was that in Simon Ogilvy that demanded perfection about him. He must have the finest clothes, the best horseflesh, and the most beautiful women, for through such things came the envy and admiration he craved—and never received otherwise. And much given to sudden enthusiasms, Simon had been inspired to whitewash his personality in keeping with that of his bride's, with the result that he began avoiding certain friends and hobbies that Alyssa might have found unsettling.

Now he dropped his burgundy satin robe and held out his arms to her. Alyssa stared at him, unable to bring herself to move. She saw that he was lean and sinewy, his skin smooth and hairless, and pale, so unlike . . .

Misunderstanding the reason for her reticence, Simon laughed softly and drew her out of the circle and poured her a glass of wine, a strong brew sure to help her overcome her maidenly modesty. Then he lifted her onto the bed, her very reluctance filling him with a wild excitement, the challenge to change that reluctance to frenzied desire. Oh, and he could! he thought triumphantly. How well he could! Had she not bathed in the special oils, drunk the special wine? Now, held within the arms of an expert in the arts of love, she would not be able to prevent herself from responding.

His mouth was hot and ravenous, his tongue forcing her lips to part, his roving fingers relentless as they slowly ravished every part of her body. "My darling . . . !" he muttered hoarsely, caressing her breasts, her stomach, his hand probing boldly between her thighs. She bit her lips as she felt his fully aroused body engulfing her own, the weight of him rising and plunging above her, the sweat from his heated flesh falling upon her own. Alyssa closed her eyes and prayed for it to be quickly over.

It was only the beginning.

Cup after cup of wine he forced on her, demanding her active participation, and as the night progressed his lovemaking became increasingly bizarre. Alyssa was relieved when the wine finally took effect and she drifted off into a hazy world where it all began to take on the aura of a dream.

In the morning she awoke to find Ogilvy examining the sheets. "You were not a virgin!" he accused.

Alyssa came awake fast. As memory of the night just passed surged back, she was filled with acute distaste. "Nor did I pretend to be," she replied coldly.

His fair skin flooded with mottled color. "You let me assume your virtue was intact."

"Is yours so perfect, sir, that you can hold me up to censure?"

"What . . . !" He came close to striking her, so great was his resentment at discovering a flaw where he imagined none existed; to realize that he hadn't been first with her. "I am a man, madam, with every right to take my pleasures where I will!"

Her own anger soared. "Aye, and after last eve I can see you have made full use of that right," she retorted cynically. "And never once did I pretend to be a virgin."

"Who was he?"

Alyssa turned her head away from the furious grey eyes. Wild horses couldn't have dragged that information out of her. Besides, it was none of his business. Had she demanded an accounting of all his affairs? So she lied, "He was a clansman from Lochmore—"

"Were you in love with him?"

"I thought so at the time," she said, and sighed.

Simon threw himself down on the bed beside her, his eyes hard enough to punch holes in the ceiling. Gradually he calmed down, reminding himself of all he stood to gain through this union, and it was reassuring to hear that she had only imagined herself to be in love with the Highland fellow.

He glanced at her from the corner of his eye, admiring the fragile profile, the long, sweeping lashes, the burnished hair fanning out over the cover. His eyes moved down the smooth arch of her throat to the swelling white breasts, and he felt desire rage anew.

He put an arm around her stiff shoulders, and feeling her resistance felt a fleeting unease. What if she left him? Aye, he could well imagine her making such a reckless move, for she was proud and determined, not one to be browbeaten or dictated to. He must tread carefully, keeping in mind all he stood to lose, at least until such time as he had gotten her with child and could use their offspring to hold her.

Swallowing his pride, he murmured, "I'm sorry, sweeting. 'Tis just that I'm mad with jealousy to think of another holding you in his arms. But . . . 'twas in the past. Now we must put it behind us and think on our future."

Alyssa examined him gravely. "I'm sorry too, Simon, and I'll understand if you wish to dissolve our marriage."

He pulled her into his arms and buried his face in her hair. "Nay, nay, you must not speak of such a thing! You are mine, sweetheart, and will remain so, and I promise to make you the most loving, devoted husband in the whole of Scotland."

The next few weeks passed pleasantly enough and only the nights were intolerable. Simon was on his best behavior, the epitome of charm itself. Glib, quick-witted, persuasive, his golden beauty and honeyed tongue had extricated him from many a mischief. As his own father had once shouted at him, "If you were to be tried for murder they would end up by hanging the judge!" He showered Alyssa with gifts and engaged a dressmaker to sew her a new wardrobe. Naturally she must have a few good jewels to complement the clothes. He was exceedingly generous, interested in every detail of her toilet, anxious that Alyssa should outshine all other women and he, through her, be the envy of his associates.

And very quickly he was. Within days of her going into society, all who saw her clamored to know who she was and where she had come from before bursting upon the social scene like a flame, casting in the shade certain ladies who until then had reigned supreme. Simon shrouded her background in mystery, recalling how this very mystery had intrigued *him*. But he also had another more sober reason for glossing over Alyssa's past, the white face of Lady Magdalen never far from his mind.

Their days were filled with activity, their evenings with banquets, balls and masks. And through all this time Ogilvy outdid himself to win his bride over and make her forget the morning after their wedding night. His wit sparkled. His conversation, as always, was sprightly and interesting, and he made it so obvious that he admired and adored his new wife that Alyssa found herself softening toward him. In spite of the ache buried inside her, Alyssa began to have high hopes for the success of their marriage, and vowed to herself that she would do everything in her power to make Simon a good wife.

The court was still at Stirling Castle where Lord Darnley had fallen ill, a situation that had Mary Stuart worried and distracted. Simon said dryly, "I hear tell that Her Majesty is dissatisfied with all his nurses and frequently attends him herself." He chuckled cynically, "And I'll wager Darnley is not so sick that he won't make good use of the Queen's tender heart."

Within days of this remark he rushed home with exciting news. The Queen had announced her intention of marrying her cousin! "All Edinburgh is agog, in a ferment of speculation. Maitland and Sinclair have been dispatched to London to get Queen Elizabeth's blessing on the union."

At mention of her former lover's name Alyssa turned away to hide the sudden color staining her cheeks. "Why . . . why would Her Grace need Elizabeth's blessing? It seems to me she must approve or she would never have allowed Darnley to come to Scotland."

"Ah! Now with that one, nothing can ever be taken for granted. Her *official* approval must be obtained if Mary hopes to be made her heir, which is nothing short of her due, for who else has a better claim? Methinks it amuses the English Queen to keep her guessing. Elizabeth, from what I heard, adores playing devious games."

Alyssa turned around and studied him for a moment in silence as the full implication of this news sank into her mind. "Then your master, the Earl of Moray, cannot be happy about this, feeling as he does about Darnley and his father, Lennox?"

Ogilvy laughed thinly. "Nay, my lord Stewart is far from delighted. Lately he has left court and retired to sulk on his own estates." He swept her into his arms and kissed her, adding gleefully, "This is the reason I have so much time to spend with you, my love, and for that I have no complaints."

Alyssa searched his face. Thinking of the money he had recently lavished about in all directions, she felt a touch of alarm. With his employer Moray now out of favor with the Queen and gone to his castle in the North, Simon was out of a job, at least temporarily. Surely it was time to drastically curb expenses.

Again Ogilvy smiled complacently while tickling her under the chin. A smart man, he said, does not put all his eggs in one basket. He had other contacts, other means of earning a living, but when she queried him about this he casually shrugged it off. "That, my sweet, you must leave to me. 'Tis my duty to provide for you, and yours to provide me with a happy home free of the stresses of business, which you have."

He kissed her, then turned the conversation to other things.

On the long ride to London the Queen's secretary, William Maitland, voiced his misgivings to Sinclair. Many of the most important nobles in the land disapproved of the Queen's marriage to Lord Darnley, chief among them the Earl of Moray himself. "Say what you will," said Maitland, "but James has been a good servant to his sister. She will sadly miss his counsel if they continue to be estranged."

Sinclair's eyes moodily roamed the wild terrain they were riding through. Moray *had* been a good servant, he thought cynically, but especially good to himself. Though a bastard, he had risen to great heights thanks to his sister. He had gained vast estates, a title, and astonishing power and wealth. His had been the hands to pull the strings to animate what he undoubtedly thought of as the royal puppet. Now, with the coming of Darnley, he was alarmed and resentful lest the interloper waste no time in cutting these gilded strings.

If forced to choose between the two men, Blake knew he would stay with Moray. Though he had his flaws, greed foremost among them, James Stewart was at least an able statesman, clever and shrewd, with a fine appreciation of the overall political situation and an astute grasp of foreign affairs. As for Darnley—and it was ludicrous to even compare the two—he was but a shallow, pleasure-loving youth with a polished veneer of culture and learning and baser instincts that he took great pains to conceal from the Queen. Many in

Scotland had reason to hate his father, Lennox. And in the short time he had been among them, Darnley himself had alienated many with his boastfulness and arrogance. But what did this matter when Mary was so besotted with him that she was ready to shout down any opposition to the match? Very gradually the girl-Queen had developed a mind of her own and she was convinced that once they were wed all the dissention would abate.

"'Tis said he has cast a spell upon her," grumbled Maitland. "By the rood, I've never seen her so smitten! Her common sense seems to have deserted her completely."

"She's young," Blake replied quietly. "And in love, mayhap for the first time. King Francis certainly cannot have stirred very much passion in her heart, and Her Grace is nothing if not a romantic."

"Love!" scoffed Maitland. "God's blood, man, we are talking about a queen!"

Sinclair shrugged. "Aye, but for all that a woman like any other. She grows tired of all this bickering over the question of a husband, and forget not how impulsive she is. Now it would seem she finally has her English cousin's approval on this. Can you wonder that she's loath to wait?"

Maitland pursed his lips. "Well, on to London! An we return with Elizabeth's official endorsement, the dissenting lords may perforce have to change their tune."

Long before Sinclair and Maitland arrived in London, Queen Elizabeth had been thoroughly apprised of the situation in Scotland. She had heard how the Scottish Protestants were fiercely opposed to a Catholic mate for their Queen. Now it seemed that Elizabeth her self was being severely castigated for having allowed Darnley to go to Scotland. There were rumblings that she had done so to snare her cousin into a disastrous marriage. Cecil himself had sighed, "I fear the blame for this matter is being hurled at your feet, madam. Why, some of our own people are muttering agin you."

Elizabeth recoiled, flustered at finding herself to be the villain. Knocked off her comfortable position atop the fence, careful never to lean one way or the other, she was desperately anxious to reinstate herself with the Scottish Protestants, many of whom had been good friends to England. And, much like her father before her, she was quick to extricate herself from a tricky situation. "Why would I sanction Darnley as Mary's consort when he sits so close to the English throne?"

Cecil coughed delicately. "There are those who read an evil meaning into you giving him permission to travel north."

"There are those who would read an evil meaning into the word of God Himself!" she retorted indignantly. And whipping herself up to a fine show of self-righteous anger, she snapped, "Methinks I smell conniving in this. Should my cousin of Scotland persist in this folly, it cannot but mean one thing—she hopes to stir up the English Catholics by linking herself to Darnley with a view to seizing my throne!"

Cecil nodded consideringly. "And there are many here-abouts ever ready to be provoked."

Now Elizabeth was frightened. She visualized a rebellion and the crown being snatched from her head. She imagined Catholic Europe, who were watching the developments close-ly, smacking their lips and congratulating themselves. She could almost hear them titter, "So Anne Boleyn's bastard daughter finally topples! Well, 'tis but meet, since Anne and Henry were never truly wed. Would it not be ironic justice to see their daughter go the same route as her mother—in want of a head!"

Elizabeth quailed inwardly. Outwardly, through long practice, none of her internal turmoil showed on her face. Her clever mind ticked furiously and all her astuteness and cunning converged to tackle the problem.

She was ready when Sinclair and Maitland arrived in London.

The Scottish lords were shown into the presence chamber to find the tall, auburn-haired monarch pacing the floor. Blake eyed her curiously, automatically comparing her with her cousin north of the border. Dressed in a magnificent gold brocade gown studded with emeralds and pearls, she bore a slight resemblance to Mary Stuart. The long nose, russet hair, her height—though Mary was taller still—all testified to the same blood running through their veins. Elizabeth too had fine white skin, though marred here and there by a blemish, a legacy from her bout with smallpox. But where his own Queen was vivacious and pretty, Elizabeth was regal and handsome, and obviously filled with a haughty sense of her own power.

She immediately launched an attack. How, she demanded, could the Scots accuse her of trying to trick her cousin into a bad marriage? "It should be obvious to all but the simple-minded that I would be opposed to her wedding Darnley for reasons of my own. Does he not stand in the shadow of my throne? Is he not of the Catholic faith? God's love, my lords, methinks your people must take me for a fool!" And while they stared at her, appalled, she swept back and forth majestically in front of them, her fair skin stained with angry color. Tapping Sinclair on the shoulder as she flounced past, she said emphatically, "You must tell the Queen of Scots that I will *never* sanction such a union! I allowed Lennox to travel to Scotland for private reasons of his own, to attend to business there. Now I have commanded that both he and his son return home immediately."

She wheeled to face them, her eyes narrow and cold, her voice dropping as she continued on a menacing note. "Should they refuse and should your Queen disregard my wishes on this matter and wed Henry Stewart, then I cannot but view it as an act of aggression against myself and all England!"

Sinclair and Maitland were dumbstruck, aghast at this sudden about-face. Blake studied her grimly, thinking that she shared at least one trait with her father, Henry VIII—a facile ability to justify all her actions, however dubious they might be. She had craftily permitted Darnley to visit Scotland at the very moment when Mary Stuart was having such difficulty in selecting a husband; when none of her own choices met with Elizabeth's approval. Then, with the advent of the handsome Darnley, what else was Mary to think but that he was her cousin's hand-picked choice?

When they returned to Scotland with the news, Mary was flabbergasted, then furious. "To think my princely cousin would trick me thus! To think she would wait to announce her true feelings until after we had fallen in love!" She burst into tears, wailing, "What now, what now? 'Tis too late to stay the great emotion flowing between us. Would she have me pluck out my heart?"

Blake exchanged a look with Maitland, then cautioned, "You must reconsider most seriously and not rush into this matter, Your Grace—"

"Not rush into the matter?" she interrupted, tears sparkling on her lashes. "Have I not already waited so long to gain my royal cousin's approval? How many more years must I dither?"

Melville, her ambassador to England, tried to calm her. "Every prince in Europe craves Your Grace's hand."

"But 'tis Henry I love!" She stamped her foot in a rare show of petulance. "Aye, and Henry I will have! I've awaited Elizabeth's pleasure on this as long as I will." She laughed shakily. "Dost she imagine all of us have blood as cold as her own? Nay, nay, I will no longer be dictated to thus." And raising her head haughtily, she cried, "Am I not too a Queen? *Twice* a Queen!" She stared at them defiantly, as if challenging them to refute it, then added meaningfully, "Can the daughter of Anne Boleyn sit so securely on her throne that she would dare give orders to one whom many believe should sit there in her place? Can this be the *true* reason she fears my marriage to Henry?"

They continued to try to reason with her, but it was useless. Feeling abused, tricked and dictated to by her imperious cousin, Mary had turned obstinate, determined to engage her in a battle of wills. It was bound to happen sooner or later, mused Blake, with two queens sharing the same small island. If Mary wanted Darnley before, she was bound and determined to have him now. What had begun as an intense infatuation and might quickly have ebbed, suddenly took on all the coloring of a grand passion that would continue forever—if only to spite Queen Elizabeth.

The court continued at Stirling. With everyone aware of Mary's bold decision, Lord Darnley became insufferably proud. By the time they moved south, about the only friend he had left was the little Italian, David Riccio, lately elevated and placed in charge of Mary's foreign correspondence.

With so much strife at court over this proposed marriage, Blake had little opportunity to attend to his own affairs, though Alyssa was never far from his mind. The day he returned to Edinburgh he learned, quite by chance, that Sir Simon Ogilvy had taken to himself a stunning flame-haired wife by the name of Alyssa, who shortly was to be presented to the Queen.

23

Holyrood Palace was very grand, rather overwhelming to Alyssa's nervous eyes. In its architecture the long connection between the Scots and French was very evident, more glittering and opulent than anything normally seen in Scotland. The palace was set in a splendid park where wildlife abounded, just outside the walls of the city. The very air was sweet and clean, bathed by tangy breezes from the sea.

Before the ball began there was a short reception, allowing those who had not already met her to be presented to the Queen. Alyssa was tense with excitement, her eyes sparkling and a bloom of pink in her cheeks. The large antechamber was crowded with courtiers dressed in the most resplendent attire; silks, satins and velvets in vibrant hues of scarlet, blue and gold and every conceivable shade in between. The white that Her Majesty so favored was also much in evidence. Alyssa was the only one present dressed in black, and felt acutely conspicuous.

She had argued with Simon over the choice of a ball gown, angry that he had presumed to buy the material without consulting her. Throwing the bolts over a table, one of the sheerest lace, the other of satin, he announced with a gleam in his eyes, "Made up to my specifications, you will bewitch everyone present. Think, Alyssa, how you will stand out in that dazzling crowd, all trying to outdo each other like overblown peacocks. This will show off your golden coloring to perfection." And he added persuasively, "You, my sweet, need no garish hue to enhance your natural beauty."

Somewhat mollified by his praise, she grumbled, "Still, Simon, you should have consulted me first."

"I wanted to surprise you, certain you would see the rightness of my choice."

Once the gown was finished Alyssa had to admit that her clever husband had been right. Except for the fact that it was shockingly low-cut, everything else about it was stunning. In an enchanting cloud of satin and lace, her white breasts rose from the bodice provocatively, her radiant coloring set off to perfection. Tiny seed pearls followed the curve of her bosom and fanned out in a spray to the hem of her dress, like the glint of pale stars against the rich darkness of the night sky. The design hugged her breasts and waist and billowed out in whispery folds to brush the floor. Her coppery hair was piled high in the latest fashion and entwined with pearls.

As they waited in the anteroom Simon took her hand, chuckling softly. "See how the other men burn with envy? There is not a one among them who wouldn't give a fortune in gold to change places with me this night."

Alyssa felt a touch of annoyance, wondering why he craved the envy of others so much. But Simon too looked his best, cutting a dashing figure in his plum-colored satin doublet lavishly trimmed with gold thread, his blond head gleaming, his fair skin and fine features enhanced by the richness of the color. Alyssa squeezed his fingers affectionately. She would do her best to make him proud of her tonight, aware of how much it meant to him for her to sparkle and do credit to the house of Ogilvy.

Aside from meeting the Queen, Alyssa was excited for another reason. Simon had made it clear that everyone of importance would be at the ball—including MacKellars. While the thought of coming face to face with Lady Magdalen made her very apprehensive, she was curious to meet Lord Thomas and perhaps others of her true family.

There was someone else she dreaded encountering at the ball, but she had made up her mind not to let him spoil this great moment. She would be cool and aloof, taking care not to let him guess how much his very name had the power to disturb her.

Alyssa started violently when a herald cried out, "Sir Simon and Lady Ogilvy!"

Simon, almost strutting, well aware that every eye was upon them, slipped a hand under her elbow and led her through the archway and across a vast room to where the Queen and Darnley sat upon a dais banked with cream-colored roses, Mary Stuart fair as an angel in a white silk gown, the handsome Darnley clad in purple velvet encrusted with diamonds.

Alyssa took one awe-struck look at the young woman who was her sovereign, then swept low in a deep curtsy. When told to rise, she looked into a pair of smiling eyes the color of molten amber; eyes that moved over her in frank curiosity, even as Darnley sat forward abruptly in his chair. Nodding to Simon, whom she had met several times before, Mary extended a long, beautifully tapered hand to Alyssa. With a soft, almost mischievous laugh and a swift sidelong glance to Darnley, she said, "Would that the men of my realm were as honest as the ladies are fair! We are charmed to have you with us, Lady Ogilvy, and wish to see more of you at court." And to Simon, "Lucky you are, sir, to have such a beautiful wife." Her eyes twinkled over his shoulder to the watching crowd. "And I would caution you to keep her close by you this night."

Simon smiled and bowed low over her hand. "Your servant, madam," he said, while conscious of Darnley furtively examining Alyssa from under lazy, half-closed lids. When she was presented to the Queen's intended bridegroom, Lord Henry was careful to display only tepid interest in the titian-haired beauty, but inwardly he marked her name well.

Moving back from the dais, Alyssa experienced a moment of acute self-consciousness, then fought it down and threw back her head, her eyes sweeping the crowd. She spotted Blake Sinclair at once, his height and vibrant good looks setting him apart from most other men, even in a dazzling crowd such as this. He was dressed grandly in a rich cream-colored satin doublet only moderately studded with jewels, the light color of his attire strongly accentuating the dark virility of his person. Blake's brown eyes raked over her boldly, a sardonic smile curving his lips. He made her an almost imperceptible bow, one rife with mockery.

Alyssa looked away. She hugged Simon's arm and gave

him her most melting smile, whispering, "'Tis the most exciting night of my life! Thank you for making it possible."

The assembly buzzed with speculation over the entrancing woman in the black lace gown. Who was she exactly? Where had Ogilvy found her? One dowager whispered to another, "I have heard, my dear, that she was little more than a common servant lass when Sir Simon discovered her."

Her companion shook her head. "Impossible! Why, she has the beauty and posture of a queen, which can only come through good breeding. Though how Ogilvy can maintain her in such style is anyone's guess."

The other fanned herself rapidly, brows drawn in disapproval. She responded acidly, "From the look of them he's managing well enough; his kind always do."

At the edge of the crowd stood two gentlemen chatting together. Like the others, they had broken off to stare appreciatively at Alyssa when she was being presented to the Queen. Watching the couple walk back, the Earl of Cassillis, from Ayrshire, was jolted. A courtly man in middle age, he was struck by Lady Ogilvy's resemblance to another great beauty, one who had been the darling of the court in his own day. He glanced at Lord Luke MacKellar, the younger brother of Lord Thomas, remarking, "By God, sir, I'll wager that lady is one of your own clan!"

MacKellar studied Alyssa closely. He was a stocky man of medium height and sported a head of russet hair and a lush, curly beard. His attire was not as elegant as the rest; not because he was short of funds, but because court fripperies held no interest for him. He had come to Edinburgh from his country estate under duress, mainly because Thomas was ailing again and might not have been able to attend the function. But his older brother, spurred on by his wife, had made the effort after all. Now that he was here, Luke steeled himself to suffer through the evening, anxious to be back on his estate with his bow and hounds.

He nodded slowly. "Aye, I see what you mean, Kennedy, but the lady is none o' ours."

"Remarkable!" Privately the earl had another thought, that she might well be one of the many MacKellar bastards.

From across the hall Lord Luke's wife beckoned to him.
Nan MacKellar was a plump, comfortable little woman in early
middle age with a blunt, forthright manner. Drawing her
husband aside, she whispered, "Yon Lady Ogilvy is a wee bit
like your niece Fiona."

"Methought she resembled Fiona's mother, our Lydia."

"Nobody seems to ken from whence she came."

He shrugged, already losing interest, his mind turning to
the sumptuous banquet soon to be enjoyed. Nan, though,
could not take her eyes off the comely Lady Ogilvy, and the
more she studied her the more certain she was that at least a
trickle of MacKellar blood ran through her veins.

Alyssa was totally unaware of the country matron's
examination. Her own attention was riveted on the Earl and
Countess of Kilgarin, conversing at that moment with the
coarse-faced Lindsay. Magdalen was dressed in her favorite
gold, and she sparkled with jewels. Thomas too sparkled, but all
the diamonds in the crown itself could not have disguised his
wan, wasted appearance.

"Ignore them," Simon muttered, feeling his wife grow
rigid beside him. "Behave as if you were unaware of their
existence—as I plan to do."

"He looks shockingly ill," whispered Alyssa, staring at this
uncle who had—perhaps unknowingly—usurped her place at
Cumbray.

"Aye, but one cannot feel too much pity for a man who
lived in such a way as to invite ill health."

Alyssa was tempted to say, "Then let that be a warning to
you, my lord," but prudently held her tongue.

The banquet hall blazed with candle and torchlight, the
tables laid with the finest damask and set with gold plate. Wine
bubbled from fonts intricately wrought in silver and gold and
studded with precious gems. One elaborate course followed
another, with interludes of entertainment in between—singers
and fools, a magician and fire-eater and even a miniature play.

Blake Sinclair, Alyssa noted, was seated at the high table
near the Queen. Mary seemed to be in great spirits in spite of
all the controversy surrounding her choice of a husband, and
time and again her merry, tinkling laugh rang out, an infectious

laugh that caused those about to laugh with her. Alyssa tried not to look in that direction, even as she felt Sinclair's eyes stray in hers. I *will* enjoy myself, she told herself grimly, and again and again lifted her goblet of wine to her lips, more wine than she had ever consumed before in a public place.

Later, the Queen and Darnley opened the ball, and a tall, handsome couple they made. Mary was an excellent and energetic dancer. Hour after hour her satin-shod feet flitted around the room, wearing out one partner after another. Alyssa too danced with so many different men that afterwards she could only recall a fraction of their names. No one seemed to think ill of the fact that most of the men flirted with her outrageously. Simon, delighted by his wife's popularity, took it all in good part.

Watching Simon Ogilvy basking in the reflected light of his wife's glory, Sinclair felt an unreasonable anger. He had never liked the knight, and liked him less now. Why, he brooded, had a man like Ogilvy gone so far as to marry Alyssa? His disreputable way of life and his indebtedness were commonly known, his need to marry for wealth so acute that it had led the knight to pursue even the middle-aged, widowed Countess McKinley, a woman so ill-favored that she had been nicknamed "the frog." Angry as he was, it alarmed Blake to think of Alyssa bound to a person like Simon Ogilvy. Jealousy flared inside him as he gazed at the lower table, his eyes on her averted profile, so flawless, delicate, and maddeningly beautiful did she look in her black lace gown. Rage boiled to explosive proportions when he thought of Ogilvy possessing the woman he loved.

Suddenly he rose to his feet and walked purposefully toward their table. Even as he reached it and bowed, Blake saw Alyssa stiffen, but Ogilvy, flushed with wine and slightly drunk, smiled congenially enough.

"May I have the pleasure of dancing with your lovely wife, Ogilvy?"

Alyssa flushed a deep pink. She refused to meet her former lover's eyes. But with everyone looking on, she had no option but to rise and allow herself to be drawn into his arms. As they tightened about her, Alyssa felt her legs sag beneath her and she almost swooned. The hard strength of his body, the fresh scent she identified only with him, and his warm breath against her forehead made her head reel so alarmingly that she almost broke free and ran from the room. Her heart lurched, and the control she had managed to exert over herself all evening completely deserted her at the moment she needed it most.

"So . . ." he growled, his lips brushing the top of her head, "it was Simon Ogilvy. Ogilvy!" he spat the name in distaste, the rocklike muscles of his arms threatening to crush the breath from her body. "And are you happy in this marriage, *Lady* Ogilvy?"

"Very happy." Her voice shook. Nervous and flustered, Alyssa knew that her tone lacked conviction.

He chuckled mockingly, and to her horror he held her tight against him with one arm and, in full view of everyone present, caught her chin and wrenched her head up to his. "Liar!" he grated, his eyes searing into hers.

"Unhand me at once!" She could feel those nearest to them eying them curiously. She could feel the sting of hot color in her cheeks. And if Simon should be watching . . .

"Please . . . !" she whimpered, horrified of causing a scene and afraid of the ruthless determination in his eyes, his arrogant disdain of the consequences. "If you ever truly loved me, take me back to the table now."

With a hand at her hips he drew her yet closer, making her fully aware of the rampant passions clamoring to be unleashed. His eyes burned across the dove-soft fullness of her breasts, raising goosebumps on her flesh, and he murmured, "Were I truly my father's son I would carry you from this room now, throw you across a horse, and lock you up in a tower room at Augusta until you came back to your senses. For even at this moment, my headstrong Alyssa, you know in your heart that Simon Ogilvy can never make you happy; never fulfill you, and—"

"And you, sir, can never make me your wife!"

"Then the name of Ogilvy means more to you than my love?"

She turned her head away, suddenly weary. "We discussed this before. You know how I feel and must accept it."

"I will *never* accept it!"

Her eyes met his angrily. "Had I been a lady of rank we would never have come to this pass. Then I would have been worthy of the mighty Sinclair."

"You mean more to me than any lady of rank."

"Your actions say otherwise."

"Then, madam, you are blind indeed!"

Alyssa laughed bitterly. "Nay, Sinclair, I *was* blind and you, sir, opened my eyes to the true way of things." They had moved around the great hall several times. Now Alyssa saw they were again near her table and suddenly pulled away from him. Blake bowed, drawling, "A great pleasure, Lady Ogilvy, and one I hope to repeat before too long."

Alyssa was trembling when she sat down, but fortunately, Simon was too bleary-eyed to notice. She had frightened herself. For just a moment, when the question of rank had been raised, she had almost blurted out the truth to Sinclair, so great was her hurt and irritation. Now, gazing about the glittering room while the flush on her cheeks cooled, her eyes searched and found Lady Magdalen—only to surprise the countess watching *her*! For a second or two their gazes clashed. All the resentment and hatred that Alyssa felt for the woman blazed in her eyes, and this time Magdalen was the first to turn away.

"Point out all the MacKellars in this room," Alyssa asked her husband tersely.

He sat up abruptly, her request slicing through his pleasant haze. "Why?"

"I would know who my people are. Mayhap one of them can tell me something of my mother, if she's dead or alive."

Suddenly cold sober and with his heart lurching in alarm, it was all he could do to stop himself from clapping a hand over her mouth. "Be silent!" Simon hissed. "Sweet Jesu, have you lost your wits! You would think of interrogating the MacKellars right under the nose of Lady Magdalen?" He glanced furtively around and leaned closer, his fingers closing painfully over her wrist. "I warned the lady to leave you alone, but if she thinks you are out to make trouble . . . !" He shuddered, his face gone tight and pale.

Alyssa bit her lip. She was seething with resentment, and frustration made more intense after her confrontation with Blake. It infuriated her to see Thomas and Magdalen MacKellar occupying a place that should rightfully be hers. Now, more than ever, she burned to set things right. Simon had promised to help her, but over the weeks of their marriage had thought of nothing but pleasure and tossing money around. Feeling reckless and determined, she turned to him and said firmly, "I would have you introduce me to some of my kin."

Again he glanced wildly around. Beads of sweat stood out on his pale brow. "Alyssa," he said persuasively, "a social occasion such as this is not the time and place. Think, lass, you cannot simply walk up to these people—total strangers—and commence to ask them very personal questions. It would be in shocking taste. They would be affronted." His grey eyes pleaded with her to be reasonable. "Would you put their backs up right from the start? Have patience, sweetheart. I promise you will meet them in good time, and where there will be no danger to you."

"I won't wait forever, Simon."

He patted her hand soothingly. "Soon, dearling, soon," he assured her.

The gaiety and sparkle went out of the evening for Alyssa. She took little notice of the gossip bandied about around her, the sly nods in the direction of a certain young matron who had recently become the mistress of the Queen's half-brother, Lord Robert, while her husband was forced to play the silent dupe, though well aware of the situation. Agitated and tense, afraid of what Sinclair might do in his frustration, she longed for the evening to end. But in Mary Stuart's court such social functions rarely concluded before dawn, since one could not depart before the Queen, and the Queen habitually danced the night away as if driven to exact every second of pleasure out of every single day, as if each one might be her last.

Alyssa kept her head turned away from the high table, but over and over his voice rang in her mind. "Are you happy in this marriage, Lady Ogilvy?" his deep voice brimming with mockery.

Across the hall, Luke and Nan MacKellar sat equally tensely with the Earl and Countess of Kilgarin, obliged to endure Lady Magdalen's patronizing manner, and she never let them forget for an instant that she considered them to be uncouth rustics who fell far short of the social graces expected at court. It might well be true, thought Nan irritably, but there were more important things in life than fancy manners and fine clothes. And who was Magdalen to criticize? Faith, she fumed inwardly, what had Magdalen and Thomas ever done for Cumbray except whittle away its assets in tasteless extravagance and ill-timed business ventures of one kind or another? Cruel and unjust to those who dared oppose them, they were far from popular within the family itself. Thomas they could tolerate, given that a weak, easily manipulated man is more to be pitied than anything else, but Magdalen they hated with a vengeance. What crimes, Nan mused darkly, had stained the lady's long white hands? How many innocents had she caused to be put to death, and how many lives ruined?

Nan thought of her old friend Lady Alicia, and the shabby treatment she had received from Magdalen after Lord Angus died. Banished to a distant convent with little more than the clothes on her back, and there left to rot. How Magdalen had hated Alicia! How she dreaded the thought of the young beauty giving Angus a son! Aye, Nan's mind ran on dourly, there was much about that period at Cumbray that wouldn't stand close scrutiny, particularly the evening when Alicia had given birth to her child; a child she swore had been born alive—and a girl rather than a lad.

Nan sighed and stared pensively across the room, her mind far away. She had not seen Alicia for years. The present earl and countess had made it clear that they desired that the lady be forgotten, and besides, Ayrshire was so very far away. The last Nan had heard, Alicia had left the convent and married a local laird, but they never came to Edinburgh.

For years Nan had felt a touch of guilt whenever she thought of Alicia, the feeling that she should have done more to defend her against Magdalen's vindictiveness. Now that

Thomas was ailing again and Luke forced to stand in for him, they had a taste of that vindictiveness at close hand.

Giving herself a mental shake to banish such troublesome thoughts, Nan glanced idly about, her eyes settling on the lovely Lady Ogilvy, and was startled at the pained expression on her face. Following the direction of her eyes, Nan saw that she was watching Lord Blake Sinclair dancing with the Crawford heiress, something of a beauty herself. For just an instant before the titian head turned away, Nan had a naked glimpse into Alyssa's soul and sensed exactly what she was feeling, and why.

24

The morning after the ball Alyssa felt unwell, too nauseated to consume her breakfast of ale and hare stew. "You ate too heartily last eve," grinned Simon, "and the food was a mite overrich to a newcomer to such fare."

But the next day she was again violently sick, also the day after. Megan watched her, and the morning when she came upon Alyssa hanging over the washbowl, white to the lips, she murmured in her dispassionate way, "My lady is fruitful."

The doctor confirmed it. She was eight to ten weeks gone with child. Simon was delighted. Finally his manhood would be vindicated! Secretly it had worried him that his various mistresses had never given him a child, and often his mind returned to the summer of his sixteenth year when he had been stricken with a virulent fever and swollen neck glands. At the time his doctor had muttered darkly that because of his illness his chances of siring young had been drastically reduced, an announcement that had cut Simon's fledgling pride to shreds. Well, he thought smugly as he embraced his wife, the old toad had been proved wrong. The Ogilvy heir—a golden child, he visualized, one who would embody the glorious beauty of his parents—would arrive with gratifying alacrity. He could scarcely wait to boast of it to his friends!

His secret meetings with Magdalen MacKellar were going well, and he continued to have the upper hand with the lady. The day after the ball she had sent for him and soundly upbraided him for daring to flaunt Alyssa at court where her in-laws would see her and possibly become suspicious. "Nonsense!" Simon had countered with a scoffing smile, and recklessly, "'Tis only your guilty conscience dreaming up ways to torment you. Why, who remembers what happened *last month*, let alone twenty years gone? Alyssa is not the only woman in Edinburgh who could be said to have the MacKellar coloring, so set your mind at ease." He went on forcefully, "We will not play the hermits, madam, for that would but arouse the suspicion of all who know me and my associates at court."

Magdalen saw the wisdom in this though she didn't admit it. "Then I hold you responsible, sir, and trust you can continue to keep your lady in check, for I like not the bold thoughts I see mirrored in her eyes."

Alyssa's pregnancy was a godsend in more ways than one. Now she would be easier to control, Ogilvy reflected, and more than ever dependent on him. At her prodding he pretended to hire an agent to look into the whereabouts of her mother, but in the meantime he had done a little investigating on his own. He had discovered that Lady Alicia was still alive, remarried, and living in faraway Ayrshire. Her new name was Cairnmore and her husband a wealthy knight. They never came to court. Wise, he thought, with Lady Magdalen at the helm at Cumbray.

On the whole, Simon was satisfied with his life, though, naturally, one could always wish for more money, particularly when no matter how much one had it was never enough. It was bad luck indeed that his employer, Moray, had lost favor with the Queen and taken himself off to his country estates to lick his wounds—at a time when Ogilvy especially longed to shine at court and gain the respect and recognition long withheld from him. All this took money; a great deal of money. He had already begun the restoration of Mordrun Hall, for a gentleman must have a luxurious retreat where he could entertain his friends. The work was going much too slowly for Simon's taste, grinding to a halt through lack of funds.

He had just about decided to pressure Magdalen for more money when he received an unexpected summons from Randolph, the English ambassador to Queen Mary's court. Randolph had some business he wished to discuss with Ogilvy and wanted to see him at once.

Alyssa was startled. "What can it mean? Why would the fellow want to talk business with you?"

Simon shook his head and shrugged—but he had more than a glimmer of an idea as to why the ambassador had singled him out.

The English statesman began the interview by politely inquiring after the health of Lady Ogilvy, and watched the young knight puff up with conceit. "Indeed she is most well, sir, and already enceinte."

Randolph, a courtly gentleman with penetrating dark eyes and a neatly clipped beard, congratulated him warmly. Like everyone else, he had been surprised to learn of this marriage. Rumor had it that the young woman, though exceedingly lovely, was from humble beginnings with neither name nor assets to commend her. For a nobleman to marry her was astounding, practically unheard of. Of such were mistresses made, not wives. It was all the more puzzling that a man of Ogilvy's extravagant tastes and straitened circumstances should go so far as to wed a woman without means. It was the talk of the court.

How, the ambassador mused, did Ogilvy mean to support her? With Moray away from town his means of earning a living would have dried up. It was this, plus his knowledge of the knight's services for Moray, that had given him an idea, one he was certain Simon couldn't afford to turn down.

Leaning forward across his desk, Randolph came right to the point. Simon heard him out in silence, smiling to himself when the older man announced frankly that he was willing to take over where James Stewart had left off. To sweeten the pot he said, "In recognition of the danger involved, you will be paid accordingly," and he named a fee that brought the knight bolt upright in his chair.

Ogilvy was sorely tempted. In spite of Magdalen's money, debts were again piling up, creditors pressing from every direction. Yet he hesitated, seeming to feel the icy kiss of cold steel against the tender flesh of his neck. It was one thing to agent himself to Moray who, in the natural course of events, had a perfectly legitimate reason for transport with England, and quite another to work for England itself.

Randolph watched him appraisingly, quickly sizing him

up, and decided to appeal to him two ways. "You were highly recommended to me by your former master," he purred, at the same time placing a heavy purse on the desk.

The praise brought a flush to Ogilvy's cheeks, the purse a bright glint to his eyes. Then Randolph clinched matters by adding, "If our plans meet with success, your part in this will not be forgotten, sir, I assure you. As a good servant to the cause, a position of power will be found for you when the time comes."

Power! The sweetest word in the English language to Simon, and music indeed to one who craved it so desperately and found it so elusive.

The two men shook hands. Simon was committed.

Early on the morning of July 29 in the year of Our Lord 1565, Mary, Queen of Scots, wed Henry Stewart, Lord Darnley. Watching the ceremony, Jason whispered to Blake, "See how sullen he is? Methinks the bridegroom is not satisfied with his new title, Duke of Albany. It would seem he hungers for more."

The marriage ceremony was conducted by the Bishop of Brechin according to the rites of the Roman Catholic church in Mary's private chapel at Holyrood. She was dressed in black, not unusual for a widow, though there were many present who read dark portents into her choice of attire. Her lovely face was pale and tense, as if she were aware that not all present wished her well, yet to Blake she still seemed radiant, if touchingly vulnerable.

Afterwards there was great feasting and dancing, "much heathenish excess" as John Knox put it dourly. Randolph was more to the point when he remarked, his eyes on the strutting bridegroom, "No good can come out of this union."

The following day the nobles, perforce, had to give Randolph's prediction more serious consideration when Mary had the heralds proclaim Darnley King of Scotland, an act of dubious legality without the approval of Parliament. Further, it was announced that from then on all documents should be signed by the pair conjointly as King Henry and Queen Mary.

This stunning development was greeted with stony silence from the lords, except for the Earl of Lennox, Darnley's father, who cried, "God save His Grace!"

Blake glanced at his cousin and growled, "My God, how much more must she lavish to his honor?" to which Jason responded dryly, "Naught remains but the crown itself."

The royal honeymoon was barely launched when a thundercloud in the shape of James Stewart, Earl of Moray, roared over the horizon with an army of angry supporters behind him. The Queen's half-brother was promptly put to the horn and outlawed. And as much as she had defended him before, Mary totally reversed her stand at this flagrant show of treachery against herself and her new husband. She set about raising an army of her own, determined to crush the rebellion.

There was little doubt from what direction Moray was receiving money to sustain his troops. With this in mind, Mary commissioned Sinclair to ride south at the head of a battalion in the event the crafty English would choose this moment to attack, and to try to cut off the lifeline that was supplying Moray with gold. "Bring these traitors back alive," she ordered grimly, "so that we might have the names of all others in my realm who secretly stand behind my brother." Angry tears filled her eyes. "My lord Moray will learn quickly enough that I am not the weak and feeble ruler he thought me to be, no longer the trusting young girl he tried to bend to his will."

It was well known that Randolph had many agents in Scotland. Identifying and apprehending them in the act of engaging in their nefarious business was quite another matter, given the wild and tractless terrain along the Scottish border. But Sinclair relished this chance for action, glad to escape, at least for a time, the problems in his own life. The storm following his separation from Elizabeth was gradually dying down. Now his family were pressuring him to select a replacement, suggesting the comely Sara Crawford as a suitable candidate when his divorce became final. Sara was dark and sultry and very, very rich, or would be when her father died. Had he not met a certain fiery lass with a will of iron and skin like warm white silk, he might have been persuaded.

One bright spark was the reemergence of young George Gordon on the scene. He had been pardoned by the Queen and his property and titles restored to him. Now George was himself raising an army, more than eager to take Mary Stuart's side against Moray, the man he held responsible for the destruction of his family.

Clad in his black and gold armor, Blake thrust all thoughts of the fair Alyssa from his mind and set out in a southerly direction at the head of his troops, Wyatt and Jason at his side. With them was a group of Morton's men, headed by one Captain Jack, a seasoned warrior and, like their leader, determined they wouldn't return empty-handed. "There are important folks in Edinburgh shielding these agents," the bearded soldier growled as they rode along in the early morning sunshine. "And the traitors ha' families, do they not, who must ken well enough what they're up to." He ran a hairy fist across his sweating brow, glowering around at the crowd gathered to see them off. "Aye, and the buggers hiding them will also pay, every man, woman and child who protects them. Ye ken Morton's methods o' dealing wi' traitors."

They all knew the Earl of Morton's methods well. Though a worthy soldier and, when it profited him to be, a strong ally of the Queen, Morton was essentially a barbarian who stopped at nothing to gain his ends, even if it meant the slaying of women and children in the most brutal way. He had appalled the Queen by advising, "Here's one sure way of making these agents reveal the names of their associates—put their wives and children on the rack and make them watch. They'll talk quick enough then, by thunder!" And until he saw Her Majesty's face, he had thrown back his head and roared with appreciative laughter, choked off abruptly at a sharp rebuke from Mary. Even then he had had the crassness to defend himself. "Madam," he said pompously, "traitors beget traitors, and leniency breeds contempt."

Remembering that little scene, Blake thought of another case in which the wife of a prisoner, hearing the soldiers riding toward her house and aware of the earl's reputation, had stabbed her five children to death and then turned the dagger on herself. Morton certainly had his methods, and the Queen was never informed as to the grim details, or what happened to the families of the doomed men—or the assets of the families.

The Queen had ordered Sinclair to bring the culprits back alive—assuming they could be found—in which case not only the agents but everyone connected to them were doomed.

The crowd cheered the troops as they rode down the Canongate, their polished armor glinting in the sun. "Down wi' the bastard Moray!" they screamed. "Hang him! Put him to the sword!" Only weeks before they had sung his praises and thrown rose petals in his path as Moray rode this same way in a ceremonial procession. Blake shook his head, musing at the fickleness of Mary's subjects, no less fickle than many of her lords. He wondered if it was for this reason that she had lately elevated the likes of David Riccio and certain other foreigners, men she had come to know and trust, much to the resentment of Maitland, Lindsay and others.

They were less than a league south of the city when a messenger caught up with them to say that the long-out-of-favor Earl of Bothwell too had been reinstated with the Queen and also taken arms in her name.

"Glory be to Christ!" laughed Captain Jack, slapping his rocklike thigh. "The day will surely be won wi' the Wizard o' Hermitage conjuring up his tricks!"

Megan scolded Alyssa for sitting at home fretting, little realizing just who she was fretting over. "You had a mind to hear John Knox preach, did ye not? Well, lady, we'll be off to the kirk on Sunday!"

The month of August dawned hot and muggy. With James Stewart on the rampage, the city of Edinburgh was tense. The average citizen had only a vague notion of the real issues involved, but until he left on a "mission" Simon had kept Alyssa apprised of the day-to-day developments. She had been dismayed the day he returned from court to inform her that he would be leaving almost at once on what he termed "the Queen's business," and that evening they had the first serious blow-up of their marriage. "Where are you going?" she demanded to know. "And what's the purpose of this mission?"

"That I'm not at liberty to tell you," he had responded

curtly, seeming edgy and distracted, almost nervous. "I've explained before that my work is secret. By the rood, woman, why must you badger me so!"

"Because I'm your wife and soon to be the mother of your child!" she shot back angrily. "If you cannot tell me the nature of your business you can at least tell me where you are going. My God, Simon, what if I should need to get in touch with you for some reason? The atmosphere hereabouts is explosive—"

"Megan will take good care of you," he interrupted impatiently, stuffing clothes into a leather satchel. "She'll know what to do and can be counted on in any crisis."

"Megan! Why should I rely on her—"

"Because I wish it!" he thundered back, and turning, he grabbed her by the shoulders and shook her violently, then threw her on the bed saying, "And I also wish you to stop pestering me about business that doesn't concern you. I will come and go as I see fit, as is meet, and you, my dear wife, will accept it and attend to the business of being a good wife, as is also meet." He leaned over the bed, his grey eyes smoky with anger and his skin flushed, and roared into her face, "Forget not that I raised you out of the gutter and honored you with my name, and as thanks must suffer your nagging tongue and less than wifely enthusiasm in the bedchamber!" Seizing her by the neck of her gown, he ripped it to the waist and his hand closed cruelly over her breast. "All that will cease here and now!"

Furious, Alyssa tried to slap his hands away. Ogilvy drew back and struck her across the face, then threw himself down beside her and proceeded to satisfy his baser desires, urges he had controlled until then.

In the morning Alyssa refused to speak to him or even say good-bye. This time he left his sullen squire Calvin at home to guard her, and spoke to both Megan and Calvin in private before departing the house.

Over the next few days Alyssa could feel the pair watching her. She took pains to conceal from them how much Simon's violent behavior had upset her, this first disquieting glimpse of the true nature of the man she had married. Frightened and disgusted, she wondered if she might have exchanged one desperate situation for another, and suddenly rued the day she had ever married him. There were bruises on her flesh, a cut on her lip, and the beginning of despair in her heart. But for the fact that she was pregnant she might have left him, for he had forced her into intimacies that revolted her. Now she couldn't leave. She was carrying his child.

Megan, her mind on that child, prodded Alyssa to walk daily in the fresh air, to eat food that almost made her gag, and to rouse herself out of the depression that had stolen over her. That Sunday they went to St. Giles and there listened to an amazing "sermon" preached by John Knox. Alyssa was startled by his daring. He rapidly turned from the scriptures to openly denounce the Queen for marrying Lord Darnley, saying, "I stand here before ye not as a servant or flatterer of princes but as an instrument bound to duty of the Lord our God, sworn to defend the rights of His Kingdom. No sovereign," he thundered, "may bind herself to an unlawful spouse detrimental to the realm, or contrary to the laws of that realm. And no sovereign may worship as she sees fit, nay, not even in private, when it goes against the religion of her people. Too long we have been tolerant of the whims of princes. Now the time has come to rise up and protest!"

Alyssa stared at him, fascinated. He held the congregation spellbound. There wasn't a sound in the church. Yet at first glance the reformer was an unprepossessing figure. About fifty years old and of medium height, he was slight of build with a narrow, ascetic face and piercing eyes that Alyssa found unsettling. His only outstanding quality was his voice—a deep, powerful voice with a persuasive ring to it.

On leaving the church, Alyssa heard someone call her name. Turning, she saw Lady Brodie, one of their best customer's at Livingstone's, with her companion, Becky Allardice.

The result was an invitation to lunch at Fairly Court.

During the meal the nosy old dowager could hardly conceal her avid interest about Alyssa's surprising marriage. When that subject was finally exhausted, much to Alyssa's relief, the elderly woman jumped to the topic that had all of Edinburgh buzzing. "To think," she sniffed disapprovingly, "that Moray would dare rebel against his sister when she's lavished so much to his honor! Now they say he marches forth with a great army, one no doubt paid for by the English Queen; the fray waged in the name of Protestantism. Ha! You can be sure Moray fights for himself, and if the English will obligingly foot the bill, so much the better!" She shook her head and went on darkly, "Randolph and his spies should be banished from court. 'Tis these same spies who carry gold from England to Moray. Mark my words, heads will roll ere this thing is over; noble heads. That fiend Morton will stage a bloodbath the likes of which Edinburgh has never seen."

The dowager's companion murmured, "They say the border is being watched."

"Eh . . . ?" Her hard-of-hearing mistress turned to her questioningly, somewhat impatient. "Speak up, Becky, speak up!"

"The border, my lady, is being patrolled, with the Queen's soldiers ready to apprehend subversive agents treating with England."

"Aye, aye, to be sure. May they catch them all, for they deserve to die a traitor's death. But let us turn to a brighter subject." Her inquisitive little eyes twinkled at Alyssa. "You must tell us, my dear, how you managed to tame the dashing Sir Simon and keep him close to your hearth. With Moray gone, the dear boy must be completely at your disposal."

Alyssa left Fairly Court feeling troubled. Contrary to what Lady Brodie thought, Simon was far from close to her hearth. It irked her that she had no idea of where he was or the work he was involved in, nor even the name of his new employer. Suddenly she recalled his recent interview with Randolph. He had returned from that meeting in high spirits, yet all he would say in answer to her questions was, "Oh, 'twas nothing, just some papers that have gone amiss—as if *I* should know aught about that!"

He was secretive and evasive. Now, after her conversation with Lady Brodie, Alyssa became convinced that he was involved in something disreputable, even dangerous.

That night she hardly slept. Megan too was restless.

Alyssa, as she tossed and turned in bed, could hear her pacing about in her room. In the early hours of the morning she finally abandoned sleep and wandered into the kitchen for a cooling cup of ale. Megan sat hunched over the table casting a horoscope and looked up with a start when she sensed her mistress's presence. Alyssa viewed her little hobby as harmless, and though she would never admit it, was mildly interested, but coming upon her like this in the middle of the night worriedly fussing with her charts and pentagrams was frightening.

"What's ado, Megan?" she asked the housekeeper sharply.

The woman jumped to her feet and hastily threw a scarf over her charts. Normally stoic and emotionless, she flushed and her sallow features tightened. "Go back abed, mistress!" It sounded like an order. "What can ye be thinking of pry— roaming about thus?"

Alyssa walked to the table and pulled back the scarf. She gazed suspiciously at Megan's handiwork, but none of it made the slightest sense to her. The housekeeper was at her elbow. Alyssa could feel her agitation. She gave Megan a sidelong glance, and with a nod to the table demanded, "Why are you working with this now, in the middle of the night?"

The other opened her mouth as if to speak, then clamped her lips shut.

"Come, Megan, I would have you answer me."

"My . . . sister is ill. I but thought to see what the stars have in store for her."

Alyssa knew she was lying. Had Megan's sister been truly ailing she would have heard about it before this. More softly she asked, "You are worried about the master, are you not?" And when there was no reply, "I'm worried about him too, Megan." She glanced back to the charts. "What do you read there?"

For a moment Alyssa thought she would refuse to answer. Then she suddenly blurted, "Pray for him, lady; pray for all of us!"

25

As they loomed over the crest of the hill the two riders were outlined against the red glow of the sunset, wild and rugged wilderness spread out all around them. A breeze soughed fitfully through the bracken, and birds, tiny black shapes against the paling sky, darted overhead and vanished to their nests in the treetops. Except for the wind it was very still, the distant howl of a wolf seeming much closer than it actually was in the pristine air.

Fisher, Simon's fellow agent, halted on the ridge and held up a hand for Ogilvy to do likewise.

"What's amiss?" asked the knight irritably, the nervousness that had been his constant companion since they left London sharpening his voice. In actuality the trip south and return journey—to that point—had been smooth and uneventful, but even so, neither man had been lulled into letting down his guard. Each of them had a small fortune in gold sewn into the lining of his jerkin, and as they neared the border each knew that the most dangerous leg of their journey was upon them.

Fisher motioned him into a stand of trees and once there said gruffly, "I wouldna halt for victuals this night, sir, but am all for pressing on."

They had not stopped to eat since nine o'clock that morning, and, hungry and exhausted as he was, Ogilvy was beginning to feel squeamish and light-headed. But better light-headed, he reasoned, than no head at all! Even to pause to eat a cold supper—neither would have dreamed of lighting a fire—was distinctly unwise at this stage of the trip.

Simon nodded and ran the sleeve of his tunic over his eyes; eyes red and sore from constantly straining to detect signs of dust or movement about them. "Curse this long twilight," he grumbled. "Mayhap we should hide here until the coming of dark."

"Nay, 'tis never wise to tarry and make o' yourself a sitting duck. We keep moving, I say, and try to ford the Tweed while we can still see. Once beyond the river I'll feel a muckle sight better. At least, should we be detected, we can give them a run for it then."

Cautiously, hugging the trees as best they could for protection, they pressed forward while the long Northern sunset lingered on in the sky, both starting violently whenever a small moorland creature scurried away before them. Neither spoke, but their thoughts ran along similar lines, both much preoccupied with what would happen should they be caught. For Sir Simon, because of his rank, it technically meant either hanging or beheading, but the Earl of Morton had a way of circumventing standard procedure by having the execution take place away from Edinburgh itself. And once far from the capital, the poor unfortunate faced the grim spectacle of a traitor's death the same as any other prisoner. He was hung, but cut down before the moment of death to have his belly ripped open and his intestines burned while he still lived. Then, when no more suffering could be wrung from him, his head was severed and his naked corpse grossly defiled.

Nor did it end there, not with Morton in charge, not when there was always the possibility of the victim's family coming forward at a later date to reclaim what was rightfully theirs. Nay, brooded Simon, Morton rarely chanced such a happening. The family too was destroyed.

Ogilvy had been well aware of the risks all along, but there lurked in him, under his surface nervousness, the conviction that he would never be caught. Had he not been engaged in one form of mischief or another since boyhood, and had not his quick wits and almost animalistic scenting of danger always gotten him off? Aye, and a man led a dull and unprosperous life if he trod the safe and prudent path, which Simon saw as a lackluster trail leading from birth to the grave. His easily bored nature compelled him to follow a different trail, as sharp and keen as the edge of a sword.

Fisher's anxiety took a more prosaic form as he constantly drew his horse up to look behind them, much disturbed by the periodic cries of wolves, which struck him as gradually closing in like a circle.

Simon brushed off his misgivings with a soft laugh. "The brutes always act thus. 'Tis their way to surround a victim." He grinned at the look on the other man's face, adding, "If wolves are all we have to bedevil us, then I'll count myself fortunate. 'Twill not be the first time I've had to tackle the scurvy beasts and lived to tell about it." He patted the saddlebag behind him. "Breathe easy, my friend, I never venture far abroad without my pitch-tipped faggots, better by far than pistol or sword."

The creatures continued to howl and Fisher to glance over his shoulder, his eyes dazzled by the setting sun as he peered to the west. Under his knees he felt a tremor pass through his horse, one that echoed inside himself. As the eerie cries grew closer, he again voiced his fears aloud. "God's blood, man, I mislike the sounds o' them! I'll wager a goodly pack be stalking us."

"Have done!" Ogilvy lost his patience, Fisher's alarm only adding to his own. "Ere we reach the Tweed they'll cease to bother us."

"Mayhap their cousins will pick up the chase on the other side."

Simon didn't answer and both fell silent. They continued on for about half a league when Ogilvy felt a strong urge to relieve himself. Fisher made no bones about his annoyance even at this short delay. "Ride on," said Simon, leading his mount into the bushes. "If I don't catch up with you shortly you'll know the wolves have made a meal of me."

The other agent grunted and in a few minutes disappeared over a hillock, not in the slightest amused.

Ogilvy was squatting in the bracken when in the stillness he heard a sharp cry. Hastily rearranging his clothing and warily leaving his horse tethered in the trees, he scrambled up the hillside and, lying flat on his stomach, peered over the top.

He was temporarily frozen into immobility by what he saw below him. Fisher, still mounted, was completely surrounded by a pack of wolves—but of the human sort. Ogilvy immediately recognized the black and gold armor of Blake Sinclair, and one of Morton's henchmen, Captain Jack. Even as Simon lay rigid, Sinclair pulled Fisher from his horse and sought to stay his hand as the agent reached for his dagger. But driven by desperation and the prospect of a long, agonizing death, Fisher evaded him and plunged the weapon into his own heart.

Ogilvy sagged with relief. Better a quick end, he was thinking, than being taken back to Edinburgh Castle to be questioned under torture, there to spill the names of all those involved.

Panic surged through the knight. He rolled down the hill, was on his feet in a flash, and bolted into the trees. The group had been small, no more than ten horse, undoubtedly out of camp on patrol, but Simon had heard of Sinclair's methods and knew there would be others not too far away—but in what direction?

For a moment he trembled in indecision, then decided that his best chance was to conceal himself as best he could where he was until dark and try to sneak away when he would be less conspicuous.

Moving stealthily, he cautiously led his mount deeper into the trees and behind an outcropping of granite, then stood stock still, his heart pounding and his face dripping sweat. He didn't have long to wait. The drumming of hoofbeats approached and in the stillness he clearly heard the jingle of spurs as Sinclair and his men rode over the crest of the hill—at which point Simon's luck deserted him. His horse, sensing other horses close by, threw back his head and whinnied a greeting.

Instantly Sinclair halted and spun around in the saddle to stare into the trees, then Ogilvy heard him bark out an order to the others. The next minute came the crashing of horseflesh through the bushes in his direction.

Ogilvy vaulted into the saddle, dragged his wide-brimmed hat down over his face, and with the blood thundering in his ears raced furiously toward the river with the knowledge that he was fleeing for his life. He glanced back only once, to see Blake Sinclair—like an apparition from hell with his black and gold armor blazing in the last rays of the sun—galloping after him.

His only hope was to make it to the Tweed and pray he lived to reach the other side.

The coming of darkness was a reprieve. Desperate, Simon evaded his pursuers by recklessly driving his mount straight to the edge of a knoll overhanging the river, at which point both man and horse sprang over the rim and disappeared.

Blake and Captain Jack arrived at the spot ahead of the others, and gazed below in the fading light to see a horse floundering in the water and a man's wide-brimmed hat bobbing away downstream. Jack cursed loudly and shook his head. "Drowned! Perished afore we could pry a name out o' the cur or even discover his identity."

"Look again!" Blake shouted against the muffled roar of the water. He pointed to a spot in the river where a pale head gleamed as it broke the surface. As the fugitive cast a terrified look over his shoulder, they caught a fleeting glimpse of his face. Then he scrambled up the far bank and vanished into the bushes.

Jack gave a start of astonishment. "Jesus and bigod, if he don't have a look o' Sir Simon Ogilvy!" He roared in fury across the ravine, "Ye can run a' ye want, ye blasted traitor, but ye won't get away. Would ye have your family suffer for your crimes?"

Blake felt the blood drain from his face and for a moment had to struggle to hide his alarm. He dropped a restraining hand on Jack's shoulder. "Easy, my friend, 'tis dark and your eyes deceived you."

The older man threw off his hand. Enraged at their quarry slipping away, he shouted angrily, "'Twas him, I tell ye!" And forgetting his place in his frustration, "God's feet, man, are ye blin'?"

Sinclair's features hardened into a haughty mask. "You erred, Jack," he repeated quietly, but with a harsh edge to his voice. "My eyes are younger than yours and that knave looked nothing like Ogilvy."

"He worked for Moray!"

"Jack"—a growl of warning—"Ogilvy is not the only one at court who worked for Moray. Would you have all these men sent to the dungeons to undergo the rigors of interrogation on the strength of that alone? And as for the light hair, why, Nesbitt is blond. Duncan Campbell also has sandy hair. Would you put them all on the rack because they had the misfortune to associate themselves with Jamie Stewart?"

Captain Jack grunted and stared hard at the bank on the opposite shore, a glimmer of doubt rising in his mind. Yet he had been so sure! The fellow had had a powerful look of Ogilvy about him. Still . . . though he was loath to admit it, his eyesight was not quite as keen of late, his marksmanship slightly off. And God forbid that he should turn an innocent over to Morton, for a man will confess to anything once the brakes have been applied to his mouth, the Dutch shoe to his feet. And Sinclair seemed so certain . . .

By the time the others rode up, loudly demanding to know what had happened, Jack stomped away and settled himself on a rock a distance from the others, there to ponder this disappointing turn of events. It was too dark now to go after the fugitive. Besides, he could not get far before dawn with no horse at his disposal.

From his perch he eyed the clan Chief consideringly, noting that Ogilvy's name wasn't mentioned as he explained the situation to the others.

Blake lay awake most of the night. He wondered if Alyssa had any conception of the danger she was in. If Ogilvy were caught and convicted there was little chance that even he could save her, providing she remained in Edinburgh. His instinct was to ride to the capital immediately and remove her to distant Augusta where, surrounded by his clan and members of allied clans, she might be relatively safe. But to leave his post was unthinkable. He had been commissioned by the Queen herself, and to leave now, with Jack still unconvinced that his eyes had tricked him, would only serve to arouse the soldier's suspicion. He thought of another way.

At dawn his squire Wyatt quietly left camp and made his way back to Edinburgh.

It was seven o'clock on the evening of September 13 when Alyssa heard a loud knock on the outside door. A few moments later a sober-faced Megan appeared to inform her, "There's a fellow in the hall wishing speech with you, lady. His name is Wyatt."

Alyssa's heart jumped. The babe growing inside her chose that moment to squirm and kick, and for a few seconds she sat still unable to move. Had something happened to Blake? Was that why Wyatt had come to see her? Oh, dear heart, she cried inwardly, please don't leave me now! Not before I can admit to my mistake; to admit that the Ogilvy name, or any other, is empty when compared to the love we used to share.

Megan helped her descend the stairs while her legs shook beneath her. A travel-worn Wyatt paced about impatiently in the hall, hurrying forward to take her arm and draw her over to the door. He saw the question brimming in her eyes and quickly shook his head, muttering, "He is well, rest assured, but you, my lady, are in great danger through the mischief of your lord. You must come with me now!" For the first time he noticed her condition and cursed inwardly, but child or no child they dared not tarry in Edinburgh. "Go hastily and pack a small bag for the journey. I will await you here."

When Alyssa turned to do his bidding she saw that the loutish Calvin had joined Megan in the kitchen doorway. Neither spoke as she hurried upstairs with her heart in her mouth. Once in her chamber she threw clothes into a bag she had pulled from the coffer, wanting nothing so much as to put distance between herself and this place she had shared with Simon Ogilvy. She hated him now. What a fool she had been to trust him, to choose him over Sinclair! Simon cared nothing for her or the coming baby, or why, by his actions, would he have put them in danger?

She was just leaving the room when she heard a hoarse cry from below, followed by the sound of a heavy object hitting the floor. Throwing open the door, Alyssa stepped into the corridor and, too late, caught a flurry of movement from the corner of her eye. Megan jumped forward and clamped a sodden, acrid-smelling cloth over her nose and mouth. The struggle was brief. In minutes Alyssa slumped unconscious in the housekeeper's arms.

By the time she woke up, they had left Edinburgh far behind and were no more than a few leagues from Mordrun Hall where, unbeknownst to Alyssa, Simon had ordered them to go in case of emergency. Alyssa found herself on a litter hidden under a pile of blankets. Her hands and feet were bound. When she screamed, the cart was halted and Megan came back to warn her, "Hold your tongue! We go to Mordrum Hall where you will be safe, and later the master will join you."

Alyssa struggled against her bonds, gasping, "Untie me at once! God . . . how you'll pay for this!"

"We'll gag you if we have to, lady," the older woman threatened. "One way or another, you will do the master's bidding."

They continued on over the rough track, every bump sending stabbing pain through Alyssa's body. She could feel the baby jumping in protest inside her and began to fear for its life. Angry tears poured down her face. She longed to scream, biting her lip until it bled, fearful that they really would gag her. What had they done with Wyatt? If they had killed him, how would Blake ever know what had happened or where to find her? Simon kept his country house a secret. As he had once told her, "'Tis not the place one cares to brag about, at least not yet. Once it has been restored 'twill be time enough to make its presence known."

They passed through a village of tumbledown cots and untilled acres, then entered a forest so dark that it was as if night had fallen, dismal as the mood that assailed her. Finally they left the trees behind and started up a rocky hillside. On its crest sprawled what at first appeared to be a ruin, from a distance its stones black and jagged, like broken teeth against the morning sky. The building was squat and not particularly large, with a square tower at one end, and narrow slitted windows seeming to peer down on them with malevolent intent.

Megan threw out an arm with a flourish. "Mordrun Hall,

lady!" and she gave an unfathomable little chuckle that chilled Alyssa's blood. "Aye," she went on after a moment, "we shall be snug here until the master returns."

Alyssa ignored the mockery in her voice and gazed at the manor in dismay. Nothing Simon had said had prepared her for Mordrun Hall. The instant Calvin helped her through the massive oak door she felt the interior dankness and smelled the unmistakable odor of mildew and rot. The roof leaked and the ancient stones of the hall oozed moisture. The only furniture was a crude board much battered and dented with time, and a high-backed oak settle drawn up before a cheerless hearth filled with the blackened remains of long-dead fires.

The door was slammed and bolted behind her. Alyssa burst into tears. She had entered a prison, her servants become her jailors, her swollen body precluding any means of escape.

26

By the time Ogilvy limped into Mordrun Hall five weeks later, the Earl of Moray's rebellion had been crushed and Moray himself was in hiding in England.

Simon returned in a deplorable state—filthy, hungry, clad in rags, his own fine leather garments long since swiped by a band of gypsies. After wolfing down an enormous meal, he toppled into bed and slept for two days. When he finally awoke, Megan apprised him of all that had taken place in his absence. Relating their unexpected visit from Wyatt, she said, "Why would my lord Sinclair think to remove her ladyship? What has he to do with her?"

Simon jumped to his feet, determined to find out.

Alyssa had been sickly ever since her rough ride out of Edinburgh, upset both mentally and physically, and greatly fearing for her child's life. She spent most of the time in her room to escape Megan's and Calvin's watchful eyes, resting as much as possible in the hopes of warding off a possible miscarriage.

When he threw open the door to her chamber, Ogilvy found his wife sitting up in bed working on fine linen to make clothes for the baby. He was a little taken aback by her appearance, since much of her old radiance had faded. Thin and pale, her normally brilliant green eyes dull and dispirited, she little resembled the vibrant beauty he had taken to the court hall. Illness had always repelled him, and after a quick, perfunctory kiss on the forehead and a few inquiries about her health he turned to the subject which at that moment was consuming him with suspicion. "What means this interest of

Sinclair's? Why did he send his squire to remove you from my house?"

Alyssa had been prepared for the question and had spent much time deciding how best to answer. Keeping her face relaxed and her mannei cool, she replied, "When we met briefly at the ball I mentioned I was from Inverness-shire, his own domain. So when Wyatt came to the apartment that evening and mentioned that you were under suspicion, mayhap Sinclair thought to get me gone from Edinburgh lest one of his own people be involved. Think how that would look to the Queen, and he so close to her? With everyone suspecting everyone else, even the Earl of Belrose could not afford to be careless."

Ogilvy's eyes narrowed speculatively, turning all this over in his mind. He knew as well as any other that no one at court could risk any connection to a traitor, however remotely. He sucked in a breath, musing about the implications for himself. So he truly *was* under suspicion! Then why hadn't the soldiers come to arrest him? Megan had told him that no one from Edinburgh had come near the estate. True, only a handful of his closest friends knew about Mordrun Hall, but the Earl of Morton had ways of loosening tongues and by this time would have discovered his whereabouts.

Simon's eyes glittered with skepticism as he stared hard at Alyssa. "Had you ever met the Chief before coming to Edinburgh?"

Her eyes widened as she feigned surprise. "Of course not," she lied. "Why are you questioning me thus?" Her face hardened. "It seems to me that *I* should be the one asking the questions. How dare you involve me in your scurrilous plots!"

He rose at last and walked to the window. With his back to her he said, "Wyatt was mistaken, but . . . if they really suspect me, why have they not sought me out?" He turned his head and gave her a penetrating look over his shoulder. "You may be right about Sinclair. He would not wish anyone remotely connected to him to be involved, therefore undoubtedly decided to keep his vile suspicions to himself." He laughed cynically but at the same time felt a vast sense of relief. At least on that score.

Alyssa had never given him the slightest cause to doubt her fidelity. She had scarcely looked at other men. And why *should* she, when he had done her the great honor of marrying her, raising her to a status that otherwise would have been impossible? Nay, nay, he assured himself, he had no cause to fret. She was his and would remain so for as long as he wished; as long as Lady Magdalen kept to her part of the bargain.

Observing how his shoulders relaxed, Alyssa felt a hot surge of anger when she thought of the child inside her and all the worry he had put her through. "I demand an explanation, Simon! Sinclair would never have sent his squire for me unless he had good reason to doubt your loyalty to the Queen."

"You demand!" In an instant he was back leaning over the bed, his face tight and his eyes cold as dark ice. "Make no demands of me, mistress! Megan told me how you were all too willing to fall in with Wyatt's plans—"

"I was in danger because of you!" she broke in furiously, color rushing into her pale face. "You cared so little about me and your child that you left me in town, even whilst knowing what happens to the kin of traitors! Aye, I would have gone with Wyatt!" she cried defiantly, throwing caution to the winds. "And I will not be kept a prisoner in this miserable house. I—I'll run away!"

For a second Alyssa thought he would hit her. Instead he burst out laughing; grating laughter that clawed at her nerves. "Have you forgotten Lady Magdalen?" he taunted.

"I'd sooner face *her* than the Earl of Morton should you be caught!"

He ran the tips of his fingers across her bare shoulder and watched her cringe at his touch, and very softly said, "You would call me a traitor and have our child known as the son of a traitor? You would have him carry this stigma throughout his life? This is what you want for your son?"

"I hate you!" she breathed, her eyes blazing. "And I never want you to touch me again!"

He straightened up, his mouth a taut line, and never taking his eyes from hers slowly began to undress, hurling her back against the pillows when she tried to run from the room. For the next week or two they lived quietly and circumspectly at Mordrun Hall, Simon ever alert for the sound of riders coming their way. By the beginning of November, starting to feel safe, he contacted a few of his cohorts in town—those who knew him too well to try to impress—and invited them out to help break the grinding monotony. Ogilvy was not a country person. Such was his nature that he must always be entertained. With Alyssa in a perpetual sulk, refusing to speak to him unless absolutely necessary, the quiet was beginning to fray his nerves.

Weekend guests began to arrive, the villagers muttering darkly among themselves and making the sign of the cross as these strangers rode through Mordrun. Sir James Balfour came with his simpering mistress. Their near neighbor, Claude de Sorley, appeared with his little mouse of a wife, Edith. There was Charles Whelty and Tim Bambridge with their latest paramours, and on a few occasions the Earl of Bothwell, a distant relative of Simon's. Others came, people with no connections at court; strange people who at first startled Alyssa, then repelled her. The little hunchback, Sceti, the grossly obese Hannah with a voice deeper than most of the men. Then the pale Tothmann with his dreamy protégé, Ruth.

During these parties much wine flowed and the conversation quickly took a bawdy turn full of mysterious innuendos. By the smirks and knowing sidelong glances passing between them, Alyssa knew that the others understood even if she felt left out and confused. Sometimes they played odd games that called to mind Megan's pentagrams and weird symbols. Claude de Sorley, a plump nobleman with soft hands and pale hard eyes, would usually officiate. "If our little Madonna will permit . . . ?" with a mocking bow to Alyssa. The lights would all be extinguished except for a pair of tall black candles, thereupon de Sorley would call forth kindly spirits said to bring good luck to their hall. Instead, or so it seemed to Alyssa, these spirits brought forth lust, since as the evening progressed the couples, pair by pair, vanished into the more private recesses of the house—not always with the people they arrived with.

"'Tis nothing," Simon laughed when Alyssa strongly objected to this form of "entertainment." "'Tis naught but harmless sport to while away the tedious winter nights. And if they wish to frolic"—he shrugged—"who are we to object if the couples are in agreement?"

But one weekend morning Alyssa was awakened in the early hours imagining she had heard a scream. Simon's side of the bed was empty. Pulling on a robe, she left the room and silently made her way downstairs. The door to the vast cellar stood ajar. With her heart in her mouth, Alyssa fearfully went down the stone steps, halting abruptly when she heard a muffled groan. A strange smoky odor, like sulphur, stung her nostrils. She could hear chanting and then a woman's shrill, excited laugh, followed by a crack like the snap of a whip.

She flew back to bed and pulled the covers up over her head, pretending to be asleep when her husband slipped into bed beside her at dawn.

Escape was impossible, her body big with child, Megan and Calvin never allowing her out of their sight. The sweating walls of Mordrun Hall were as dank as any prison, the countryside around it a wilderness where, as winter progressed, wolves roamed in savage packs, hungry enough to venture into the manor grounds itself.

Ogilvy too grew increasingly restless and morose, Alyssa's coldness infuriating him. He curbed his anger because of the child. He wanted this child badly, and because of that—and her delicate health—took himself out of her bed. Nothing must harm his son, this golden babe who would set his deepest fears to rest. Though he had been sexually active from a very young age, none of his paramours had ever come to him asking for money to help raise his bastards. He never forgot the doctor's remark after his youthful illness, to the effect that he would be unlikely to ever sire young. Shortly he would prove the old leech wrong, and God forbid that he himself should cause the infant's destruction.

But . . . a man must have his pleasures. It was natural and right. Alyssa was beautiful even with impending motherhood upon her, and daily he was forced to look upon that beauty and deny himself the joy of possessing it. Her very coldness had added an unexpected thrill to their union, filling him with a virile sense of power as he overwhelmed her, forcing her to intimacies that he knew she detested.

In the second week of December Ogilvy risked a trip to Edinburgh, there to visit Magdalen MacKellar and some of his old pleasure haunts. He tarried in the capital for a week gambling and wenching and was in the bed of a harlot the night his squire Calvin burst into the room to tell him that Alyssa had given birth.

Ogilvy threw the woman aside and jumped out of bed, shouting as Calvin stood frowning at his boots, "Well . . . what is it, you clod, a lad or a lass?"

The young squire wouldn't meet his eyes. "A lad, sir."

His master swelled with pride and gratification. "To Mordrun Hall! I must see this fair son of mine and introduce him to his sire."

Calvin looked at him from under his brows. "Your lady is very weak . . ." but Simon wasn't listening. He was already in the hall, his companion of the night calling after him that she hadn't been paid for her services.

An inscrutable Megan put the blanket-wrapped bundle in his arms, then wordlessly drew back the flap that partially covered its head. Simon sucked in a startled breath and almost dropped the baby. After a moment when he stood gazing at it in perplexity, his eyes rose questioningly to the housekeeper's face.

Megan nodded. She touched the infant's cap of curling black hair, murmuring, "Remember the night Sinclair sent Wyatt for your lady? I thought it odd then; now . . ."

Ogilvy thrust the tot back into her arms and stormed up to his wife's bedchamber, thinking, No golden child this! He found Alyssa lying limp and exhausted, her face startlingly white against the cloud of red/gold hair tumbling about her, the cold sweat on her brow glistening in the candlelight.

He screamed at her in outraged pride. She had tricked him into marrying her, lied to him, made a mockery of his fine name. He would be the laughingstock of the court when this was discovered, for there was not an Ogilvy alive with such soot-black hair—nor a MacKellar!

"Whore!" he shouted into her ashen face. "Gutter

harlot!" Incensed, he grabbed her by the throat and squeezed and might have gone on squeezing if both Megan and Calvin hadn't burst into the room and dragged him away from her while he roared that he would kill both Alyssa and the child. In the corridor Megan reminded him of who had sired the child and Sinclair's influence with the Queen; of how the Chief had protected him, only because of Alyssa.

"Mayhap this misfortune can be turned to your benefit," she suggested slyly. "Forget not that this babe bears your name and cannot be taken from you. This tool might prove useful some day." And patting his hand, "Come away to the hall and I'll pour you a dram, then ye can think this through and see how it might profit you."

After several stiff drams Simon indeed saw how it might profit him. This child of Sinclair's would provide an excellent lever if ever he had need of help in the future, and in the meantime, aware of the type of woman he had married, things would be different in his house. Knowing her for the whore she was, why should he continue to treat her like a lady? Now he had a handy little instrument through which he could make her obey.

In the morning he returned to Alyssa's room and announced that he had selected the child's name. "He shall be christened Alexander, after my grandsire, one of the meanest curs who ever trod Scottish soil."

Alyssa sighed wearily. "Why not just release me from this vile farce of a marriage?"

His eyes glittered like cracked ice and he laughed. "Release you! Do you propose to leave Mordrun Hall and bid farewell to your son? Forget not, my dear, that his name is Ogilvy. He is my property and remains with me." Enjoying the dismay on her face, he added another barb. "Oh! I almost forgot. My agent in town had information about your mother. She died years ago in the convent," he told her brutally, "so you had best forget any notion of being restored to your birthright."

Alyssa turned her head on the pillow and closed her eyes. Simon returned to the hall and drank himself insensible.

* * *

There was a rude shock awaiting Sinclair when he returned to Edinburgh. Confident that Alyssa and Wyatt were long since safely installed at Castle Augusta, he discovered instead that his squire was still in town recovering from a severe blow to the head that had fractured his skull—and that Alyssa had disappeared. Wyatt had another startling piece of news for him. "She's pregnant. About five or six months gone when last I saw her."

"What?"

The older man nodded. "And married or no', she was perfectly willing to go wi' me, which leads me to wonder if all is well betwixt her and Ogilvy."

Blake's mind turned back to the night they had spent together at the Hare and Hound and he made a quick calculation. Would it be Ogilvy's child or his? His senses vaulted with hope and excitement, then just as quickly were dashed. If the child were his, and Ogilvy became suspicious, how might he react? He had to find her, and quickly. Fearing for her, and recoiling at the thought of his babe going through life saddled with the Ogilvy name, he removed himself from court and the duties awaiting him there and devoted all his time to combing the city, questioning all who knew the couple in the hope of discovering their whereabouts.

In December he paid a brief visit to his solicitors in the hopes of spurring them on. "Patience, my lord," they advised. "You know these things cannot be hurried." And the younger partner pried, "Is there perhaps a special reason as to why you want the divorce hastened?"

"My freedom is reason enough," Blake replied curtly, chafing at the interminable delay, thwarted too in his attempts to locate the Ogilvys. Their apartment was closed, the neighbors ignorant as to where they had gone. None of Simon's associates at court knew either, and his friends shrugged and shook their heads, whether because they spoke the truth or hoped to shield him, the result was the same. No progress.

Blake became painfully aware of the passing of time. With each day ending in failure, his alarm increased. He found himself almost wishing for the child to be Ogilvy's. At least then she would be safe. But he had heard many foul tales of the knight and his habits, and that, coupled with his own contact with him, though brief, kept him awake at night dreading what might happen to Alyssa should her husband discover that the babe was not his.

By the time baby Alex was two months old, life at Mordrun Hall had become intolerable for his mother. Simon had returned to her bed, nightly subjecting her to the disgusting spectrum of his lust. By day he took pleasure in calling her vile names, in taunting her and glaring into the cradle, an expression on his face that chilled her to the bone, as if he could barely restrain the impulse to wreak havoc on the innocent reminder of where his wife's love really lay.

Alyssa forced herself to eat well, to take daily exercise in the clean, cold air. She climbed the stairs over and over to strengthen her muscles, and took a fierce joy and pride in her son's size and voracious appetite. Cuddling him close to her, smiling into the eyes that were gradually changing from brown to green, she whispered, "Grow quickly, my lamb, so we can escape this evil place."

In his own way Ogilvy was as oppressed by Mordrun Hall as his wife, and almost as eager to leave. But it was still too soon to risk a move back to the city. The reports he received from Edinburgh were disquieting. Morton was staging large weekly executions and many heads were rolling on the merest hint of guilt. Sinclair, he could depend on to keep silent, but what of Captain Jack? Aside from that, the city was reeling from the news that the Queen and her consort were quarreling openly, Mary resentful because Darnley was more interested in pleasure than in helping her tackle matters of state. When Bothwell paid them another visit in mid-January he said with a dry chuckle, "The King indulges himself in sports while the Queen struggles to rule the country, angered that her mate will not help her share the load. He's a young fool! And if he hopes to gain the crown matrimonial—which he most certainly does—then he has a peculiar way of proving his worth."

"Is it true that Maitland is out of favor with the Queen?" Simon asked curiously.

Bothwell nodded. Many formerly close to Her Majesty

had lately fallen under a cloud, he said. Ever since Moray's rebellion, Mary appeared to have taken a harder look at her nobles as if wondering who might betray her next. Bothwell growled, "And that wee scab, Davie Riccio, has managed to worm his way into high places. 'Tis he more than anyone who drips his crafty venom, poisoning Her Grace agin many of her ministers. Darnley and Riccio are no longer friends. Christ alone knows where it all might end."

Alyssa looked up from her chair by the hall fire. "Then the King cannot have many friends left now that he's lost David Riccio? Forsooth, the Protestant lords hate and detest him."

Bothwell turned to her with a smile, his brown eyes softening as they always did when he beheld fair women. "Nay, my lady, he of a sudden finds himself flush with friends—some of them these same Protestant lords who formerly shunned him." Chuckling at the confusion on her face, he explained, "With so many out of favor with Her Majesty, and Darnley being one of them, it would seem they have all banded together to lick their wounds."

"Holy Mother!" Simon stared at him searchingly. "Methinks that sounds . . . ominous."

Bothwell inclined his head. "Aye, that it does. Now they stroke and flatter the young fop and he, being a prideful fool, laps it up like a starving cur. Mary Stuart has many enemies, and these same enemies have scented her weakness—the King. And weak as he is, craving the crown matrimonial which she continues to deny him, they see King Henry as a very useful tool in their schemes."

"Schemes?" Alyssa echoed, exchanging a look with Simon who sat back with a thoughtful expression on his face. She could almost read his mind. He was wondering how this unexpected turn of events might possibly benefit him.

It was James Balfour, Bothwell's friend, who answered. Being the shrewd lawyer that he was, he was typically evasive. "Who can read the minds of the likes of Morton and Lindsay? Aye, and James Stewart too. You can be certain he's kept well abreast of the situation in Newcastle, sifting and weighing how best to react."

Of all Simon's friends Alyssa could tolerate Bothwell best.

He was always polite and considerate and treated her most graciously. Interesting and dynamic, he was nevertheless not a particularly comely man, and as she studied him Alyssa tried to puzzle out what it was about him that had women flocking to him in droves. He was only of medium height, broad in the shoulders but otherwise wiry, his somewhat sallow visage dominated by a large, crooked nose. His eyes, however, were arresting. Dark and alert, they were very expressive, lazy as a warm caress whenever they turned in her direction. A man of action, he was much given to the use of body language when he spoke, especially when he spoke to women.

It was during that brief visit that he made a comment that Alyssa was to remember later. "'Tis a pity," he said, "that the Queen should have the feckless Darnley by her side instead of a strong, supportive husband. With the right man beside her, Mary could sweep away all the troubles besetting her kingdom."

Alyssa had enough troubles of her own to beset her without worrying overmuch about the Queen. Though she tried to conceal it, she was growing increasingly afraid of Simon and his erratic moods, fearing particularly for little Alexander. It had been a bitter disappointment to learn that her mother had died before they had the chance to get to know one another. Now, it seemed to Alyssa, her last faint chance to prove her identity had vanished. So she must look to the future, to the safety and prosperity of her son, and at long last she faced the fact that she could not make a life for him on her own. If Mary Stuart with all her wealth, position, and countless ministers and advisers *still* needed a strong man beside her, then how could *she* dream of coping by herself? Scotland was a harsh country, the times turbulent and uncertain, and women—even Queens—mere pawns to be mercilessly manipulated at the whims of men.

Somehow she must take Alexander to his father. With the might of Augusta behind him, even a bastard son would have nothing to fear. And as for herself . . . nay, she would not think of that now. The immediate goal was the thing she must fix in her mind, and all else would follow. Carefully she prepared, waiting impatiently for the right moment. Simon was talking of returning to Edinburgh in April to sniff out the lay of the land. April, then, Alyssa promised herself. She would wait for a day when Calvin hunted for game, then knock Megan unconscious if she had to. One way or another, her baby must be removed from the malevolence of Mordrun Hall.

Fate, as often happened, stepped in to abruptly change Alyssa's plans. Snow was still on the ground and the wintry wind still howled through the glens when in late February the moment was suddenly upon her. It was a Monday evening, Simon still sleeping off the effects of a wild weekend party, one Alyssa had refused to attend. She was in the nursery after supper playing with the baby when she heard what sounded like the rumble of thunder reverberating across the hill. Jumping up, she ran to the window and peered out into the darkness to see a blaze of torchlight bobbing up the hill. A group of irate villagers boldly knocked on the door of Mordrun Hall, bellowing for Simon to show himself. "For you an' the swine de Sorley and the rest o' yer vile crew, did kidnap and violate MacAlpine's daughter. Open up!" they roared, battering the door. "We come for vengeance long overdue!"

While Simon, Calvin and the remaining guests hastily scrambled for swords and pistols, the door burst inward and the furious mob poured into the hall. With the entire household hard-pressed to subdue them, even with their superior weapons, and Megan downstairs with them doing whatever she could, Alyssa—for the first time in months—found herself completely alone. Knowing it would take them some time to route the angry horde, if they ever did, she seized upon that moment to escape. She dressed the baby rapidly, bundling him into warm clothing, then quickly pulled on the moleskin breeches and thick woolen cloak she had hidden away in an old chest under the window. With the blood thundering in her ears, her heart in her mouth, she slipped out of the room and down the back staircase and cautiously opened the door that led out to the stables. The building was empty except for the horses, the grooms of de Sorley and others having dashed into the house to help their masters.

Moments later she led Calvin's mule, Doughty, out of the stables and, once away from the yard, mounted him and turned his head south. The night was bitterly cold, a few inches of snow on the ground, and as occasional blasts of frigid air penetrated his little cocoon of blankets, Alex began to wail in protest. Alyssa rode on into the moonlight. Come what may, she would never go back, and never forgive Simon for the way he had exposed her to danger by involving himself in Moray's rebellion, then subjecting her to the degradation of his lust when she upbraided him.

If God willed it, both she and Alexander would reach Edinburgh safely, and if He did not . . . to die was better than to live with Simon at Mordrun Hall.

Turning of the Tide

27

Edinburgh and Lynnwood
1566-1567

The Queen was pregnant by a man she no longer respected or loved. She had quarreled with many of her most important nobles. In the years she had been in Scotland she had developed a mind of her own and a better understanding of the lords around her, beginning to look at them with a stern, appraising eye, misliking what she saw. She complained to Sinclair, "Methinks many of my lords are overly ambitious, more intent on building up their own fortunes than in helping to strengthen the crown. I cannot forget the ones who have risen up agin me, nor others whose loyalty wavers with the tide. They should have a care," she continued darkly, "for I have others I can turn to, men ready to put their Queen and kingdom before aught else."

Maitland was in the room at the time and Blake could see he was furious at this slight, which was perhaps overly harsh where he was concerned. Yet Blake could well understand Mary's jaded attitude, soured as she was by the ingratitude of Moray, Darnley and others. He studied her sympathetically as she continued to berate these men openly, even with Maitland and two pages present. This marriage, he thought, had taken much of her sparkle away, and Moray's rebellion had hardened her. Pregnant and frequently ill, her normally lustrous hair was dull and her white skin tinged with a yellowish cast, no longer able to compete with the white roses which, as ever, surrounded her. Just past her twenty-third birthday, she looked older than her years, beginning to show the effects of the endless strife plaguing her country. It had been months now since he had watched her dance the night away or listen to her sing along with her musicians. Unable to find a happy outlet for her naturally vivacious nature, her energy had turned in upon herself, leading to frequent hysterical outbursts of temper.

Just the same, it was unwise for a queen to show her feelings too openly, so when she announced her intention of attainting Moray and the other rebels when Parliament convened in March, Sinclair asked her to reconsider. He found the mood at Holyrood disturbing, and explained that though they might deserve such punishment, these lords would be most unlikely to sit back and let their lands and titles be taken from them. They still had powerful connections in Scotland, large families or clans who would rise to support them, and at that particular moment in time—with many turning away from her—Mary could not afford to challenge them. "Hard as it might be to swallow," he advised, "it might be more prudent to make up with Lord James and allow him to return to Scotland bringing the others with him. Then they would be in your debt, beholden to you, and by skillful handling Your Grace could win them back to her side. You worked well with him once," he reminded her as he saw her frown. "And Moray, to my way of thinking, is preferable to others at this moment struggling to take his place."

"Why will *you* not agree to take his place, Sinclair?" she queried peevishly, raising a subject they had discussed recently on more than one occasion. Always he fended her off. The more he saw of the political machinations in Edinburgh, the less he liked it. He had his own family, his own clan, a small world of his own to govern at Augusta. Since coming to the capital at Mary's summons he had neglected that world, forced to leave those less capable in charge. He had never intended to remain in the city for more than a year or two. His idea had been to remain in the city only long enough to help Mary establish herself firmly on her throne, a task that was taking far longer than he had anticipated.

So again he smilingly declined. "Your Majesty is gracious, but eventually I must return to my clan."

"So you would desert me too!" Sudden tears sparked her eyes.

"Nay, madam, not while you have need of me." He took her hand and carried it to his lips, wondering at the same time if her cousin across the border would have revealed such touching vulnerability. When she relaxed, smiling slightly, he pressed again for Moray's return, saying, "It would be prudent to set your own personal feelings aside for the moment and allow your brother back."

At once her smile vanished. And being a woman who found it well nigh impossible to set her feelings aside, she cried out, "Nay! That I will never do, Sinclair! He hurt me deeply. He took arms agin me. Now, from England, he calls me foul names behind my back. He, as much as Darnley, hungers after my crown." She burst into tears, sobbing, "Is there no man in Scotland who will love me for myself! Must a Queen always have these vultures about her!"

Everyone commented about the strange atmosphere at court, the illusion of a dark ferment seething under the surface quiet. Because of her pregnancy the Queen was often ill, sometimes too ill to conduct business, and in her absence the conspirators worked diligently. Morton took Darnley aside and hinted that the reason his wife was so cold might lie with David Riccio. The "vile foreigner" had poisoned her heart against him and, though ugly and far from being Darnley's equal in looks or intelligence, had cast a spell over her with a thought to taking the King's place in the royal bed. Rumor had it that they were already lovers. Some had gone so far as to suggest that the child she was carrying was no issue of the King's.

Darnley's tawny eyes blazed with fury. His touchy pride erupted in an outpouring of threats. "He shall suffer for it! Aye, and so shall she!"

Morton hid a smile of gratification, thinking that many would like to see Riccio suffer, to pay for casting them in the shade with the Queen. Falsely grave, he went on, "We grieve at your misfortune, Your Grace, that your marriage should come to this pass—and you a King!" Then he added the words that brought the young man's eyes leaping back to his face. "Many are with you. 'Tis agin the natural order of things that a woman should stand at the helm of a country, steering a course with her feeble woman's hands. Is it any wonder that Scotland is in such turmoil?"

Once more Darnley's golden eyes blazed, but this time

with ambition. Long tired of taking a back seat to Mary, and prodded constantly by his father, Lennox, he felt himself ready, willing and able to snatch the helm from his wife's hands, confident that he could steer a steadier course, particularly now that he seemed to have all the important lords behind him.

While aware of the undercurrents at court, Blake was distracted with worries of his own. From an associate in town he had been able to discover that Simon Ogilvy had a place in the country. "Nay, I know not where it is," said the fellow with a shake of his head, "though I don't think it's very far from Edinburgh."

Then in late February Sinclair finally got the lead he had been waiting for, and from an unexpected quarter. He was dining in Bell's Tavern with George Gordon when the subject came up of Bothwell's forthcoming marriage to Huntly's sister, Jean. Blake remarked that he hadn't seen Bothwell much about court in the last week or two, to which George responded with a dry chuckle, "Aye, he's making the most of his freedom while he can, for 'tis certain our Jean will have none of his antics once they're wed. He's gone off to Balfour's place and doubtless they'll pay a visit to Ogilvy's moldering estate—"

Blake grabbed his arm. "*Simon* Ogilvy?"

"The same."

Blake could hardly contain his relief and excitement. "And where is this estate located?"

Gordon stared at him curiously, taken aback by his intensity. "Out by Lethington way, near the wee village of Mordrun." And when Sinclair rose abruptly, "Why . . .what ails you, man?"

He laughed and slapped him on the back. "Nothing, George! You have just taken a great weight off my shoulders."

The temperature dropped steadily as Alyssa rode through the dark countryside, the track in front of her lit only by the moon, and urged Doughty on for all he was worth. Alex lay against her breast, tucked into a sling made out of a shawl. He had long since cried himself into exhaustion, a warm but heavy bundle for all his small size, and growing more so as the hours dragged by. Alyssa prayed constantly that her infant would survive the rough ride, and that Simon and his villagers would battle far into the night.

The baby began to whimper as a tepid sun sent tentative fingers over the crest of a distant hill, touching the surface of the snow with a spangling of silver. The wild landscape was a study in black and white—the carpet of snow, the bare gnarled branches of the trees, and the crumbling remains of an old chapel on a hill against the sky. Alyssa prodded the tired mule uphill in the direction of the ruin with the intention of sheltering from the biting wind while she fed and cleaned the baby. As she neared the building, she sniffed a tang of soot in the air, wafting to her on the breeze. Then as the sun rose higher she saw that the chapel had been burned.

Dismounting, her bones aching and stiff, her neck and shoulders slumped from carrying the weight of the baby, she approached the building cautiously, hoping to find some safe nook where she could rest and put Alex to the breast. Her feet crunching the snow, and the freshening wind, were the only sounds to break the silence.

Pausing before the great arched doorway, cut from solid granite and still intact, she peered into the church. The interior was a fantastic jumble of blackened timbers, fallen beams, and piles of sooty debris. Anything of value had long since been taken. Picking her way warily over the rubble to an overturned pew, or what was left of it, Alyssa sat down with her back to the altar. She unwrapped the baby and examined him anxiously.

His tiny face was red and fretful, his eyes shut tight as he moved his head back and forth eagerly searching for his breakfast. She laughed and cuddled him close, immensely proud of her baby's stamina, thankful that he seemed none the worse for the long, bumpy ride. Kissing the top of his curly dark head, she murmured, "Just like your father, the Chief, and tough as a wee oak sapling! We're safe, my lamb, or—God willing—soon will be. Then you must be bathed and powdered and made bonny as a prince to meet your sire."

While Alex tugged hungrily at her breast, Alyssa sat back, and a feeling of peace replaced the stonelike cold that had gripped her from the moment she stepped inside Mordrun Hall. It was there that the real Simon Ogilvy had revealed himself, breaking out of his handsome, courtly facade. It seemed incredible to her now that she had ever chosen him over Blake—marriage or no marriage, for the ring on her middle finger might just as well have been around her neck. She had not loved him, a fact she had made clear from the first. But then neither had he loved her; she doubted that he was capable of loving anyone. Why had Simon gone so far as to marry her? Surely it was out of character for a man of his type. This question perplexed her now as it had over the past few months.

She leaned her head back against the pew, listening to the wind whistling through the broken rafters overhead, musing as to how Blake would react once he learned that he had become a father. Alyssa visualized his astonishment when the baby was placed in his arms. "Your son, my lord," she would say. "Does he not look just like you?"

Thinking of him, she felt a savage yearning that brought sudden tears to her eyes, crying for the happiness they might have known together had he made a different choice that day at Lynnwood. Now she had given him a bonny, healthy son, a lad fine enough to be any Chief's heir—but their first-born was a bastard!

When a feeling of bitterness stole over her, Alyssa thrust the thought away. Taking Alex from her breast, she opened the bag she had kept packed over the last few weeks and set about cleaning him.

A thud resounded behind her from the direction of the chancel. Alyssa twisted about, her eyes narrowing to pierce the dusting of soot stirred up by the breeze. Something, perhaps a timber, had been blown free by the wind, and the increasing turbulence without was beginning to make the building unsafe.

Tucking the baby hastily back into his sling, she started to rise, when a fresh blast of air swept through the chapel rattling the rafters overhead. Something broke loose high above the altar and swung at the end of a rope over her head. Transfixed, Alyssa peered up through the gloom and saw the moldering corpse of the priest, his tattered robes fluttering on a blackened carcass that had been reduced to bones.

She shrieked in horror and stumbled back, dislodging a

tangle of broken roof supports. A crack rent the air as the charred beam split in two . . . and began to fall. Screaming, Alyssa ran for the door even as the shadow of the timber streaked across the floor and overtook her, snapping her ankle as it crashed to the floor. Alex was catapulted from the sling on impact and landed ten feet away in a mound of ashes, midway between his mother and the door.

A thick pall of dust rose in the air: The body of the slain priest swayed back and forth at the whim of the wind like a ghastly angel, his robes billowing around him, but otherwise all was quiet.

28

It was daylight before Simon and his friends were able to suppress his villagers, killing the ringleader and one other before sending them back to their cots literally licking their wounds. Claude de Sorley too had been wounded, and the little hunchback Sceti had his thumb lopped off.

Then no sooner had the chaos died down and his friends gone off to recover in their own abodes than Megan came running to say that Alyssa and the infant had disappeared. After a quick search of the house and grounds it was obvious what had happened. Simon slammed his fist angrily on the board, shouting for Calvin to saddle up the horses, reasoning that Alyssa could not have gone far carrying the baby as she was. And she must be found; returned to Mordrun Hall before Lady Magdalen got word of what had happened. If Alyssa had thought of Mordrun Hall as a prison before, Ogilvy raged inwardly, then it truly would be one once he had moved her quarters into the cellar.

At first they concentrated on the land between the manor and the village of Mordrun, unable to follow her tracks because of all the recent activity back and forth. Gradually they widened their search, combing the more rugged territory between Mordrun and the hamlet of Waterside. It was while they were making inquiries at the inn there that Blake and his squire passed by.

Sinclair reached Mordrun Hall at two o'clock in the afternoon to find only the stone-faced Megan in residence, her face betraying none of her inner turmoil. The master and his lady were visiting Sir Simon's brother in the Highlands, she lied. And nay, she had no idea when they would return.

Drawing their swords, Blake and Wyatt brushed past her and stepped into the hall, and it was as if a hurricane had passed through the interior. What little furniture there was was in a shambles, and the grey flags were spattered with blood. In the nursery they came upon the cradle. It was empty.

"Where is she?" Blake shouted into Megan's rigid face. "A fight has taken place here, and recently, so speak up, woman, and it had better be the truth!"

When she refused to answer, Wyatt got behind her, his arm encircling her neck. With his dirk poised against her throat, he growled, "Give the word, sir, and I'll slit her from ear to ear."

But Blake had a better idea. "Nay, I can think of a certain way to loosen her tongue. We'll take her back to Edinburgh and turn her over to my lord Morton. Doubtless he would be much interested in any information she could give him concerning the recent activities of her master." He eyed her coldly, his voice dropping to a near whisper. "Tell me, Megan, have you ever heard tell of the Iron Baron? Now *there* is a lover you would not care to know! Women have gone mad in his embrace—and not with pleasure—and by the time *he* takes his pleasure they are not fit to be called women anymore."

When he reached for her arm, she commenced to babble. There had been a fight and in the course of it the lady ran away, taking the babe with her. "Your son!" she spat, "even though he bears my master's name." And as Sinclair stood watching her while trying to control his emotion at this wondrous news, she said that at nine of the clock or thereabouts Sir Simon and his squire had gone looking for his lady. "And when he finds her," she continued grimly, "she'll have reason to rue the day she ran away."

Wyatt hurled her to the floor and they hurried back to the horses. They decided not to waste time by searching the estate itself, since Ogilvy would already have done so. "She would have tried to reach me in Edinburgh," Blake said with certainty. "We must pray that Ogilvy doesn't find her first."

They mounted and set off at a gallop, Wyatt worrying the inside of his lip. Megan swore that the lady had departed sometime during the night, yet they had not encountered her along the track. Surely, he thought, even inexperienced as she was, she would not have left the road and wandered onto the moor.

As they combed the territory on either side of the track, Blake began to wish he had not set off so hastily, but had waited to gather his men and bring them along to help in the search. Miles of wilderness lay about them in all directions, and there were countless small villages and hamlets to be gone through as they continued south. Blake's concern mounted as the daylight hours flitted by without revealing a trace of Alyssa.

By three in the afternoon the tepid sun had disappeared and a few flakes of snow wafted down from a steely sky. Shadows lengthened like a dark stain across the frozen landscape, and both men were acutely conscious of the fact that in little more than an hour it would be dark. With the coming of darkness it would be impossible to follow tracks in the snow and too dangerous to probe the forests or venture out into the moor, that bleak wasteland where many an unwary traveler had come to grief. It was small comfort to know that if they encountered trouble they were prepared. They had their blades, bows, and a goodly supply of pitch-tipped faggots packed in a roll behind their saddles. But what chance was there for a lone woman and a child?

A league from the village of Gowrie, Wyatt, an expert at tracking, spied fresh spoor in the snow. "Well, what are they?" Sinclair turned to call over his shoulder.

His squire hesitated, then lied, "Fox. A muckle crew o' them. Must be a den somewhere hereabouts."

A few minutes later Sinclair spotted a blackened ruin on a hillside. As he lifted his arm to point it out to Wyatt, they heard a horse nicker close by. Both men drew up, slid from their mounts and quickly led them into a nearby thicket. Drawing their weapons, they moved stealthily into the wood and tethered the horses to a tree, then started down an embankment toward the gurgling sound of a river. They came upon Ogilvy and his squire resting on the bank.

The thin wailing of a child echoed mournfully in the ruined chapel. Alyssa awoke to pain, pain so fierce she could barely stop from crying out. She couldn't move. The beam had fallen across her foot, pinning her against the wall, and she had no option but to lie helplessly listening to the hungry cries of her baby without being able to bring him comfort.

A wave of panic rolled over her as she contemplated their plight. Either they would die here of cold or starvation or she would risk attracting Simon to them by calling out for help. She shouted until her throat was raw, then when nothing happened broke into hysterical weeping, pushing and tugging the beam frantically until her hands were covered with blood. The mule long-tethered outside grew annoyed and impatient. He added his braying to her shouts, but still no one came.

The cold pressed in on her, the pain in her ankle bringing out an icy sweat. Alex thrashed about angrily in his blanket, and though he too was cold and hungry it comforted his mother to see he was none the worse for his fall. He lay no more than ten feet away in a shaft of pallid sunlight shining down through a break in the roof; perhaps the sunlight would provide a little warmth for the infant.

Seizing a broken post near to hand, Alyssa tried to wedge it under the beam, hoping to lift it just enough to be able to drag her foot free. It was past noon before she gave up and again turned to calling for help. She tried praying, and soothed herself by thinking that sooner or later someone would ride along and spot the mule tied to the hitching stone beside the ruined church.

She talked to Alex softly; she sang to him for a while — and never once allowed herself to look up, or even at the shadow that the priest's carcass cast on the floor. Finally, exhausted from her efforts to free herself and dizzy from pain, she lapsed into unconsciousness early in the afternoon.

When Alyssa woke up it was dark, the interior of the chapel filled with a preternatural hush. "Alex?" she called softly.

The baby stirred . . . or something did.

She stuffed her knuckles into her mouth, her eyes slowly circling the chapel. There was an aura about that filled her with a creeping apprehension. Something had awakened her; some high-pitched sound. Had the baby been crying, or—

Alyssa froze as a long, savage howl drifted across the breast of the hillside, echoing and re-echoing through the glens, to be joined by others in the distance. In the yard Doughty brayed with fright, stamping and straining desperately at his rope as he sought to break free.

"Quiet!" Alyssa called to him sharply, her heart constricted with fear. Now she prayed aloud, "Dear Lord, don't let the mule attract them to this place! Make him be silent, and make someone ride by and find us—even if it be Simon."

She listened breathlessly, wanting to scream as Doughty nickered and wrenched violently at the rope each time a fresh chorus of howling erupted across the moor. It roused Alex and he mewled piteously. ·The infant lay between her and the church door.

Pawing the nearby ground until her hand closed over the post, Alyssa pushed against it with a superhuman strength born of terror, even as the wolves streaked across the frozen moorland toward the hapless creature tethered like a sacrifice by the church door.

Calvin heard them first and shouted a warning to Ogilvy, who had been tightening the girth on his horse. Running back with his sword in his hand, Ogilvy found Sinclair standing in the clearing, his face a study in controlled violence in the fading light. Simon's own features tightened and his fair skin flooded purple with rage. Confronted by the man who had his wife's affections, together with everything else in the world that he craved—rank, power, the respect of his peers—black hatred pounded in Ogilvy's head. He didn't stop to consider the Chief's reputation in battle, or the fact that his own young squire was no match for the experienced Wyatt. So when Blake offered him the chance to drop his weapon he rushed forward instead, slashing wildly with his blade.

Blake avoided him by nimbly leaping to the side. Simon spun about and with a shout of fury lunged with his weapon poised for Sinclair's chest. This time Blake didn't step away. He parried the thrust easily and brought the flat of his sword crashing down on Ogilvy's wrist. The impact sent a shuddering wave of pain racing up Simon's arm to his shoulder, yet somehow he retained a frantic grip on his weapon and swung desperately for Blake's throat. The Chief raised his arm high to deflect the blow, hardly noticing when the tip of Ogilvy's rapier nicked him on the forearm. He moved in grimly, seeing that resentment had only lent stamina to his opponent's anger and that the knight seemed prepared to fight to the death.

The clearing rang with the cold clash of steel and the ferocious yells of Wyatt as he battled nearby with Calvin, yet above the noise Sinclair heard another sound that caused him even greater alarm. Turning suddenly, he pounced on his adversary with a mind to ending the fray quickly, bringing his sword down at an angle across Ogilvy's shoulder. The blade sheered off leather, linen, and a slice of Simon's hide. Ogilvy's sword flew out of his hand, and with a cry of pain the knight staggered back, a hand clapped to his shoulder, and crashed headlong into the bracken.

When Blake turned, he found Wyatt kneeling over Calvin. "Dead, by the look o' it," said his squire with satisfaction. "What of Ogilvy?"

With the toe of his boot Sinclair turned the knight over. Gazing down at the handsome face, his eyes grew pit-dark and his blood cold. At his feet lay a man who had betrayed Queen and country; a man who had used his wife so ill that she had run away into the winter night with a small child in her arms without protection of any kind . . . and there lay a man who would forever stand between him and his deepest desires.

Sinclair raised his sword—

"Hark!" shouted Wyatt, distracting him. Lowering his weapon, Blake cocked an ear in the direction his squire was pointing. He heard the frenzied braying of a mule over the hunting cry of the wolves; it seemed to be coming from the direction of the ruin he had spotted on the hill. Wyatt was already racing up the incline. He called back over his shoulder, "Some poor sod must be up there yonder with that mule! Holy Mother, might it be—"

With a swift, dark look at Simon, Sinclair unhitched his horse and vaulted into the saddle, and both men galloped off across the moor. The clear winter's night resounded with the howling of the wolves, bouncing back at them from the granite hillsides like a demonic chorus from the gates of hell. In the bright moonlight they could see the predators streaming down from the hills, eager to reach the mule rearing and tugging against his restraints.

Jumping off their mounts outside the chapel, they dragged the pitch-impregnated faggots from their saddle rolls, seasoned oaken posts about two feet long and five inches in diameter. Setting them alight, they ran around the building depositing the flaming posts in a circle, then proceeded to set fire to the piles of tinder—some of which refused to ignite—liberally strewn about the ground.

But the wolves were not easily deterred, driven to desperation as they were by hunger. They ventured close to the ring of fire, their yellow eyes blazing with a savage light, enough of them to chill the heart of any man. "Jesu!" breathed Wyatt, his eyes on one enormous brute, larger than the others, that commenced to slink around the perimeter of the circle searching for a break where he might venture through. With a last flash of slavering fangs he vanished from sight to the rear of the building. Wyatt, in all his experience, had never seen such a large pack before. He glanced at their dwindling faggots, the sputtering little bonfires they had set, much of the wood wet, and muttered, "None o' this will burn for very long, and the brutes seem prepared to wait it out."

"Keep an eye on them," Blake growled. Sword in hand, he disappeared through the arched door and moved warily into the chapel, eerily illuminated by the glow outside.

Alyssa had fainted. Her frantic attempts to dislodge the beam had only succeeded in damaging her leg more. She woke up at the smell of burning to see the interior of the church flickering with a dull orange light. At a sound from the back of the chapel she turned her head and caught a quick flurry of movement near the broken back door. Out of the gloom crept a hideous creature, a nightmare of shaggy grey fur and glistening fangs, working his way toward her with his belly close to the ground. For one shocked instant their eyes met. Alyssa stared into soulless orbs of yellow fire—and screamed.

Launching himself to spring, the wolf was distracted by the appearance of another to his feast. Instantly he changed directions and sprang at Blake instead. Sinclair was knocked backwards by the weight of the creature, which instantly and instinctively lunged for his throat with a vicious snarl that resounded throughout the building. Blake's sword flew out of his hand and clattered into the shadows somewhere behind them. Jerking up his arm to protect his face, he gouged his elbow into the animal's neck with all the strength of his muscular body behind him. The beast rolled away, but was back on its feet in an instant and again crouched to spring. This time Blake had his dirk in his hand when it pounced, and the six-inch blade sank to the hilt in the creature's belly.

Bleeding himself, and with his jerkin hanging in shreds, Sinclair bounded over the debris and knelt down by Alyssa's side. Their eyes met, but hers were blank. Recognizing the symptoms of shock, Blake wasted no time in trying to bring her out of it with the howling outside rising to a deafening crescendo. Straining hard, he managed to lift the beam the few inches necessary to release her foot. He swung her up in his arms and ran with her to the broken stairs leading up to the belfry where she would be reasonably safe, at least for the time being. Laying her down gently, he returned to the ground and searched about for the infant. When he found him, Blake was certain he was dead.

One by one Wyatt watched the fires die down, the faggots sputter out. The wolves moved closer. He could almost smell them now. With a sigh he glanced at the mule, drew his dagger and sliced through the rope that held him fast. As he had anticipated, the poor demented animal immediately bolted for the hills, the wolf pack after him.

Praying for time, Wyatt hoped the mule was fleet of foot and would lead them far away before they inevitably finished him off and returned to the chapel for the rest of their meal. He plunged inside the building, shouting for his master to make haste. Within minutes all four of them were riding furiously away from the ruin toward the village of Barnstable with its stout stone inn and the promise of shelter and food, and hopefully a leech or midwife who might tend Alyssa's injured foot.

They discovered that there was no doctor in the area, but

an elderly woman was brought to the inn, a crone who ministered to the villagers through all manner of ailments from birthing babies to curing mysterious bellyaches and hysterical afflictions of the mind. Her prognosis was grim. Pointing to Alyssa's foot, she said, "Your lady will n'ere walk on *that* again, my lord, and it will ha' to come off. Her mind too is gone, poor soul." Then at the shocked expression on his face she added a word of cheer. "But the bairn is none the worse for wear. Ye ha' a right fine lad there, sir!"

Once he had ascertained that the baby was alive—*his* son he had no doubt by his shock of curly black hair—and had arranged for him to be fed and cared for, all Blake's attention had gone to Alyssa. The gravity of her condition filled him with dread, but when the old midwife said, "We'd best send for the barber, my lord, for the sooner that foot comes off the better," he shouted, "Nay! Christ's blood!"

Two days later, as soon as she was able to travel, he took her back to Edinburgh to consult with his own physician.

Now he had another problem. Where should he take her? They could not go to Clairmont with his divorce in progress without stirring up damaging gossip, nor could he take her to his apartments in Holyrood. A good tavern such as the Hare and Hound was a possibility, but there wasn't a tavern in the world that could offer the constant loving care, the tender comfort and peaceful surroundings that he wished for the woman he adored. Finally he sent Wyatt on ahead of the litter with a message for Jason. As he pulled into town, his squire met him at the gate to say that they might go directly to Highfield, Jason's mansion in the city.

Both his cousin and his French wife, Lizette, were waiting to welcome them when they arrived. The couple's four young children inquisitively craned their necks over the gallery rail until their nurses shooed them away. Lizette was just as curious as she gazed upon the dazed woman who was her brother-in-law's mistress. Looking from the white-faced beauty to the infant tucked into the crook of her arm, she felt a touch of sympathy.

Lizette was small and dark, with a pointed chin and bright

hazel eyes. She had been terrified when sent to Scotland at the tender age of sixteen to marry a man she had never seen. After the first strangeness wore off, she had not only fallen in love with her good-looking husband—but with her brother-in-law too. They had been good to her. Now it was her turn to be good to them.

Alyssa was installed in one of their grandest bedchambers and the baby carried off to the nursery, there to be fussed over and spoiled by his four older cousins. When Gilespie arrived to examine the sick woman, he too looked grave. She was deeply in shock from her hideous experience, and her ankle, he discovered, was badly twisted and broken in two places. At his suggestion they called in one Benito Greer, a doctor who was part Scottish and part Italian and had studied at the great teaching university of Florence. "He is an expert with the bones, my lord, and if you will permit a consultation—"

"Send for him at once!" said Blake, brushing off Gilespie's efforts to examine the livid cuts and scratches on his hands and face, a legacy from his struggle with the wolf.

Greer presented himself at the door of Highfield the following day, bulky leather bag in hand; Sinclair could hardly conceal his anger and dismay. The fellow looked like nothing so much as a black-eyed tinker. Small, wiry, stooped in the shoulders and with his swarthy face surrounded by a frizzy mane of coarse black hair, he was clad in a shabby, badly stained doublet and grimy hose.

His manner too left much to be desired. With a faint cynical smile at Blake's expression, he snapped, "I'm Greer. Now, if you will kindly lead the way to the patient . . . ?"

All the time he examined Alyssa, Sinclair hovered suspiciously at his elbow. When she cried out in pain as he ran skilled fingers over her injured foot, Blake almost wrenched him back from the bed. Then when Greer leaned over her, gazing deeply into her eyes, the Chief finally exploded. "What in Christ's name are you doing? 'Tis her foot that ails her, not her eyes!"

The little man straightened up with an exaggerated sigh of exasperation. "Stand aside, my lord, if you wish to see this lady walk again. I cannot treat her with you snorting and huffing over me like a—a crazed bull. The time has come for me to set the breaks, so kindly take yourself from this room."

Such insolence from anyone else would have merited instant punishment, but the words, "if you wish to see this lady walk again" loomed above all else in Sinclair's mind. And something about Greer's steady gaze and air of authority in the sickroom inspired confidence.

Without a word Blake stalked from the room. A sympathetic Lizette joined him in the hall, and squeezed his arm when a scream shattered the quiet of the house. After a long time the doctor beckoned them back into the room. Alyssa appeared to be sleeping peacefully, which astonished Sinclair after what she had just been through. There was a strange iron brace around her ankle, not unlike the infamous Dutch shoe he had once seen when visiting an imprisoned friend in Edinburgh Castle, though the inside of *this* contraption was padded and covered with silk.

"Now!" began the officious little doctor briskly. "The bones have been set and now must be left to heal. She must be kept quiet and relaxed so that her mind might heal also." Producing a greyish powder from his cracked leather bag, he handed it to the Chief, instructing, "Mix a spoonful of this in half a cup of water three times a day and make her drink it. She will seem unusually sleepy most of the time, but try not to be alarmed. During this tranquility her mind is resting." The black eyes bored into Sinclair's. "And try not to weary her with your well-meaning but tiresome fussing."

Greer visited his patient every day. Blake stayed away from court to sit by her bedside. Though Alyssa didn't respond, he spoke to her softly, tenderly, sometimes leaning forward to brush a kiss over her softly parted lips. Her continued remoteness worried him in spite of Greer's assurances, and he held himself responsible for forcing her into the situation that had led to her present condition, wishing he had taken the time to run Ogilvy through.

Once he went to the nursery when the older children were at lessons and stood by the cradle gazing down at his son—his bastard son—though technically the child was

Ogilvy's. The dark-haired infant, as fine and sturdy a babe as he had ever laid eyes on, brought home his mistake forcefully. This lad was his first-born. He filled his father's heart with tenderness and pride, but he also made him painfully conscious of his folly.

Glancing around to make sure they were really alone, Blake reached into the cradle and gingerly picked the boy up and held him nervously in his arms, terrified that the tot would cry or wriggle or somehow slip out of his grasp. Alex yawned, flexed his arms, and slowly opened his eyes. They were turning more and more green, veering away from the brown tone he had been born with, and he gazed up at the dark head bending over his with what seemed to Blake to be accusation. "You'll not suffer for the circumstances of your birth, my son," he promised very low. "You and your mother will have every honor and advantage I can give you." Then somewhat self-consciously—for he'd had little contact with infants— Sinclair kissed the child on the forehead and returned him to the cradle.

He left the nursery feeling troubled.

It was Bothwell who forced him out of the sickroom. He sent a message by Jason to say that he must see Blake immediately "on a matter of great importance."

"You must go," his cousin urged. "The Queen is annoyed at your long absence. Something is underfoot at Holyrood, and with Parliament due to open in a few days . . ."

Blake completed the remark in his own mind: ". . . and with Moray and the other rebels due to be attainted, whatever is underfoot bodes no good for Mary Stuart."

29

The three noblemen conversed in Bothwell's quarters in Holyrood, and Blake discovered that much had happened in the time he had been away from court. Some sort of plot was under way involving Morton, Maitland and Moray, together with other Protestant lords who resented the commoner David Riccio's swift rise to eminence. "And there's little doubt but that Darnley is with them," said George Gordon, looking more like his father than ever since he'd begun to put on weight. "Though Morton and the others secretly loathe him, they have lately attached themselves to the King like lamprey to trout. It was Morton or Maitland, I'll warrant, who filled the young pup's ears with tales of Her Grace's supposed revels with Riccio."

Bothwell suddenly roared with laughter, thumping the table with a clenched fist. "Och, can you imagine a more ill-matched pair, Mary tall as a giraffe and wee Davy scarce higher than a dwarf!" And with the coarse sense of humor for which he was notorious, Hepburn added, "Dear sweet Jesus, the poor wee gent would need a ladder to properly service her!"

Sinclair grasped the situation at once. If the Protestant nobles could prove, by fair means or foul, that Mary was guilty of adultery with her secretary, her crown could be taken away and placed on the puppet, Darnley, and through this weakling the old band would be back in power.

It all hinged on the opening of Parliament, due to take place two days hence. If the Queen persisted in her plan to attaint Moray and the other rebels, the plot would go forward, Blake was certain.

He set about sending word to all the loyal lords to come to Edinburgh immediately, feeling they would have need of every hand they could get if trouble did break out. And until this session of Parliament was over, he, Bothwell and Gordon would remain close to the Queen in Holyrood at all times. Sinclair felt that he could trust Gordon and Bothwell totally. George Gordon, the new Earl of Huntly, had every reason to hate Moray and wish to see him brought low, and Bothwell despised the Hamiltons, who were known sympathizers of the rebels.

Parliament was opened on March 7 by the Queen herself, looking resplendent for all her sickness of mind and body in a glorious gown and mantle of silver and gold, anxious that her people gathered to watch her ride by should have the fine show they expected from a monarch. When she had passed, the citizens of Edinburgh muttered among themselves. "Where is the King, her husband? Why does he not ride at the side of his Queen?"

The reason for his insulting absence was soon clear. Darnley, as he anticipated, was not granted the crown matrimonial and in his anger and arrogance preferred to stay away, biding his time. At Mary's insistence a bill of attainder was to be passed against James Stewart, Earl of Moray, and his fellow conspirators on March 12. During the weekend preceding this event the entire city seemed to hold its breath.

In her private apartments at Holyrood the Queen paced back and forth, stricken by last-minute doubts. She wept a little, recalling how much she had once loved this brother she was about to deprive of everything he owned in Scotland; deprive him of his right to live in Scotland itself. She fretted over her husband, Darnley, whom she had loved in reckless defiance of all her advisers, and because of that love had honored him with the title above all others: King.

Gazing through her window that Friday evening, watching the mist roll in from the nearby firth, Mary wondered how Maitland could possibly be jealous of her little servant and former musician, Davy Riccio. It was Davy who had brought her some lighthearted pleasure through his music and sprightly conversation, treasured moments that for a short while took her mind off the serious business of ruling the state. Vile rumors had been spread about her and her private secretary, but surely no one in their right mind could possibly believe them? Aside from aught else, was she not six months pregnant with the royal heir!

The palace was so quiet, the court muted, the city itself shrouded in the fog drifting in from the sea. Standing at her window, the young Queen suddenly broke into hysterical laughter, thinking that the mist was like a symbol, signifying her continuing perplexity about these nobles of hers. The Scottish court was nothing like the France she had grown up in and come to know so well, nor were her ministers here remotely like her dear Guise uncles who had always stood solidly behind her and counseled her most skillfully along the way. Even the husband she had chosen to help her share the burden had proved as insubstantial as the fog swirling beyond her window!

Seton, Bothwell and Sinclair were loyal, of that she had no doubt, but at that moment she was a little annoyed with the handsome Earl of Belrose who had often absented himself from court in the last few months. His marriage was over in all but name, she had heard, but such a man would never lack female companionship. Mary, in a truthful moment, recognized that she was jealous of these shadowy women, even though her brother James had once scolded that queens should be above such earthy emotions.

But that Sinclair could have been her mate! How different things might have been, strong and loyal as he was . . . and passionate. Of that she had no doubt, smiling slightly as she thought of his dark, glowing eyes and wide, sensuous mouth.

Mary sighed heavily and dropped a hand to her swollen stomach with a touch of guilt, half-envying her English cousin her ability to control her feelings and never for a moment place the woman before the Queen.

Late in the afternoon of the following day, Saturday, Wyatt arrived at Holyrood with a message for his master. The Lady Alyssa had that morning been taken off her medication and had begun to speak for the first time since she had arrived at Highfield.

"She asks for you, my lord. Could you not come back to the house for an hour or two?"

Blake was torn, longing to see Alyssa, and thrilled that she had at last returned to the world of the living. There was not much stirring at Holyrood and the Queen's only plans for the evening were a small dinner party in her own quarters with close friends. The temptation was too great to be overcome. After a word with Gordon and Bothwell, who intended to remain on guard for the evening, he had Fleet saddled and rode eagerly back to the house.

Lizette Sinclair had been busy. Though basically practical and realistic, there was a spark of romance in her nature, and the fair young creature awakening like a flower unfolding in the upstairs chamber had fanned this spark into a full-blown flame. Alyssa must be bathed and dressed in one of her own most alluring bedgowns, a frothy thing of palest green chiffon with narrow satin ribbons the color of spring-fresh mint holding the low-cut bodice closed over her lush white breasts. She must be set upon fresh silken sheets, and the chamber itself filled with flowers. Scented candles too, she thought excitedly, rushing to have everything ready before her brother-in-law arrived home.

"He may not come," Alyssa suggested, a tremor in her voice. Lizette had been at her bedside when she opened her eyes once the drug wore off, and the two women had spent the day getting to know one another. Alyssa had tried not to be too disappointed to find Blake gone, especially when Lizette explained the reason for his absence. As time wore on and he still didn't appear, the older woman had sensed her yearning and disappointment and took the liberty of sending Wyatt to Holyrood.

Now Lizette patted her hand reassuringly. "He will come, chéri!" And with a throaty little laugh, "Mary Stuart herself could not keep him away!"

Both looked up sharply when they heard the clatter of hoofs against the cobbles. A great burst of relief swept through Alyssa when she heard Sinclair's deep voice bark out an order to a groom. Then he was in the doorway, big, dark, and glowing with virile good health, bringing a clean rush of cool air with him. In three strides he was at the bed and Alyssa in his arms. "Thank God!" he said, a tremor in his voice as he noted a touch of color in her cheeks and some of the old shine back in her eyes.

He kissed her deeply, trying to control his emotion at finding her improved, striving to be gentle when every nerve in his body cried out to crush her against him and taste her sweetness, which he had begun to doubt he would ever enjoy again. She had come back to him! And she would never leave his arms again, nay, regardless of whether Ogilvy was alive or dead. When she clung to him crying in relief, he kissed her tears away, soothing, "You are safe now, my love, and God help Ogilvy—or anyone—who tries to harm you."

A delicious supper was sent to their room, and at his urging, Alyssa ate a little to please him. They talked of their son, Blake's face flushing with pride as he said, "A Sinclair through and through! Lizette tells me he's already lusty and demanding, the wee rascal, and has all the other bairns dancing attendance on him."

"His name is Alexander," she told him softly, her heart swelling with joy at his delight.

Sinclair made no comment, aware of who had chosen the name, thinking, It should be as mine, and *would* have been had she stayed with me!

Conversation turned to her injured ankle, which Greer felt was healing well. Finally Alyssa herself brought up the subject of that fateful night when she had made up her mind to leave Simon and never return. "I was . . . wrong," she admitted, searching his face. "I know my son belongs with his true father—"

"As well as the lad's mother," he broke in soberly, watching her just as closely.

"What if I never walk again?"

"Then I will carry you."

She went into his arms and buried her face against his chest.

In her private apartments at the palace the Queen and her guests were enjoying a quiet supper. It was a small affair, the type Mary most liked now that she was clumsy with child, and included her half-brother and sister, Robert Stewart and Jean, Countess of Argyll, and a few others. David Riccio, of course, had been included to add his stimulating conversation and the music that Mary so loved.

In the cozy room hung with wine-red and green, the ominous pall about Holyrood was shut out, the atmosphere within warm and relaxed. A narrow staircase led from the Queen's quarters to her husband's on the first floor of the palace. As the company supped, Darnley himself suddenly rushed up the stairs and burst into the room, startling everyone present. Normally he scorned these little parties as being tedious and boring, so at the sight of him Mary asked uncertainly, "What brings you thus, my lord?"

Before he could reply, the debauched Lord Ruthven appeared. To the astonishment of all, they saw that he was armed. Ruthven's feverish eyes jumped from the Queen to David Riccio and he demanded in a loud, strident tone, "We would have yon foreigner come forth from your apartments, madam. He will not tarry here again!"

Mary was shocked and indignant. She answered haughtily, "How dare you, Ruthven! David is here at my invitation."

He sneered into her angry face, "So you admit to this shameless indiscretion? You would allow this—this churl to sully your honor? Madam," he shouted, "you are not fit to be Queen!"

Feet pounded on the stairs and a band of men barged into the chamber, all armed, some with swords drawn. The dinner guests jumped up from the table, which was overturned by Lord Lindsay, and moved back in terror leaving the pregnant sovereign to face them alone. Pointing to Darnley, who had also moved back and looked as nervous as the guests, she cried, "This is your doing, my lord!"

David Riccio scurried to the window as if he would throw himself out rather than face the vengeance of the mob, and when Ruthven drew his dagger and made to follow him, Mary stepped forward and barred his way. As he ducked around her, the Queen's own servants rushed into the room, but it was already too late. Riccio tried to save himself by clinging to Mary's skirts, but George Douglas—a relative of Morton's—

dragged him away. At the head of the stairs Riccio was stabbed viciously again and again and his bloody corpse hurled to the floor below.

Pandemonium broke out in the palace, and presently the Common Bell boomed out in the city itself. People rushed to Holyrood, and a huge, unruly crowd shouted up at the windows, demanding to see their Queen. When Mary would have obliged, almost faint with fear as she was, Lord Lindsay wrenched her back, threatening to cut her to pieces if she didn't hold her tongue. "It is not over for you yet, madam," he warned grimly. "Do you not understand that you are now a prisoner inside your own palace?" And he laughed at the look of shock on her face.

Within the hour the conspirators had taken over Holyrood. With Mary secure, they set about searching for the nobles who had supported her, intending to kill them on the spot. Huntly and Bothwell made a daring escape by vaulting over the lion pit, choosing that as the lesser of two evils. Immediately they set off at a gallop to drum up support for the Queen and stage a rescue attempt.

That night Mary was locked into her own bedchamber with only the aging Lady Huntly, widow of the former Earl of Huntly, for solace. Luckily for Mary, this venerable lady still had all her wits about her. She advised the weeping Queen, "Your lord the King is weak and dithers one way and then the other, so for your own sake, ponder how you might win him back to your side."

Mary stared at her in amazement. "What? I want no more of Darnley! I detest the knave. Did he not cause my good servant to be slain before my very eyes? Did he not bring risk to my child and my own life through this shock? You would ask me to win back the affections of a murderer!"

Lady Huntly nodded wisely. "One needs do what one must, Your Grace. The King wavers with the wind. Did you not say he turned green when his former friend Riccio was done to death?" She caught the younger woman's arm, stressing, "A monarch must sometimes swallow a bitter pill for the sake of hanging onto her crown."

Mary had grown to like and respect the older woman.

Now that her son George had been restored to his father's title and estates, Lady Huntly seemed to harbor no grudges over the past. That, Mary often reflected, took great strength of character and equally great wisdom, and the Queen had always been inclined to listen to those who had won her affections.

Swallowing the "bitter pill," she set about wooing the mercurial Darnley back through flattery and seeming understanding. The older lords, she said, had cunningly lured him into this grave mischief for their own ends, and would dispatch him as swiftly as they had Riccio when they considered him to be of no further use to them. She would forgive him, she promised, if he would only come back to his senses. "I fear for you, my lord, running as you are with a pack of jackals."

Darnley thought this through and could not but see the sense in it. These lords, he recalled, had recently despised him. Now, of a sudden, they would be his dear friends. He remembered how Moray had always felt about the Lennoxes, and such a man—now that he considered it soberly—was not like to change his position.

He fell on his knees before her and kissed her hand. He had been a poor husband, he admitted, but from then on would dedicate himself to her wholeheartedly and denounce these traitors who sought to topple her from the throne. Mary, Lady Huntly and the King put their heads together to think up a plan of escape, made that much more difficult because of the Queen's advanced pregnancy. Finally it was Mary herself who thought of a way to turn her very condition to advantage. While Lady Huntly smuggled a message out of the palace, the younger woman pretended to go into premature labor. At this her guards were forced to leave her chamber, and when the midwife had temporarily left the room, she and Darnley hurried down their private connecting staircase at midnight, crossed the graveyard of the abbey, and made their escape on the horses provided by those who had received Lady Huntly's message.

Blake was torn from Alyssa's bedside by the clanging of the Common Bell. Riding down the Canongate with his men, he met Bothwell and Huntly racing to warn him. The Queen was a prisoner, Riccio slain, and Lord Lindsay had sent troops to round up all the loyal nobles and forthwith put them to death. The night about them was sulphurous, the stink of pitch hanging in the air from the blazing torches brandished by what seemed to be thousands of uncertain citizens, angry and confused as to what was going on.

"We must off to Seton Castle!" shouted Bothwell over the roar of the crowd. "Faith, but we cannot serve the Queen or mount a rescue while in want of our heads!"

Blake sent Wyatt and some of his men to get Alyssa, Lizette and the children and take them immediately to Seton by a circuitous route, for if the women were to be seen with them they too would perish. Wyatt rode away none too soon. As Blake's party passed Blackfriars Wynd, a contingent of Lindsay's troops suddenly burst out of the narrow close and engaged them in battle. Lindsay, no friend of Sinclair's from the time of the elder Huntly's rebellion, had given his men specific instructions to hunt Sinclair down and kill him, thereby settling their old score.

The fighting was ferocious, and within minutes mutilated bodies and rivers of blood ran through the little street. Hemmed in by the buildings that all but hung over the wynd, and jostled by the plunging and rearing horses, Sinclair found it difficult to maneuver the big, muscular Fleet. When his horse was killed from under him, he leaped out of the saddle and continued to battle on foot, four of Lindsay's henchmen surrounding him and forcing him back against the side of a building. Swinging his sword in a deadly arc, he decapitated their leader, but as he wrenched his weapon free of bone and muscle, the man behind him sprang to the side and struck him on the shoulder, the blade shearing perilously close to his throat. A chunk of heavy padding flew off his tunic, and Blake felt the fiery kiss of steel gouge his flesh, a touch that was no stranger to a man who had fought at the head of battalions from the time he was seventeen years old. When his opponent again raised his ax, bringing it down savagely with the full force of his weight behind it, Sinclair ducked and the fellow went sprawling over his shoulder, slamming into the door of the nearest house. Those behind were engaged by some of MacKellars' soldiers before

they could close in on their prey. Blake paused for a second to
test his arm, and finding it still basically intact if bleeding
profusely, plunged into a group of Lindsays surrounding Jason.

When the cry had gone up that the Queen was a prisoner,
the nobles still loyal to her had mustered to her defense.
Thomas MacKellar, recently confined to bed, had sent his
brother Luke in his stead. Riding along the Canongate with his
men, Luke had at first entertained the notion of storming the
palace, then had come upon the fray in Blackfriars Wynd.

The fighting continued until the litter of bodies and dead
horses clogged the narrow street, making it almost impossible to
move. Seeing they were getting the worst of it, Lindsay's
survivors hastily fled into the dark and mingled with the crowd,
hoping to make their way back to Holyrood for reinforcements.
The royalists started for Seton Castle immediately, racing to
leave the city before the gates were blocked.

Darnley too was desperate to leave Edinburgh behind,
trembling to think of what the rebels would do once they
discovered how he had tricked them. The ride to Seton and
then Dunbar Castle, a near-impregnable fortress on the coast,
was a long distance away for a woman in frail health and heavy
with child. For all that, the King insisted they proceed at top
speed, shouting, "'Tis easy to get another child if this one dies,
but impossible to get another head!"

At Seton were gathered a large contingent of loyal nobles
and their followers, and during her brief respite there Alyssa
met Mary Stuart for the second time. Finding a woman lying
on a litter in the crowded hall, the Queen walked over
inquiringly and gazed down upon Alyssa and little Alexander.
Mary remembered this beauty, a woman not easy to forget.
Finding her in the care of her favorite minister—whose child
she suspected the infant to be—she realized at once why
Sinclair had been so frequently absent from court.

Mary was not especially surprised that the Chief would
have taken Lady Ogilvy as his mistress. Her own father, King
James V, had had as one of his mistresses the Lady Margaret
Erskine, at that time married into the powerful Douglas family,
and her half-brother Moray had been the result. Such arrangements were commonplace. But, being Mary, she could not

now hold back a sharp little pang of dismay, which she admitted to herself ruefully was most unqueenly.

Nevertheless she smiled down at Alyssa and bent to examine the baby. "A fine, lusty lad!" she said with a heartiness she didn't feel, and with an impish sidelong glance at the proud father. "Forsooth, my lord, you have indeed been well occupied while away from my court!"

The Queen spoke kindly to Alyssa. Always sympathetic to the sick and infirm, she promised to send her own physician to examine her injury "If God heeds my prayers and restores me to my rightful position."

Alyssa kissed her hand and promised to add her own prayers to the cause, and wished the Queen well in her upcoming confinement.

After a short time at Seton the royalists rode on to the more secure Dunbar Castle, where even more supporters were awaiting them. When on March 18 Mary reentered Edinburgh triumphantly at the head of a large army it was to find her half-brother Moray waiting to greet her. Since he had only just arrived back from England, the Queen did not connect him to the rebels. They had a touching reunion wherein Stewart confessed to regret that he had ever caused his dear sister "such sore grief." In a mellow mood, Mary pardoned Moray and the other lords who had taken part in his rebellion, known as the Chaseabout Raid, provided they help her bring to justice the murderers who had killed the hapless Riccio.

In the meantime, the latest conspirators fled the capital when they got wind of Darnley's defection. Most of them, including Lindsay, Morton and Ruthven, raced over into England. Darnley, newly reinstated with his wife—a wife who could not help but be suspicious of his loyalty—had a fresh chance to prove himself in her eyes. Her nobles were not so charitable. To a man, they despised and distrusted one whom they considered a weakling and turncoat. Erratic and unstable emotionally, seething with lofty ambitions and with scant regard as to whom he had to mow down to achieve them, he was viewed as a serious threat to their own ambitions. Darnley was too proud and arrogant to try to win them over, and within weeks of their reconciliation he was again causing his wife anxiety through his behavior. A rumor came to her that the King was hatching a new scheme to seize her crown.

While Mary wept, her ministers put their heads together. All agreed that something must be done to curb Darnley's penchant for treachery and to stop him from further disturbing the Queen. The question of a divorce was put forward, but—as all knew—divorces took so long. Aside from that, there was no guarantee that the Pope would grant one. Had not Henry VIII tried and failed?

"Some other way, then," said Bothwell firmly, and the other lords nodded slowly, avoiding each others' eyes.

30

Blake held his breath as Benito Greer removed the cast.

Alyssa stood up cautiously. She took one shaky step, then another. Without being conscious of it, Sinclair held out his arms as she slowly limped toward him, her eyes never leaving his face, taking strength from the love and encouragement she saw there. When she was several feet away, he swiftly closed the distance between them and swept her up in his arms. "Thank God!" he breathed. "Thank God . . ."

Greer scorned his gold. "Pah! Money cannot buy my skill, so do not try to corrupt me with this." And he tossed the purse back, adding in a tone of affront, "A haunch of venison or keg of ale, if it please you. The money you may donate to the beggars at St. Giles."

The little doctor then proceeded to give imperious instructions for Alyssa's convalescence—the type of food she should eat, how much exercise she should get, and so forth. "It will be some time before she walks as she did before, so you must be patient. A change of air would be wise, somewhere tranquil. And now"—he snapped his medical bag closed—"I must perforce leave her in your hands, my lord."

With a doubtful look at the Chief he shook his head and swaggered to the door.

"Insufferable little wretch!" Sinclair growled under his breath, but at the same time he was eternally grateful to the abrasive little doctor.

Blake made up his mind to take Alyssa and the baby to Lynnwood. The air in the North was much healthier than in Edinburgh, and the lovely, peaceful surroundings would do them good. His own shoulder wound was healing well, but he too looked forward to a sojourn away from the constant demands on his time at court. Alyssa, he noticed, seemed unusually quiet and preoccupied ever since they had returned from Seton Castle. They had very little privacy at Highfield, where the entire Sinclair family frequently gathered. During these times Alyssa usually remained in her room. Blake suspected that she was embarrassed at her position in his life, not made any easier by the stern, disapproving glances of his uncle Harry Sinclair.

They had heard or seen nothing of Simon Ogilvy, but Blake knew that Alyssa lived in dread of him putting in an appearance. She never asked about Elizabeth or how their divorce was progressing.

She seemed a little distant, and it bothered him. They needed time alone, he felt strongly, confident that that was all that would be necessary to reestablish their former closeness. Because of the awkwardness of their situation at Highfield and the fact that she had been ill, he had stayed away from her bed. This alone caused a certain tension between them, one that mounted daily as her health improved. Sinclair looked forward to remedying this situation at Lynnwood, the one spot where they could be truly alone.

He made arrangements to leave for the Highlands the following week.

Alyssa was relieved. She was quietly desperate to get away from the city and the possibility of Simon tracking her down, even though Blake swore he would kill him if Ogilvy made any attempt to remove her from his protection. This was the very thing she dreaded most, a confrontation between the two men in her life. In that type of situation Sinclair couldn't win, since to kill Simon would make him a murderer.

She had a secret. She had hugged this secret to her ever since their brief stay at Seton Castle, not quite sure how she ought to proceed. Among the other lords she had met there had been Luke MacKellar, a gruff but kindly man who told her with a grin, "When I first beheld ye at the court ball ye reminded me strongly of my sister, Lydia. My lady wife too remarked at the resemblance."

Her heart had begun to race, but she replied carefully.

"I'm from Inverness-shire, my lord; the little village of Lochmore."

"Sinclair's territory. Ah . . . I see," and his eyes had gone to the child. When she blushed, he hastily returned to the former subject. "Well, lass, ye may not be a MacKellar, but for a' that ye're welcome to visit our house." And with another glance at Alex, "And bring the bairn. My lady is muckle fond o' weans and never could have none of her own, so she'd give ye a right hearty welcome."

Alyssa had thanked him warmly, barely able to conceal her excitement, and promised to pay them a visit. Now she seethed with indecision, not sure what to do, yet thinking that here was her chance to make a positive connection with her own family—even if they didn't yet realize she was one of them!

Always her mind returned to the original problem, how to prove her claim, made that much more difficult, if not impossible, since learning of the death of her mother. There was no one in the world she could point to and say, "He or she will vouch for me." Or even, "My mother will tell you what she heard that night at Cumbray, that her child was a girl; a girl who was born alive and vigorous."

A hundred times she had been about to confide in Sinclair, but the very fact that she had waited so long to take him into her confidence went against his believing her story. Now there was another complication, stemming from her state of mind after her ordeal on the moor. She had overheard Greer tell Blake that it would take time for her to recover completely, not only physically, but mentally too. Since then she had often turned to find Blake studying her soberly. Once, he said, "You seem a little . . . depressed. I won't have you fretting, Alyssa! Stop conjuring up wild happenings in your mind. I'll take good care of you, my darling, so trust me and stop brooding."

There were times when she felt that the best thing she could do all the way around was to forget that she had been born a MacKellar and accept her identity as Alyssa Dunne. It was too late to set things right—and much too dangerous, not only for herself, but for her son. She had no fear of Lady Magdalen as long as she stayed with Sinclair and did not press her right to Cumbray. She was recognized now as the Chief's mistress, Alexander his bastard son, and as such they would both be safe. This then was the price she must pay, to accept a role her very bones stiffened against in rebellion; that together with the permanent loss of her true identity.

Alyssa could not bring herself to query Blake about Elizabeth, or how the divorce was coming along, for inevitably it would lead to another, more disturbing, question: what would his plans be once he was free? It was impossible to live at Highfield without becoming aware of the desires of the family, particularly that of Blake's oldest uncle, Harry Sinclair. They were hoping for a match between their Chief and the comely Crawford heiress, a union that would bring much good to the clan—and greater strength and wealth.

Alyssa tried hard to push these troublesome thoughts from her mind and concentrate on getting well, since her very fragility only increased her feeling of uncertainty and vulnerability. Jason's wife was sweet and kind to her, as well as Jason himself, but certain other members of the family, Alyssa was certain, viewed her hold on the Chief with resentment, seeing in her an obstruction to their plans.

She had become close friends with Lizette. While Blake was off on court business they had spent many an hour chatting around the hall fire. When Lizette made friendly inquiries about her background, Alyssa answered carefully, telling her exactly the same things she had told Sinclair. After she had related her life with Isa Dunne and said she was not sure of her true parentage, Lizette leaned over and kissed her on the cheek. "Ah, chéri, life has not been easy for you, but now you are well loved by a great Chief close to the Queen herself. Without rank or wealth you have won the adoration of a man sought after by every woman at court!"

"He is not truly mine, Lizette," Alyssa responded with a sigh.

The older woman put down her needle, caught by the anguish in Alyssa's voice, and studied her sympathetically while wishing there was something more positive she could say to soothe her. There was nothing. Alyssa spoke the truth. As Lizette well knew, a mistress held a very insecure position in a man's life, particularly a noble lord who was the chief of a powerful clan. The French woman enjoyed romance as well as any other, but underneath there was a strong streak of realism in her nature. During her years at court she had watched great passions flare . . . and inevitably cool with the passage of time, that great destroyer of romantic love. In the end a mistress frequently had nothing to show for her devotion but a clutch of bastard children, many of whom grew up to blame their mother for their ignoble lot in life.

She mulled the situation over as she continued with her embroidery while Alyssa did likewise on the other side of the hearth. Sinclair was very attached to this woman, she was thinking. She had never known him to be quite so engrossed in the past. Her mind turned to the impending divorce, then mentally she shrugged. Even had the fair Alyssa been free, Blake could not possibly marry her. Even now there were plans underfoot within the family to bring about a match between the Chief and Sara Crawford, and it would be an excellent match indeed! Sinclair, having been raised from infancy to understand that duty to the clan came first, could not dispute its suitability without risking turmoil and violent opposition within his own house, the sort of strife that could split a clan into warring factions that inevitably led to its own destruction, and that he would never do.

Lizette offered Alyssa the only comfort she could. "We must make the most of whatever happiness comes our way, savoring it to the full. Who among us, wife or no, can predict what tomorrow holds in this troubled land, or how long any of our men will be with us?"

As the wife of a nobleman, Lizette was involved in various charitable ventures, the latest of which was a Hospice Fund, a unique concept to bring shelter and health care to the city's poor. One day she came home from a meeting with the news that Lord Thomas MacKellar, the Earl of Kilgarin, was again seriously ill. She sighed and shook her head as her maid removed her cape. "Should aught happen to the earl, I doubt that Lord Luke will relish inheriting all the responsibility of Cumbray. His wife confided that he pines sorely for their country place and detests court life." Lizette chuckled dryly.

"I'll wager the Lady Magdalen does not make it any easier for them. There's bad blood there, you can be sure, though I suppose Sir Simon has told you about the dissension in the family?"

Alyssa had been feeding the baby. Now she took him from her breast and raised her head to the older woman in confusion. "Simon? What would he know about that?"

"Then he's not close to his cousin Lady Magdalen?"

Alyssa stared at her. "His . . . cousin?"

Lizette laughed. "Then he didn't tell you of this connection? 'Tis not surprising. From what I know of the countess, she'd have scant patience with a man of Ogilvy's type unless she thought he could be of some use to her. She's not a woman to put much stress in kinship—"

Alyssa had stopped listening. She hung her head over the baby in a state of shock, her mind reeling. Simon and Magdalen related! Why had he never mentioned this? Was it because of his connection to the countess that he had been able to prevail upon Magdalen to leave her alone? A great doubt rose in her mind when Alyssa considered the type of woman he would have had to deal with—as Lizette had remarked, one who had scant regard for kinship. Alyssa could not imagine anyone, related or not, being able to prevail upon Magdalen MacKellar to do anything against her will.

She could hardly wait to be alone to think things through. Later, in the privacy of her room, her mind went back to the night Simon had asked her to marry him. It had been *after* he learned of her true identity. He had promised to protect her from Magdalen and help her locate her mother—but only if she would consent to marry him. Yet marriage hadn't been on his mind, she was certain, until he discovered who she really was.

What had he hoped to gain, knowing it would be almost impossible to establish her claim to Cumbray? Short of funds as he had been before—and she recalled the bill he had run up in Livingstone's—he had suddenly been flush with coin after they were wed, lavishly throwing money in all directions. Where, she asked herself, had this wealth *really* come from?

A dark suspicion entered Alyssa's mind and at the same

time solved a puzzle, suggesting the real reason he had married her—something that had startled everyone at court at the time. Was it possible that he had blackmailed his powerful cousin, threatening to reveal the truth unless she paid handsomely for his silence?

It fit in well with what she had learned about her husband's character. Gain was the motivating force in Ogilvy's life, and for that he had been willing to sell out Queen and country, so why not his wife?

She hated him. And how she rued the day that her son was saddled with the Ogilvy name, one he would have to carry for the rest of his life. And if the time came—and it could at any moment—when Simon grew brave or reckless enough to demand the return of his "son," the law required that he be turned over to his "father."

"I'd kill Simon first!" Alyssa breathed through clenched teeth. Or, more likely, Blake would do it for her.

Was it possible that Simon was already dead?

Two days later they left Edinburgh for Lynnwood with Wyatt and a score of Blake's men in attendance. Word had been sent on ahead to Mistress Keane to have everything ready and the old nursery aired and made comfortable for Lady Ogilvy's baby. The ride north went without a hitch, and four-month-old Alexander took it in stride, showing a great interest in everything that went on around him. He was big for his age, with a goodly mop of curly black hair and long-lashed green eyes a shade darker than his mother's. For all his curls, no one ever mistook him for a girl. To his doting parents he was the finest lad in all of Scotland, and Alexander accepted their homage as his due, every inch the first-born of Augusta.

When they rode into familiar territory and saw the manor below, placid as always in its verdant green dell and beautiful gardens blazing with daffodils and multihued tulips, a welter of bittersweet memories rushed back to haunt Alyssa. Involuntarily she turned her head, and as her eyes met Sinclair's she imagined a glint of triumph in the sable-brown depths, the proud look of the victor. He had won! She was here in the capacity he had had in mind for her all along, and all that remained was for her to accept it with as much grace as she could, keeping in mind the most important thing—that she loved him.

"My lady . . ." Blake waved her on ahead of him.

Alyssa hesitated only a moment, then nodded and started off down the hill. Keane was waiting at the door to welcome them, a smug little smile on her face.

A strange, soft melancholy stole over Alyssa the moment she entered the beautiful house with its delicate pastel-tinted walls and exquisite furniture, each room filled with fresh flowers from the gardens. She remembered the first time she had entered it, as an innocent, trusting girl of seventeen; a naïve girl who foolishly believed that anything was possible.

Blake sensed that she wanted to rest. Fortunately, the chamber Keane led her to was a different one from her previous visit, even more sumptuous, with a great carved oak bed draped in shimmering lavender silk and a muted Turkey carpet on the floor. The walls were hung with tapestries depicting scenes from Greek mythology, their theme being domination and surrender, which to Alyssa seemed all too appropriate. A massive bowl of lilacs sat on a table under the window, the sweet, fresh perfume filling the air.

Alyssa undressed, bathed, and lay down across the satin cover, her eyes fastened on a slanting beam of sunlight streaming through the window. She tried not to remember all she had hoped and dreamed when first she had come to this place. One thing had not changed. She was even more in love with Blake Sinclair than she had been then, and he had demonstrated over and over that he loved her too. It was enough, she told herself, heeding Lizette's sage advice; she would savor whatever happiness came their way and try not to think of tomorrow.

Alyssa was awakened hours later by a furtive rustling sound in her room. Opening her eyes, she saw darkness beyond the window. The candles had been lit in her chamber, the scent of lilacs everywhere, and as she stretched, feeling rested and suddenly happy to be back at Lynnwood where they could be blissfully alone, she found herself looking forward with excitement to the evening ahead.

When she sat up, Alyssa saw the gown spread across the foot of the bed, the most beautiful gown she had ever seen—and in her favorite color. With a sense of awe she examined it, touching it lightly with the tips of her fingers. It was of emerald-green satin, the gathered skirt and flounces delicately traced with fine silver thread, the underskirt a froth of the sheerest cream-colored lace.

Slowly her eyes moved to a nearby coffer. Perched on the lid were a pair of satin slippers the exact shade of the dress, and beside them a long, narrow box inlaid with mother-of-pearl.

She laughed in delight and pressed both hands to her flushed cheeks, her heart melting with love. Blake had remembered! And as she touched the rippling folds caressingly, her mind went back to the day he had come upon her unexpectedly at Gower Castle preening and bowing before the guest-room mirror, wondering how she would look in such a gown. Now she would soon find out!

Keane herself appeared to help her dress for supper, which she informed Alyssa was to be an intimate affair set on a small table drawn up before the library fire. Seated before the looking glass, Alyssa tried to explain to the housekeeper how she had lately worn her hair, piled high in a style much favored at court.

"Nay, my lady, wear it loose this eve," the older woman coaxed softly. "Let it tumble like molten gold across your shoulders . . . like it was the other time." Picking up the inlaid box beside the slippers, she extracted a long, creamy rope of pearls. "We'll brush your hair until it glistens and twine these pearls about the curls."

Dressed to Keane's satisfaction at last, the housekeeper stood back to survey the results. "Ravishing! Truly ravishing. The vibrant green o' the gown looks wondrous when contrasted with the whiteness o' your skin and bonny golden hair."

The gown fit perfectly too. Now she knew why Lizette had insisted on taking her measurements some weeks past, announcing that she would have her seamstress make Alyssa a dress. This creation was a work of art, the daringly low-cut bodice molding her bosom, the wide, scalloped skirt outlined in silver tracery, swishing gracefully with the slightest movement. Tiny pearls dotted the rich material, cunningly swirling around to outline each breast, the creamy fullness of her flesh rising from the bodice bewitchingly in the candlelight.

Blake was standing by the fireplace when Alyssa glided into the room with her heart fluttering madly but satisfied that she had never looked better. She paused in the doorway to the library and gazed admiringly at the tall, broad-shouldered man leaning indolently against the mantel—and promptly forgot herself. Firelight played across his strong, deeply tanned features and reflected twin bonfires in the sable brown eyes that quickly moved over her gown, then leaped hungrily to the excited flush on her cheeks. He too, she noted, looked rested and refreshed, and handsome in his dove-grey velvet doublet, a color that emphasized his dark good looks to perfection.

Sinclair crossed to her quickly, took her hand and carried it to his lips, his eyes burning into hers as he studied her appraisingly from under his brows, as if trying to gauge the receptiveness of her mood. It was not the grandness of the gown that stirred the Chief's admiration and devotion, but the gift that God himself had bestowed on her, the rare beauty and radiance of her face and form, the mysterious allure of the woman herself.

"Enchanted," he murmured, elegant as any court gallant. Then with a husky laugh he caught her to him and kissed her lightly on the lips. After the briefest contact he stepped away, saying, "First we dine . . ."

He pulled out a chair at the small table before the fire. Feeling like the most cherished woman on earth, Alyssa waited for him to take his seat opposite her, but he continued to hover behind her chair. She gave a little start as she felt something cool and whispery slide around her neck; felt him fasten the clasp, even as she tilted her head back to look up at him questioningly. Bending, Blake kissed her parted lips with breathtaking passion. Holding her head gently between his hands, his eyes locked to hers, he said softly, fervently, "I love you, dear heart, now and for always."

Raising her up, he pushed her in the direction of the gilt mirror hanging over the reading table. Alyssa gasped at the flash of diamonds and emeralds that met her gaze in the looking glass. The necklace was like a waterfall of glistening gems, dipping to a large teardrop emerald in the center, sparking cool green fire back into her eyes.

Sinclair came up behind her and put his hands on her shoulders. "So it pleases you . . . ?" he asked softly, pressing a quick kiss to the top of her head.

Sudden tears rushed into her eyes, even though she was smiling. "Thank you," she whispered, "for remembering the gown, for this lovely necklace, for you most of all."

Blake turned her to face him and looked deep in her eyes, seemed about to say something, then kissed her instead.

They partook of a miniature feast, with a variety of wines to stir their palates, and the nearness of each other to put fire in their blood. Blake was at his most amusing, entertaining her with funny little incidents from his life. Alyssa kept him laughing as she related Isa Dunne's determination to find her a husband and the various unlikely candidates who had passed through her life. And each time their eyes met, both felt the jolt of acute awareness and need for each other; each time their hands touched, it sent the warm blood pounding through their veins. They had not known each other intimately for over a year, a year that had been agony for both of them. It was a pleasurable kind of agony now, knowing that the lack would soon be rectified.

This is my life, thought Alyssa as Sinclair plucked a rose from the centerpiece and tucked it playfully behind her ear; this is the path I must tread, since every other I take inevitably leads back to him.

Sinclair's patience ended long before the meal. He took her hand, and without a word they rose together and quietly, arms entwined, climbed the stairs to their room. He closed and bolted the door behind them, then turned and held out his arms to her, and Alyssa saw such a force of emotion in his face that she felt ashamed of her niggling doubts.

His mouth burned down on hers and as she was swept against him in blissful rapture her own clamoring heartbeats betrayed how urgently she too had yearned for this moment. When they were both naked, Blake lay down beside her and crushed the full length of his hard, muscular body against her trembling flesh, claiming her lips with a kiss that was almost savage with pent-up hunger, but one Alyssa responded to with a need equally demanding. A wave of sweat broke out across his tawny skin as he tried to restrain his ardor, his mouth roving her face and hair, lingering on her ear, then brushing downward over her arched throat to the firm swell of her breasts. Gently he nuzzled a dusky-rose tip, then bathed it with the moist heat of his mouth, his tongue lightly stroking and caressing as his warm hand leisurely roamed her body.

"Oh, my love . . . !" Alyssa moaned as he inexorably sought and found the inflamed core of her, teasing her flesh with strong, experienced fingers until every nerve in her body was aquiver with a wave of ecstatic fire. Their lips met in a surge of bruising passion, and as her trembling fingers moved frantically over his back, seeking to draw him yet closer, Sinclair was suddenly between her thighs, the hard shaft of his manhood thrusting downward to fill her sweet softness.

A wild urgency swept both of them as Blake whispered hoarse endearments. Moaning love-words of her own, Alyssa moved against him in total abandonment, her fingers in his hair, her lips and tongue devouring his, her body turbulent as they soared together to breathless heights, then spun off into a world of pulsing rapture.

Blake kissed her over and over as they lay back together, her hair a tumbled coppery mass mingling with the curling dark pelt on his chest. He murmured in her ear, "I feel like a parched man who has just been given a sip of nectar."

"A sip?" She laughed. "Then indeed you must be parched."

His eyes adored her. "Ah, but the night is long and the well deep, and who says a man must stop with a sip?"

Alyssa smiled contentedly into eyes burning with love for her. She teased, "I'm sure you have not gone athirsting during your long separation from . . . from Elizabeth."

A shadow moved across his face, but he replied lightly enough, "If you recall, I *did* say nectar, and that is not so easily found."

Alyssa lowered her cheek to his shoulder, hiding the fierce

stab of jealousy that might have shown in her eyes, vague images of shadowy women rising in her mind to taunt her, especially the sultry Sara Crawford. Nay, nay, she thought hastily, nothing must intrude to spoil things! She must keep in mind that he was here with her now because he wished to be. Twice he had saved her life. He had defied convention by flaunting her in the face of his family at Jason's house, and at this very moment was neglecting his duties to Queen and country just to be alone with her. These were the sweet facts she must cling to, all the rest dread imaginings that might never come true.

Alyssa saw that his eyes were dark as wine, drowsy with desire. Kissing him, she touched the tip of her tongue to his while at the same time sliding her hands over the rocklike muscles of his back to his hips. She proceeded to kiss all the many battle scars on his body until, with a muffled groan, Sinclair rolled her on top of him, driving every thought from her mind with the force of his need for her.

"Is this not more pleasurable than any potion Greer could have prescribed for you?" he commented afterwards with a grin.

"Aye, you are a very good doctor, my lord."

"And at your service night and day, my lady."

Alyssa slapped him playfully. "If it were left to you, I would never step forth from this room."

Sinclair laughed, his eyes smoldering. "Ah, but I'm only harkening to the instructions of the good doctor, and he made me promise to see to it that you had plenty of bed rest—"

"Rest! At this rate I shall need another holiday once we return to Edinburgh. What will you tell Greer then?"

"To mind his own business and stop poking his long nose into our private affairs," he growled. "He meddles far beyond the point he should, the obnoxious wee churl! I half believe he hankers after you himself."

It pleased her to find a spark of jealousy lurking in his heart, even though she took pains to soothe it in a way that would please him best. They made love until dawn, and slept through half of the following day only to begin the delicious process all over again. "I've always loved Lynnwood," said

Blake, finally rising to bathe and dress before dinner. "Something about the air hereabouts brings out the best in me, or mayhap you would say the beast."

"A nice beast." She rose too and stepped naked into his arms.

"God's blood . . . !"

They dined that evening in their room.

31

It was mid-May before Simon Ogilvy's wound healed completely and he felt it safe to return to court, where he reinstated himself with his old employer the Earl of Moray, now back in favor with the Queen. His close brush with death had sobered the knight, taking the wild edge off his recklessness. Now he lived for one thing, to find his runaway wife and take his revenge on her powerful lover. He was no longer so foolhardy as to challenge Blake Sinclair face to face. Another way would be found, he promised himself, and he would force himself to bide his time.

The court was in a state of uncertainty over the Queen's intentions toward her husband. Privately Ogilvy learned from Moray that she now heartily detested Darnley. To embarrass her the King had taken to roistering openly in the pleasure dens of Edinburgh itself. "'Tis plain she would fain be rid of him," Simon overheard Moray confide to the Earl of Huntly. "She would be relieved if he moved abroad until after the heir's birth."

The court—and all of Europe—watched and waited as the birth of the Queen's child was calculated to be just weeks away, whispering and speculating among themselves as to what might become of the child's father once Scotland had its heir.

A few days after Ogilvy returned to the city, Lady Magdalen sent for him.

She sneered at him, "So . . . your lady has left you for richer game." And when he opened his mouth to explain, "Nay, do not waste my time by denying it. What we must do now is to put our heads together and see how the situation can be remedied. From now on you will be honest with me, sir knight!" The gaunt lines of her face hardened. "The marriage is in ruins, is it not?" And when he hesitated, she leaned forward and rapped him smartly on the knee. "No more subterfuge! If you value your life and comfort you had best speak plain."

There was little need for him to speak at all. Within minutes Simon discovered that she was well informed in regards to his marital situation. Gloomy dismay ebbed slightly when she said, "I have a good, productive estate at Thornburn that brings in a tidy income, more than enough to subsidize your, er . . . extravagant mode of living. It can be yours, Ogilvy, *provided* you agree to my plan." She paused for a moment, watching him closely, then announced in a harsh, implacable tone, "The lady must be found! And destroyed."

Simon nodded slowly. He hated Alyssa; hated Sinclair. He lived in dread that his wife might ruin everything by divulging the truth to her powerful lover.

But Magdalen smiled tightly and shook her head. "He would never believe such a seemingly wild tale, and well she knows it. The girl is many things, to be sure, but a fool she is not. Still," she reflected aloud, "we must be careful. When the time comes to act, the MacKellar name must never be tied to her downfall."

"Nor the Ogilvy name," he said dryly.

The countess laughed and placed a cool hand over his. "Trust me to handle it, cousin, and both of us shall come out of this most satisfactorily."

The moist green days of spring sped by all too swiftly for the lovers at Lynnwood. As Alyssa grew stronger, they rode around the estate, amused themselves at bowls and archery, and spent a long weekend exploring the ancient city of Aberdeen. In the evenings they sat over the chessboard, or Blake strummed the lute while Alyssa sang off key. Sometimes they wandered along the banks of the loch in the gloaming, talking softly together, her hand in his, while watching the last rays of the sun swallowed up in the dark waters of Loch Ness.

They had Alexander with them often, much more than was fashionable among people of Sinclair's rank, and they crowed over their son. Was he not the biggest, brightest, most energetic child of his age in the whole of Scotland? "Aye," laughed Alyssa somewhat ruefully, "and according to his nurse, already the most spoiled."

Sometimes they roamed the moorland and when the mood struck them made love in a bed of primroses, the heat of their passion mingling with the wild essence of the flowers. Lying in Blake's arms afterwards, Alyssa gave voice to a thought beginning to nag at her mind. "Oh, if only we need never return to the capital!"

Messengers arrived at Castle Augusta every few days bringing news from Edinburgh, and after one such occasion Sinclair surprised Alyssa by remarking of the Queen, "She has that within her to bring much mischief to herself."

"What do you mean?"

Laying aside the parchment he had just received, he replied thoughtfully, "She inclines to rashness and impetuosity and is apt to plunge wholeheartedly into a situation when it would be more advantageous to hold back. Darnley is a case in point. The honeymoon was hardly over when she realized her folly. Even with Riccio she made a grave mistake. A more canny monarch—like her cousin, Elizabeth—would have realized the danger in elevating the Italian at a time when many of her own nobles felt less than favorable toward her."

Alyssa sighed, "Ah, poor lady, she cannot hope to please them all. From the sound of it, her lords are a scheming, ungrateful lot."

"Mayhap, but she needs them just the same, and should set her personal feelings aside and learn how to handle them by cleverly pitting one against the other without taking sides."

"Easier said than done."

"Aye," he sighed wryly, "but great things are expected of a monarch. Like it or not, they are expected to be above the failings of ordinary mortals, nor are their mistakes so easily rectified. Queen Elizabeth avoids such pitfalls by never committing herself. *That* she leaves to her ministers!" he went on with a harsh laugh. "'Tis *their* mistake when aught goes amiss, never hers. Elizabeth learned much from her insecure youth, first under her father, then her brother and sister, and what she learned was the danger and folly of allowing anyone access to the private workings of her mind."

Alyssa made a face. "I would not live thus for all the jewels in the royal crown, never able to trust anyone or truly speak one's feelings frankly. 'Tis akin to being in a prison."

Blake laughed and threw an arm around her shoulders. "Ah, but as I said before, a Queen is no ordinary woman, my love, and must pay a price for her high position if she hopes to keep a firm grasp on her crown—which Elizabeth most assuredly does. She, unlike Mary, is a true politician and an expert at setting up a smokescreen with words, which those about her may decipher as they will. And if they read her awrong, is that any fault of Queen Elizabeth's?"

Alyssa thought about it for a moment, then slowly admitted, "She is clever—but I could never like such a woman!"

"The woman in her takes a poor second place to the Queen, and 'tis the Queen who will be remembered in history."

They had many discussions during the long, tranquil days at Lynnwood. Neither, as if by tacit agreement, brought up the subject of their respective spouses or what the future might hold for them as a couple. Alyssa sensed that Sinclair was striving to make their holiday as relaxed and pleasant as possible and quickly steered away from any subject that might lead them into turbulent waters. Most of the time they were alone, and as the weeks went by, Alyssa wondered if her lover missed the company of others. She had a clear view of her place in his life and the narrow boundaries enclosing it. Blake could hardly flaunt his mistress in the grand houses in the North any more than he could in Edinburgh. He wanted her with him, but always she must stand in the shadowy background.

By the end of May even the nights had turned mild. One evening as they lay together in a light embrace, warm and relaxed after the turbulence of lovemaking, Blake told her that he had bought a town house for her on the outskirts of Edinburgh. She would have her own household, servants, men to guard her, and whatever else she required. He would join her there whenever he could get away from Holyrood.

Alyssa nodded slowly and turned her face to the gentle breeze wafting through the bedchamber window, blinking rapidly to fight back the tears welling into her eyes. It was happening just as she had imagined, and some spark of defiance flared to challenge this role that fate had forced upon her, this position she was made to occupy in the life of the man she loved. She thought of Lady Magdalen and all that the countess had taken away from her, and inwardly she raged, so that when Blake turned her face toward him and asked, "Are you not happy that we can be together even in town?" Alyssa could do nothing but nod, not trusting herself to speak.

The night before they returned to Edinburgh, Sinclair outlined his plans to protect her. Wyatt and several of his most trusted men would be on hand at all times at Beckford Lodge, the small estate he had deeded to her. Because of the uncertainty of the situation with Simon, he went on gravely, she must promise never to venture out alone. In the meantime, he would have a talk with his lawyers to see if there was some way she might have her marriage to Ogilvy dissolved.

"And what of your own marriage?" she asked boldly, tired of skirting the issue.

He sighed and rubbed a hand over his jaw. "These things take time, Alyssa, and we must try to be patient." He kissed her and added softly, "But what does it matter, my darling, when we already belong to each other?"

It was not quite the answer she longed for, and she voiced her deepest fear. "What if something should happen to part us?"

Blake drew her head to his muscular shoulder, his arm tightening about her. "Nothing short of death will separate us, Alyssa, and in that unlikely event I have made provisions for you and the babe—"

Swiftly she kissed him to silence as a chill swept over her. "Never speak of such a thing, dear heart! Oh God, why must we return to Edinburgh?" Alyssa raised anguished eyes to his face, and every line of that tanned face was achingly dear to her. If she should never see it again, she knew that she wouldn't want to live. "The Queen has many others to advise her," she burst out. "Your son and I need you much more than she does."

Sinclair smiled gently. "Would you have me go back on my word? Long ago in France—I've already told you the story—a wee auburn-haired lass gave me a wild rose she plucked from the garden hedge, and when she presented it to me in sweet impulse, I made her a promise, mayhap just as impulsively but a promise nevertheless." Dark eyes looked into green ones soberly as he added, "I hold myself to it, Alyssa."

Her raw nerves snapped. "Then you are a fool, Blake Sinclair! You were but a lad when you made that pledge. No one in the whole of Scotland doubts your honor. Have you not proved it time and again on the battlefield? Please"—she swallowed back tears, the chill premonition that they should not move South—"please . . . let us stay here!" The tears spilled over onto her cheeks as she added, "You said yourself that the Queen has a knack of embroiling herself in trouble, nor is so ready to take advice. I feel—I sense great strife ahead and you will be in the thick of it, and if anything should happen to you . . ." Alyssa was unable to go on.

Sinclair kissed her tears away. He smiled at her coaxingly and assured her with his usual confidence, "Nothing will happen to me. Have faith! And when the day comes that Mary Stuart sits firmly on her throne, we will leave Edinburgh and return here to pursue our life together, both of us satisfied that we have done what we must. You, sweet, have the harder part of the bargain since waiting is the devil's own tool to torture man—and woman." He hugged her fiercely, adding, "You must find it in your heart to be brave and to trust me."

Alyssa wondered gloomily if the day would *ever* come when Mary Stuart sat firmly on her throne, and mused over the nature of Sinclair's unique relationship with the Queen. But since she seemed powerless to change it, as powerless as she was to alter her own relationship to the Chief, she tried to resign herself to do as he asked.

They arrived back in Edinburgh a week before Prince

James's birth to discover that in his absence the Earl of Bothwell had become much closer to the Queen. It was on Bothwell's advice that Mary had been installed under heavy guard inside the stout walls of Edinburgh Castle, rather than having her baby in the birthing suite at Holyrood.

Mary's first words to Sinclair were, "Ah, so you finally return! Bothwell has been a good counselor while you were away, my lord. His own moss troopers have sworn to guard me and the babe with their lives." Though pale and with lines of strain about her mouth, she took his hand and smiled sweetly. "Now that you too are back with your men I'm much relieved." She examined him closely. "You *will* remain in the castle until after the child's birth?"

Sinclair could not bring himself to deny her.

The court was never static. It was in a constant state of change with one faction rising or falling, this or that person or group in or out of favor with the Queen. Various schemes or plots were always underfoot, for many among the nobility were enemies of longstanding in a country noted for never forgetting a grudge, any more than they forgot a favor. The newest star on the ascendant was the Earl of Bothwell, these days rarely far from the Queen's side. Sinclair admired the vigorous James Hepburn as a fine soldier and a man who could be counted on to speak his mind, but at the same time he saw a ruthless, self-serving side to the earl's character and a certain baseness to his habits that left much to be desired.

The courtiers watched and waited, and the consensus of opinion was that Bothwell would enjoy but a brief flowering at Holyrood. He had nothing in common with Mary Stuart, they whispered. The Queen was naturally refined, intellectual and cultured, and though Bothwell was intelligent, well traveled and equally well-read, there was an innate roughness and crudity to his nature.

"Ah, but they share one character trait," Blake remarked to Alyssa after explaining the new turn of events at court. "Impatience."

Prince James of Scotland was born on June 19 after a long and difficult labor that left his mother in a state of collapse.

Scotland rejoiced, Queen Elizabeth seethed with envy, and Darnley—largely ignored—was left to ponder on the role he might occupy in his wife's life now that he had fulfilled his duty.

32

Alyssa was not displeased by Beckford Lodge, though neither she nor Blake saw the house prior to purchasing it, this done for Sinclair through his lawyers. It was built of multicolored stone and had many dormers overlooking a steep wooded valley only half a league from the city; the rooftops of Edinburgh were visible on a clear day. The property had pleasant gardens within a high stone wall and stout padlocks placed on the gates. Guards circled the house day and night.

By July of 1566 Alyssa walked with scarcely a limp, and a complete return to good health brought the rosy blush back to her cheeks. Unfortunately, it also brought an increasing restlessness. She spent much time with Alex, her embroidery, and slowly wading through the books that Blake brought from Clairmont. He was able to spend several evenings a week with her and most weekends, and at such times Alyssa listened avidly to all the news from court. Aware of her near-isolation at Beckford Lodge, Sinclair shared his experiences generously and took great pains to make her understand the convolutions and nuances simmering about Holyrood.

The Queen was more popular than ever with the common people since the birth of Prince James, but the strain of the year she had just lived through plus her husband's scandalous behavior had taken a delayed toll on her nerves. "All agree that something must be done about Darnley and again the question of a divorce has been raised. The trouble is that such things take so long—as I well know—and there are those about the Queen who cannot bear the thought of the situation dragging on."

"Such as Bothwell?"

Blake nodded. "He above all others."

"Nevertheless there is nothing else that can be done."

Shortly after their return to Edinburgh, Sinclair ran into Simon Ogilvy at Holyrood. The two men came face to face in a narrow corridor off the audience chamber. "I think you have something that belongs to me, my lord," Simon growled, his grey eyes cold as ice. "And you would do well to return it."

Blake grabbed him by the shoulder and thrust him through the nearest door into a small storage room, kicking it closed behind them. Wrath blazed in the Chief's eyes as he advanced on the blond knight and forced him back against the wainscotting. Striking the wall over Simon's head with a clenched fist and using his arm to block all means of escape, he said, "Listen to me, knave, and harken well. What I have belongs to *me* and always has, and the day you are rash enough to forget it is the day you will die! So for the sake of your own miserable health, forget this folly that I have stolen something that you never owned in the first place—regardless of the words babbled over you by some preacher. The lady and I made our own vows long before, which makes any exchanged with you invalid."

Angry as he was, Ogilvy hesitated to betray it. He saw murder in Sinclair's eyes and sensed that any untoward action from him might be to invite sudden death. He could almost taste Sinclair's urge to kill him at that moment.

With a snort of disgust Blake hurled him into a stack of boxes, and by the time Simon extricated himself and rose shakily to his feet the room was empty. As he rearranged his clothing and smoothed down his hair, Ogilvy burned for revenge. But Magdalen was right, he thought judiciously. It must be done in such a way that neither of them would be suspected.

To spare Alyssa anxiety, Blake never told her about his encounter with her husband, but there was no way he could avoid relating the outcome of his inquiries as to her chances of obtaining a divorce. As both had feared, the answer was negative. Ogilvy, in the eyes of the law, had fulfilled his husbandly duties by providing her with a home, sustenance and support. Most damaging of all was the fact that *she* had left *him*. That Alyssa had been driven to do so out of self-preservation interested the law not at all, particularly when her charges against Simon could never be proven.

"Put him out of your mind," Blake said forcefully. "You are free of him now and will remain so."

Their only visitors were Lizette and Jason, but at first this mattered little. Beckford Lodge was their home. They delighted in the privacy and enjoyment of their son, and for months it was enough. Lying in her lover's arms, Alyssa could think of nowhere else she would rather be. Those first few weeks at Beckford it was easy for her to pretend that the near-idyllic life they were leading together would continue indefinitely, since both of them wished it so much.

Then in October the Queen fell desperately ill, so ill that her doctors feared she might not survive. After a brief visit to her bedside, Darnley returned to his own pursuits of hawking and wenching, so much so that his behavior was now known to commoner and noble alike. Again Mary's ministers gathered to discuss a situation they could no longer brush aside, particularly as the Queen's doctors laid the blame for much of the monarch's health problems on the actions of her husband. First they tried to talk to Darnley with a view to settling their differences, but the King sneered contemptuously at the lords gathered together for the sole purpose of trying to salvage the marriage, and without a word stalked haughtily out of the room.

The newly reinstated Maitland turned to Blake and commented angrily, "If he refuses to bend, then mayhap he must break."

A proposition was put to the Queen when she slowly recovered from her illness. If she would only agree to pardon Lindsay, Morton and the others involved in David Riccio's murder, the lords would all band together to support her in finding a way for her to obtain a divorce.

When Mary reluctantly gave her consent, a meeting was scheduled to take place at Craigmiller. All her ministers were required to attend.

For several weeks Sinclair had been compelled to spend more time at Holyrood and less at Beckford Lodge. Alyssa understood, but understanding did not make her loneliness any easier to bear. She could spend only so much time with Alex, with her reading and embroidery. As autumn turned to winter, on long evenings sitting alone before the hall fire, she had more time to think. For all Blake's assurances, fear of Simon nagged at the back of her mind. She brooded about Sinclair's own divorce and what would happen once he was free. Though she tried to resign herself to the loss of her birthright, the wrong she had been done by Lady Magdalen simmered like a cauldron of acid deep inside her, pushed to the back of her mind but never able to be forgotten.

Sometimes she threw open the lid of her coffers and gazed at the beautiful gowns Sinclair had given her. In her jewel case lay many valuable gems against their nest of rich black velvet. Blake—and occasionally Lizette and Jason— were the only ones who ever saw her wearing this finery, the latter the only guests entertained in her house, perhaps the only kin of Blake's who would *ever* condescend to visit them at Beckford Lodge. As the weeks went by, Alyssa wondered if Blake regretted the lack of hospitality in the home where he now spent most of his spare time. Whenever conversation lagged or he seemed restless or preoccupied, the fear would gnaw at her mind. Even the closest of couples, she realized, needed outside stimulation to enrich their lives, and while Blake had his work at court, she—shut away like a pampered prisoner behind the high walls of Beckford—had nothing.

What if he grew bored with her, a state that signaled the beginning of the end of most relationships such as theirs? Worse, she was beginning to grow bored with herself!

Wyatt protested vigorously when Alyssa announced her intention of paying a visit to Elmwood, the city home of Luke and Nan MacKellar, but Alyssa was adamant. She remembered Luke MacKellar's kindly interest when they had met at Seton Castle, even though he obviously understood her position in Sinclair's life, and thought often of the invitation he had extended to her to visit their home. There was a danger in accepting such an offer if Lady Magdalen ever got wind of her trying to forge a connection to her family, but she had allowed the countess to dictate the direction of her life for far too long.

Dressed in her best green velvet riding habit lavishly trimmed with miniver, Alyssa set off with her escort for Edinburgh in a mood of determination and defiance.

Nan MacKellar, normally affable and easygoing, marched around the kitchen of Elmwood finding fault with the preparations for supper. The meat was too stringy, the sauce too flat, and the cream for the strawberry tarts seemed already slightly sour.

The servants bore her complaints stoically, aware of the reason for their mistress's disgruntlement. She was like this whenever Lady Magdalen came for supper. They eyed Nan's stout little body encased in a new crimson silk gown, a far more fashionable—and uncomfortable—creation than anything they had seen her in previously, and sympathized. They had heard that the countess was dissatisfied with their rustic attire and had ordered them to dress in a manner more suitable for life at court. Nan's plump cheeks were mottled with indignation as she fretted and fumed over the menu, certain that that too would not meet with approval in the eyes of their esteemed guest.

Nan was startled when a footman appeared in the kitchen to announce that she had an unexpected visitor. "Lady Ogilvy awaits speech with you in the hall, my lady."

The moment Nan bustled into the hall, Alyssa remembered seeing her at Holyrood the night of the court ball. "Aye," the older woman chuckled, "that was a wondrous evening. Marry, but you, my dear, cast all the other ladies in the shade!" She examined Alyssa with frank interest, recalling her husband telling her that the beautiful Lady Ogilvy had become the mistress of the Earl of Belrose. Further, that she had borne him a son.

Her first interest in Alyssa was revived and she fairly crackled with curiosity. Observing her at close hand, Nan was more than ever convinced that she had some distant connection to the MacKellars.

They sat down on either side of the blazing hall fire while a servant brought them each a glass of claret. Alyssa had already thought up an ostensible reason for her visit. "I understand that you are involved in the Hospice Fund, and I would like to offer my support. I—I hope I haven't inconvenienced you by stopping by—"

"Nay, nay, lass, I'm delighted," Nan assured her warmly, leaning forward to pat her hand. "And believe me, we can use all the support we can get. Do you know that there are those in this city—wealthy folks—unwilling to share as much as a crust of bread with the poor?" She didn't add that her haughty sister-in-law was one of them.

For a little while they talked about the recently formed charitable organization and the assistance it had already been able to provide in the way of a soup kitchen set up in one of the churches as well as emergency medical attention for the most needy. It was Nan herself who brought the conversation around to more personal matters by inquiring with a smile, "And do your folks visit ye often here?"

Alyssa hesitated only a second, then replied boldly, "I have no real family, unfortunately. I was raised by an elderly woman in Lochmore, brought to her late one winter's night by a masked rider. He gave her some gold and ordered her to raise me as her granddaughter, but . . . my true parents remain a mystery."

Nan was taken aback by this response to her polite inquiry and stared at Alyssa doubtfully, then broke into a cheery laugh. "Och, but ye do spin a fetching tale, Lady Ogilvy! But I assure ye, my dear, that my intention was not to pry."

Now was the time to pull back from the rash step she had taken; to slam the lid on the past and join her laughter to Nan's, passing it off as a joke. Something propelled her forward. "I was not jesting, my lady. The story is true enough."

The older woman sobered. "Then ye were fostered out. Aye . . . 'tis a common enough practice, one I don't hold with, mind ye. Now, if I'd had a bairn . . ." She broke off and waved the thought away, thinking that she had *not* had a bairn and should have been resigned to her childless condition long since. "And ye have no idea who or where ye came from?"

Alyssa hesitated. She could feel her face burning with excitement and her heart clamoring madly in her chest. The hand holding the wineglass trembled as Davie Weir's warning shrieked in her mind, "Don't think o' trying to prove your claim. It would be impossible . . . and dangerous." The Wier brothers had died because of their connection to her past. Their mother had also perished. And though she was drawn to trust the motherly Nan MacKellar as she had her kindly husband, still . . . they were kin to the woman who had brought about her ruin.

Now Nan was gazing at her curiously, perhaps sensing her inner turmoil. "I—supposedly they are a well-known family in Scotland," Alyssa said. It was as if another identity had taken over and spoken the words her conscious mind feared to utter.

Nan sat back in her chair, in her own way as agitated as her guest. From the moment she had first laid eyes on the enchanting Lady Ogilvy, she had sensed that she was linked in some way to her husband's family. The resemblance to the MacKellars was too pronounced to ignore. She thought of Luke's brothers, all dedicated wenchers in their youth—as some still were in middle age!—and was positive now that Alyssa was one of their bastards—mayhap even one of Luke's! "How . . . how old are ye, my dear?" she inquired unsteadily, wondering if her fondest prayer was about to be answered, for a bastard child was vastly better than none at all.

Alyssa was almost light-headed with tension. "I know I was born during the battle of Ancrum Moor in 1545, though the exact date remains uncertain—"

"Ancrum Moor!" All thought of bastard offspring was blasted from Nan's mind as her memory carried her back more than twenty-one years to a day when Lord Angus had bid farewell to his pregnant young wife and ridden off to battle at the head of his men. She had not been present at Cumbray Castle when Alicia's babe had been born, but the servants had whispered of dark deeds carried out that night—before they had been mysteriously silenced.

It was several moments before either woman became aware of the footman standing in the doorway. Coughing discreetly to get their attention, Jennings announced, "Lady Magdalen and her daughter are just arriving, madam."

Alyssa sprang to her feet, color draining from her face. Seizing her astonished hostess's arm, she asked, "Is there another way out of the house?"

"Lass . . . !" A hundred questions rose in the older woman's eyes.

Alyssa squeezed her arm frantically. "Please! I—I have no desire to meet the lady."

Nan could taste her fear and nodded briskly, thinking that she was not the only one who avoided Magdalen when they could. She led her out of the hall and in the direction of a door at the end of the corridor, then held her back for a moment. Looking squarely into the younger woman's eyes, she said, "We must meet again soon. You and I have much to talk about, methinks."

Alyssa outrode even Wyatt on the way back to Beckford Lodge, the cold wind off the sea drying the sweat under her clothes, her heart pounding so hard she could scarcely draw a deep breath. For once she was glad of the long hours Blake spent at Holyrood, and once they reached the house she ran directly to her room and threw herself across the bed. She had set something in motion today and, afraid as she was, could not pull back now, nor would the woman locked away inside her for so long permit it. The time had come to get to know that woman, and, once sure of her, introduce her to Sinclair. Then for good or ill the sham existence she had known from birth would be over. And she would finally be at peace with herself.

Luke MacKellar rubbed a hand wearily across his face as he listened to his wife babble excitedly about Lady Ogilvy's visit and the young woman's mad flight when the countess was announced. Luke nodded now and then and tried to pay attention. He had had a long, annoying day at court and an even more annoying evening in the arrogant Magdalen's company. Now he longed for nothing more than to put his head on the pillow and drift into blissful sleep and, hopefully, dream pleasant dreams about being back on his country estate.

Nan bent over him as they lay together in bed and shook

...m by the shoulder. "Can we not at least look into it, sweeting?" she begged. "You must admit that her background is intriguing."

"And no doubt concocted to obscure her humble beginnings."

"She was born at the time of Ancrum Moor," Nan persisted. "Luke, what if she's really your own brother's child?"

"Nonsense!" he laughed, though not unkindly, conscious that Nan had always harbored a certain amount of guilt about Alicia, feeling they should have stood up for her more against her cunning predecessor. To please her he said, "I promise to make inquiries, but don't get your hopes up, henny, for I'll wager you're destined to be disappointed."

MacKellar had more trouble falling asleep than he imagined. He blamed it on his irritating day at Holyrood and then coming home to face the likes of Magdalen. Was it any wonder he sought repose in vain?

Thinking of the countess brought Simon Ogilvy to mind, and Luke recalled that they were cousins. And Simon Ogilvy was wed to the fair Alyssa, a marriage that had astounded everyone at court. It seemed incredible that the penniless Sir Simon would think to wed an equally penniless wife, one with neither dower nor title to bring increase to his house.

Odd, thought Luke as he shifted restlessly in bed, and even more odd that Ogilvy had suddenly seemed flush with coin immediately after this unlikely union. While visiting his sick brother Thomas recently, Luke had arrived at Cumbray Court just as Sir Simon rode away from the house, yet Thomas had made no mention of their visitor, leading Luke to believe that the knight had stopped by to see Magdalen in private. Strange, he reflected, when he had heard that there was bad blood between them.

What had happened between Lady Ogilvy and her husband to drive her into the arms of Blake Sinclair? And why had she fled their home earlier today minutes before Magdalen's arrival?

Aye, he thought with more interest, it might indeed bear looking into, though in truth there were few servants at Cumbray Castle today who went back to the time of Ancrum

Moor, and servants were always the best source of information, if they could be persuaded to talk.

Blake did not return to the house that night. He had been detained at Holyrood for the past five days, involved in arranging the upcoming Council Meeting at Craigmiller, when they would discuss the Queen's divorce.

Alyssa lay awake in the huge bed, her eyes on a shaft of moonlight slanting through the window, trying to decipher a curious change she felt in herself. She was still lonely without Sinclair and still very conscious of inhabiting a backwater of his life, and afraid too of the action she had taken that day, but mixed in with these emotions was a spicy splash of elation, the satisfaction of having done something positive for her own life. It was an intoxicating feeling, one that transcended fear, and something she must do on her own.

After a long time Alyssa closed her eyes and dreamed of the day when she would go to her lover, not as Isa Dunne's granddaughter or Simon Ogilvy's wife, or even Blake Sinclair's low-born mistress, but as Alyssa MacKellar, his equal.

Alyssa awoke just after five in the morning with a gnawing pain in her back which she blamed on her rough ride back from Elmwood. It was only when she threw back the covers and swung her legs over the side of the bed that she saw the blood on the sheets.

Her maid took one knowing look and sent a stable lad galloping into the village for a midwife.

Late that night Alyssa again lay alone in bed, wan and exhausted, weeping for the child she hadn't even known she was carrying, convinced that this was God's way of punishing them for the sinful life they were leading. She was weak from loss of blood and sank down into a deep well of depression, in sharp contrast to her mood of the previous evening. Once again, she brooded, fate had stepped in to make a mockery of her plans, to scorn her dreams, thwart her chances of seeing Nan MacKellar in the near future.

By the time Blake rushed into the house the following morning he found Alyssa white and remote, gazing blankly at the wall with hot, dry eyes that alarmed him far more than any outburst of hysteria. After the village doctor had examined her, Sinclair took her in his arms, assuring her that no permanent damage had been done. "With rest and plenty of good red meat you will soon recover, my love." Brushing the long red/gold hair back from her pale forehead, he whispered, "Alex will yet have a brother or sister, never fear—"

Alyssa shook her head and burst into tears.

"Let her be, m'lord," advised the midwife. "Women are oft like that when they lose a babe. It will pass once she rests awhile and regains her strength."

Sinclair paced the floor, raking fingers through his hair. "Why won't she speak to me? I like not this—this distance."

"Though she has no heart to respond, she kens you are there, sir, and that is enough for now."

There was no question of him going to the meeting at Craigmiller under the circumstances, and Blake proposed to send Jason—his heir—in his place. His uncle Harry Sinclair objected strenuously. "Are you out of your mind! You know the importance of this meeting; that they need every sane voice they can get." His florid face darkened with anger. "The Queen will expect your presence, and because of your *mistress*"—he spat the word—"you would put personal matters ahead of the crown!"

"I have lost a child," Blake reminded him grimly, "and the mother of that child is ill." His voice rose. "I will not leave her, crown or no crown!"

The tall, heavy-set nobleman sputtered, "Then you are indeed a fool, for Her Grace will not forget this slight, nor will her brother Moray!" And he stomped out of the room.

Jason left for Craigmiller the following morning.

Alyssa's depression hung on, made worse by a sense of frustration, and try as she might, she could not seem to shake it—until the day Blake carried Alexander to her chamber just before the noon meal and craftily set him down on her bed with the remark, "He has missed you of late . . . just as I have."

The eleven-month-old baby gave her a winsome smile, displaying a brand new tooth, and Alyssa felt the cold lump lying like granite in her chest begin to loosen and melt. With a low sob she gathered her son into her arms and hugged him fiercely, thinking that he was growing more like his father every day and, as he wriggled to get out of her rather stifling embrace, already showed the same energy and vigor. Burying her face in his soft, dark curls, she was reminded that the same God who had seen fit to take their latest baby away had also given them Alex, a child to be proud of and surely proof that their love was not looked on with total disfavor.

Blake watched her closely. "I thought we might all dine together. Hopefully he won't make too much mess."

Their eyes met above the baby's glossy curls, and she saw in Sinclair's face that he too had suffered from this loss and longed to share her grief, even as he tried to share every other aspect of his life with her. She had been selfish! she thought with a pang of shame, and rarely considered how much their relationship cost *him*, nor all he had done and risked, both privately and professionally, to make her happy.

Wordlessly Alyssa held up a hand to him, her eyes brimming with tears of love and contrition, as firmly committed to this love as she had ever been, and as ready to accept the pain along with the ecstasy.

Blake bent swiftly and kissed her on the lips, sparking the fire that had died down to a dank ember under the weight of guilt and fear of divine retribution. He caught her pale, tear-streaked face in his hand and looked deep in her eyes. "I love you, my darling, and together we must put this sadness behind us and not allow it to cloud the future, nor read dark meaning into the loss."

Alyssa smiled shakily. "You must have read my mind."

He sat down on the side of the bed and slipped an arm around her shoulders while Alex busied himself by pulling apart the silken tassels tying back the bed curtains. "When a man and woman are as close as we are, they can often accurately gauge the workings of each other's minds." He grinned suddenly, a flash of white against his strong, dark face, the old mischief leaping up in his eyes. "Sometimes that is good, but at other times . . . most inconvenient."

"What have you been up to at court, my lord?" Catching his mood, Alyssa pretended suspicion.

He waved airily, "Oh, wenching and dicing and all the usual pastimes. You know that courtiers have naught better to do."

Alyssa's smile faltered, even as she knew he was joking. Blake laughed and his eyes grew lazy, smoldering over her shoulders and fastening on her partially exposed breasts rising like luminous white globes from the flimsy material of her bedgown. In a swift movement that brought a gasp to her lips he brushed the material aside, bent his head and kissed each rosy peak, the tugging heat of his mouth wrenching her back from the cold world she had been inhabiting for the past two weeks. With a sob of a different kind, Alyssa clutched him to her, her fingers in the thick black hair, her cool flesh straining against the vibrant warmth of his. "Alex . . ." she whispered. "He must not see this."

Sinclair hid a smile as he felt her response to his touch, thankful that the crisis was over.

Blake never learned of her visit to the MacKellars, overshadowed as it was by the miscarriage. Wyatt forgot to mention it, much to his mistress's relief.

With Blake by her side, Alyssa recovered quickly. They walked in the garden, often with their son, and rode along the seashore when she felt strong enough to ride. At Sinclair's insistence they slept apart. "Because," he grinned wickedly, "I don't trust you to remember you are a sick woman."

"You can at least hold me in your arms!" Alyssa protested, her eyes moving over the broad shoulders and flicking to the muscular thighs boldly outlined by the tan riding breeches.

"Nay, I fear you might take advantage." His expression was falsely grave, even as his eyes teased. "We both know you are a hot-blooded, lusty creature, while I am but a helpless slave of your passion."

Alyssa slapped him, none too gently, her senses beginning to rebel against the enforced abstinence and his amazing control, even while aware that he denied himself out of concern for her health.

"Very noble!" she snapped, her green eyes sparking, embarrassed at revealing how much she needed him.

Sinclair swept her a low bow. "Thank you, my lady, and rest assured that I will continue to strive to protect you from your, ah . . . more earthy instincts."

Their very nearness became sweet torture for Alyssa, her mind tormented by vivid images of their more fiery encounters. It was a period of rediscovery when she became acutely, achingly aware all over again of the things that had first attracted her to Sinclair. At table she would study his strong, rather aquiline profile that made her think of the predatory eagle and had always given him a hint of ruthlessness, a side of him he had never permitted her to see. She gazed at the dark olive skin and recalled the firm, smooth feel of it under her fingers. Again and again, as they walked on the shore or sat together over a game of chess, Alyssa felt her eyes drawn to the thin, sensuous mouth that so blissfully ravished her with kisses, to the broad, tanned hands that could stir her body to such frantic desire. He could not cross a room but her eyes darted after him, hungrily moving over the tautness of his hips, the muscular thighs, until with an inward groan of frustration she looked hastily away.

Alyssa, hoping to distract herself, took to exploring the more distant nooks and crannies of the house, spending long hours in the sprawling attic examining furniture and other relics from a bygone age. As she was returning from such an exploration one late afternoon, Blake met her on the stairs. Grinning, he reached to pluck a cobweb from her hair, remarking, "Are you trying to avoid me, my lady, or mayhap something within yourself?"

She felt a sudden flash of anger. "Don't flatter yourself, sir! I can find much at Beckford Lodge to interest me other than your noble self."

His smile faded but the knowing gleam remained in his eyes. Tossing her head, Alyssa flounced past him, angry at herself much more than with him. But she needed the physical reassurance of his love as balm to soothe the underlying uncertainty of her position, even as she resented this need and the eternal insecurity of her situation. No matter how often he confessed his love for her, the doubts lingered on, the question of what he would do once finally free of Elizabeth.

Blake never talked about it, and his very silence on the subject struck Alyssa as ominous. She understood only too well the thinking of his family, that they resented the time and attention he gave to a mere mistress—and a low-born one at that.

Or so they thought.

Oh, the sweet satisfaction of being able to hurl the truth in their haughty faces, Alyssa fumed inwardly, her indignation focused on Lord Harry Sinclair, a man who steadfastly refused to set foot in Beckford Lodge or make the acquaintance of his little grandnephew Alexander. Tossing and turning in bed at night, Alyssa wondered over and over how Sinclair himself would react to such a revelation, assuming the day ever came when she could prove who she really was. Would he be quite as reluctant *then* to discuss his future plans? she mused peevishly. More to the point, could she be truly happy with a man who married her, not for herself, but for what she stood for?

As the December weather grew cold and blustery, so did the raw sexual tension build to explosive proportions between the man and woman forced to spend most of their time shut up inside the house. Her growing doubts made her irritable, and inevitably sharp words were exchanged. Blake took to spending hours at a time closed up in his study. Alyssa, when not with Alex, continued her detailed examination of the house, particularly the interesting contents of the attic.

One stormy afternoon found her in the attic poring over the contents of an ancient coffer, the candle propped on a shelf beside her flickering in the draft blowing in from the sea. An early dusk had fallen, and the candle did little to chase away the heavy shadows encroaching in all directions.

On the floor beside Alyssa lay a pile of quilts, each of which told a story, wrought in pictorial squares, detailing events in the lives of the former occupants of the house. Births, marriages and deaths were vividly set down in silk thread that must once have been bright and colorful but which had faded with time. She saw that a Preston son had gone to sea, been taken captive by pirates, but escaped by jumping overboard and swimming to an island inhabited by savages. Another Preston, she saw, had been hanged, and yet a third knighted by what appeared to be a former King.

Lifting a new quilt from the trunk and smoothing it on the floor, Alyssa was startled to see depicted in a center panel a dark-haired woman tied to a stake, flames leaping up all around her, an expression of agony on her face. Underneath this horrifying picture was the brief inscription worked in dark red silk: Lady Glamis. The next panel showed a ghostly figure floating over the battlements of a great castle, obviously meant to portray the same woman returning to haunt those who had condemned her to such a fate.

Alyssa dropped the quilt and spun around at a sound from the door, a gasp escaping her parted lips when through the gloom she spied a blob of white where none had been a short time before. The eerie silence of the attic rushed in on her as she jumped nervously to her feet, straining hard to see through the cobwebs and dust motes eternally waving in the musty air.

"You . . . !" she whispered as Sinclair moved away from where he had been lounging against the door, watching her in some amusement as she bent intently over the quilt. He was dressed casually in form-fitting tan riding breeches and an open-neck white shirt with loose, flowing sleeves, and in the semidarkness of the attic his skin looked dark as bronze, ruddy from the hours he had spent outdoors, hours which she had shared until recently.

Alyssa raised a hand involuntarily to her throat as he crossed the distance that separated them in his long, easy stride, bringing with him a salty tang of the sea. He stopped before her, the candle at his back, the hard muscles of his shoulders and arms outlined in fire.

"You frightened me," Alyssa accused, unreasonably angry and not sure why. "How long were you spying on me from the door?"

Sinclair regarded her steadily without answering, his eyes moving lazily from the flush on her cheeks to the feverish shine in her eyes to the velvety-soft cleft between her breasts. Then he glanced down at the quilts piled about the floor. "So . . . ," he drawled, "this is how you amuse yourself while avoiding my company." He stooped and picked up the quilt she had just been studying, glancing from the embroidered picture of the unfortunate Lady Glamis to Alyssa's sullen face. "Do you know this story?" he asked gravely.

"How could I?" she retorted. "I'm only an ignorant village wench!"

33

A tense silence fell between them. The musty air in the attic was suddenly stifling and thunderous. Into the quiet they heard violent gusts of wind battering the house and the sound of the waves lashing the rocks at the bottom of the nearby cliffs, a turbulent force that Alyssa felt echoing in her own heart.

For a second or two his shadowy face was like that of a stranger, the line of his jaw taut, his mouth drawn into a hard line. He inhaled deeply, even as a pulse throbbed to life at the side of his jaw, and after a long pause he went on as if she hadn't spoken. "The lady was Janet Douglas, wife of the Lord of Glamis Castle, said by her enemies to be a witch and to have used sorcery to try to kill our present Queen's father, James V."

Alyssa gazed back at him stonily, clenching her teeth to keep from screaming, What do I care about Janet Douglas? I want to talk about us! I want to discuss our future together—if we *have* a future together!

Sinclair propped a booted foot on a nearby coffer and continued relentlessly, as if immune to the chaos churning inside her, "This was in 1537, and Janet was the great beauty of her day from all accounts, also the wife of a powerful nobleman. But, alas, nothing could save her. She was convicted and burned at the stake, wrongly as it turned out later when William Lyon, her chief accuser, confessed to having lied." His voice dropped eerily. "Now her ghost is said to haunt Glamis Castle every year on the anniversary of her death." He glanced around the gloomy spaces under the eaves. "This house too is rumored to have its ghost. I wonder that you'd risk coming here alone."

The teasing cadence of his voice angered her. "No doubt your uncle would relish accusing *me* of witchcraft, of keeping you bound to me by sorcery, and would gladly see me burned at the stake!"

Blake grinned, candlelight reflected in his eyes. "He may be right. I've long thought of you as an enchantress."

Exasperated, she stamped her foot, sparks flying from her eyes, and struggled in vain against the urge to goad some sort of admission from him, even while aware that she was venturing onto dangerous ground and might hear something that would devastate her.

"Why must you always jest when I would be serious?"

He put his arms behind his head and leaned back against the wall, the very picture of ease and relaxation while Alyssa stood before him with her hands on her hips, tension in every line of her body. He studied that body leisurely for a moment before answering casually, "When a man must deal with serious matters at work, he looks forward to lightness and pleasant diversion at home—"

"Pleasant diversion! Is that all I mean to you?" And before he could answer, she went on, "Aye, I can see that it is! We discuss everything and everyone while avoiding the subject most important to us—ourselves!" Tears spattered from her eyes and splashed down her cheeks. "D-doubtlessly you think it a waste of time—or unnecessary—to speak frankly to me—"

In a swift movement that caught her by surprise, Sinclair grabbed her by the wrist and tumbled her down upon the stack of quilts beside him, pinning her there by throwing a leg over her hips and silencing her with a bruising kiss. As she thrashed beneath him and tried to jerk her head away, he sank long fingers into her hair, tightening his grasp until he rendered her immobile, then with his tongue forced her lips to part. As he slowly teased the sweet interior of her mouth, Alyssa lay rigid for a moment, fighting not to respond, even as every cell of her body cried out for the hard heat of his now pressing urgently against her.

Yet still Alyssa made the pretense of rejecting his lovemaking, gasping, "Nay . . . ! If you think this will solve everything then . . . then you are wrong! I want to talk—"

"You want this!" He caught the neck of her gown and ripped it to the waist, a burning hand covering her breast, his lips and tongue caressing a nipple until a shuddering thrill ran through her bringing with it a desire for more. Yet she sought to push his hands away as he tore the clothes from her body, then held her down with elbow and knee as his own garments dropped to the floor. Catching her flailing arms by the wrists, he held them above her head with one hand while with the other began a slow and relentless exploration of her body.

He knew her too well. As his skilled hands sought and found, as his lips and tongue teased and caressed, Alyssa sobbed aloud in a kind of helpless agony as she felt all resistance melt away. Suddenly her fingers were in his hair, her mouth raised breathlessly to his, her limbs arching to meet the hardness of his thighs even as he whispered in her ear, "Do you still want to talk?"

Sinclair's voice seemed to come from a great distance, from somewhere beyond the blood pounding in her ears, the mad clamoring of her heart, the sweet violence of their lovemaking merging with that of the storm raging about the house. There was little tenderness in their coming together, nor did Alyssa crave tenderness at first. As Blake rose and fell above her, his tawny flesh glistening with sweat in the candlelight, the ghosts in the attic were the only witnesses to the pent-up passion that sought many directions for release.

"Wanton!" he breathed against her ear afterwards. "A man can only withstand so much. Now I must suffer the hard edge of the good doctor's tongue, beast that I am."

Alyssa grinned, raising herself on an elbow, soft masses of dark gold tresses spilling over her shoulders and breasts to touch the curly dark mat on his chest. "Do I seem sick to you, sir?"

"Aye—sick of waiting!" he replied with a chuckle, brushing aside the curls obscuring her breasts so that he might feast his eyes upon their firm white perfection. Cupping one in his hand and lightly stroking the nipple with his thumb, he gave her a smoldering look from under his brows. "I should leave you now before . . . before too much damage is done."

"Stay!" It was a cry from the heart, and unconsciously Alyssa caught his arm, blushing as he studied her with sudden gravity through eyes that saw far too much. "I'm as fit as a fiddle," she rushed on lightly with a brittle little laugh that she hoped would mask her underlying concern. "You know I don't break so easily."

Sinclair continued to examine her soberly. "What are you so afraid of, Alyssa?" His deep voice seemed to rise from a well, echoing in the dark chambers of her heart, touching specters that she tried to keep buried there. Now, perversely, *she* was the one reluctant to confront them; loath to look into the future, afraid of what she might hear. A little while ago in a fit of bravado she had accused Blake of taking refuge in frivolity to avoid serious discussions. Now that he seemed deadly serious as he awaited her answer, Alyssa was terrified.

She loved him so desperately, too completely to bear the thought of sharing him with another woman. He had been finished with Elizabeth—whom he readily admitted he had never loved—before she came back into his life. Elizabeth had had nothing to do with *them*. She belonged to Sinclair's past. But a new wife—

"Darling"—Blake took her hand—"what troubles you?"

"Tomorrow!" she blurted, fighting tears. "Tomorrow troubles me." Alyssa swallowed hard, her pride shrinking as she saw him raise a dark eyebrow quizzically, and above all dreaded to glimpse pity in his eyes. It was this possibility that helped her control the emotion that threatened to boil over in a flood of humiliating tears. If she was destined to suffer because of this love for him, then she was determined that he would not witness it.

Alyssa raised her head and forced herself to meet his eyes; to withstand whatever she saw there. She reminded herself that this was the moment she had waited for—however nervously —for four and a half years. Through all the difficulties of those years, even when she thought she had lost him, she had never ceased to love him, and never would, but neither would she share him with another woman.

Her body grew taut and still, her hands clenched into fists at her side, but she kept her eyes fixed searchingly on his. "Your family resent my place in your life," she began stiltedly, her heart fluttering. "I—I know they feel you could be making better use of your time in deciding on Elizabeth's replacement."

Alyssa stopped, every nerve in her body shrieking, her throat too constricted with dread to continue.

Blake gave her a penetrating sidelong glance that seemed to pierce her soul. He moved away slightly, shifting position to prop his back against the wall. He smiled faintly. "Don't lump my entire family in with Uncle Harry, a man who follows the old rules out of habit more than anything else. In his bluff, misguided way he imagines he's doing his best for me. I may listen—but in the end I make my own decisions."

They looked at each other while the candle flickered down to a nub. Sitting apart from him, longing for the comfort of his arms around her, Alyssa had never felt so totally naked in her life. Her hand reached out for the security of a quilt, then drew back as if she had been stung. She could feel him reading her eyes, her expression, with the easy wisdom he had gleaned through the years.

"Jason doesn't resent you," he pointed out gently. "Nor Lizzie or Adam or most of the others. And as to how they think I should best spend my time, they may think what they will. I'm here with you, Alyssa," he went on forcefully, his face suddenly harsh, his eyes intense, "because I would rather be here than anywhere else. This should be obvious after all this time. Nor can I think of replacing a wife I'm still tied to by marriage, if not by desire, shunting one out and another in like so many brood mares!"

"Why . . . why are you so angry?"

Blake was about to reply when they heard the clatter of riders turn into the courtyard far below. It was his cousin Jason returned from Craigmiller to report that he had been barred from the meeting and Sinclair severely criticized for not appearing. Though not allowed into the council itself, Jason had stayed at the castle to learn all he could from servants and retainers, who rarely missed anything that went on.

"It seems that some sort of document was drawn up by Sir James Balfour and signed by those in attendance, including Maitland, Bothwell, Argyll and others," he said after he had gulped down a long draught of ale. "This bond was to the effect that steps were to be taken to remove Darnley from power on the grounds that he debased the honor done to him and daily embarrasses the Queen with his conduct."

Blake threw him a startled look, part of his mind still lingering in the attic where he had taken a hasty departure from Alyssa when Jason was announced. "Treason!"

"Aye," the younger man nodded grimly, "it would seem so, and, to be sure, he has given enough cause." Jason sought to describe the strange aura of secrecy he had found at the castle, wondering aloud if he might have imagined it. "The Queen seems to have made it clear that whatever was decided must have the endorsement of Parliament, though I think none wish delay, particularly Bothwell. You can be sure that Darnley will be brought speedily to trial, and that will be the end of him."

"If he lives long enough to stand trial," growled Sinclair, thinking of the nature of Bothwell, the man who now, in a sudden shift of power, stood closest to the Queen; a man with a decided penchant for taking matters into his own hands, as his past history amply demonstrated.

While the men conversed in the hall, Alyssa ordered the tub brought to her chamber and hot water for a bath. As she soaked among the perfumed suds, the last of her tension ebbed away. Blake loved her; she had never doubted that, and, calmer now, she smiled remembering his remark about brood mares, of shunting one wife out and another in, much as a country squire might restock his stable.

Nay, she mused, he was not so insensitive. And he had matured since that long-ago time at Lynnwood when he had taken so much for granted, so certain she would fall in with his plans and agree to an arrangement that he had been raised to think of as normal. This time, Alyssa was confident, he would make no hasty assumptions, any more than he would a hasty marriage—family or no family. He had learned, or so she hoped, that even a man in *his* position could not have it all.

When Alyssa joined them in the hall, bathed and glowing and radiant in a turquoise velvet gown, Jason rose swiftly and bowed, raising her hand to his lips. Smiling into the brilliant green eyes provocatively uptilted at the corners, he had no trouble at all in understanding Alyssa's long hold over his cousin, reasoning that their uncle must be blind—or mayhap jealous!

"Tell me of the meeting," she asked with great interest. "Is there to be a divorce?"

The two men exchanged a look and Jason replied carefully. "Darnley will be removed, that much is certain, with none caring to speak up for him. But the young dolt brought it on himself! His own stiff pride will be the weapon to break his back." He took another thirsty gulp from his tankard, having ridden directly back from Craigmiller through the storm without stopping for refreshment, much to the annoyance of his men who were at that moment slaking their appetites in the kitchen. Wiping his mouth carelessly with the back of his hand and looking boyish with his black hair tousled and damp around his lean Sinclair face, a face softer and less forceful than the man leaning indolently against the mantel, but alike enough to be brothers, Jason continued, "Nothing, of course, will be done about the King before Prince James is baptized. Blessed Mother, there can be no questions raised about his legitimacy!"

Alyssa nodded and looked away, her mind turning to her own fine son, and she felt the usual twist of pain in her heart whenever this touchy subject was mentioned. She had not as much as glanced at Sinclair since entering the chamber, even though acutely aware of him watching her, the unresolved outburst in the attic still heavy between them. Now Alyssa raised her head and gazed in his direction. His strong, dark face was sober, almost austere, but she saw understanding in his eyes; that he shared her regret concerning Alexander. It eased the hurt inside her, to know he suffered for this too, and unconsciously she gave him a faint, wistful smile. The change in him was instantaneous, his features softening in relief, ready to forget the painful and awkward subject she had raised above-stairs.

Aye, thought Alyssa ruefully, he would be glad to thrust it aside. Being a man used to having his commands obeyed and his desires quickly gratified, he was unused to being challenged and made to account for his actions, particularly by a woman.

She had pressured him and, typically, he had resisted with anger. Alyssa wondered if his anger had its roots in the fact that he had not come to a decision about her, aware now that there could be no easy solution.

Sleet spattered against the walls of the manor while they dined, sharp gusts of wind blowing puffs of smoke from the fireplace to give the hall a damp, peaty odor that was not unpleasant. The conversation revolved around the new difficulties rising up to confront the Queen, and Alyssa took some grim comfort in realizing that even a monarch was not immune from conflict in her love life. Indeed, she mused, was any woman?

After the meal, Jason climbed with her to the nursery to play with his nephew for a rambunctious half-hour before Alex went to bed. Next to his father, this was the man Alex most adored—but then he had contact with so few of the Sinclair men.

"Ah, he's a grand lad!" Jason draped an arm casually around her shoulders when they closed the door of the nursery behind them, adding easily as if it were the most natural thing in the world, "Alex will have fine sport with his cousins when you come to us for Christmas. Lizette is arranging an exciting mask for the children, with a fiery dragon and a giant with two heads, one evil and the other good, with a prize going to the bairn brave enough to steal up behind the monster and drape a noose over the wicked head."

Alyssa stopped, her mouth working. "Jason, we—I cannot join your Christmas revels—"

"None of that!" he protested vigorously, his arm tightening about her. "You would not deny your son much fun with his family, nor us the pleasure of your charming company?" He smiled into her eyes and went on more softly, "You will come, Alyssa, and sit on my left at the board—across from the Chief—because you are one of us and Lizette and I greatly desire you to be there."

Tears pricked her eyes. "But—"

"Courage, sweeting. You must not back away." He caught her chin in his hand and smiled encouragement. "Some among the family have never met you. Would you have them learn about you second-hand, mayhap through one less than . . . ah, favorably inclined toward you?"

Alyssa glanced away, biting her lip, quailing at the thought of having to appear at a huge family gathering where every eye would be upon her, the woman they had heard had bewitched their Chief so that he was content to live in an illicit relationship instead of forging a legal one that would bring increase to their house. Imagining those cold, condemning eyes fixed upon her, with Blake to witness her mortification, made her physically ill. Yet . . . they loved each other and, unlike many of them, had made no secret of the fact. They had not taken their pleasure furtively and by so doing imbued their love with shame. She felt no shame at loving Blake Sinclair and stood ready to defy anyone who dared consider their own life so spotless that they would try to sully it.

There was a hard gleam in her eyes when they turned back to Jason, and her voice was firm when she said, "Thank you for the invitation. I shall be delighted to accept."

Then she rose on tiptoe and kissed him on the forehead.

The two men lingered downstairs talking long into the night. In her chamber Alyssa waited, wondering if Sinclair would join her. When she heard the door open quietly in the early hours of the morning she didn't move, but Blake could tell by her breathing that she was still awake. Yet when he stretched out beside her, Alyssa didn't speak, nor as she customarily did—even instinctively while sleeping—curl happily against his chest. Sighing deeply, Blake turned his head and gazed at the faint outline of her delicate profile in the darkness. "You are upset still, Alyssa?" he inquired in a voice carefully checked of emotion. "My assurances to you in the attic were not enough?"

"You were angry, my lord—"

"Angry that you should doubt me!" he broke in harshly. "That you should make certain demands of me at a time—"

"And, doubtlessly, I have no right to make any demands at all?" she retorted hotly. "I am to remain here"—her voice cracked—"compliant and unpresuming, like a—a puppet ready to jump at your every whim for as long as it pleases you to pull the strings!" She gulped in a ragged breath, angrily ignoring the little voice in her mind warning her that she was being unfair. "Have I not a right to question where this love of ours might lead us?"

"You are not my prisoner, Alyssa," he told her quietly. "There are no bars on the windows of Beckford Lodge, nor locks on the doors. Just as I am here because I wish to be, so, I understood, were you."

His meaning was clear. He was telling her that if she truly desired to leave, he would not force her to stay. It was a stark reminder that they were there by choice; that nothing else bound them together. His cool words struck at the very root of her uncertainty, unleashing her deepest fears.

In the strained silence Alyssa became conscious of the cold in the room, the distance between them as he lay apart from her, the chunk of ice crushing the breath from her lungs. He would be prepared to let her go if she tried to force him to make a commitment. This then was where their great passion had led, much as Davie Weir had predicted long ago. Either she would accept what he could give her of himself—what he was *prepared* to give her—or remove herself from his life.

So great was her hurt that Alyssa was momentarily rendered mute. Numbly, shivering with cold, she felt him shift restlessly beside her, a hard thigh brushing her hips, a muscular arm thrown casually behind her pillow.

"Were you truly listening downstairs?" Blake asked impatiently. "Can you not comprehend the crisis looming up at Holyrood?" When she didn't reply, he went on, "You, who spend your days in tranquillity here at the manor have naught to ruffle you but private concerns, the weaving of pretty plans for the future—a future that might not exist if this country cannot be stabilized behind the Queen." He stared at her irritably in the darkness. "I have sworn to support Mary Stuart for as long as she remains in Scotland, to take up arms against her enemies should the need arise, which means that I am hardly in a position, considering the state of the country, to look very far ahead—"

"You—you think there might be fighting?" Alyssa interrupted, alarm for him overriding other concerns.

He sighed. "I like not the sound of the meeting that took

place at Craigmiller. I sense fresh intrigue hatching among the lords hovering about the Queen. Bothwell is a bold and courageous solider, but as a statesman . . . ! From what I know of him he's a man who tends to act first and think later, a character trait that some might think to make use of to Mary's detriment. Already he's made many enemies, nobles resentful of his new lofty position, and James Hepburn is no diplomat, not the type to try to win them around.

"We live in troubled times, my sweet Alyssa, when perforce we must live from day to day and seize as much happiness as we can, while we can." His arm came down about her shoulders, and very gently he drew her against the lean, hard length of his body. "I'm not angry at *you*, dear heart, but . . ." he drew in a deep breath and admitted, "there are times when I rail against the situation I've pledged myself to at Holyrood, when I must stand by and watch the Queen act in a way that can only damage her crown. Poor lady, she is tugged one way and then the other, yet . . . I'm but one voice at Holyrood and"—he chuckled dryly—"not mayhap there as often as is meet."

Because of me, thought Alyssa, and felt a sharp pang of contrition.

Sinclair bent his head and brushed her lips with his mouth. He kissed the pulse at her throat, the silken hollow of her shoulder, the marblelike fullness of her breast. With a sigh Alyssa put her arms around him, then tightened them fiercely to hold him fast to her heart as a memory came back from her childhood, her first horrified glimpse of a battlefield following a war between the clans. She could still hear the wailing of the women as they searched out husbands and sons from among the broken, mangled bodies strewn across the plain. She remembered the unnatural color of the earth, dark brick-red and damp with blood. Staring with dead eyes at the sky were the white faces of vigorous young men cut down in their prime, noblemen reduced to the same level as their men by that great equalizer—death.

Shivering, Alyssa caught the dark face of her lover between her hands. "Nothing must ever happen to you!" she cried softly, hating herself for her selfishness, her lack of understanding, even as she crushed her mouth to his and clung to the vital warmth of him while trying to shut out memory of the mourning women clinging hopelessly to the cold, rigid corpses of their loved ones.

That night Sinclair's lovemaking was infinitely tender, their union transcending the mere gratification of the flesh to a communion of spiritual ecstasy. He murmured very low, his voice husky with emotion, "And nothing must ever come between us, my love, for though you may not be *my* prisoner—I am yours, and gladly so."

Alyssa's heart swelled. Tears overflowed. She felt joyful and humble at once, and deeply ashamed of the devilish doubts that periodically rose to plague her and taint their love, vowing to give them no quarter from then on. "Would that we could return to Lynnwood," she breathed fervently, chilled by the fresh storm clouds rising on the horizon, a storm that might sweep him away from her.

"We will, darling. I look forward to that day as fiercely as you do." And with an unexpected touch of impatience and exasperation in his voice, "Pray God Her Grace can be steadied on her throne and spring of the new year finds us back in the Highlands."

Buoyed up with fresh confirmation of Sinclair's love, Alyssa determinedly prepared for the Christmas celebrations, which because of the Chief's marital situation would that year be held at Highfield. Blake presented her with exquisite bolts of ice-blue taffeta and tissue-of-gold for a new gown, and Alexander—approaching his first birthday and already walking steadily—was to have a scarlet doublet and his first white silk hose. Surely, thought his fond parents as they prepared to depart for the ride into town, he was the most handsome child in the world with his ebony ringlets surrounding plump rosy cheeks and sparkling green eyes brimming with mischief, his tall, sturdy little body already hinting of the proud physique of the man he would one day be. Blake's eyes moved from the child to the child's mother, and pride blazed in his eyes.

"You are the most beautiful woman in Scotland," he told Alyssa, meaning every word of it, for he had seen none fairer.

She laughed nervously and glanced down at her gown, a

stunning creation of cool, shimmering silk overlaid with gold as fine as gossamer, sapphires—her Christmas gift from Blake— flashing at throat and ears. "You say that with every new dress."

"I'm not thinking of the dress."

Swallowing her apprehension, Alyssa smiled at him flirtatiously from the corner of her eyes, her gaze moving from the broad shoulders encased in crimson velvet and moving down provocatively over the snowy white lace at his chest and cuffs to the shining Spanish leather of his shoes. "My lord is most handsome as well as gracious. Scarlet becomes you, as it does Alex."

He bowed, grinning, and moved behind her to drape her fur-lined cloak over her shoulders, leaning down to whisper in her ear, "Stay close to me during the revels. Sinclair men are lusty and I would not have anyone forget you belong to the Chief."

And many will not care to be reminded of that fact, my lord, Alyssa thought grimly, concealing her uneasiness with a smile; many will castigate you in private for daring to flaunt your mistress in the face of your haughty family—but if you are willing to brave it, so am I!

34

They set out with Alex and his nurse and a dozen of Sinclair's men early on the afternoon of the twenty-fourth, the horses' hooves crunching on the snow, puffy white flakes falling softly from a heavy slate-grey sky. Alyssa sat stiffly erect on her palfrey until she consciously relaxed her shoulders and fixed what she hoped was a calm smile on her face. She would not anticipate what lay ahead, but concentrated on getting through it with as much dignity as she could summon, so that Sinclair would have no cause to rue the day he had ever taken this bold step in presenting her to his family.

Church bells pealed joyously all over Edinburgh and the city blazed with candles at every window and lanterns twinkling a welcome beside every door. Tantalizing odors of roasting meat, nutmeg and cinnamon floated in the air, mingling with the peaty scent of the fires, and ruddy-cheeked pedestrians bustled about doing their last-minute shopping. Alexander stared at everything with huge, wondering eyes, pointing from the castle lit up with torches on its crag high overhead, to the brightly lit shop-fronts displaying their colorful wares, to the chestnut roaster on the corner, his brazier flaring cheerily in the snow. There was excitement in the air; even the beggars looked less doleful than usual, many with arms full and gums munching, whether because of a shamefaced generosity on the part of more prosperous citizens or through theft, Alyssa could only guess.

Her eyes met Blake's over the awestruck face of their son, who sat before Wyatt on the saddle, his head swiveling in one direction then another, shouting for them to "Look! Look!"

whenever something interesting caught his eye, which was every other minute.

Sinclair winked at her and blew her a kiss as they turned the corner and saw Highfield directly ahead of them. Dredging forth all her courage, Alyssa flashed on him a brilliant smile, one that might have been tinged with bravado. When he lifted her from the saddle, Sinclair put his face close to hers and murmured, "A yuletide to remember, my love. Our first together."

And pray it not be our last, she thought shakily, her eyes moving beyond him to the house.

The next twelve days passed in a shimmering wave of color, of sights and sounds, of smiling faces and others stiff with icy reproof. There was hearty laughter, and sly whispers, eyes that looked on her with curiosity and admiration, others with resentment and hostility. From the moment Sinclair strode arrogantly into the hall with Alyssa on his arm, his expression daring anyone—guest or family alike—to challenge her right to be there, Alyssa determined that, come what may, she would enjoy herself, that nothing would be allowed to spoil this first Christmas they celebrated together.

Over the next days, none present could honestly fault her deportment. She was beautiful, intelligent and gracious; she ignored slights and quickly charmed those who showed the slightest hint of acceptance. And by Twelfth Night the latter were in the majority. Though they might not approve of the arrangement between herself and the Chief, they found it difficult to dislike her as a person. Nor could any resist Alexander.

After the first stiff bow and muttered words of greeting, Harry Sinclair behaved as if she did not exist, his meek little wife, Sadie, compelled to follow his example. But on the afternoon of the childrens' mask, watching Alex toddle fearlessly over to the "giant" and struggle to put the rope about his neck, she cried out softly, "Oh, is he not the most darling child!"

"Hush, lady," her husband growled under his breath. "You twitter like a magpie."

But he stared hard at the boy, surprised that one so young should be so quick to ape the older children and understand what was expected of him. Nobody objected when the giant obligingly lowered his head so that Alex could encircle it with the noose. A burst of applause rang out from the adults watching the game, and the tot was pronounced the winner and presented with a toy sword.

Alex grabbed it by the hilt and swung it about as he had seen his father do, much to the amusement of the onlookers. Delighted at finding himself the center of attention, he spied a big, portly man with greying black hair and a grizzled beard, the only one in the hall who happened to be frowning at him.

Raising the sword, Alex ran to the man's chair and lunged in the direction of the rotund stomach. Taken by surprise, Harry jerked back just in time, whipped away the tiny weapon with one hand and scooped the child up with the other. Plunking Alex on his knee, he wagged an admonishing finger an inch or two from the twinkling little face, which bore an uncanny resemblance to Blake at the same age. Except for the green eyes sparkling with deviltry. *Her* eyes, he thought, and his expression again grew stern. "Methinks you are a wee rascal," he told the child, "and have scant respect for your elders."

Quick as a flash, Alex pulled his beard and wriggled out of his grasp and ran to hide behind a screen. Somebody shouted, "Concede defeat, Harry. You make poor sport for a lad who just tackled a giant."

With his lips twitching, Lord Sinclair glanced at his wife from under his brows. She quivered to control her mirth, gasping, "He's a Sinclair, my lord. What else can you expect from him?"

But he was *not* a Sinclair! In the eyes of the law he was an Ogilvy. The nobleman felt a surge of outrage that this should be so, and with a glance at the Chief, who stood watching from across the room, he could not but feel pity for Blake. Had the boy been a bastard, he might rightfully have been raised under the protection of his father, but legally he was the son of Sir Simon Ogilvy, one of the more disreputable elements at court.

Why, Harry railed inwardly, could Elizabeth not have been the mother of Blake's son! Why did the Chief continue to squander his manhood on a woman who could do nothing for Augusta, let alone give him an heir? Bigod, he fumed, this nephew of mine has lost his head as well as his heart, behaving for all the world as if she were his lawful lady with a right to stand by his side. Worse, most of those present, including many of their own family, seemed to accept the situation, if not approve of it.

This amazed and perplexed Sinclair. In my time, he thought, a man had the grace to be more discreet. As he watched Blake leaning over Alyssa's chair, the couple chuckling as if at a private joke, his mind flashed back to a time when he too had been faced with the same dilemma over the daughter of a tutor. Yet . . . he had had the fortitude to do the right thing! He had triumphed over his weakness. Aye, and proceeded to wed the silly, empty-headed Sadie, who had subsequently presented him with five daughters and a stillborn son; a woman who exasperated him more than anything, as their daughters exasperated him, caring for nothing but clothes, gossip and romantic intrigue. Had it not been for his nephew Blake, destined to be Chief, and all the joy and bright hopes he had long harbored for the boy, Harry's life might have been disappointing indeed.

Over the last few days Blake had made no secret of his anger at Harry's treatment of his paramour. *She* had caused that too, the first rift in their warm relationship, for he had been more of a father to Blake than his own cold, aloof father had been. Yet how in the name of the Blessed Mother could he be expected to honor a woman who could but damage their house, regardless of the dignity and beauty she possessed? Blake could *never* marry her.

The evening of the grand ball, his wife wheedled, "'Tis yuletide, my lord, or have you forgot the season?" And when he glowered at her, "Can you not unbend and find it in your heart to give our Chief the gift he most craves?"

"Nay," he muttered stubbornly, "he expects too much."

"You would let this destroy the love between you?"

Harry sat at table with a brooding look on his face as he gazed from under bushy brows at the glittering throng, watching the men of his family dance one after another with

Alyssa, stunning in a midnight-blue chiffon gown trimmed with silver, elegant from the top of her fiery head to the dainty silver slippers. He recalled that his nephew the Chief had haughtily ignored him for the past few days. Even Jason had been cool. A pox on her! he fretted.

Harry kept motioning a servitor to the table to refill his goblet with wine, but the merry mood that all others seemed to be enjoying evaded him. Sadie drew back, startled, when he suddenly sprang to his feet and, without pausing to think about it, strode to the high table and bowed stiffly before the woman seated across from the Chief. "May I have the honor of dancing with you, my lady?" he choked out gruffly, his face brick-red and almost grim.

Alyssa's face lit up with a brilliant smile. Harry saw the young couple exchange a quick look of relief. When he took her rather awkwardly into his arms, her supple body felt warm and fragrant, her hand firm in his, her hair silky as a babe's when it brushed his cheek. He kept his gaze fixed straight ahead as they slowly circled the room, nodding but not listening as Alyssa sought to engage him in conversation until she too fell silent and grew tense in his arms.

Alyssa glanced up at the averted face, realizing with a pang of disappointment that he had only asked her to dance for form's sake and to appease the wrath of his nephew, and for the first time that week she felt her constraint threaten to snap. Alyssa surprised herself as well as the nobleman by saying coldly, "You need not have condescended to recognize me, my lord, for we deceive no one by dancing like this."

His eyes jumped to the high table where he saw Blake watching them grimly.

Now Harry steeled himself to look into her face, even lovelier at close range than he had imagined. No ointments or powders masked flaws in that white skin, nor did the blush on her cheeks come from a box, such as he had seen scattered across his wife's and daughters' dressing tables. The brilliant green eyes, with their tangle of long dark lashes, held his steadily. No shrinking violet this! he thought, a touch of admiration mingling with his resentment. Aloud he said, "I would wonder that you could be so bold."

"Love makes one bold, sir! Have *you* ever known true love, my lord?"

He snorted, his dark eyes raking over her face as if he would have liked to shred the white flesh. "If you truly loved my nephew you would not demean him thus."

Her eyes flared with anger. "Blake does not consider our love demeaning or he would not have brought me here, but what can you know of a man's heart having none of your own!"

They were passing an archway leading into a corridor running from the front to the rear of the house. Instead of turning, Sinclair propelled her straight ahead and finally released her in the passageway in the shadow of the stairs. He half-expected her to flee back to the safety of the hall, but Alyssa stood her ground, her eyes betraying a hint of mockery. "You wish to speak to me in private, sir?"

He bristled at her sarcasm, annoyed that she didn't back away from the confrontation. "I hear, Lady Ogilvy"—and he stressed the Ogilvy—"that at this very moment your husband is searching for you, anxious that you should return to his house, where you belong."

"That is not your business, my lord!"

"And I wonder what will happen when he locates you," he went on as if she hadn't spoken, "and tries to remove the boy from Beckford Lodge. Do you think my nephew will stand aside and allow his son to be taken away? Have you considered the consequences of this association?"

Sinclair had the satisfaction of watching the fight go out of her and a shadow chase the angry shine from her eyes.

He nodded gravely. "I understand more than you think," he continued more softly, unaware that his tone had gentled. "I too was a young man once, subject to . . . to the usual temptation and choices, forced to make decisions I would sooner have avoided." Without thinking, he put a hand on her arm, and his eyes were beseeching. "If you love him—and I do not doubt that you do—retire from the forefront of his life and content yourself with seeing him in private, otherwise this love may destroy both of you."

Alyssa watched him walk away. She sat down on the stairs

and rested her forehead on her hand, trying without success to dredge back the anger and resentment.

Blake was furious after forcing her to repeat the gist of this conversation. He would have gone to his uncle had Alyssa not pleaded with him to let it rest. "He—he has a point, sweeting—"

"Pah!" He slashed the air swordlike with his hand. "Do you think I worry about a confrontation with Ogilvy! By God's blood, I would welcome it!" His eyes narrowed and he struck the table with a clenched fist. "Aye, and this time we would settle the matter once and for all, and the sooner the better—"

"Nay, darling, don't talk thus!" Alyssa ran to him and buried her face in his chest, feeling his taut muscles tense beneath her hands. "I would rather retire to—to Lynnwood than be the cause of such an encounter. Your uncle means well. He wants only the best for you."

Blake slid a hand under her chin, his expression suddenly tender as he murmured, "And I for you. Lynnwood is too distant from Edinburgh."

They returned to Beckford Lodge two days later, Alyssa with mixed emotions, not at all certain that they had done the right thing by appearing together at Highfield.

They celebrated the coming of 1567 quietly. Soon, Alyssa knew, Blake must return to his duties at court and she herself continue her quest begun just before the miscarriage. She thought of Nan and Luke MacKellar often, convinced that if she were ever to unlock the door to her past, these two would be the key, because who else would be likely to help her? During the Christmas celebrations at Highfield she had learned all she could about the couple. Rough-hewn though they were, they were well thought of at court, much to Lady Magdalen's dismay. The countess was said to resent their popularity, chafing that her husband continued to ail, and waited impatiently for his recovery so that she could dispatch them back to the country.

Only a few days into the new year Alexander came down with a severe cold and fever. By the end of the week the child was delirious, the doctor fearing that the disease had affected his lungs. Alyssa and Blake were frantic. Sinclair sent for one doctor after another, impatient and alarmed when the boy's fever and hacking cough lingered on. Finally he swallowed his pride and bade Wyatt seek out the abrasive Dr. Greer.

After the little man examined Alexander he proceeded to bark out orders to the servants, ignoring the frantic parents standing by impotently wringing their hands. Steaming kettles must be brought at once to the lad's room. The fire must be kept blazing and wet sheets hung to dry before it, sending moist heat into the air. He applied a poultice to the tiny chest and forced a spoonful of vile-looking liquid down Alex's throat, then finally seemed to remember the parents, who had watched it all in dread.

"He will recover in a week or two," Greer announced smugly. He snapped his bag closed and swaggered from the house.

In a week Alex was eating normally, and days later was trying to get out of bed. By the end of January he was running around the nursery engaging in all his usual tricks and a few new ones besides, much to the mingled relief and exasperation of his nurse.

Alyssa was surprised at how many members of Blake's family came to visit Alexander during his illness, even some she had thought hostile, and by the time he recovered, the nursery floor was littered with new toys. Harry Sinclair did not come—but he sent a gift, a tiny suit of armor, beautifully etched and gilded, "For the Knight who slew the Giant at Highfield."

"That," laughed Blake, examining the card, "must go into the Sinclair Chronicle for posterity."

But Alyssa was touched. "Don't be too hard on him, my sweet," she said gently. "He worries about Alex . . . and about you."

On the afternoon of February 9, the first day their son had been allowed out of the house to take the air, they received a disquieting message from Jason in Holyrood. It appeared that the King, furious at being ignored at his son's baptism in December, had stalked off in a huff to the domain of the Lennox Stewarts in Glasgow. There, so the rumor went, he soon engaged in fresh plotting to seize the crown, but before he could put his plans into effect he had fallen seriously ill with another attack of the pox. In the meantime, word of his intrigues had found there way back to Mary, and, long suspicious of her husband since his involvement in Riccio's murder, she harkened to Bothwell's advice and coaxed Darnley back to Edinburgh where they could keep him under close observation. Jason wrote, "Why the King fell for this lure is hard to fathom, since in Edinburgh he's surrounded by those who hate him, including Morton and Lindsay lately back from exile. Huntly maintains she got him back by hinting she'd give their marriage another chance, and Darnley is just fool enough to believe it!"

Sinclair raised his head from the parchment to Ratcliffe, Jason's squire. "So . . . the King is back at Holyrood? Amazing!"

Ratcliffe laughed and shook his head. "Nay, my lord, he stopped short of walking into the lion's den and chose to be lodged at Kirk o'Field, Jimmy Balfour's place out by St. Mary-in-the-Field."

"Kirk o'Field!" Blake was more astounded than ever. "Christ's soul, surely 'tis mean quarters for a King?"

"Comfortable enough, sir," replied Ratcliffe tonelessly, "and close-guarded by its owner, James Balfour, friend of my Earl of Bothwell."

Sinclair turned cold. He knew the slippery Balfour, a lawyer who in the past had had a checkered career and had used his wits and legal skill to worm his way out of many a ticklish situation. Now this same Balfour, whose reputation was far from spotless, had entrenched himself with the man at the right hand of the Queen, a man whose restless character would chafe at the idea of a long, tedious divorce, if divorce would even be granted.

Ratcliffe broke into his thoughts, "My lord bids ye come to Holyrood immediately, sir. He feels the Queen may have need of ye."

Blake nodded. He gave orders for the horses to be saddled and sent a messenger galloping for Augusta where he had left a large force to guard the castle, with instructions to be on the alert and ready to move south the moment he commanded it.

Then he went upstairs to take leave of Alyssa, and found her in the nursery removing Alexander's outdoor clothes.

Something in his face, a certain distance, as if his thoughts were already elsewhere, brought her quickly to her feet. "Nay, there's no cause for alarm," Blake lied quickly at the fright leaping up in her eyes. "You knew I would have to return to Holyrood shortly."

"The Queen sent for you?" she asked in a sinking voice.

He smiled slightly. "'Tis not a royal messenger downstairs, only Ratcliffe. He tells me there's some pother with the King, who's installed himself—undoubtedly to embarrass Her Grace—in the old provost's house at Kirk o'Field, hardly suitable for one of his rank and position. Now we must see if we can persuade him back to the palace before this foolishness is bruited about and misconstrued." He grinned, striving to make light of it. "We cannot have it said that Her Majesty shunts her ailing husband to a doghouse, cur though he may be."

Alyssa did not smile. She gazed up at him keenly, sensing the urgency he was striving to conceal, his eagerness to be gone. And misunderstanding the reason for it, she spoke sharply without thinking. "Then go! You would not wish to keep Her Most Gracious Majesty waiting, pledged as you are to defend her with your life."

His smile froze. The dark eyes were suddenly cold. Leaning forward stiffly, he brushed his lips across her forehead, then turned swiftly to embrace his son, hugging the boy fiercely to his chest.

From the nursery window Alyssa watched them ride away, breaking into a gallop once clear of the courtyard. She stood with tears streaming down her cheeks long after they had disappeared from sight, and for the first time recognized her *true* adversary, the woman she most had to fear, one with the power to part them forever, though Sinclair's lover she could never be.

Mary Stuart.

Fickle Winds

35

Kirk o'Field
1567

When Blake and his men reached Holyrood, the atmosphere was deceptively quiet. They were informed by a page that Her Majesty was attending the wedding of Bastion, one of her valets, and from there would go directly to a dinner given for the ambassador of Savoy. Bothwell, Moray and Huntly were also absent. "The Earl of Moray left the city this morning, my lord," said the page, "and my lords Huntly and Bothwell are both with the Queen."

"When do you expect them to return here?"

The man hesitated, finally saying somewhat reluctantly, "Very late, sir. I believe they intend to visit the King at Kirk o'Field afterwards. Mayhap Her Grace will remain there overnight and return with His Majesty in the morning."

Sinclair stared at him, taken aback. "Then Dar—the King means to return to Holyrood?"

"Aye." The page smiled dryly. "His apartments are being readied now on the Queen's instructions."

Sinclair and his men conferred in his own quarters at the palace. Harry, leary of trouble over the touchy situation between Mary and her errant husband, said, "All seems well enough. Mayhap they have indeed reconciled, and I see no reason to linger here tonight."

Blake was silent, thinking that it was always possible, if unlikely. He had not seen Mary in weeks and was aware of her mercurial temperament, her penchant for pardoning those who had in the past done her ill—her own brother being a prime example. It was unfortunate that neither Huntly nor Bothwell were around to bring him up to date on the state of the royal marriage, and he found it faintly disquieting that none of the lords closest to the Queen were available for questioning.

Jason said, "I agree with Uncle Harry. Mayhap we were anxious for naught. Think of it, would Moray have left town if some crisis were brewing—"

"Aye!" Sinclair fairly shouted. Jason had just put his finger on the crux of a situation that most troubled him. "Has that not always been Moray's pattern, to set the stage and absent himself when the curtain rises?"

The men around the table shifted uneasily. Adam Sinclair reminded his cousin that Moray was but recently reinstated with the Queen and dare not risk engaging in questionable activity, nor would Morton and Lindsay, newly back from England.

Harry nodded. "They may be ambitious but not fool-hardy."

"What of Bothwell?" asked Blake quietly.

Several chimed in at once to assure him that over the past few weeks the border lord had become exceedingly unpopular with the other nobles through his overbearing tactics, and could not risk moving against the King without the support of the most powerful lords in the country.

Sinclair remained unconvinced. He knew these men and how devious they could be, particularly Moray and Morton, how they seized on a man's weakness and used it against him, as they had once used Darnley to rid themselves of David Riccio. Now that Darnley himself had become superfluous in the eyes of so many, means must be found to remove him, and another scapegoat would have to be found if it were to be accomplished speedily. A hideous thought struck him. What if they intended to use the Queen herself!

At nine o'clock that evening Sinclair and his retinue rode up to the old provost's house at Kirk o'Field. It was a pleasing enough residence, built in a small square above the Cowgate and hard by the town wall itself, with a gate leading into its own attractive garden, now covered by a few inches of snow. Beyond the city wall stretched orchards and fields.

It was a cold but bright evening, and as they approached the house they saw signs of a great deal of activity, with horses and grooms cluttered about the yard. Candlelight blazed from every window and cheerful music flowed out into the darkness, with every sign of a party in progress, undoubtedly for the amusement of the convalescing King. Blake banged determinedly on the door and demanded admittance from Nelson, Darnley's servant, who opened it after several minutes had gone by. Before Nelson could decide what to do, Bothwell himself appeared, clad in the black and silver costume he had worn to the pre-Lenten carnival earlier. For an instant he seemed nonplused at the sight of Sinclair and his men, then relaxed, grinning, "Greetings, stranger! So you have finally come out of your love nest to see how us less favored mortals are faring?" And as Blake made to step forward, Bothwell's arm came up to bar the door. "Sorry, my friend, but Her Grace will not see you. She would have you await her pleasure, as she awaited yours this long while past—"

"I would hear that from her own lips," Sinclair interrupted curtly.

Bothwell's smile faded. "I have leave to speak for her, Sinclair, and she refuses to see you."

With a growl of impatience Blake shoved him rudely aside, but as he stepped into the foyer he was instantly surrounded by a dozen of Bothwell's moss troopers left there to guard access to the apartment above, torchlight glinting off the weapons in their hands. Bothwell dusted himself off and chuckled with no outward show of ill feeling. With a nod at his men he said, "They have their orders, laddie, and they come from the Queen." And as Blake's face turned dark with anger, "Be at ease, my friend, she's just a wee mite miffed at your neglect, but never fear, she'll get over it in time," adding with an edge to his voice, "We all ken how she canna resist the Sinclair for very long."

Blake's eyes roamed over the heads of the soldiers, and in a corridor leading away from the stairs he suddenly spotted James Balfour and, for an instant before he ducked into a nearby chamber, the golden head of Simon Ogilvy, Balfour's longtime cohort. Blake turned back to the border earl sharply. "Why was the King brought to this place?"

Bothwell shrugged. "At his own request. Her Majesty

would naturally have preferred Holyrood, but . . . you ken the willful nature of His Grace."

"I would like a word with you in private."

The smaller man heaved a sigh of regret. "Alas, it must wait. I've absented myself overlong as it is." And in a rush as Sinclair reached to grab his shoulder and the troopers sprang forward, "Be at peace, man! God's blood, don't do something you'll regret and destroy the warm feelings the Queen has always harbored for you and your kin." He backed away cautiously. "Meet me at my apartments in Holyrood before noon tomorrow, and in the meantime"—he winked—"I'll put in a good word for you with Her Grace."

As Bothwell clattered up the stairs, his soldiers edged the Earl of Belrose in the direction of the door, where Harry Sinclair stood sweating profusely, the others behind him. His uncle caught his arm, muttering under his breath, "Have done, lad! Jamie's right, you'll only antagonize the Queen more by turning their revel into a brawl. And tomorrow is but a few hours away."

A crowd of curious grooms had gathered near the door to watch the outcome of the confrontation, disappointed when the earl and his men mounted their horses and rode away when a good fight would have been just the thing to drive the chill from their limbs. Among them was a brawny giant in a stained leather jerkin, who was joined a few moments later by another with flaxen hair that glinted in the torchlight.

"Should I follow them, sir?" Bruno asked the newcomer, looking at the satin-clad dandy with tiny eyes that held a hint of contempt. "He might lead us back to the lady."

Simon Ogilvy smoothed down the folds of his lavishly embroidered doublet, shivering a little in the cold night air. "Aye, though 'tis certain he'll remain in town this eve, given that he seems mighty suspicious."

Bruno doffed his broad-brimmed leather hat, managing to convey more scorn than deference in the gesture. "Your servant, sir!" he sneered, and heaved his increasing bulk into the saddle, turning his mule's head in the direction of the road. Simon called after him softly, "Take good care to stay out of sight."

Bruno didn't bother to reply, except to hawk loudly over the flank of his mount, simmering with resentment that he now must take orders from the perfumed dandy as well as his own hated mistress, Lady Magdalen, whom it would have given him immense pleasure to kill had he not needed her protection.

As the MacKellar squire left the square, a keen pair of eyes thoughtfully observed his departure. Another MacKellar squire, Hamish, in the service of Lord Luke, felt certain that his master would be much interested in the little scene he had just witnessed, particularly since Luke had had both Ogilvy and Lady Magdalen watched for the past several weeks.

Less than an hour passed before Hamish Whittier saw the Queen herself emerge from the house, together with her nobles. Luke MacKellar puffed over, looking alien and out of character in a blue brocade doublet trimmed with brilliants, his greying russet hair and beard neatly clipped, his appearance overhauled on express orders from the countess. He complained irritably, "Well, Hamish lad, it seems there's to be no peace for us this night. Just when we thought Her Grace would retire at Kirk o'Field and return to Holyrood with the King in the morning, Bothwell reminded her that she had promised to attend Bastian's and Christiana's wedding masque, so afterwards she'll bide the night at Holyrood."

Whittier told him about Ogilvy and Bruno. Luke was silent for a moment or two, stroking his beard, then ordered, "Until I say otherwise, I want ye to stick to Bruno like a nit on a head o' hair."

MacKellar's company was the last to ride away from the square by the town wall. Darnley's own grooms, MacCaig and Glenny, watched them go. Inside the house where the King was recovering were seven or eight of his personal servants, his valet, Taylor, sharing the King's bedchamber. The young King grumbled peevishly, "A murrain on them for departing so soon! Her Grace, my wife, had promised to stay the night until that rogue Bothwell lured her away. Am I not of more import than an idiotic wedding masque?"

"Most assuredly, Your Grace," murmured Taylor from the window, where his eyes were scanning the yard, the torches having been doused.

"I like not how Bothwell puts on such airs. 'Tis overweening and insulting to my person, how he clings like a leech to her side. By the rood, I could swear the warlock devised spells that I should not recover from this ailment."

There was no response from his valet.

Darnley raised himself on an elbow, his tawny hair boyishly rumpled, his fair skin flushed from the heat in the chamber, lending his appearance a womanish delicacy in sharp contrast to the pugnacious virility of his competitor, Bothwell. "What are you gaping at yonder?"

Taylor hesitated, then shrugged, reluctant to confess the uneasiness that had come over him when their company had broken up so abruptly, as if on cue. "Nothing, my lord . . . nothing."

Bothwell escorted Mary to Bastian's wedding masque and afterwards saw her safely back to her private apartments in Holyrood. The moment he left her he rushed to his own chambers and threw off his fine clothes, replacing them for sober attire less conspicuous in the dark. With two of his most trusted servants beside him, the earl left the palace and, taking a circuitous route through the winding back streets of the city to avoid running into the watch, arrived back at the house at Kirk o'Field.

The conspirators were waiting for him in the shadows— those recruited to put the crime into effect—while the real architects of the murder, with the exception of Bothwell, lay far away from the scene tossing anxiously in their beds. Around the border lord were George Dalgleish, his tailor; his former servant, Paris; and several of the Earl of Morton's most dependable kinsmen—plus Sir James Balfour and Simon Ogilvy. Like the others, Ogilvy was dressed in black with a thick woolen cap pulled down over his fair hair. In the darkness his eyes gleamed with excitement as he watched Bothwell himself light the fuse to the gunpowder already laid down. There was no mercy in Simon's heart as he thought of the man lying abed inside the house. His obliging mind assured him that they were doing the right thing to rid the Queen of this scourge blighting her life.

But as the fuse finally caught, sending orange sparks flying up into the darkness, Ogilvy spied the blur of a face at the King's chamber window, those inside perhaps alerted by furtive sounds in the yard. While the conspirators waited tensely for the explosion they were aghast to spy two figures in white bedgowns suddenly rush out onto the balcony attached to the town wall. Throwing down a chair attached to a rope, this pair scrambled to safety seconds before the blast went off. Jumping to their feet, the intended victims fled into the nearby garden, Darnley's white bedgown flapping about his legs, the frantic figures outlined violently in the blast.

Drawing his dagger, Ogilvy and several of Morton's men raced after them, determined that the King not escape. They turned a deaf ear to Darnley's last cries for mercy, while Sir James Balfour and Bothwell hastily departed the scene, the latter returning to his own quarters in Holyrood.

It was Alyssa's first evening alone for weeks. After a solitary supper she sat in the hall gazing dully into the fire. Blake's cool leave-taking was very much on her mind, and she blamed herself for that—but she also blamed Mary Stuart. But for the Queen they might have been at this very moment living happily together in the Highlands, far away from the eternal strife and intrigue bubbling at court. Yet . . . by an ironic twist of fate it was through Mary Stuart that she might finally untangle the web of deception surrounding her birth, and she remembered her first meeting with her uncle, Lord Luke, on the night they all fled to Seton Castle.

Alyssa could not find it in her heart to hate the Queen, a woman with troubles surely too desperate for any mortal to bear. Upon meeting the young, warmhearted monarch, she had found it impossible to truly dislike her. Perhaps this winsome quality was one reason why Elizabeth of England had long avoided a personal confrontation with her cousin, and perhaps it was why Blake was so attached to her. And Alyssa knew she could not fight such an attachment, defying as it did all the usual reasons why a man would bind himself to a woman.

But there was a battle she must wage for herself, and by

calling Sinclair away Mary had paved the way for Alyssa to visit Elmwood.

Alyssa made up her mind to ride into the city the following day. With that decision made, and steadfastly refusing to be intimidated by the consequences, she climbed the stairs at ten o'clock and within half an hour had fallen asleep.

Alyssa was roused abruptly shortly after two in the morning by a great commotion in the yard below her window. Straining to see, she glimpsed Wyatt and several of the guards shouting and gesturing wildly in the direction of the city where a ball of flaming orange lit up the night sky.

The explosion rocked Edinburgh, spilling the good citizens and nobles alike rudely from their beds. Blake had been merely dozing. He was up and partially dressed when Jason and Lord Harry and a dozen of his men burst into his chamber. Sinclair's first thought was for the Queen, not quite sure at that point what had happened. They found her standing in the open doorway of her suite, surrounded by a nervous crowd of minor courtiers.

"Oh, Sinclair!" she cried in relief when she saw him, her white face brightening. A trembling hand reached to grip his arm. "Has the end of the world come then, just as Knox predicted? Forsooth, I have never heard such a din!"

Blake herded the Queen and her ladies back into their apartments and posted an armed guard at the door, and then left, promising to find out where the explosion had occurred. As they were mounting their horses in the courtyard, George Hackett panted over with sweat streaming down his face. "The King is dead!" he shouted. "The house at Kirk o'Field is no more. I'm on my way to wake Bothwell now. As high sheriff of Edinburgh he must—"

"Wait up, man!" Sinclair grabbed his arm and spun him around. "Hepburn is in Holyrood?"

"Aye!" the harried man assured him. "He returned here last eve wi' Her Grace, Huntly and others."

Blake let him go.

By now the courtyard bustled with a chaotic mass of people, none quite sure of what had happened or what they should do. Torchlights sprang up in the city itself, the common folk rushing out into the winter cold in their night attire to clog the streets. Waving an arm for his men to follow, Sinclair rode to the Canongate and through the Netherbow Port to Blackfriar's, where he was forced to slow to a walk because of the crowd, frightened men and women jostled roughly by those on horseback, their faces—studies of fear and uncertainty—illuminated by the flames.

Kirk o'Field had been reduced to a pile of smoking rubble. "By the Blessed Virgin . . . !" Sinclair breathed, sliding off his horse to approach on foot. In the garden beyond the town wall a crowd surrounded two corpses, those of the King and his valet, Taylor.

Sinclair gazed down at Darnley, startlingly boyish in his crumpled white bedgown, amazed to see that the body was intact in spite of the blast. Bending to examine him, he noticed the marks on his neck as Bothwell rode up with his soldiers, shouting to his men to apprehend anyone who seemed in the slightest suspicious.

After one swift look at the dead King, Bothwell left Blake to send for a physician and have the body carried to a nearby house while he and his troopers went about making haphazard arrests. He was absent when the doctor announced that Darnley had been strangled. On learning this, an old woman in the crowd about the door suddenly screamed, "'Tis not the poor folks who had a hand in this! Nay, ye maun look to the proud nobles aboot the Queen, to the yin wi' most to gain."

Others took up the cry, "Bothwell! Bothwell!"

Sinclair turned grimly to Jason. "I must warn him; speak to him." And this time, he determined, there would be no excuses.

Leaving Jason and his men where they were, Blake rode out alone to avoid drawing attention. The crowd were angry, ready to attack nobles and soldiers alike. Though they had learned to despise Darnley for his brazen conduct and disrespect of the Queen, they made excuses for him now that he was dead, suddenly remembering that he was but a lad who had been led astray by evil company—no doubt by the very lords who had plotted his demise!

Blake moved through the horde warily, a hand at his sword, and left the square without mishap. But as he turned into Blackfriar's Wynd a blazing torch was suddenly hurled in front of his horse. Fleet II reared, toppling Sinclair from the saddle, and before Blake could stop him the terrified animal raced away into the night. As he started to rise, a brawny figure sprang from the shadows. There was the faint glint of a dagger, then Sinclair felt a searing pain slice through his left forearm. He rolled to the side as the assassin made to launch himself upon him, and Bruno went sprawling on the cobbles. When Bruno jumped to his feet, Sinclair stood facing him, rapier in hand.

For all his size, the MacKellar squire was nimble on his feet and danced out of reach as the sword whistled through the air a foot from his shoulder. In the light from a lantern hung by the lintel of a nearby door, Bruno saw that the Highland Chieftain's tunic was rapidly becoming drenched with blood. He grinned, sure his blade had nicked a major vein or artery. Once Sinclair was sufficiently weakened from loss of blood it would be a simple matter to move in for the kill. So each time the younger man lunged, he chortled and leaped to the side, moving around in a circle, faster and faster, waiting for the moment when his victim would become dizzy and lose his balance. So intent was he on watching his prey, never taking his eyes off the sword, that the squire failed to notice the puddle of blood forming at his feet.

There was a shout from the end of the wynd, and a group of citizens ran toward them to see what new mischief was afoot, but neither man noticed their presence. Blake was waiting his chance, his left arm hanging uselessly at his side, and when next Bruno jumped away, his foot shooting out from under him on the wet cobbles, Blake sprang forward and drove the point of his blade through the man's heart.

A cheer went up from the onlookers. Blake heard it as if from a distance through the ringing in his ears, the ground wavering beneath him as he bent over the fallen man and ripped aside his outer jerkin to uncover the MacKellar blazon patched to his vest. He froze, wondering if his dimming eyes could be deceiving him. The MacKellars and Sinclairs, enemies in the past, were now allies and had been for a number of years. He shook the mist from his vision and stared hard at the badge, and saw that there was no mistake, that the long truce between the clans had gone down before yet another act of treachery.

He straightened slowly as a voice cried out from the crowd, "Seize that man! He's one of the scurvy crew involved in the death of the King!"

Blake turned his head sharply in the direction of a tall, lean man whose face seemed very white under his dark woolen cap. His fine features, though blurred, struck him as familiar.

"Restrain him!" the fellow commanded when no one moved. And at the drumming of hoofbeats on the nearby street, "Soldiers! Soldiers! Hasten before he makes it away!"

The crowd scattered in all directions as the troops converged on Sinclair. Blake tried to lift his blade, but it was struck from his hand, and from a long way away rang an authoritative voice, crying, "Take him to the Castle!"

36

Alyssa's plans for the day were blasted when a messenger rode up to Beckford Lodge shortly after nine o'clock the following morning to say that the King was dead and Sinclair arrested and implicated in his murder. Also, he panted, the Chief was wounded and incarcerated in Edinburgh Castle.

The blood drained from Alyssa's face. She would have fallen if Wyatt hadn't jumped forward to support her. "Wounded . . . how badly?" she whispered, her first tortured thought being that she hadn't kissed him good-bye.

The sweating clansman shrugged. "We know not, lady. No one is allowed to see him." Then he turned urgent eyes on the squire. "I believe ye have your instructions and know what ye must do?" Wyatt nodded, impotent tears in his eyes. "Hasten, man!" the clansman made bold to say. "There's no time to lose."

Aware that he lived in constant danger, Sinclair had left instructions that if anything should happen to him, Alyssa and his son were to be taken immediately to safety at Castle Augusta, but when Wyatt sought to propel her toward the stairs to make ready for the journey she pulled away, crying, "We cannot abandon him! Would you ride away to safety and leave him to his fate?"

"I would fain be with him," said the squire, emotion roughening his voice, "but he entrusted you to me, lady, and I will see the task done. Please go" — he motioned to the stairs. "Pack quickly. You cannot help him by tarrying here. 'Twould only add to his worries."

Sobbing, Alyssa turned and flew up the winding stairs,

thinking that with their Chief in prison the entire Sinclair clan would be under a cloud. But Blake had powerful friends and allies. There were the MacKellars—and Bothwell. James Hepburn and Blake had been friends. They had fought together behind the Queen during the time of David Riccio's murder. And the border lord, so it was said, was now the most powerful nobleman in Scotland. She would go to him and beg on her knees, if necessary, to have her dear one released from the vile charges against him. It was unthinkable to hide away behind the walls of Augusta while Blake might be put to the rack.

Alexander! Dear God, she thought, trembling with indecision at the top of the stairs. She dare not leave her child here to risk being kidnapped by Simon, or worse, taken by Morton's men! And the hyenas would surely move in once news of Sinclair's arrest reached certain interested ears. Without his father's protection, Alex was as defenseless as a kitten—as she was.

Thinking of the motherly Nan MacKellar, Alyssa came to a decision. She went into the baby's suite and found the nurse standing anxiously at the window with Alex in her arms. Taking him from her, she said, "I would be alone with my son for a little while. Go to the kitchen and tell them to pack enough food for the ride to Augusta, then ready yourself to leave."

The moment they were alone, Alyssa dressed the toddler warmly and ran with him back to the chamber she shared with Blake. Throwing open the lid of one of his coffers, she dragged out attire he usually wore when hunting. The kidskin jacket and breeches engulfed her slender form, and Alex laughed gleefully at the sight of his mother in such unlikely attire. Kissing him quickly on the tip of his impish nose, Alyssa stuffed her long tresses under a wide-brimmed hat, grabbed the boy and stole out onto the gallery. In the hall below, the messenger gulped refreshments while Wyatt hovered by his elbow, together with the other men, hanging on his every word while he related the events of the previous night before hurrying on his way.

By taking the back stairs, Alyssa and Alex left Beckford

Lodge unobserved. The stables were temporarily empty, all the help having rushed into the house intent on hearing the newcomer's story.

Within minutes the woman and child were riding swiftly away from the manor, Alex laughing in delight at this unexpected adventure, blissfully ignorant as to the reason for it and not in the least frightened by their frantic pace.

Nan MacKellar was astounded when Lady Ogilvy burst into the house with the child in her arms. Within minutes she had the story out of Alyssa, sighing, "Marry, if only Luke were at home!"

Like the other lords, he and his men were at Holyrood, ready to defend the Queen if trouble should break out. The citizens of Edinburgh were in an ugly mood, roaming the streets fighting and looting, resentful of being kept in the dark over the death of the King and demanding that his killers be brought to account.

Nan had heard only the hour before that Sinclair had been arrested. "He's innocent!" Alyssa cried, trembling on the brink of hysteria. "I know him, my lady, and he would never do anything to cause hurt or dishonor to the Queen. Means must be found to help him and set this hideous mistake aright." She gazed pleadingly at the plump face, her eyes brimming with tears. "I intend to see my Lord Bothwell, but must be certain that Alex will be left in safe hands. Will you keep him for me, Lady Nan?"

"See . . . Bothwell?" Nan was shocked. According to Rab, her cook, who had ventured into the streets for news, Hepburn was the name the crowds screamed vengeance on, maintaining that the boy-King's blood stained his grasping hands. Rab had reported that placards were being nailed up all over town to the effect that the border lord had bewitched the Queen into straying from the virtuous path she had always followed, and that Mary must be freed of his evil spell "but dire means if necessary."

"Listen to me, lass." Leaning forward anxiously, Nan put a comforting hand on her knee, as Alex sat listening to the tense conversation with huge, solemn eyes. "You dare not try to see James Hepburn, nor even venture out into the streets in such a wicked time. When my lord returns—"

"Nay! By then it could be too late." Alyssa jumped to her feet, a wild determination in her eyes. "I cannot sit idly by while my lov—while Sinclair lies injured in prison awaiting a traitor's death."

As she started for the door, Alex in her arms, Nan hurried after her puffing breathlessly, uncertain of whether she was more afraid of having Alyssa walk out of her life or of involving her family in this dangerous situation with Sinclair, the first nobleman to be arrested in the death of the King.

Less than an hour later Alyssa rode away from Elmwood clad in a gown borrowed from one of Nan's waiting women, a lady whose slender figure corresponded to Alyssa's more closely than her mistress's did. She was escorted by three MacKellar retainers in full livery, the family badge prominent on their arms. It was this badge that made it possible for them to get past the guards—Bothwell's men—who barred the gates to Holyrood. Once in the palace, Alyssa was shown into a crowded anteroom crammed with excited, chattering people all waiting impatiently to see the man who now seemed to be in charge. As the minutes and then hours crawled by, she heard snatches of various conversations. One voice murmured that at that moment the King's body was in the process of being embalmed, another that many arrests had been made, chief among them Sinclair himself. She sat in rigid silence, sick with impatience and dread as another complained of the long wait, "Marry, but at this slow pace many of us might not manage speech with my Lord Bothwell today."

This proved to be correct. At four o'clock a steward appeared in the doorway to announce that his lordship could grant no more audiences, a statement that met with angry protests from those who had waited hours to see him. As the disgruntled crowd filed from the room, all but pushing the unfortunate steward aside, Alyssa ducked through an archway and boldly opened the door leading into the audience chamber itself.

Bothwell, on the point of leaving the room, stood at a table in company with Maitland and Huntly and several others whom Alyssa didn't recognize. James Hepburn spun around warily, a hand dropping to his dagger as the door banged wide behind him, then laughed in relief as Alyssa threw back her hood. "Lady Ogilvy! God's wounds, what do you here?"

Ignoring the others, Alyssa walked up to him and dropped a respectful curtsy, the folds of her brown velvet cloak falling open to expose the low-cut gown below. As she straightened she saw Bothwell's bright hazel eyes linger appreciatively on her breasts. He took her hand and kissed it, saying to the others who hovered about suspiciously, "You may safely leave us. Lady Ogilvy is a friend of mine."

He drew her to a window seat and they sat down side by side, the earl turning so that he was looking directly into her face, closer than he had ever dared approach her during his visits to Mordrum Hall. He had heard that she had left Ogilvy and become the mistress of Blake Sinclair, and guessed why she'd come, but pretended ignorance as he let her explain, finding it a pleasant respite from his worries to sit back quietly while feasting his eyes on her charms. Had he only know that she had been tiring of Simon—

"Oh, my lord, you must know that a great injustice has been done!" Alyssa sobbed, tears like drops of crystal flowing from her eyes. "Sinclair is your friend. Like you, he would do nothing to cause grief or dishonor to the Queen."

The nobleman hastily removed his eyes from the lovely, pleading face. He shifted uncomfortably, thinking that he could never stand the sight of a weeping woman. Suddenly that woman seized his hand and pressed it to the velvety bosom. "I beseech you, help him!"

Bothwell melted. "So you love this man?"

"Aye," Alyssa admitted without a moment's hesitation, "I love him desperately and will be forever in your debt if you right this wrong."

The earl sighed, envying Sinclair such passionate devotion. He pursed his lips considerably as he reviewed the situation. He knew Sinclair was innocent, but how to avoid those who would ask, "How can you be so sure?" Just the same, clemency might be advisable. If his own grand ambitions were to come to fruition he would need all the support he could muster from the nobility, well aware, that under their thin veneer of friendship, many among his rank were envious and resentful of his sudden eminence, and could turn on him as swiftly as they had done with Darnley. And ticking away at the back of his agile mind was a plan to draw up a bond boldly stating his suitability to rule at the side of Mary. If he could manage to persuade most of the lords to sign this document it could but advance his suit with the reluctant Queen. And the handsome Earl of Belrose stood high in her estimation.

He leaned forward, taking the liberty of kissing Alyssa on the lips, promising, "I will do what I can—"

"And may I be allowed to see him?" she burst out hopefully. "I would know how badly he's been hurt."

Slowly the earl shook his head. "Nay, my dear, at least not yet, but never fear, I shall guarantee he will receive good care and get word back to you as soon as I can."

Alyssa gave him the MacKellars' address, and at his look of surprise explained that they were friends. "They would not have me living alone during this difficult time."

There was no mention made of Simon Ogilvy, but Bothwell could have told her that it was Simon who had accused Sinclair of treasonable conspiracy in the death of the King. Though they were distantly related, Bothwell considered Simon of small consequence when pitted against the might of the clan Sinclair, potentially of much greater use to him. Aside from this, Ogilvy's nature was such that he tempted shrewder minds to take advantage of him. Moray and Randolph had done it, so why not Bothwell?

"You will bide here with us until this is over," Nan insisted again when Alyssa returned from Holyrood. "We can keep each other company since my lord too must remain at the palace." And giving the child in her arms a quick cuddle, "Alex and I are already grand friends, and dinna fret about Lady Magdalen stopping by. She and I have had a tiff!"

Alyssa looked at her sharply, this seemingly casual remark delivered with light-hearted satisfaction momentarily distracted her from thoughts of Sinclair. She whispered, "Lady Nan . . ." color rushing into her pale cheeks, her heart beating fast.

Nan gave her a comfortable smile and patted her hand. "Not now, m'dear. Poor thing, ye look about all in. There will be time for discussin' later, when my lord comes home. In the meantime, 'tis wondrous that Bothwell has promised to help ye try to free Sinclair. Now ye must sup and retire early. I'll wager ye're about dead on yer feet."

Two days later Bothwell sent a message to Elmwood. Though brief, he had infused it with hope. Blake's wound was not serious, he wrote—though he had not had time to check this out for himself—and he was receiving good care. "On the morrow I plan to visit him myself and see what can be done."

"There!" laughed Nan with satisfaction, noting the tears of relief in Alyssa's eyes. "If anyone can help him, that man is Earl Bothwell. I think ye need not have too much to worry about."

Early on the evening of February 10, James Hepburn set off, as he'd promised, to visit Sinclair.

There was nothing heartening about Edinburgh Castle, that dour ediface looming on the hill known as Arthur's Seat, casting its grim shadow over the city of Edinburgh. And there was nothing cheering about the deep bowels of the castle, or the dampness that trickled from the walls in cold green slime, the cries echoing eerily through the twisting passageways, and the smell of death rising into the shadowy air like a pall.

As he waited for a guard to unlock the last door into the dungeons, even Bothwell shivered, though clad warmly in a heavy fur-lined cloak, thinking that it hadn't been so long ago when he too had known the untender hospitality of the castle, every bit as grim as his stay in the infamous Tower of London. Now here he was, the most important noble in Scotland, and about to be more powerful still, assuming he could acquire the backing of the other lords—or most of them.

The gate clanged open and the guard stepped back, holding his lantern high, rats scurrying away as their footsteps rang in the corridor, a foul odor emanating from the streamlet of moisture running along the center of the floor, a sudden shriek resounding from beyond a door at the end of the passageway.

The turnkey glanced at the earl with a gap-toothed grin. "He likes not the fit o' the Dutch shoe, from the fuss he makes."

"Hasten!" Bothwell ordered grimly. "A man could expire from the very air in this place."

"Aye, but usually the rack gets them first!" the other cackled.

They halted before a large, dank chamber where beyond the grilled door the earl espied a wretched huddle of humanity, perhaps two dozen prisoners awaiting their turn in the nearby torture chamber. The gloom in the cell made it hard to see clearly, but from a pallet of straw in the far corner rose a tall, dark man with the arched brows and strong features that stamped him unmistakably as a Sinclair. After one swift look at Jason's wrathful face, Bothwell wheeled on the startled guard and shouted indignantly, "Who gave the order for the Earl of Belrose to be brought to this stinking hole?" Then before the man could answer, for the turnkey knew well enough that Bothwell had known about it, "Unlock this door immediately and make arrangements for Lord Sinclair to be removed at once and carried to suitable quarters upstairs."

At this outburst Jason's fury was somewhat mollified. "Over here," he waved. "Come hither and see how Scotland treats its heroes, for by the Blessed Virgin, if my cousin dies I'll turn my back on this vicious land forever."

Sinclair lay unconscious on a rude pallet of lice-infested hay, his clothes stiff with encrusted blood, a grimy bandage tight about his arm. The wound had not been too serious—had it been treated properly—but now poisoning had set in. The Chief's face was white in the gloom, his breathing shallow and rapid. Bothwell had looked upon many a dying man in his time, and now, as he bent to examine the young nobleman, he was convinced that he was gazing at another of them. Dismayed, for he had liked and admired Sinclair, he rose and draped a comforting arm around Jason's shoulders, promising, "I'll do my best for him, laddie. I only discovered today that Morton had had him arrested on a charge from Ogilvy, who swore he saw him running from Kirk o'Field minutes after the blast went off."

"He's innocent!" Jason cried, "And that whoreson Ogilvy will pay for this—"

"Aye, aye, to be sure, but first we must get your Chief out of here and find him a doctor."

Bothwell supervised everything personally. Sinclair was taken to a comfortable room in the castle itself, where a blazing fire crackled cheerfully in the grate. The filth of the dungeons was washed from his body and Blake's own doctor permitted into the castle to treat him. Somehow word leaked back to the Queen, who had been kept in ignorance of the developments. "I would have spared you this," Hepburn defended himself quickly when she railed at him. "You seemed so cast down at the death of your own lord that I thought to spare you more grief." And when she cried that she would go to see Sinclair personally, "Nay, nay, Your Grace, 'twould not be seemly for a Queen to consort with one implicated in her husband's murder—though wrongly, of course," he added hastily at the look on her face. "The process of law must be observed, to appease the people if naught else . . . but there's every chance that Sinclair will be released."

Mary sent her own physician, Arnault, to the castle.

While the doctors fought to save the Chief's life, Bothwell took Jason aside, saying, "I will do my utmost to see that the charges agin him are dropped."

Jason wrung his hand, then overcome with emotion, embraced him. "The Sinclairs will be forever in your debt."

The earl nodded, well satisfied.

Alyssa could think of nothing but Blake. Over and over she reread Bothwell's latest message, saying that the Chief was holding his own and receiving the best of care, but until he was formally cleared of the charges against him, no one could visit Sinclair except his immediate kin.

Her own plans and aspirations seemed suddenly trivial with her dear love's life hanging in the balance. Realizing this, Nan MacKellar never mentioned the suspicion lately uppermost in her mind, that Alyssa was one of their own and by rights the real Countess of Kilgarin. Until the shock of the King's death, her husband, Luke, had been busy making his own secret investigation, and after weeks of painstaking sifting and probing had unearthed an old retired servant, formerly at Cumbray, who had been wardrobe mistress at the castle at the time of Lady Alicia's confinement.

Bella had been most reluctant to talk. Even after so many years she still feared Lady Magdalen. But she was ill, dying of a humor that caused a painful lump to grown on her breast, and after many assurances from Lord Luke that he would respect her confidence and protect her, if necessary, she told her story about that far-off night.

"When the appointed midwife took sick at the last minute, Lady Magdalen found another, Caitlan Weir. We was a' sent below-stairs when the poor lady's pains began. Only the midwife and twa serving lassies were wi' her. But a scullery lad swore he saw Lady Magdalen an' her young squire, Jock Semple, riding furiously awa from Cumbray when it was a' over. He kenned Semple weel from havin' been sweetheart's wi' the squire's sister."

Luke had been greatly excited when he related the gist of this conversation to his wife. Now they had a name to go on—Jock Semple, and Semple might still be alive, unlike so many other potential witnesses he had managed to track down, only to find them lying in long-forgotten graves. But, naturally, there was an obstacle. MacKellar learned that Semple had left the village abruptly shortly after Alicia gave birth, and had not been heard of for years, until a traveling preacher had brought his father a Christmas message five winters ago. The older Semple, confused as to why Lord Luke was interested in his son, said proudly, "He sent word that he had a braw farm jist ower the border, forebye a wife and twa bonny laddies. Och, I always kenned he would gan awa to try to better his lot. Jock was the maist ambitious o' a' ma lads."

The old man had no idea where this farm was located, and "ower the border" covered a vast stretch of territory. But Luke was not daunted. There was nothing he liked better than a chase, his only regret that he was not free—because of his older brother's illness—to search for himself. This task he was forced to relegate to his trusty squire, Hamish Whittier, together with a dozen of his most loyal clansmen. He told no one in the family itself, afraid that through some slip or a careless word Magdalen might get to hear of it. To Nan he warned sternly, "We might still be wrong about Lady Ogilvy. True, she bears a strong resemblance to the MacKellars, and from what she divulged about her background, it could be so, but at this point 'tis merely supposition. We need a witness to say that the crime truly did take place. *Then* we will question Lady Ogilvy more closely. In the meantime ye must promise to say nothing."

So while both their men were absent and Alyssa so distracted with worry, Nan kept her promise to her husband, though it wasn't easy. The two women, over the long evenings they sat together before the hall fire, rapidly became close friends, and Nan adored the little Alexander. Gradually, warmed by the older woman's kindness and interest, Alyssa talked a little about the cause of her breakup with Simon. Then one night she confessed that she had first met Sinclair years ago in Lochmore, and though she had tried to put him out of her mind, been in love with him ever since.

Nan clucked sympathetically. "His wife, they say, is demented, following Knox about in a coarse grey robe, with her hair cropped like a—a monk's, denouncing the Queen as a sorceress to anyone who will listen. One wonders why her uncle doesn't have her locked away before she can do mischief to herself or others."

Alyssa sighed and turned her head to look into the fire. "The marriage will soon be ended . . . " she said faintly, feeling sudden pity for Elizabeth, who never fully understood Blake's unique relationship with the Queen. "I hope he lives to enjoy his freedom."

Nan leaned forward and squeezed her hand. "Take heart, my dear. You must not lose faith now. And until he returns to you, you and Alex are safe at Elmwood, since none know where you are. My servants are discreet and loyal. They . . . they understand," she added pointedly, her mind on Magdalen and the instructions she had given them -should the countess take it into her head to pay them an unexpected visit, always a possibility for all that they'd quarreled.

As it happened, Lady Magdalen was too worried and disgruntled to think of visiting anyone. Her fool of a squire was dead, slain by the man he had been sent to follow, rather than kill. What, she fumed, had possessed Bruno to attack Sinclair before the Chief had led them to the girl?

Imbecile! she raged inwardly as she paced the floor of her upstairs solar. Would that Bruno were here now so she could have him flayed alive!

The squire was the least of her worries. Of more danger was the fact that her cousin Ogilvy had plunged himself into another rash adventure, going so far as to openly accuse Blake Sinclair of treason, with the result that the Chief was now incarcerated behind the bars of Edinburgh Castle.

Who would lead them to the wench now? And by recklessly denouncing Sinclair, Simon had set something in motion that might not be so easy to stop. God's feet, the world was full of idiots, men chief among them, ever slaves to their own pride and vaulting ambitions! How she rued the day she had ever tied her fortunes to that of Simon Ogilvy, nor would she have but for the threat of the letters he had supposedly left with someone at court.

Something must needs be done about Simon . . .

As she stalked back and forth across her chamber, her mind grew cold and pristine-clear, as it always did when she felt danger hovering. At any time her ailing lord might expire. Even so, as the Dowager Countess of Kilgarin she would still be a rich and influential woman, nor so old that she might not make another advantageous marriage.

If all went as she planned. If no one came forward to point an accusing finger, as happened so often in her darkest nightmares.

First, the wench, undoubtedly in hiding now that Sinclair could no longer protect her, must be found and dealt with, then Simon's incriminating letters located and destroyed. To discover the whereabouts of these she would require the assistance of some high official at court since her own lord was powerless to help her, and Lord Luke disinclined. Her mind turned to Bothwell, her kinsman, now the mightiest noble in the land. "Would that I had taken the trouble to nurture better relations with the rogue," she muttered ruefully, scolding herself for being so careless.

Magdalen was aware that at this moment Bothwell had pressing troubles of his own. Billboards were nailed up all over the city accusing him, together with Balfour and Morton, of murdering the King, and requesting that witnesses step forward to support the King, and requesting that witnesses step forward to support this charge "in the name of justice, the Queen, and in the eyes of God who will not fail to punish severely those who know and would remain silent."

She had heard that letters of condemnation were pouring into Holyrood from abroad, even from the Pope himself, decrying this vile outrage and demanding death for the guilty. The Earl of Lennox, Darnley's father, was understandably loud in his grief, nor hesitant about pointing a finger. Bothwell's troopers, huge force though it was, was hard-pressed to keep order in a city trembling on the verge of revolt. The boy-King, despised in life, was speedily being whitewashed into a near-saint in death as people recalled his youth, his beauty— his innocence!—contrasting these tender qualities with the harsher ones of the man who now stood arrogantly by the side of the dead King's wife.

Magdalen's spies kept her well informed. One of them had returned to Cumbray Court only the previous day to report that a new, more ominous tract had been posted to the door of St. Giles church, this one stating that Mary Stuart herself might have known about the plot to take her husband's life "but been rendered mute through witchcraft at the hand of said Bothwell, long known to practice the Black Arts." Again the unknown author of the plaque appealed to witnesses or any with special knowledge about the crime to step forward so that the "wicked demons" could be brought speedily to trial.

Aye, thought Magdalen dryly, her kinsman Hepburn had his problems and must—for all his arrogance and courage—be quailing inwardly lest some witness be found.

On the second of March she requested a private meeting

with the Earl of Bothwell, deeming it most urgent that he comply.

The earl, though intrigued, came to see her reluctantly. These two ambitious, strong-willed people had always been wary of each other and usually kept their own counsel. "Since we are related and I would not wish our family to be drawn into a disastrous situation," the countess began, thinking that he looked tired and thinner since she had last seen him, "I thought it only right to warn you of a rumor that has come to my ears. It seems that the same man who accused Sinclair will stand up before Parliament and name others involved in the plot to kill Darnley. The Earl of Lennox, seemingly, has promised this informer a sack of gold and a manor in France if he will help bring his son's murderers to justice."

"From whence came this information?" asked Bothwell noncommittally. But his flesh turned cold. He was aware of Magdalen's formidable talent for ferreting out news. It suddenly struck him too that Simon had been avoiding him, nor had been seen about court of late.

The countess chuckled cynically. "Ah, now that I cannot divulge. You have your spies and I have mine. However," her face darkened, "I have it on good authority that Ogilvy has left certain letters in the hands of a court official should anything, ah . . . happen to him, and these letters, my dear cousin, should be found and destroyed immediately. If you cannot see to this yourself, busy as you are, then for your own safety you must make your agent swear to burn them without reading the contents."

When Bothwell returned to Holyrood, his first order of business was to send for the lawyer James Balfour, a man with every reason to be as nervous as himself. They talked in private for half an hour while the Queen lay in a darkened chamber close by, her delicate health cracking under the strain of her husband's murder, horror descending on her from all sides, much of it involving her own nobility.

Beyond her window she could hear the voices of the common people shouting as they waved their torches, "Justice! Justice for the King! Hang the traitors and an eternal curse on the bloodthirsty pack!"

Weeping from red-rimmed eyes already swollen from tears, Mary drew a pillow over her head and wondered whom she might turn to; whom she could trust. Sinclair was in prison. Moray had left the city prior to Henry's murder. Seton had stayed on at his castle after she had visited there for a day or two, hoping the change of air would clear the shock from her mind. It was difficult to think clearly, her distress made worse by the recurrence of the old ache under her ribs, the feeling that a net was closing about her; that there was no way out.

There was one. Thinking of this, Mary lay very still, the tears drying on her cheeks. As the widow of Francis she was Queen Dowager of France, with family and property there and many friends to welcome her. In France she had been most happy. Ofttimes she thought of the country with yearning, remembering the sweet years of her childhood, so different from the troubled ones in Scotland.

Yet she was born to rule Scotland. Was it meet that she should turn tail and flee from the land of her father, and her father's father? Who were these nobles that they imagined they had a better right to her throne than she did; never had she known such harsh, arrogant men! Even the low-born Knox had dared to criticize and upbraid her—and she a Queen! Why, her father would have had him beheaded long since!

In one of her passionate shifts in mood, Mary's misery changed to anger. She rose from her bed and stood at the window with clenched fists, watching the torches bobbing about in the darkness, the irate cries of her people ringing in her ears. She did not blame her subjects that they screamed thus. What, after all, did they know of the true situation, the factions buffeting her throne? These people loved her. After their first wariness upon her return, they had melted and accepted her with open arms. Nay, she thought grimly, the people were not her enemies. The difficulty lay in the grasping lords fighting to get blood-stained hands on her crown.

Would that she had a standing army! her mind ran on. During her long absence in France her mother, then regent, had tried to get Parliament to agree to finance such a force. Naturally, the suspicious nobles had read ominous portents into such a request and had voted it down. Cannily, they wished no powerful force of fighting men standing between them and the Queen; a force that could turn on them and compel them to obey.

Mary gripped the window ledge until her knuckles shone white. She was the true anointed Queen! This was her country. And though she might be a woman and frail in body, her spirit was strong. They would not drive her away nor wrest the crown off her head, and, army or no, she would find the means to fight them. Bothwell had many men at his command, and James was more than willing to support her, yet—her face sobered, the anger turning to uncertainty—James Hepburn was the very name the people decried, the man Lennox held chiefly responsible for Henry's death.

The fire went out of Mary abruptly. Under her ribs the pain throbbed with fresh vigor. She sat down on the side of her bed and put her head in her hands, again succumbing to a state of confusion, uncertain of which way to turn, if indeed there *was* a way out of her dilemma.

37

Simon Ogilvy was pleased when James Balfour and a dozen or so of his men rode out to visit him at Mordrun Hall early one blustery March evening. He hurried out to the courtyard to welcome them, glad of the diversion.

Upon accusing Sinclair and having him thrown in prison to await trial, Simon had hastily retired to the country, a little unnerved at the step he had taken in the heat of his resentment and anger, intending to lie low until such time as he must appear to testify at the Chief's trial. Then, after his enemy was condemned and executed he would return to Edinburgh to the bright future awaiting him there under Bothwell, for the earl would not forget what he had done for him at Kirk o'Field. In the meantime, he was safe enough at Mordrun Hall, or as safe as it was possible to be short of leaving Scotland. Yet . . . he was bored and apprehensive, time weighing heavily on his hands, and the sight of his old friend Balfour was just the thing he needed to cheer him.

"Ho! How goes it in town?" he greeted the lawyer when he dismounted. And waving a hand to the open door, "Come in, come in, I need merry company this night." He added with a bitter laugh and a glance at the glowering sky, then the walls of his ancient manor, "There's little hereabouts to distract a man from care now that all my friends are either in hiding or not of a mood to indulge in hearty pastimes."

Balfour stepped up to the door and gave him a long, measuring look from under his brows. "Greetings, Ogilvy," he responded soberly. "Then you have no other company to-night?"

The knight shook his head, peering over the lawyer's

shoulder. "What! So many lads and not one lady? I swear you too, my friend, have fallen prey to the surly mood besetting Edinburgh. But come in, come in!" And once the company had entered the hall, "Megan! Our best ale for our party."

His housekeeper nodded, her dark eyes moving over the group searchingly as they stood about somewhat tensely gazing at the fire, the walls, at anything but the master. During past visits these same men had always been loud and boisterous, delighting in shocking her with their crude jokes and, like great overgrown boys, engaging in horseplay with Sir Simon, arm-wrestling and the like. Now they stood about in awkward silence.

Once the ale was served, Megan made to depart, whereupon Balfour rose from the board and requested that she take his chair. The servant sensed trouble before her master and she declined, explaining that she had tasks to do in the kitchen, when in reality she was thinking of a certain cupboard where she recently had hidden a pistol.

Balfour seized her by the arm and pushed her into his chair, drew his own pistol and pointed it at Ogilvy's chest.

"What's this?" Simon laughed, well used to his friend's little practical jokes. "Have done, man! You'll frighten Megan out of her wits."

Sir James didn't return his smile. Suddenly a great pregnant hush fell over those around the board, and his former companions were staring at him out of hard, implacable eyes that struck a chill into his heart. Simon bolted from his chair, only to be thrust back by the nozzle of the pistol. Balfour nodded quickly and several of his men rose, one of them uncoiling a length of rope from his waist, and while two held the knight fast, the third draped a noose around his neck.

Ogilvy turned ashen pale. He cried, "Jamie, Jamie, be done with this farce! Come, man, are we not friends?"

"*Were* friends," the lawyer replied, and grinned, the smile falling short of his eyes.

With Simon and his housekeeper tied fast to their chairs, the interrogation began. Taking a dagger from his belt, Balfour leaned close and drew the tip of his weapon slowly across Ogilvy's cheek, leaving a thin red smear behind. "We would know the whereabouts of certain letters said to be writ by you and given to another in the form of insurance. Speak up!" he snapped when Simon hesitated, gaping at him in horror, his mind swerving from Bothwell to Lady Magdalen. Sir James shifted the dagger to Simon's other cheek, his eyes crawling mockingly over the handsome face. "You're a comely man, Ogilvy, at least on the surface. While we wait for you to remember where you hid the letters, it might be amusing to scratch that bonny surface and see what lies below."

As warm blood ran into his mouth, Simon screamed, "There are no letters! I—I lied. I swear to you they do not exist."

"He *swears*!" another man chuckled cynically, glancing up from where he had been entertaining himself by slicing away Megan's clothes to expose her scrawny, sallow body. "Faith, but he'd lie to Christ Himself to save his miserable hide." And with a glance back at the woman who sat stoically in the chair with her eyes fixed unblinking on the opposite wall, Balfour's squire suggested, "Mayhap we should give him time to consider while we amuse ourselves with Megan, giving her a taste of the iron baron, or his close cousin, the hot poker," he finished with an excited guffaw.

"Nay!" Ogilvy shrieked, blood and sweat mingling on his cheeks, his eyes bulging from his head in horror. "She's but a servant; she knows nothing. Dear God in heaven—there *are* no letters!"

"You lie, knave," said Balfour quietly, and nodded to his squire.

When Megan's ghastly torture was over, the lawyer whispered in Simon's ear, "Your turn now, my friend. We would see if the iron baron fancies your charms as well as those of your housekeeper."

They took him and hurled him on the table.

Afterwards, one of the men overturned a candle. Another knocked a torch from its bracket on the wall, sending a shower of sparks against the old wood molding. Within minutes the gloomy chamber glowed in crackling orange, the flames reflecting in Simon's eyes as he lay where they had left him, unable to move because of the nature of his injuries. Out of dull, glazing eyes he watched them leave. At the door Balfour called back, "Farewell, traitor! We trust our visit amused you to your satisfaction."

The door slammed shut and hoofbeats thundered away into the night. The group paused to look back from a distant hill, gratified to see the manor in flames, certain the destruction would be complete.

Luke MacKellar came home to break the news to Alyssa in person. When he finished, she sat for a long time gazing silently into the fire, the strain of the past few weeks evident by the lines of tension on her face, unable to believe that Simon was really dead. She hadn't been prepared for this. All her thoughts had been for Blake. Simon, wily animal that he was, seemed indestructible, always managing to save his neck on the very brink of disaster. And now . . . to die thus!

She shuddered. "How, think you, did the fire start?"

Luke shook his head. "No one knows for certain. The house was very old and mayhap one of them grew careless with candle or torch." Reaching to cover her cold hand, he said quietly, "And there is always the chance that it was set. Ogilvy was known to have many enemies."

Many enemies, MacKellar thought soberly, and even more debts. How in the name of God could this poor girl hope to settle them?

He put an arm about her shoulders, hating to broach such a crass subject but, certain that Ogilvy's creditors would be seeking her actively by the morrow, he said, "I know your lord left you poorly provided for, but Nan and I want ye to ken ye are welcome to bide here with us for as long as ye wish," he assured her, lapsing into the broad Scots with which he was most comfortable, even if the countess didn't approve. "I hear tell that Sinclair is recovering, but no word yet of his release." He didn't tell her that earlier that day twenty men said to be implicated in the King's death—mostly lesser gentry and servants—had at Morton's command been hung, drawn and quartered at the Cross.

Alyssa pressed his hand to her cheek. "You've both been so kind to Alex and me!" She added without thinking, "You could not have done more if you'd been my own flesh and blood . . ." and suddenly broke off and held her breath, aware of what she'd said.

There wasn't a sound in the room. When Alyssa finally raised her head it was to find the couple staring at her, Nan with a bright gleam in her eyes. Looking from one to the other, loving them both, she was suddenly weary of waiting. Very deliberately, with her heart beating fast, she went on, "And mayhap you *are* my kin. I truly believe that."

Nan sucked in a breath and pressed a fist to her heart. Luke pulled up a stool close to Alyssa's chair and sat down facing her intently. He had planned to wait, to take this step by step, to find Semple if possible and proceed cautiously—since so much was at stake—but all that crumbled under the soft pleading in the wide green eyes; eyes like those of his brother, Lord Angus.

He was suddenly short of breath. "Alyssa, I would have ye tell us everything ye know about your background. Leave nothing out, no matter how insignificant it might seem. Ye trust us, don't ye, lass?"

"With all my heart."

The story unfolded while the couple hung onto her every word, Luke occasionally interrupting to ask a question. When she came to the part about Davie Weir's death and her suspicion that Bruno had murdered him, Nan cried, "I knew it, I knew it! Magdalen knows the truth and views Alyssa as a threat—"

Luke held up a hand to silence her. "Let the lass talk, woman, and dinna jump to conclusions. What *you* think or suppose will hardly bear much weight in a court o' law. There's such a thing as proof."

Spurning modesty, Alyssa pulled back the skirt of her gown and showed them the brand on her thigh. "Nan could be right. Why else would Lady Magdalen try to kill me? I'm certain too that Simon was later involved in her plot, the main reason he married me."

Luke pursed his lips, nodding slowly as he mulled it over. He rose and nervously paced about the hall, and finally turned to ask, "Does Sinclair ken about this?"

Alyssa shook her head. "I was afraid that if I told him he might think I was trying to trick him into . . . into marrying me." She turned away, flushing.

MacKellar smiled slightly. "A good point. What else *could* he think? If a bonny lass came to me wi' such a tale I'd be mighty suspicious, given that it sounds preposterous." He scratched his head, his mind turning to his own family. They detested Magdalen as much as they despised Thomas, who had given them absolutely no reason to respect him as Chief, but by the same token they would never dream of ousting him—nor could they—without substantial proof that he was an impostor. Thinking of the conniving nature of the woman his brother had wed, Luke was inclined to believe that Thomas had been kept in ignorance of his wife's crime. A man in his cups as often as Tam had been before his illness would have been bound to let something slip.

He returned to the stool and sat down, regarding Alyssa gravely. "Lass," he said, "we think we might have a witness," and told her about Jock Semple and his efforts to find him. "And if it takes a year or five years, I won't rest until I do. My brother Thomas is dying," he went on more quietly, "and as it stands now I will succeed him. But," he went on with a wry grin, "I'm too auld and cantankerous to relish the thought o' having to give up my peaceful life and simple pleasures to bear the responsibility o' Cumbray—or to dress up and play the part o' the court dandy when the need arises." He turned to his wife with a fond smile. "We're country folk, not fancy at a'—"

"Do ye think she canna see that, lad?" Nan broke in with a merry laugh, pointing to his rumpled doublet and stained hose.

"As a' was saying, we're simple people. We are also childless." Luke leaned closer and took Alyssa's face between his hands, his touch infinitely gentle. "We'll unearth the truth, sooner or later, but until we do you must be patient and mention this to nobody—including Sinclair. And if ye really are ma' niece I have a wondrous surprise for ye. The Lady Alicia is still alive!"

Alyssa caught his hands by the wrists, her grip fierce, wrenching hope in her eyes. "Simon swore she was dead. Oh, dear God, are you sure?"

He nodded.

"I must write to her! See her—"

"Nay, henny, not yet. Until we are certain, we must raise no false hopes, least of all in that poor lady's heart, for she suffered much when she lost her babe."

Tears started from Alyssa's eyes and coursed down her face. "Please tell me all you know about my mother."

For over a month Jason Sinclair had not been allowed into Edinburgh Castle to visit the Chief, nor had he been able to see Bothwell personally, which did not surprise him, considering the earl's personal problems. Bothwell, however, had sent him a message. Blake was on the mend, he assured Jason, but for reasons he could not set on parchment it was thought expedient that he receive no visitors for the present. "Bear with me," he wrote, "and by spring, if not sooner, your Chief will be released."

Edinburgh was in a state of turmoil, bold placards posted in every public place demanding that the Queen bring her husband's killers to account. Darnley's family accused Mary of protecting the murderers, hinting that she was an accomplice. Critical letters and messages poured in from abroad.

The Queen had no choice. On April 12 the Earl of Bothwell was tried for the King's murder, but the man who formally accused him, Lennox, failed to appear at the trial. This was far from surprising since Bothwell arrived with a huge retinue of troops, over four thousand men, and some of the most powerful nobles in the kingdom.

He was acquitted.

To celebrate, the earl treated his friends and supporters to a grand banquet which at first he intended to hold at Holyrood, but at this blatant show of supremacy Mary balked, stating firmly that it would be unwise, not to say dangerous, to so brazenly raise himself above the other nobles.

The site of the banquet was moved to Ainslie's Tavern.

In the course of the celebration much wine flowed. A jubilant Bothwell, in an indulgent mood, rewarded Sir James Balfour for his part in drawing up the Craigmiller bond and personally organizing the King's destruction, with the wardship of Edinburgh Castle itself. To Jason Sinclair he dangled the promise of another gift, though he failed to state the reason for his generosity. Clapping him on the back, he announced heartily, "By the end of the month your cousin will be free, restored to you hale and fully exonerated of all charges against him, as I promised."

"Why cannot he be released now? With Ogilvy dead, who is there to speak out agin him?" asked Jason, confused.

Bothwell leaned forward to murmur, "Patience, my friend. This must needs be handled cautiously, so that no backlash can occur; no cries of favoritism, if you take my meaning."

Jason nodded slowly, not understanding his meaning at all but having little choice in the matter.

"Drink up! Drink up!" laughed his host as Jason frowned dubiously. "You too have reason to be of good cheer this night."

Near the end of the evening, Bothwell produced a document which he asked the assembly to read and sign. By this point in the festivities even the nobles who *could* read were drunk. When it was passed to Jason, he stared at it through a haze, the words written there swimming like tadpoles before his eyes. He too had freely imbibed and he turned to Huntly sitting on his left. "Have you penned your name to this?"

"Aye," George Gordon nodded, "everyone present has, even the bishops at yonder end of the table," and he gestured vaguely to a group of men laughing and joking and every bit as drunk as the rest of the party.

Yet Jason hesitated. He wished the Chief were there to advise him. As far as he could make out in the smoke-filled room, the bond had to do with the fact that the Queen was once again a single woman and in need of a strong, supportive husband, but the rest was so shrouded in convoluted legal obscurities, with a reference now and then to Bothwell, that with a snort of impatience Jason finally gave up.

He wrote "Sinclair" under all the other names, thus committing his house to supporting a marriage between Bothwell and the Queen.

On April 21 Blake Sinclair, now fully recovered, paced his room in Edinburgh Castle like a caged beast. By bribing one of his guards he had managed to keep up fairly well with the news. He heard that Simon Ogilvy was dead, that Bothwell had been acquitted, and that there had been a spate of executions—none of anyone of great importance—following King Henry's death.

Gripping the bars at his window, Blake gazed down upon the city, wondering again why he had not been released and why Jason had not been allowed to visit him over the past weeks. Most of all he worried about Alyssa and their son.

Now and then he had had a message from James Hepburn asking him to be patient, full of assurances that once his own problems were under control he would see to it that Blake was released. The last contact had been two weeks ago.

Sinclair rattled the bars furiously, almost mad with anxiety and frustration, and seething with a lust for revenge when he considered how the MacKellars had betrayed him. Why had they tried to kill him? On the face of it, Blake could not imagine what they felt they stood to gain—but he meant to find out the moment he was released from this accursed place!

Finally the moment he had been longing for came, and that very same evening. It was than that his cousin Jason told him that Alyssa and the boy had disappeared—and that he had signed the Ainslie Bond in his name.

Afraid that the MacKellars, failing in their attempt to kill him, might have gone after Alyssa and their son, he rounded up as many of his men as he could locate in the space of an hour and started immediately for Cumbray Court.

38

A groom flew into the hall blubbering, "Lady, the h-house is surrounded by heavily armed clansmen; Sinclair's men! They caught us by surprise, stealing up in the dark wi' their horses' hoofs muffled. They—there's naught we can do."

The countess started up from her seat by the fire, flustered for one of the few times in her life, but she had only taken a few steps toward the stairs when Sinclair himself burst into the room, a dozen of his men crowding in behind him. A pair of murderous dark eyes froze her in place. "Sit!" he commanded, pointing to the bench. "I would have a word with you and your lord."

Recovering herself quickly, Magdalen didn't move. "By what right does an accused traitor force his way into my home and make demands of me and my sick husband?" she asked haughtily.

Blake smiled grimly. "Tell me, madam, do you find yourself in want of a squire?"

She concealed her terror, shrugging coldly. "You speak in riddles, Sinclair—"

"A squire by the name of Bruno, the fellow sent to kill me last February tenth."

The countess made a fine show of astonishment. "We live quietly here, my lord, ever since the earl has been so ill. Have you not heard that Lord Luke is temporarily in charge of the affairs of Cumbray? You must take this matter up with him."

Leaving two of his men to guard her, Blake and Jason made a thorough search of the house. In a lavish upstairs chamber they came upon Lord Thomas, or what had once been Lord Thomas, lying in a coma in his great poster bed.

Shocked, Blake drew back, his nostrils offended by the foul odor in the air. The Earl of Kilgarin had been reduced to a yellow husk covering a pile of bones, glazed eyes staring out of a bony skull, an enormous array of vials and powders set out on a table beside the bed.

This man, Sinclair saw, was long since past the stage of giving orders to anyone. The treachery, then, had come from the direction of Elmwood. This confused and surprised Blake, since he had always had good relations with the younger MacKellar brother, but with Alyssa and his son unaccounted for he was in no mood to ponder the vagaries of the human heart.

Returning to the hall, he bowed sardonically to Magdalen and left without a word of apology.

She watched them go, smiling thinly, in no doubt that Elmwood would be their next destination. Good! she thought with a chuckle. Mayhap Luke and Sinclair would destroy each other. Her brother-in-law and his wife were fast becoming a mite too popular at court.

Sinclair and his men met more resistance at Elmwood, though it was late in the evening by this time and again they caught the household by surprise. But with Lord Thomas's life hanging by a thread, Luke MacKellar was now Chief in all but name, and as such entitled to keep a large personal guard at his residence. Seeing that their former allies were heavily armed and in a belligerent mood, Luke's soldiers rallied from the surprise swiftly and drew their weapons, their leader shouting, "State your business here, my Lord Sinclair."

The door of the house flew open and Luke MacKellar peered out into the yard. In the torchlight by the stables he saw dozens of angry clansmen, their Chief with a sword in his hand. Startled, the older man growled, "What means this intrusion, Sinclair?"

Blake shouted back, "I come here through your own treachery, MacKellar! And I demand satisfaction. So step outside, or would you have me cut you down inside your own hall?"

Luke was completely mystified, his bewilderment obvious to the tense group of men waiting in the yard, but Blake, certain he was trying to bluff his way out of a confrontation, reminded him sarcastically, "It was your man, was it not, who tried to assassinate me on the night of the King's murder? The MacKellar badge was on his chest."

"You ere—"

"Nay, I think not. Come out! Or must we fight our way in?"

The older man heaved a sigh and stepped back from the door, commenting with a droll smile, "For the sake of the long truce between us these many years, I trust we can parley before you cut me down?"

Blake entered Elmwood warily, glancing about into the shadowy corners of the hall, then his head jerked up abruptly at a soft cry from the gallery above. At sight of Alyssa's titian head Blake misunderstood. With a snarl of fury he wheeled on MacKellar with his sword raised to strike, his only thought to kill the knave who, not content with trying to assassinate *him*, had kidnapped Alyssa and the baby. Luke stumbled back, his face grey, an instant before the blade whistled past his shoulder. As Blake raised his arm for the second time, Alyssa flew down the stairs, screaming, "Stop! Please, stop!" and ran between them.

"Get back!" Sinclair shouted. "Are you out of your mind?"

She pushed the arm holding the sword violently aside. "Nay, you must not. I—I came to Elmwood of my own free will."

Blake hesitated, his eyes flickering from Alyssa to her uncle. Luke nodded slowly, a little color creeping back into his white face, and suggested gruffly, "Be at ease, my lord, for this is not how it seems, and if you will be seated"—he waved to the hearth—"we will try to explain."

Sinclair dropped his sword but did not sheath it. With his free arm he drew Alyssa to his side, looking down avidly into her pale face, his eyes warm and questioning at once. She clung to him, tears of relief flowing, yet in another way she was nervous too, wondering how they would possibly explain this without giving too much away.

She need not have worried. Her uncle, with a warning sidelong glance, seeing that she was wavering and inclined at that emotional moment to blurt out the truth, quickly took over, for even her lover must not be brought into this until they were sure.

The story he delivered was plausible enough since it happened all too frequently within noble families. From the moment he had met Alyssa at Seton Castle, he said, he had suspected that she might be a MacKellar bastard, especially once he learned of her background. Putting a hand on the young woman's arm, he continued, "I believe she might be my own daughter, but we thought not to disturb you with this until we were sure—or as sure as 'tis possible to be after all this time."

Blake was clearly astounded. His eyes jumped from the older nobleman to Alyssa's sheepish face, and he burst out laughing. "Ridiculous!"

"Take a close look at her, Sinclair," urged Luke. "You know our family. Mayhap you recall my sister Lydia when she was so much sought after at court? 'Twas some years gone, and you were but a sapling lad then, but—"

"I recall her well," Blake interrupted with a slight smile, and gazing at the woman he loved he felt as if a veil had been whipped from his eyes. The hair was the same, the flirtatious slant of the eyes, and the tall, regal carriage. He passed a hand across his face and shook his head, bemused by this unexpected turn of events and annoyed that Alyssa had not thought to confide in him. "A—a coincidence," he suggested, though no longer so sure. "God's blood, you cannot think to base kinship on appearance alone!"

MacKellar assured him smoothly that that was not the case. He had *other* reasons for believing that Alyssa might be one of the family and was at that moment investigating, but, naturally, until this had been completed the matter was to be treated in the strictest confidence. When Blake gave Alyssa a cool, measuring look that held a tinge of disapproval, MacKellar soothed, "She would have told you once we were sure, but until then I made her promise to keep this secret lest both of us be proved wrong."

Sinclair removed his arms from Alyssa's shoulder, rose and prowled about the room, this startling piece of news distracting him from the main reason for his visit to Elmwood, never dreaming to find Alyssa there. A MacKellar bastard! Well, he mused, calmer now, it was not so hard to imagine. The MacKellar brothers had been comely men in their youth and as lusty as any other, and if Lord Luke—childless— thought to warm his old age by claiming one of his blood, albeit from the wrong side of the blanket, what was the harm? But secret or no secret, he was disappointed that Alyssa hadn't confided in him!

Blake glanced over his shoulder as she sat apprehensively by the fire watching him nervously, sensing his hurt and displeasure. Alyssa had grown thin and pale, he noted with a pang, her old radiance greatly diminished, and he knew why. As their eyes met, hers softly pleading for understanding, Blake melted. She was safe here! His son likewise. For that alone he owed Lord Luke a debt that could never adequately be repaid.

Sinclair stopped before her chair and drew her up into his arms and kissed her on the mouth. With a sob of relief Alyssa clung to him, burying her head in his chest. Luke would have left them alone had Blake not stopped him. There was still the matter of the MacKellar squire who had attacked him the night of the King's murder.

The moment he began describing the would-be assassin, Luke sighed. "Bruno . . . lately with my sister-in-law, Magdalen."

When Sinclair returned to Cumbray Court, half-expecting to be met by a large force, he was taken aback to find the mansion quiet. Magdalen had had ample opportunity to prepare her story. "He has not been in my employ for some time," she lied of Bruno. "I rid myself of the cur months ago for the very reason that I brought you here, that I could no longer trust him. The last I heard, he was in service with Sir Simon Ogilvy."

Blake had no way of disputing her, and it might well have been the case. Ogilvy had certainly had every reason to want him dead. And wily rogue that he was, could have made the squire continue to wear the MacKellar badge as a precaution, lest he were caught and the crime traced back to himself.

Sinclair's next thought was to get Alyssa and the boy out of Edinburgh, and as soon as possible, anticipating trouble ahead. Both well might have been acquitted of murdering the King, but the common people remained unconvinced. An undercurrent of violence hung over the city. And the nobles, according to Jason, were rapidly growing more resentful of Bothwell's authority, so much so that his cousin suspected some new plot hatching to discredit the border lord.

If trouble came, Blake knew he would be called to defend the crown. He wanted his little unofficial family settled far off in the Highlands, hoping they could spend some time alone together before he had to return to Edinburgh. MacKellar made no protest at this arrangement, and though she knew she would miss them terribly, Alyssa longed for complete privacy as avidly as did her lover. While at Elmwood there was always the threat of Lady Magdalen discovering her whereabouts. In the North she could breathe easier and enjoy peace of mind, knowing that her son would be safe even if his father had to be away.

Luke and Nan promised to keep in touch. As yet, Luke's men combing the border region had met with no success. "Have faith, lass," he told her privately before she left. "We've moved the search into England and won't give up until we discover if Semple is alive or dead."

They left Edinburgh almost at once, on the morning of April 24, both looking forward to at least a few tranquil weeks together at Lynnwood. As they traveled steadily north, ridding their lungs of the pungent, sooty atmosphere of the city and the tension and explosive aura focused on Holyrood Palace, Alyssa sighed deeply and finally began to relax. Her first sight of the mountains and the sweeping, heather-clad moorland brought a wrenching pang of nostalgia, and she thought of her old friends Davie and Robin, and a certain dreamy-eyed lass who had dared to wish for the stars for all that she had only a comely face and quiet determination to recommend her.

Had that been only five years ago? It seemed a lifetime!

Alyssa glanced at her lover, who seemed to be preoccupied with thoughts of his own, and felt a sense of awe that they were still together considering the trials and separations that had beset their relationship from the first. Now a new element had come between them, though Blake might not be aware of it. Guilt! Because of her, Bruno had sought to kill him, and had come close to succeeding. And as if that were not enough, she had badly lied about her connection to the MacKellars, going along with Luke when he pretended that she might be his bastard daughter. As long as Blake had known nothing about her past, Alyssa had managed to convince herself that her secret was best kept hidden away where it could do no harm to anyone. Now she had blatantly deceived him, her dearest love, and she despised herself no matter how passionately she tried to justify it.

Her shame too must remain a secret. Blake longed for this holiday together and needed it desperately, and Alyssa was determined not to spoil it because of her own shortcomings, yet she dreaded to think how he might react if Lord Luke succeeded in finding Semple and Blake discovered the truth. The irony of it appalled her, that her own personal triumph might bring about that which nothing else had been able to do, the destruction of their long relationship.

On the crest of a hill the company paused to give the winded horses a brief respite, and there below them was Lynnwood, timeless and untouched by the violent machinations of the world beyond the mountains, serene in its golden dell as it had always been.

Absently Alyssa noticed that each time Keane greeted her it was with increasing warmth. Now, instead of referring to her as "mistress," the housekeeper dropped a respectful curtsy and welcomed her with a genuine ring of honesty in her voice. "Ah, my dear lady, 'tis grand to see you again." And at sight of Alexander, "Holy Blessed Virgin, I'd swear 'twas his lordship all over again, long ebony curls and a'!"

Blake smiled into Alyssa's eyes, reading her heart, and his strong, tanned fingers closed tightly over hers as they walked over the threshold and entered the sweet-scented hall, both with the thought that they had come home.

That night they made love with shameless urgency—the first time. The second time was sweeter, more intense, each touching new depths of ecstasy and taking the time to savor it more. Blake kissed her lips, her breasts, the strange little scar within her thigh, pausing for a moment to examine it thoughtfully as he always did. This time, touching it reflectively with a fingertip, he mused aloud, "Could this mayhap have been done to you deliberately, rather than caused through some childhood accident?"

Hating herself, Alyssa shrugged, "Mayhap . . ."

He took the candle from the bedside table and leaned closer, frowning while she lay very still, wondering why one lie always must lead to another, and another, each one shoveling another spadeful of dirt from the hole she was digging for herself.

After a minute he said, "This might well have significance, Alyssa, in light of what MacKellar believes about your birth. Ofttimes the bastard children of nobility are marked in some way so that later—"

Alyssa caught his face between her hands and kissed him into silence. She teased, "Will you babble with me all night about something I know nothing about, sir? I can think of many more *interesting* ways to pass our time."

His eyes gleamed. "Would you care to show me, my lady?"

"With pleasure, my lord."

Within minutes her hands and lips had driven all thought of bastard children from his mind, but it was obvious the next morning while they walked hand in hand on the moor that he hadn't forgotten. Again he returned to the subject Alyssa had begun to dread.

"What think you about this idea of MacKellar's?" Blake asked her curiously.

She turned away, her eyes following the flight of a hawk as it hovered in the cloudless sky over a mountain tarn, its graceful shape reflected in the water below. "It would be wonderful to belong to someone," she replied quietly.

"You belong to me, Alyssa." Blake sounded slightly hurt.

"I know, darling!" She hugged his arm, closing her eyes as

she went on softly, "I meant, it would be nice to know where I came from; to find my true family."

His arms came around her, and with his fingers in her hair, which she had left unbound that morning to please him, he held her head against his heart and tried to imagine what it must feel like to be rootless. It was difficult for Blake to contemplate, he who had always been surrounded by kin—many of them, each supporting the other and pulling together as a team. The Sinclairs had always been close, raised to present a solid front to the outside world, regardless of the occasional differences of opinion between them in private. There had been few splits in his family, and none in recent times. He could name his ancestors going back countless generations, and though his father had been a cold, distant parent with little patience for young people, he had always been there to represent protection and security.

"Luke MacKellar is a good man," he said, "much respected at court—unlike his brother, Thomas."

It was the opening Alyssa had been looking for. "Blake, I don't trust Lady Magdalen!" She had to warn him. "Promise me when you return to Edinburgh that you'll be careful?"

He seemed a little taken aback by her vehemence. "The fellow Bruno no longer worked for her. He was with your, ah, husband, Ogilvy, who had every reason to want me dead."

"She may have lied."

Blake gave her a puzzled look. "And why would she lie? What sense does it make? It's to her advantage too that we are allies."

Alyssa bit her lip, her mind racing. Somehow she must find a way to put him on guard. Oh God, she thought, what have I done? If all else failed she would have to tell him the truth, breaking her promise to her uncle, for she would not allow him to return to the capital unaware of the danger.

"Remember, Magdalen and Simon were kin. And they were alike in many ways, both devious and scheming." She swallowed and hurried on while Blake stared at her quizzically so that she wanted to cringe. "Mayhap Simon told her about us, and, being kin, she sympathized and thought to help him by . . . by having you killed."

He laughed aloud. Such reasoning was naive and highly unlikely. Magdalen MacKellar, from what he knew of her, was much too shrewd to cause a clan war over the marital troubles of a lowly cousin. But at the anxious expression on Alyssa's face he sobered. "Magdalen and Thomas have returned to Cumbray, so I doubt I have anything to fear. Nonetheless, I promise to be most careful."

"Do you mean it, Blake?" Her grip was fierce on his arms.

"Aye, sweeting"—he kissed her—"I mean it."

Much of her uneasiness melted as they embraced.

The days passed pleasantly at Lynnwood and Alyssa prayed that these golden hours together would go on and on, but late on the afternoon of May 2 a messenger rode furiously into Lynnwood with very disturbing news. Bothwell had kidnapped the Queen—with or without her consent, no one seemed sure—and taken her to Dunbar Castle where he had coerced her into agreeing to marry him, perhaps by showing her the Ainslie Bond signed by many of her most important nobles to the effect that they believed the border earl to be the right man to stand at her side. But now these same lords, according to the courier, regretted signing and deplored Bothwell's dramatic rise to power, accusing him of drugging Mary to preclude royal opposition to his outrageous plans.

"But . . . my Lord Bothwell is *already* married!" Alyssa burst out in confusion.

"Not for long." The newcomer brushed the sweat off his brow with his sleeve, continuing darkly, "He's taken steps to have his marriage to Huntly's sister dissolved immediately, or those in charge of it will suffer the consequences." His worried gaze moved to Sinclair. "This could lead to civil war, my lord, for now even the common people are turning away from the Queen, seeing that she would bind herself to one they still consider to be her husband's murderer." Then came the words Alyssa had been dreading. "You must return to Edinburgh at once."

For a moment rage boiled in her heart against Mary Stuart, even if it was unreasonable, even as she knew that in many respects Mary was a helpless pawn surrounded by self-seeking vultures quite willing to manipulate her for their own ends. And it never stopped. Nor, Alyssa was beginning to suspect, would it ever end. How much longer could she stand mutely aside while Blake was called away at a moment's notice to her service, forced to live by the sword, and perhaps die by it in her name? He loved her and their son, it was true, yet the Queen stood between them . . . and perhaps always would.

Blake tried to keep Alyssa informed of the situation while he was away. In his first letter he told her that the Queen and Bothwell had been married in Holyrood Palace on May 15, "and a more sober bride I have never seen," he went on, "going through it all in a daze and with a strange show of indifference." And most startling of all, he continued, it had been a Protestant ceremony. "God's soul, one must wonder if she has lost her mind! Now the people shout agin her, calling her whore and other evil names, but nothing seems to penetrate this fog about her. Bothwell, though, is triumphant . . ."

Alyssa could tell that Sinclair had great reservations about this hasty marriage to which the nobles had formally given their approval by signing the Ainslie Bond—an act most of them now regretted. Jason Sinclair too had signed while the Chief was shut up in Edinburgh Castle. Bothwell might be a fine soldier, Blake went on in his letter, but as the man most closely associated with Darnley's murder he was a disastrous choice of a husband for the Queen, nor would the people accept him. He continued grimly, "Bothwell, now the Duke of Orkney, is well aware of these humors and become surly and and wary, even of his friends. He keeps Her Grace shut away from her nobles and under heavy guard, not trusting any near her lest they poison her agin him—if he has not already done so himself through his mean deportment."

Blake added wistfully, "Mary has lost much of her beauty and all her gay nature, taking no interest in music or dance or any former pastimes. I'm certain she rues this rash step . . . even if her lords at first seemed to approve of it."

He finished on an ominous note. "In spite of everything this marriage might succeed, given time, but I fear time too is against them. There's rumbling of some plot hatching. Morton is said to be behind it. Maitland, too, hating Bothwell as he does, and he's rarely seen about court of late. As for Moray, her brother, well . . . we all know how jealous he is of the new Duke of Orkney. One must wonder if even Bothwell's old friend James Balfour is still as staunch in his cause, even though his was the name most closely linked to Bothwell's in the death of the King."

Later Alyssa was to discover that it was the chameleon Balfour, granted the governorship of Edinburgh Castle by Bothwell after the King's murder, who again shed his skin and became instrumental in the Queen's downfall by siding with the new group of rebels forming to oppose her marriage to Bothwell. On the promise of gathering a large army to support the Queen and her new husband, Balfour lured them out of their secure position at Dunbar Castle and back to the capital.

By the time they reached Leith the newlyweds realized they'd been led into a trap, and here on June 15, in sweltering heat, they were compelled to stand and fight. Mary and her paltry troops took up position on Carberry Hill with a hot sun streaming down out of a hard blue sky, the warm breeze fluttering the Queen's pennant, the Red Lion of Scotland. Pale to the lips and with her eyes now dry, long drained of weeping, Mary Stuart gazed across the waving banners to where the insurgents mustered on a nearby ridge and saw there men she had honored and raised high; men she had naively hoped would help her govern her unruly country . . . all against her now.

Mary cried bitterly, "Why do they hesitate? They are not blind and can see we are vastly outnumbered."

Blake removed his helmet and wiped his sweating brow. "Aye," he agreed grimly, "but who among them have the nerve to give the signal to attack? Remember the ilk of men we are dealing with, Your Grace, and spineless as they are, they have enough wits left to recognize when they are in the wrong."

This might be true, but as they day wore on, more and more of the royal troops slunk away, convinced they would be defeated. Finally Bothwell took Sinclair aside and suggested they slip away and try to rouse the nearby country people to the

Queen's cause. Mary had another idea, one that might prevent bloodshed. She offered to give herself up to the rebels in exchange for Bothwell and Sinclair being allowed to leave unmolested, hoping they could drum up greater support while she returned to Edinburgh, and later join her there at the head of a large army.

Sinclair violently opposed the idea, but Bothwell remarked ruefully, "'Tis our only chance, and surely better than none."

Blake took the Queen by the arm and beseeched her not to go through with the scheme, whereupon her husband cried, "Let her be, Sinclair! They dare not harm her with the eyes of the world upon them, and if you and I can but make it safely to Dunbar she will not tarry with them long, I promise."

Mary kissed both men and bade them leave while they still could, and when Sinclair adamantly refused, she said, "Faith, my lord, but you are more good to me alive than lying dead at my feet in a pool of your own blood. So hasten!"

As the sun sank in the west they left her sitting astride her horse with her banner drooping in the early evening stillness, a solitary figure, yet proud and regal, standing out vividly from among her meager soldiers.

Blake looked back once, his eyes misting, then spurred his horse and thundered away after Bothwell and in minutes vanished in the gloaming.

Mary Stuart was seized roughly and taken into Edinburgh as a captive, a city that had been bombarded with propaganda, all of it adverse and calculated to turn her people against her. As she rode past, her head high in spite of her mud-spattered clothes and with her glorious auburn hair loose and tumbling over her shoulders, the citizens of Edinburgh eyed her coldly, wondering what had become of the virtuous young monarch they had adored. She heard the words "whore" and "wanton" and her expression froze, but she was too dispirited to weep at this ultimate betrayal. How could she blame the people, fed so many evil lies about her? Nay, nay, she still loved her subjects and would soon enough win them back if Bothwell and Sinclair were successful. For if it took a day or a year, she knew these men would do their utmost to restore her or die in the attempt.

To shame her, the Queen was lodged in the provost's house, an indignity that turned out to be a mistake for the rebels. When Mary appeared forlornly at the window, obviously in a sorrowful state, the citizens were made uncomfortable and finally moved to tears. Pointing to the lords who held her captive, they wondered if *their* conduct was so spotless that they should dare point fingers at the Queen.

The pendulum swung back in favor of Mary.

Rioting broke out in the city. Afraid their prisoner might be rescued, the Queen's jailors moved her to remote Lochleven Castle in the middle of a deep lake. As she gazed out of an upstairs window of her new quarters, Mary's spirit finally crumbled. Nothing short of a miracle could save her now.

39

One sultry afternoon in late June, Keane came running into her mistress's chamber. "Riders approach the manor, my lady!" she cried excitedly, having already recognized the Sinclair pennant.

Blake swept Alyssa off her feet and kissed her in full view of the servants while they stood watching with abashed grins. He was as brown as a gypsy, lean and sinewy, and by the look of his clothes had recently spent much time in the saddle.

This proved to be true. After he had bathed and dined he told Alyssa about the recent happenings. Setting off in different directions, he and Bothwell had ridden all over the country doing their utmost to stir up support for the Queen, and though the response had not been as good as they had expected, they were gradually meeting with some success. Even a few of the rebels had repented and offered to join them. Now Blake hoped to do even better with some of the local nobles, many of whom owed him debts for past favors.

Everything went well during his time in the Highlands until they heard that Bothwell had been outlawed, and all his possessions seized. When this news seeped out of Edinburgh to the more remote sections of the country, the army that Sinclair had managed to put together drifted away. Even Huntly gave up at that point. "It's a lost cause, and well you know it, Sinclair. Word has it that Bothwell has taken ship for Norway." And at the determined expression of Blake's face, "God's teeth, man, daily executions are taking place in Edinburgh, poor unfortunates slain for public consumption to distract from the *real* culprits in Darnley's murder, for if Bothwell was indeed guilty then he wasn't alone." He sighed and shook his head. "'Tis time to lie low in the North and watch developments. Mayhap at a later date something more positive might be done."

Reluctant as he was to bide time, Blake saw the wisdom in this. If he persisted openly and was also outlawed, then he would certainly be of little good to the Queen. He had plenty to keep him busy between Augusta and Lynnwood and his other estates, business that he'd been forced to delegate to others during the time he was in Edinburgh.

There was another matter grating on his nerves—the divorce. Because of Elizabeth's unorthodox behavior, a question had been raised about her sanity, and for a while there had been a distinct possibility that Blake's freedom would be delayed for a very long time, assuming he ever got it at all. But his latest communication with his lawyer had been more hopeful. His wife, it seemed, had been unnerved by his imprisonment in Edinburgh Castle and later his involvement in the fray at Carberry Hill. Afraid of being associated with one who stood an excellent chance of being outlawed—therefore losing everything he owned—she was now pressing for the divorce as actively as he was, desperate to regain the large dowry she had brought to the marriage while she still could. So for the moment he had heard that she was living quietly with her uncle, whether because he had ordered her to change her behavior or risk losing all she had, or on advice of her lawyer, Blake wasn't sure. He was certain her control would not last long, but prayed it would continue long enough for the divorce to go through—and it must go through!

Blake, typically, kept these worries to himself, relieved that Alyssa avoided the subject and seemed to have accepted their present mode of living. Since there was no question of him installing her at Augusta, it was convenient that Lynnwood was only an hour's ride away, and Lynnwood was where Sinclair spent every spare minute of his time over the next few weeks; pleasant weeks for all the turmoil in both his private and public lives.

Alyssa, though, quickly sensed his underlying restlessness. He seemed always slightly on edge, as if ready to spring up and ride away at a second's notice should there come word of a rescue attempt being organized on behalf of Mary Stuart. Sometimes she almost hated the Queen, who had the power to steal away his thoughts as she had so often taken him away in person. When they heard that she had miscarried Bothwell's child and hourly lived in fear of her own life being taken, Alyssa was ashamed of such thoughts, and tried not to resent the unfortunate lady.

Then came disastrous news. They learned that the Queen had been forced to abdicate, and on July 29 baby Prince James had been crowned King of Scotland, with the Earl of Moray as regent during the prince's minority.

Blake slammed the parchment on the hall table with such violence that Alyssa jumped, crying, "Well, now it is over! You must accept it and go on with your own life."

He stared at her as if she had lost her wits, his rugged face grim, dark eyes blazing. "It's not over," he grated harshly. "She was *forced* to abdicate, so whatever she signed is not legal, and well that whoreson Moray knows it!"

"There is nothing you can do," Alyssa said sharply.

"Not for now, but this matter is far from resolved."

She thumped down her tankard of ale, splashing the contents over the parchment, two spots of flaming color blazing over her cheekbones. "Nothing is *ever* resolved! From one day to the next there can be no peace in our lives, and all because of Mary Stuart! I grow weary of it. As long as there was a chance I—I could understand, but now"—she gulped in breath—"you've fulfilled your promise to her. She is no longer Queen of Scotland!"

Sinclair eyed her coldly. "You are wrong, Alyssa. A Queen forced to give up her throne by having a pistol held to her head has legally given up nothing."

And with that he strapped on his sword and without another word rode off to parley with George Gordon at Strathbogie.

The day after, Blake came to Alyssa and told her that he was off to France and regretfully could not take her and Alex with him. He would be on the move constantly trying to drum up a rescue attempt for the Queen, but shouldn't be gone more than eight or nine weeks. Since Wyatt was going with him, Alyssa would be left in charge of the under-squire, Thorpe, together with most of his men then in the Highlands, and would be safe enough. These men had promised to guard her with their lives.

So with her anger still unresolved, Alyssa reluctantly bade her lover farewell, never dreaming that months would pass before she saw him again.

When the Chief returned in March, he found Alyssa quiet and unusually subdued. For all his efforts on the Queen's behalf, he returned empty-handed. No French troops would come to Scotland to mount a rescue attempt. "If Her Grace is to be delivered, then it must be done by us alone," he told Alyssa grimly, after embracing her fiercely and kissing her over and over, with the air of a man whose senses were parched.

Alyssa barely returned his kisses, and as the days passed it became clear that a wall had formed between them. Blake was concerned; from the moment of his return he had detected a change in her. She struck him as being cool and oddly remote. "Nothing ails me," Alyssa insisted sharply each time he probed. "And please stop badgering me!" Then with a touch of indignation in her voice, "You cannot expect to be gone for four long months and come back to find everything the same, my lord."

"What do you mean?"

She felt helpless, never knowing when Blake would have to leave again, or even if he would return to her. She knew Blake felt he could not desert his Queen, yet she was tired of coming second in his life. There was hostility inside her, a fierce, hot anger that she couldn't quite control. It made no difference to tell herself that she was being unfair; that she had known from the start that Sinclair had other important responsibilities besides herself and would never be the type of man to sit comfortably by the fireside as one of her own rank might have done once his daily tasks had been attended to.

Alyssa had a stark view now of the gulf that separated his world from hers. His interests were such that he would often have to be gone. Life for Sinclair didn't begin and end at

Lynnwood—or even Castle Augusta . . . or revolve around her.

The coolness between them persisted and came to a head in late April when, after a visit from George Gordon—which was conducted in private—Blake announced that he was leaving for Seton Castle and might be gone for a week or two.

Alyssa nodded stiffly. "Then I would like to return to Edinburgh to live with the MacKellars."

"What . . . ?" Sinclair gazed down at her stony face in astonishment and dismay. "In God's name, why?"

"Because I wish it!"

He grabbed her by the shoulders and shook her a little, his own anger rising. He had tried to be patient, to wait out whatever dark mood had fallen over her—to discuss it if she would!—all to no avail. Now he meant to get to the bottom of it.

"You are going nowhere," he growled, his face as hard as the granite mountains surrounding his castle. "We will have this out, my lady, once and for all!"

"You will keep me a prisoner, then?"

"Alyssa, Alyssa, have done with this." His tone softened. "Tell me what troubles you, darling. Come, we love each other, do we not?"

Her eyes were determined, implacable. "Aye, we love each other—but mayhap it's not enough. From first we met, you, my lord, have been the center of my existence, but I know now that *I* can never be the center of yours. I've lived my life through you, like a—a star spinning around the sun, but now I think I must not depend on you for heat and light and must—"

Sinclair burst out laughing. "Christ's soul . . . what has gotten into you?" A mixture of amusement and surprise glinted in his eyes. "Have you become a philosopher, then, mayhap through reading too many dry books in the library whilst I was gone? Forget this foolishness. Spinning around the sun, indeed!" He grinned down into her sullen face. "Come upstairs now and I'll show you just how warm the sun can be, and be done with this cloud hanging over us."

Alyssa went rigid under his hands at this unfortunate remark, meant to be taken teasingly. Under the circumstances she found it far from amusing. Her eyes narrowed. "I have a life of my own to see to, just as you have, and must look to it now."

Sinclair's hands dropped from her shoulders, the smile dying in his eyes. "I warn you to reconsider," he said ominously.

"Nay, my mind is made up."

He gazed down at her, suddenly haughty. "My son stays here."

All the color drained from her face, but her eyes did not soften. She drew in a harsh breath. "I have never asked anything of you, my lord, but not I implore you to grant me this boon—let Alex stay with his mother?"

For a moment Alyssa was certain he would refuse, which he had every right to do, but then he nodded. "He may stay with you . . . for now."

That night they slept apart. Lying dry-eyed and numb in the huge carved bed, Alyssa sought to understand herself, and failed. During Blake's long absense a part of her had switched off while another had flared to life to take its place. She couldn't seem to feel—a strange sensation for one who had been governed by emotions all her life. Her mind was alive, more keenly alive than it had ever been, and she considered things with a clarity that hadn't been possible before, when her feelings had colored everything.

How long, she asked herself, could she be content to live her life through Blake Sinclair?

40

In April—while Alyssa was still at Lynnwood—Luke MacKellar's men were on their way back from England, where they had spent more than a year searching for their quarry in vain. They had investigated every tiny village and hamlet on either side of the border, stopping at countless farmsteads along the way. They had talked to innkeepers, stable stewards, squires and grooms, to barmaids, ministers of the local churches, town headles and even vagabonds they ran into on their route. No one had heard of Jock Semple. Either he was dead, reasoned Hamish Whittier, or he had moved much deeper into the heart of England, in which case he would never be found.

Passing through Carlisle on the way home, Whittier and his men stopped at the Tusk and Hoof. When the bartender plunked tankards of ale before them, Hamish took a grateful swallow, grimaced, then spat the brew out on the rushes. "'Tis sour as piss," he complained loudly, drawing a disapproving scowl from the innkeeper, who retorted, "You Scots are all alike, bragging that everything is better north of the border. If it's so blasted good up there, why do so many of ye settle here among us, eh?"

Whittier sneered. "Them that do must be daft, or forced to flee—" He broke off and stared hard at the innkeeper. "Be there Scots folks hereabouts?"

"Aye, and ye can see for yourself come market day if ye plan to tarry awhile." That's when all the local farmers brought their beasts to town for auction, he informed them, and about the only time they ever saw Scots Johnny from Danbury Farm. "He's quiet, like, a fella who likes to keep to himself—"

"What's his last name?" Whittier broke in, forgetting all

about the sour ale as he eyed the other man intently, wondering if they were off again on another wild goose chase, as had happened numerous times before during the past year.

"Johnny Templeton. A big fella, somewhere 'bout forty of mayhap a little younger. Is the name familiar to you?"

Hamish shook his head—but he made up his mind to remain in Carlisle until market day, and in the meantime they could do some discreet investigating on their own, including taking a ride out to Danbury Farm.

In the next three days Whittier learned quite a bit about Johnny Templeton, thought to be originally from Glasgow in Scotland. The farmer had lived in the Carlisle area for about twenty years and had bought Danbury Farm from the Gilchrist family thirteen years ago. He was said to be quiet, hardworking, married to an Englishwoman and the father of two sons. In all this time south of the border he had never lost his Scottish accent and, as far as anyone knew, had never returned to his homeland for a visit.

On market day Hamish and three of his men were stationed near the door of the inn while the others, well armed, waited tensely outside. Many people came and went that afternoon, Whittier and his companions sitting forward expectantly each time a tall man entered the noisy, crowded common room. Finally, when they had almost given up hope, a big red-faced farmer strode in with two friends, and they heard the tell tale burr in his voice. Whittier gave the party time to down their first brimming tankards of ale, then turned to their table with a grin. "You're from Scotland?" And when the big man didn't respond, "We couldna help overhearing, and by the sound o' your voice I'd guess ye hail from the Highlands."

An instantaneous change came over Templeton, his eyes wary, meaty fist tightening on the handle of his mug. "Nay," he said, "I'm from Glasgow."

Hamish feigned surprise. "Are ye, bigod! Well, a man's ears will sometimes mislead him. Have ye lived in these parts long?"

At this, feeling superfluous and convinced that Templeton would be anxious to catch up on all the news from his homeland, his friends finished their drinks and, clapping him on the shoulder, left. Without waiting for an invitation, Hamish and his men moved quickly to occupy the chairs just vacated, and the squire came right to the point. "Mayhap, knowing the territory well, ye can help us, sir. We've come south to locate a man by the name o' Jock Semple. Have ye ever run into anyone by that name hereabouts?"

The farmer's eyes flickered away and he shook his head.

"Well, we ken he's been hiding here for a great many years and owns a farm outside Carlisle, and we also ken that he thought it prudent to change his name in the foolish hope that he would never be traced." The squire, convinced that they had found their man and tired of parrying, dropped a heavy hand on Templeton's arm with the words, "We know who you *really* are, so 'tis useless to deny it." And he lied, "We have muckle evidence to back it up, and a hundred men stationed outside the inn lest ye entertain notions of making a run for it. Ye won't escape us this time, Jock Semple."

The big man said nothing. All the life had gone out of him. Deep inside he had always known that sooner or later this day would come and he'd be brought to account for his crime. He had dreamed of it happening over and over. For more than twenty years nightmares had haunted him, giving him no real peace. Now he felt resigned to his fate and when Whittier and his men rose he followed them like a wraith and allowed them to escort him from the inn, only half-listening when the squire assured him that in exchange for the truth he might be permitted to return eventually to the new life he had forged for himself across the border. Thinking they were really Lady Magdalen's men, Semple didn't believe it for a minute, certain he was doomed.

True to her threat, Alyssa left Sinclair and returned to her kin in Edinburgh on May 1. Two days later Lord Luke MacKellar rushed home to Elmwood with astounding news. The Queen had somehow escaped from Lochleven and asked that all her faithful supporters meet her at Niddry, Lord Seton's place, where a large army was gathering.

Alyssa's heart again swelled with terror, knowing that Sinclair would be among them, certain that he had been one of those who had helped engineer her escape from the island. Her prediction, then, had come true. The turmoil and violence surrounding the Queen would never end, not as long as she lived to breathe visions of valor and glory into the men around her, a lure so few of them could resist.

Alyssa had spent countless hours examining her feelings for Mary Stuart, surely a woman like no other. She was not jealous of the Queen or the powerful emotions she inspired in Sinclair, and others, but she was afraid that those emotions would be the means of their destruction. Unlike Sinclair, she could not continue to live her life in the shadow of death, acutely aware that each moment they shared might be their last together, so when Luke raced home with his news, Alyssa tried to convince herself that she was well out of it and had done right to leave him, all the more so since he had refused to commit himself where she was concerned.

Luke MacKellar left with most of his men for Niddry. His youngest brother, Stephan, was left in charge of Elmwood, and Stephan made no secret of the fact that he resented his tame mission when so many more exciting events were taking place. Within days the young man began spending more and more time at Holyrood, neglecting his duties at home as he tried to keep abreast of the developments.

Amid all this furor, Magdalen and Thomas MacKellar returned to Edinburgh almost unnoticed.

The Queen's army clashed with the regent Moray's in the small village of Langside, where Lord Hamilton spurned Sinclair's advice to avoid the area and ride hard for the stronghold of Dumbarton to raise more troops for the cause. As Blake had feared, their men were wedged into the tiny village street, attacked at one end by Kirkcaldy and at the other by the Earl of Morton's men. The royal soldiers fought savagely, trying to hold them off until the Earl of Arbyll arrived with his own army, as he'd promised. Finally some did arrive—but without their Chief.

At this betrayal, Mary's army scattered in all directions.

Sinclair, fearing for the Queen's life as she sat astride her horse on a nearby ridge, hacked his way toward her and reluctantly gave the signal for his men to retreat. While they galloped away for the Highlands, Blake remained at the Queen's side and tried to persuade her to go to Dumbarton and from there take ship for France. Instead, she decided to ride south to Lord Maxwell's castle of Terregles.

After an arduous journey to distant Terregles in the company of Sinclair and Maxwell and a few other loyal nobles, Mary shocked her company by suddenly announcing, after a short rest, that she wished to continue over the border into England.

Her supporters were speechless with horror. Blake thought she was joking, then noticed the stubborn expression on her face. He was appalled, realizing that she was serious.

"Put such an idea out of your mind!" He was more angry with her than he had ever been. "You can expect no help from the English monarch and must turn to France instead."

Mary threw a wild-eyed glance at the disapproving faces around her. With her long auburn hair cropped close to her head to conceal her identity during her trip south, and still wearing her torn, mud-splattered clothes, she looked more like a pale gypsy than the glorious and beautiful Queen all of them remembered so vividly during her first years back in Scotland.

She sighed and shook her head. "You misjudge my cousin Elizabeth. Did she not rail against Moray for his part in the Chaseabout rebellion? Did she not put forth a critical outcry against any daring to rise up against their sovereign? Think of it, my lords, she *must* support me in this crisis, if only with a mind to discouraging those in her own country who might be nourishing plots against herself. I have her friendship ring"— and she held up a hand no longer smooth and white, but red and chapped—"as well as a kist full of her loving correspondence. We might not agree on everything, but she is still of my blood and we are in complete accord when it comes to treasonable acts against the crown."

The others turned away from the entreaty in her eyes as she appealed for their understanding, but Sinclair caught her by the shoulders and shook her a little in his alarm and exasperation.

"Madam, you are fatigued and overwrought. Rest awhile

and ponder this again once you can think clearly." He inhaled deeply, his temper rising when he caught the determination in her eyes. "You must not take this disastrous step!" he shouted.

The Queen was clearly miffed, even as the others were uneasy and embarrassed, amazed that Sinclair had stepped so far out of line, though they well understood his reasons for it. Mary tossed her head proudly and sniffed, "I'm not afraid, my Lord Sinclair, nor will I flee this island like a—a whipped cur. I am the Queen of Scotland." She paused for a moment to let her words sink in, as if feeling that he needed reminding. "I will not give up my crown while there's breath in my body to fight for it. My cousin of England can understand my plight and imagine herself in my position, for the simple reason that it could so easily happen to her, her own crown being not overly secure, and because of this she'll be forced to assist me."

Blake's hands dropped from her shoulders. "God help you," he muttered, and strode out of the room.

41

For one of the few times in her life, Magdalen MacKellar felt completely blocked. She had recently quarreled violently with her sister-in-law Lady Nan, and Nan had had the temerity to say that Magdalen was no longer welcome at Elmwood and would not receive her there unless on express command of Earl Thomas—who had long since passed the stage of being able to command anything.

Magdalen was beside herself with rage, rage she had been forced to choke down because of her precarious position within the family. By and large, the MacKellars detested her. Already it was as if Luke were Chief and dumpy, homespun Nan his countess. But, furious as she was, the cool reasoning side of Magdalen's mind recognized the fact that she had made a serious mistake where the family was concerned. She had always been too proud for her own good, no great sin when one was on top, in a strong position at Cumbray as she had been when Thomas was in better health. Now he lay close to death in an upstairs chamber at Cumbray Court, their mansion in Edinburgh. This in itself would not have troubled her over much—had the family rallied around her in her coming bereavement. That they did not boded ill indeed.

And something underhand was going on, she was certain of it! Her keen, sharply honed instincts read much into furtive glances, whispers hastily broken off when she appeared, and, most disturbing of all, the fact that Luke's head squire, Hamish Whittier, had been dispatched to the border on some vague mission over a year ago.

She had been unable to infiltrate Elmwood with a spy or two since they refused to take new help into the household. All their servants had come from the country manor and all were staunchly loyal and impervious to bribes. So she had no recourse but to set some of her own loyal retainers to watching Elmwood from a distance, to try to mingle with Luke's men then in Edinburgh and report back to her any tidbit of gossip they overheard. None of it bore fruit until the time the Queen made her dramatic escape from Lochleven. In the ensuing confusion, one of her spies raced back to tell her that he'd heard that a fair young woman and small child had arrived at Elmwood and been welcomed into the family. The woman's escort had worn the badge of the Sinclairs.

Instantly everything was clear, the reason for Hamish Whittier's long absence on the border explained. Magdalen experienced a deep chill, but she was not so frightened that she couldn't make plans. Through an agent she immediately arranged to have money and jewels transferred to France and a manor purchased for her there under another name. Then she looked into shipping schedules departing from the nearby port of Leith.

She should have fled at once, but there was that in Magdalen MacKellar's nature that railed against anyone getting the best of her, especially another woman. *That* she could never tolerate and hope to live in peace with herself; her pride simply wouldn't allow it.

She pondered for an hour or so and came up with a way to taste the sweetest revenge, but to put her plan into effect she needed someone like Bruno; someone ruthless and desperate enough to follow her instructions to the letter, and the ability to slip past the sentries guarding Elmwood.

There was one place where she might find such a man.

Magdalen's visit to Tolbooth Prison, ostensibly to inspect the conditions there as a member of the Hospice Fund, proved highly profitable, as it had done years before with Bruno. The thought foremost in her mind as she looked over the poor wretches incarcerated there was that a man will try hardest when he's desperate. Most of those she saw were very desperate indeed, many condemned to die within the week. But she had in mind a very special type.

Wrinkling her aristocratic nose in disgust at the smell, she waved a glove sprinkled heavily with perfume in the direction of a fetid cell where two evil-looking creatures were chained to a wall.

"I would know what crimes these fellows committed." she asked the turnkey imperiously.

He grinned lewdly. "Rape, lady, and o' a most unnatural kind—"

"Aye, aye," she cut him off impatiently, "then they deserve to die. I trust a suitably cruel end has been arranged for them?"

"Och, that it has, yer ladyship!" he wheezed with malicious glee. "They'll get a taste o' their own medicine on the morra when they fall afoul o' the embrace o' the iron baron."

They moved on down the slimy passageway.

A claw-thin hand groped at them through the bars of a small, square opening in an otherwise solid door. Magdalen drew back, sniffing in distaste as the filthy fingers brushed her elaborate headpiece, an anguished voice crying from inside, "Mercy! Mercy for an innocent man unjustly accused."

"Open the door," the countess ordered.

Though he was naturally in awe of this grand lady who had so unexpectedly paid a visit, the guard slowly shook his head. "Nay, lady, ye widna want tae see in there—"

Magdalen drew herself up haughtily, her black eyes chilling. "Open up unless you have a mind to share his quarters!"

The turnkey shrugged and grinned and obligingly held his lantern high to illuminate the shadowy interior of the cell. Pressing her glove to her nose, Magdalen saw that there were three men in the cell, though two hung suspended from metal caged high overhead and had been reduced to little more than skeletons, bloated purple tongues protruding from mouths that had long since forgotten the taste of nourishment.

She dismissed these two and turned to the third. He was shockingly thin and clad in rags, but, from what she could see in the gloom, basically intact. He stood shaking before her, head turned away from the lantern, then suddenly sank to his knees and clutched at her skirt. "Help me, I beg of you! I swear I had naught to do with the attack on my Lord Morton's life. I was not even at Langside on the afternoon in question. Lady"—his sob caused one of those suspended overhead to jerk and croak, rattling his cage—"if you will speak up for me, I vow to serve you for the rest of my life."

Magdalen's interest quickened, especially when the guard informed her that the fellow was scheduled to be drawn and quartered at dawn the following day. Was it any wonder that he looked up at her with such heart-wrenching hope, ready to do anything to spare himself the worst agony that a mortal could endure? Yet there was something about him . . .

Magdalen motioned the turnkey closer with his lantern until the light shone directly on the upturned face. The countess sucked in her breath, gasping, "God's suffering soul, what happened to his eyes?"

"They be put out a week ago," the guard replied complacently, "when he refused to confess."

Exasperated and disappointed, she thrust the young prisoner away so that he tumbled back, arms flailing wildly, and landed on his swarming pallet of bug-infested straw. They hurried out and slammed the door, his shrieks of despair ringing in their ears.

In the end Magdalen had almost settled on a hard-eyed creature much like Bruno, when she spied the boy sharing the same cell. In spite of his tender years, he too was scheduled to die the following day. The lad, it seemed, was an incorrigible thief. To the street people he was known as the White Eel because, it was said, he had the uncanny ability to slip into any house in the city, regardless of how well fortified, and make off with whatever of value he could lay his hands on.

"Aye, and I'll cheat the gallows the morrow too!" the teen-age urchin cried defiantly, alert blue eyes snapping in a sharp, dirt-streaked face, his wiry body springing away with astonishing speed when the warden made to cuff his ears.

"I'll take him!" said Magdalen with a decisive nod of her head, and when the guard protested that he was a condemned prisoner, "One so young deserves another chance to reform."

Then for the lad's benefit she added a warning, "I'll return him to you the moment he disobeys."

The Countess scrawled her name on the necessary documents and, mainly because he was only fourteen years old, young Toby—or the White Eel—was released into her custody.

Three days later, on the evening of May 13, Alexander's nurse left him playing happily with his toys in the upstairs nursery at Elmwood while she hurried to the kitchen to arrange for his bath. When she returned ten minutes later, the child had vanished.

A search was made of the house and garden, then of the street itself. An elderly flower-seller on the corner informed them that not long before she had noticed a youth galloping past her stall with a wriggling sack slung across the saddle in front of him. "Methought it funny," she said. "He was such a scury laddy tae be riding such a fine horse. And he had something—some *living* thing—struggling awa in his bag."

"Lady Magdalen!" Alyssa cried. "Who else would have reason to kidnap my baby?"

Nan burst into terrified tears. Who else indeed? And all the men were gone with Stephan to Holyrood, leaving only the house servants at Elmwood. "Now ye ken why I scolded Stephan for tarrying away so much," she sobbed. "His duty was to guard us lest something like this happened."

"Send for him at once!" Alyssa choked, then flew upstairs to her room. But she had no intention of waiting for Stephan to return, which could take more time than they could afford. She could not bear to think of her darling son at the mercy of Magdalen MacKellar, a woman who hated her and would enjoy venting that hatred on her helpless child, aware of the anguish this would cause his mother. And Blake! When he discovered she'd been so careless as to allow the fruit of their love to be kidnapped that love would turn to hatred and he'd rue the day he ever met her.

While chaos reigned downstairs, Alyssa slipped along the corridor to Luke and Nan's bedchamber. She plucked a pistol and dagger from the weapon rack on the wall, and rifled through a kist for riding breeches and a leather jerkin. Dressed in the too-large clothes, she donned a hat and pushed her long hair up under the brim, then, with the pistol tucked into her belt and the dagger into the sleeve inside her deerskin boots, she slipped down the back staircase to the stables at the rear of the mansion.

Daylight still lingered in the sky as it did until past ten o'clock at this time of year in these northern climes. High above stood the dignified grandeur of Edinburgh Castle, tonight seeming more threatening than comforting to the woman who rode far below. The great royal park of Holyrood Palace was enveloped in mist, the building itself obscured, as if shrouded in a grey pall of mourning for its lost Queen.

Alyssa was filled with an icy resolve, her thoughts far away from the absent Mary Stuart. She would kill anyone, if necessary, who stood between her and her son. She had no fear for herself, for what would her own life matter if she could not save Alexander? She *would* free him or never leave Cumbray Court alive.

The Sinclair family lawyer brought the documents to Clairmont and accepted the glass of claret that Harry Sinclair offered him, remarking with satisfaction, "Well, my lord, it is done. Your nephew is a free man. His lady, latterly, wanted the divorce as actively as did he, afraid of being associated with one who stood an excellent chance of being outlawed and losing everything he owned, including the large dowry she had brought to the marriage. As instructed, this has recently been returned to her intact."

Harry nodded soberly.

When the family lawyer left, Harry continued to sit on behind the desk, gazing off into space, musing at how much life had changed since his own youth when a man conducted his life along certain circumscribed lines. Now everything had changed and it was so very hard to get used to, just as it was difficult to get used to the fact that he was no longer fit enough to ride out with his men.

He suffered frequently from shortness of breath and

stabbing pains in his chest, and therefore had to be content with remaining in town to look after the family headquarters. Now he had the responsibility of seeing to it that his nephew received word of the latest development as soon as possible and must dispatch a courier south within the hour.

There was a time when he could have predicted what a man in Blake's position would do once he got word of this . . . but no longer. The turbulence of the times had spawned a different breed, and he could not understand them.

With a glance at the sealed documents he sighed, "What now, what now?" and felt age pressing heavily upon him.

42

Late that afternoon, pretending to receive a message from Lord Luke, Magdalen sent her house guard galloping in the direction of Jedburgh. Shortly afterwards she startled most of her servants by giving them the rest of the day off, all but her four loyal retainers who would accompany her to France.

They were leaving later that evening from Leith—taking the Sinclair bastard with them. At that moment the child was drugged and curled up in a wicker basket at her feet, waiting to be strapped to the back of one of the pack mules in the lane at the side of the house. The White Eel, young Toby, had admirably lived up to his reputation, but now she had no further use for him. He too lay trussed up at her feet before the hearth, his foul, demanding mouth silenced with a gag.

Magdalen smiled down into the fierce blue eyes under the shock of straw-colored hair. "You see, lad, 'tis never wise to be overgreedy. I might have sent you on your way with a gold piece or two had you accepted it with the proper gratitude and not seen fit to threaten me, but then you had no way of knowing what happened to the last man who thought to blackmail me."

The boy lay very still, glaring up at her.

She chuckled softly, somewhat ruefully. "He died in a fire, a more painful end than the one you so recently escaped from." Her eyes slid from the young face and rose to the newly lit torch on a nearby wall, a look of such dread significance that the youth's face turned the same yellow-white shade as his hair.

"Accidents happen, my bold young friend, though I must confess to having no great love for this house—nor anything in it. And I think you'll appreciate my need to send up a smokescreen"—she burst into sudden, shrill laughter, controlling it with an effort as she added—"to conceal the fact that I departed from here alive."

And with that she went upstairs to dress for the journey.

Very slowly Toby let out his breath and allowed his muscles to relax, causing the rope that bound him to losen. It was an old trick he had learned long ago, to puff oneself up to the limit when being tied, allowing for a little slack afterwards. And sometimes that tiny bit made all the difference. Toby had noted at once that the steward who secured him had been a novice at the job and had not taken the time to be thorough, obviously nervous and anxious to be gone before the child's relatives traced him to Cumbray Court. He chuckled inwardly, thinking that better men had trussed him and *still* he had escaped. Why else had he been nicknamed the White Eel of Edinburgh?

It was one of the two maids who spied him worrying his bonds, and forthwith struck him a crushing blow to the side of the head with the brass bed-warmer hanging from the nearby mantel.

As always, Lady Magdalen took great pains with her toilet, perhaps even more than she used to now that the signs of advancing years were so markedly upon her. She had her own special concoctions—the lead paste tinted with essence of gilly-flowers, the rare imported cochineal powder so useful for adding a dusting of rose to dry white cheeks. She selected a gold gown made from tissue of taffeta, her mind momentarily flitting to the dying man in his chamber along the corridor, then with a shrug of her thin shoulders just as quickly flitting away. Nay, she thought, the only one she might miss in Scotland was her daughter, Serena, though she had changed a lot since marrying Sir Edward Grant and become almost as sanctimonious and hypocritical as her husband. In time, if it seemed safe to do so, she could contact Serena privately and mayhap arranged a meeting somewhere—but not at her new home in France.

No one would ever be able to trace her or prove that she had kidnapped the Sinclair bastard, and that boy, she vowed grimly, would live to curse the day his mother had ever had aspirations on Cumbray. Aye, and the boy's father would curse her too, in the end. Each time they looked at each other they would be reminded of their lost child—until they would not be able to stand the sight of each other at all! There would be no peace or happiness for the pair as they brooded over the fate of their firstborn, sacrificed for his mother's lofty ambitions on Cumbray.

Alyssa tied her horse to a tree in St. John's Yard and entered a narrow lane that ran behind a row of impressive mansions. A high brick wall separated the lane from the private gardens and through gates in the wall Alyssa spied elegant courtyards, well-tended flower beds and fountains, the water tinkling softly in the still evening air. Overhead, swallows darted and swooped between the high gables; she sniffed columbine and myrtle on the breeze and the more pungent odor of the stables.

Alyssa stood hidden in a clump of rhododendron and peered through the massive iron gate that opened into the rear garden of Cumbray Court. Three pack mules waited patiently at the side entrance to the house and several horses were tied to the hitching post, saddled and ready to go. It was obvious at a glance that the owners were about to embark on a journey.

Alyssa pressed a clenched fist to her heart. Magdalen had guessed the real reason she was staying at Elmwood, and meant to escape while she still could—but where was Alexander?

The gate was stoutly padlocked. Grasping the rails firmly, Alyssa proceeded to climb, then dropped hastily to the ground when a retainer left the house carrying on his shoulder a large wicker basket, which he carefully positioned atop one of the mules as if it held something of great importance. Once satisfied that it was stable, he tied it down with thick leather straps, then patted the basket and chuckled, "There ye be, safe and sound," and with a shake of his head returned to the house.

Alyssa's attention riveted to the hamper. The house carl had behaved as if it had an occupant! She frantically climbed the gate and tumbled soundlessly onto the thick, velvety grass on the other side, her legs like feathers, her heartbeats echoing like drumbeats in her ears. Sticking to the protection of the trees and bushes as much as possible, she found herself opposite the mule, then with a quick spurt across the courtyard, at his side.

Desperately she wrenched at the straps holding the basket, certain that her son was concealed inside from the remark the servant had made, and because it made the perfect hiding place for spiriting the toddler out of town. Her nails splintered as she tore at the straps frantically, rivulets of icy sweat running down her face, expecting to hear a shout from behind her at any second. One of the bindings came free, and then another. The hamper teetered, then slid sideways into her arms. It was remarkably heavy, and for a moment Alyssa staggered under the weight, but terror lent her strength she hadn't known she possessed. Setting the container on the cobbles, Alyssa knelt and breathlessly tugged on the hasp. Throwing back the domed lid, she saw her baby lying curled up inside. For a second she thought he was dead, so pale and still did he seem, his long black ringlets damp against rounded ashen cheeks.

"God . . . !" She whispered involuntarily, choking back a scream. She plucked him from his small prison and pressed an ear to his chest, then raised her head abruptly when she smelled smoke—and saw Magdalen MacKellar standing in the doorway with a pistol in her hand.

A malicious laugh shattered the quiet of the evening. "So . . . we meet again, Lady Ogilvy. For a moment I was not certain it was you." Scornful black eyes moved over Alyssa's breeches and jerkin, pausing at the weapons tucked in her belt, and when Alyssa fumbled to reach her own pistol with Alex a dead weight in her arms, Magdalen said, "Nay! Do not try anything so foolish, wench, unless you relish the thought of seeing your bastard's head blown into pieces against your breast."

Servants crowded into the doorway behind the countess, eyes widening with astonishment when they spied Alyssa in her incongruous male attire, the boy cradled tight against her breast. Thick grey smoke billowed out from behind them, and one of the men cried, "My lady, we must hasten whilst we can!"

Magdalen kept her eyes fixed on Alyssa. "This makes for a slight change of plans. The boy will not go with us. Methinks his mother would prefer to keep him close." Her shoulders shook with stifled laughter. "Bring them into the house, Raby."

Struggling between the two male servants, Alyssa and Alex were dragged into the hall, where flames flickered eerily against the wainscotting, ignited by a flaring torch carelessly left lying near the base molding. Even as they entered, a beautiful tapestry of a hunting scene exploded into orange fire. They were all coughing now as the men wrestled Alyssa to a bench and proceeded to tie her down. At that her nerves cracked, and Alyssa heard herself pleading with the tall, dark woman who stood watching with a fold of her gold silk cape held over her nose. "Spare my baby! Take him with you if you must, but I beg of you, get him gone from this house!"

Smoke swirled around Magdalen's head. Within it her face was a white blur, her eyes dark hollows in the gaunt features, like twin pits. "Nay," she said, "'tis right and meet that a child bide with his mother—and right and meet that you, upstart, should burn. From the day of your birth you have cast an evil spell over my life"—she was seized by a spasm of coughing—"and as a witch it is fitting that it end thus."

"Sinclair will pursue you, hound you for the rest of your life!" Alyssa screamed as the servants, terrified as the beams overhead ignited, flew ahead of their mistress to the door, shouting for her to hurry.

Magdalen chuckled. "Would that I could tarry to watch you roast alive . . . Alyssa MacKellar. Aye," she nodded, taking malicious pleasure in admitting it now, when it could do no good. "I knew who you were from the moment I first set eyes on you at Gower Castle. The likeness to your father, Lord Angus, was too strong to ignore. Would that I had killed you with my own two hands that night of your birth at Cumbray, rather than entrusting the task to Caitland Weir! I should have known that she would deceive me and try to turn it to her own advantage, curse her soul—"

"Lady, come now!" shouted Raby from the door as a beam fell with an ear-splitting crack and the flames roared through the ceiling to the floor above.

The noise seemed to bring Magdalen to her senses, and though she could hardly tear herself away from the pleasant sight of her enemy's anguish, it was dangerous to linger. "Farewell," she choked, her voice muffled behind the fold of her cloak. "'Tis regrettable that you will not live long enough to enjoy that which you craved. I trust your end will not come *too* hastily."

Horrified, Alyssa watched her toss her head and saunter away, stately and arrogant as ever, not deigning to hurry for all that the fire had spread halfway around the room. Alex stirred in her arms. He took a deep breath, gagged, and convulsed in violent coughing.

"Help us! Dear Lord, help us!" Alyssa shrieked, struggling so desperately to free herself that her bench overturned and sent them crashing on the floor. It was then, to her astonishment, that she noticed they were not alone.

The youth lay near the hearth, partially hidden by the huge oak settle, a fierce-looking lad with the sharp features of a fox and eyes blazing with hatred as they riveted on Magdalen's back.

From the moment Alyssa and the child had been brought into the hall the others had forgotten him. Toby, the White Eel, had made good use of the distraction. Rolling behind the settle, he held his bound wrists to the torch left casually on the floor until the rope singed, then with a tug, snapped. After that it was easy. Within seconds he was free. Yet he had stayed where he was, perfectly still, patiently waiting for his opportunity.

Lady Magdalen was no more than ten feet away when the flaming torch was in Toby's hand. When Alyssa opened her mouth to ask him to untie her, he put a finger over his lips. Springing to his feet, the nimble youth flew after the countess and caught up with her before she reached the door, and thrust the torch into the billowing taffeta folds of her gown.

Magdalen spun about with a startled screech—then felt the sudden heat licking at her legs. Looking down, her eyes bulged from her head. In the breeze wafting through the open door the tissue-fine material of her gown burst into a sheet of fire. She jumped, screaming, then began to run wildly and mindlessly about the hall while her servants stood transfixed in the doorway—until they heard the riders clatter into the lane.

Toby had Alyssa and the baby free and partway to the door when Stephan MacKellar and his men burst through the entryway. Though her head was reeling and she could barely speak for coughing, Alyssa gasped, "Upstairs . . . Lord Thomas!" But when they found him, Thomas MacKellar, like his wife, was dead.

Stephan took young Toby back with them to Elmwood for questioning, and in the course of it the boy repeated Lady Magdalen's last words, which he had clearly overheard. "She admitted that this lass"—pointing to Alyssa—"was really Alyssa MacKellar; that Lord Angus was her father."

Stephan was flabbergasted. "The lady was mad!"

But the following afternoon Luke's squire Whittier arrived back in Edinburgh with Jock Semple, who resignedly confessed his part in the crime. By the time Luke himself returned to interrogate him, it had dawned on the rest of the family that they might have a new Chief, and this time a woman, though, of course, the legalities must be gone through to ascertain that there was no mistake, however unlikely it now seemed.

This process would have to wait. Luke brought back disquieting news, news that caused the family to pack quickly and bid Edinburgh a hasty retreat, their destination Cumbray Castle in the Highlands.

With no one quite sure what had happened to the Queen, or even where she was, the leaders of the insurrection had seized power under the Earl of Moray and immediately set about arresting Mary's supporters, some of whom—lesser nobles—had already gone to the block. In the Highlands they would be relatively safe. Cumbray Castle was well equipped to stand a long siege, if it came to that, and there they were surrounded by their own people and many allies who had no reason to love Moray. Aside from that, a solid wall of mountains, excellent terrain for conducting guerrilla-type battles, stood between them and Edinburgh.

At the age of twenty-three Alyssa had finally gained what was rightfully hers, but she had scant time to enjoy her moment of triumph, nor even time to reflect that she was ill prepared for the great responsibility now upon her, because of the circumstances of her upbringing. It was enough for the moment that Alexander was safe and recovering from the effects of smoke inhalation, that her most virulent enemy was dead, and she herself beginning to be accepted into the bosom of her true family at last.

Yet even then there was no peace in her heart. The satisfaction and relief she imagined would be hers completely escaped her. From the moment she left Lynnwood she had heard nothing more from Sinclair and now began to fret that she never would. He was a proud man and their parting had been a cold one, a chill air of finality in his voice when he had bid her farewell, as if to imply that she had made her choice and he was prepared to honor it.

Her uncle could do little to soothe her troubled mind, except to say that Sinclair had ridden away from Langside with the Queen and undoubtedly was still with her. Aye, Alyssa thought with a curious mixture of admiration and bitterness, and he'll bide with her to the end no matter where it might lead him, and no matter how far it might take him away from herself.

She had never quite been able to understand her lover's unique relationship with the Queen, except that it transcended the ordinary attraction between a man and a woman and left her powerless to compete. Worse, not even sure she had the right to try to break such a bond, an almost spiritual link forged long before she had met him, and though she sometimes resented it, even raged against it, deep in her heart Alyssa accepted it as being inviolate, a thing apart from the love the two of them had shared. The memory of that love brought Alyssa a fierce, wrenching ache that grew steadily more acute as they rode away from Edinburgh, and even her first sight of mighty Cumbray Castle, the home of her ancestors, did nothing to abate it.

More than anything in the world she wanted Sinclair back. Cumbray, for all its grandeur, was no more than a massive, inert—and cold—pile of stones.

43

Blake received the long-awaited documents at Terregles Castle on Saturday, May 15, the official notification that his marriage had ended. His own reaction to the news surprised him. He gave no great shout of joy, nor did he feel a wild surge of elation, the urge to gather his men together for a grand celebration to mark the conclusion of a frustrating mistake, one that would never be repeated.

Rather, he was filled with a deep and profound sense of relief.

After a moment he turned his attention to a letter from Lord Harry, informing him of the reprisals taking place in Edinburgh against the Queen's adherents. Because of it they were returning posthaste to Augusta, as many another royalist had thought it prudent to flee. "Given time," wrote his uncle, "Moray's fury agin his sister's supporters must wane, since as regent he will have his own troubles ruling Scotland, assuming that Mary fails in gathering an army to win back her crown. Aye, you can be sure Moray will soon need all the help he can get and be more than glad to let bygones be bygones, as many another has done afore him. He has his faults, but a lack of expediency is not one of them."

Near the end of the letter Harry wrote, "I thought to send you the documents thinking it would cheer you, rather than waiting for you to return. Send word back with the courier as to what is happening. We cannot be at peace through worrying least you end up in exile in France—or mayhap in Hell!— following the enchanted trail of your royal Lorelei."

Blake smiled tightly at that last remark as he drew quill and parchment toward him, pausing for a moment to consider how best to describe the incredible turn of events at Terregles. He made three attempts before thrusting the writing materials away from him, too restless to concentrate. Strapping on his sword, he left the castle alone for a solitary walk along the shore.

Across the Solway Firth lay England. He could just make out, a darker line against the sky, distant Cumberland. Blake sat down on a chunk of driftwood and rested his chin on his hand, still unconvinced that Mary meant to carry through her outrageous plan of turning to her cousin Elizabeth for assistance. The previous evening he had had another heated encounter with his "Lorelei" when he pointed out that Elizabeth, a Protestant, could hardly embroil herself in a plan to install a Catholic Queen in a Protestant country. Even if she wanted to—which seemed highly unlikely—her own people would never countenance such a thing. And above all others, Elizabeth loved her people and craved their approval and goodwill. For them she had given up everything—husband, children, the dearest and warmest of the basic human pleasures in life, so that they should know and never doubt that she esteemed them above all others, however mighty, who touched her life.

And Mary Stuart represented a serious threat to the English Queen. There were many militant Catholics in England who viewed Mary as their rightful Queen, and with the help of a Guisard army from France, led by her own relatives, would do their utmost to knock Anne Boleyn's bastard from her high place and at the same time restore the true religion to their country.

"Vague, improbable schemes such as all monarchs must contend with!" had been Mary's response to this reasoning. And with a rueful chuckle, "God's blood, Sinclair, I have enough trouble holding onto my *own* crown that I should crave hers! Nay, nay, of more immediate concern to my cousin will be the fear that if England won't help me then there are others who will, eager to seize this excuse to set foot in this island of ours." And she added confidently, "By August I will be back in Scotland at the head of an army!"

It was then that she had asked him to follow her across the border, saying with a hint of her old beguiling smile, "Don't look so grim, my lord. It ill befits that handsome face to scowl so. I need your optimism and courage now more than I ever have before, and your broad shoulder to steady me if I should falter." And when he said nothing, the amber eyes beseeched him, "Stay by me, dear Sinclair! We must see this through together."

At that she had reached for his hand, and Blake had flinched to find it icy cold for all her great show of bravado, desperation in the fingers that pressed his so urgently. Inwardly he melted and found himself wavering, and restrained an urge to reach out and pat the short-cropped auburn curls that lent her a boyish, sweetly vulnerable appearance; an urge to assure her that of course he would remain at her side as he had done from the moment she returned to Scotland.

"You will not change your mind?" he asked instead.

Slowly the Queen shook her head.

Now, gazing somberly out to sea to the distant coast of England, Blake was faced with a choice, to pursue the elusive dream of what the Queen considered to be her destiny or to return to the challenge of his own. There was no doubt in Sinclair's mind which step was the more important to him or which route he would take.

The following day, May 16, Mary Stuart's nobles escorted her to the tiny port near Dundrennan Abbey, and there, accompanied by the Lords Maxwell, Hamilton and others, she embarked on a simple fishing boat for the short trip across the Solway Firth to England.

Blake Sinclair remained on the shore.

As he took his final leave of the woman he had always thought of as being as wild, beautiful and unpredictable as Scotland itself, his attachment to her bound up in his loyalty to his country, he kissed her hand and then, in a burst of emotion, embraced her fiercely, praying that he would be wrong and that her quest for English aid would meet with success. But whatever happened, Blake had made up his mind to retire from the political scene in Edinburgh and concentrate his energies in his own affairs and in strengthening ties with other clans. Mary had represented a grand vision of uniting the turbulent factions that for centuries had torn Scotland apart, but, being of a turbulent nature herself, she had sown the seeds of her own undoing, never outgrowing a tendency to view political maneuvers in personal terms. Her vibrant, highly emotional temperament had worked against her from the start, and her grasping nobles had quickly learned how to turn this flaw to their advantage. Might a different personality have managed to overcome the great odds, perhaps a woman as subtle, enigmatic and oblique as her cousin Elizabeth, Blake pondered; a woman never known to commit herself irrevocably on anything, therefore always leaving open a means of retreat. Aye, he mused, perhaps Mary could learn much from the English Queen . . . were she given the opportunity.

Sinclair watched the boat until it was swallowed up in the mist that hung over the water; until the tearful waving figure of Mary Stuart—still holding in her arms the bouquet of white roses he had given her—vanished from sight. Mary had been the dream of his youth. Now, as a man, other dreams clamored, perhaps less altruistic ones, but for all that no less dear to his heart.

The riders waited on a ledge where a narrow pass cut through the mountains, a gorge that opened into a wide green valley where a gushing river flowed, the water sparkling in the mellow June sunshine. Behind them on a high ridge sat Cumbray Castle, a flag fluttering in the breeze to signify that its Chief was in residence. Wild flowers covered the hillsides like a bright fragrant mantel, and in the rocky places sturdy gorse bushes had burst into golden bloom. There was tranquillity in the air, but under it a pulsing excitement.

Luke MacKellar's courier had delivered his message to distant Ayrshire more than a week ago, and that morning an outrider had arrived at Cumbray to say that their visitors were no more than a few leagues away, having responded to the message immediately. Alyssa had dressed with great care in a new mint-green riding habit, a matching hat set perkily on her elegantly coiffured hair, and started out with her uncles and men to meet their guests and escort them personally to Cumbray.

Now, mounted beside Luke MacKellar on one side and

Stephan on the other, she was silent and pale, her heart beating so swiftly and erratically that she felt she might faint. This was the moment she had waited for all her life. Now that it was upon her she was terrified, dreading the ultimate rejection, warning herself over and over not to expect too much from this stranger she was about to meet, and having no idea what she would say to her.

A shout went up from the men, and Whittier pointed to a trail snaking through the hills where a small party could be seen moving in their direction. Alyssa closed her eyes and waited. She wanted to pray, but could find no words to express the raw, tumultuous emotions inside her. Indeed, at that moment she found it impossible to think coherently at all.

The wait seemed interminable as the newcomers covered the last half-league and drew up on the crag. In a daze Alyssa rode forward to meet them, woodenly uttering the expected greeting, "Welcome to Cumbray," her eyes quickly passing over the men and riveting on the tall, fair woman in the blue silk cloak. She was hardly aware of Stephan helping her down from the saddle, or the tension that gripped both parties as the older woman too dismounted and approached Alyssa on foot.

The mother and daughter examined each other in silence, eyes damp and questioning, searching avidly for some special sign in the other's face, assurance that at last the long years of yearning were over. There were streaks of grey in the older woman's hair and fine lines about her eyes and mouth, yet she was still a handsome woman. And she too was afraid, Alyssa saw with a pang, one that gave her the courage to reach for her hand and press the icy fingers to her lips, then to her cheek, until with a small choked sound Alicia put her arms about her and drew the bright head to her breast.

"If you could know how often I've longed to do this," breathed Lady Alicia, tears on her cheeks.

"And if you could know how often I've dreamed of it," whispered Alyssa, her arms tightening to wrap her mother in an embrace while drinking in the special scent of her, surely sweeter by far than the costliest perfumes mysterious Arabia had to offer, and far more unique.

The men about them slowly relaxed, exchanging warm,

foolish smiles foreign to such rugged features, waiting patiently while the women drew back again to look at each other, and again embraced, this time with a joyous mingling of laughter, words bubbling over as they tried to give voice to their emotions.

At last Alyssa took her mother home to Cumbray.

44

News came to them at Cumbray Castle of the Queen's flight into England and that some of her most loyal nobles had gone with her, including—so it was first thought—Blake Sinclair.

Alyssa was not surprised. All along she had tried to resign herself to the possibility of this happening; that the almost mystical lure of Mary Stuart would steal him away in the end.

So it is done, she thought when Nan brought her the news, and now, somehow, she must find the fortitude to put him behind her. She reminded herself that she had much to be thankful for. God had been good to her, and no one had a right to expect the gratification of all desires.

Alyssa spent the rest of the day alone in her private solar.

Mercifully, it was impossible to brood at Cumbray. There were her mother, Nan, and Stephan's quiet little wife, Sarah, and rarely a silent moment with years of catching up to do. Nan and Alicia quickly renewed their old friendship, cut off so abruptly when Magdalen had banished Alicia to Our Lady of the Well in Ayrshire scant weeks after Lord Angus was killed. Yet sensitive Nan was careful to see to it that Alyssa and her mother had many private hours together, gentle times of discovery when the two women sought to forge bonds that should have been established when Alyssa was a child.

They discovered many things in common. Both enjoyed music and literature, and both shared a mutual concern over social issues, especially the plight of the country's poor. "I know what it is to go in want," Alyssa said, and proudly outlined the principles of the Hospice Fund, financed—not without a struggle—by wealthy merchants and the nobility, the latter putting up the most resistance.

"My dream is to eventually open chapters all over Scotland."

Her mother squeezed her hand. "A wondrous dream indeed, but one that might well take a lifetime to realize." She smiled, "'Tis as well you have much of your father's drive and energy, his determination to see a thing through, for the greater the obstacles put in his way, the more resolved he was to knock them down."

Gradually, through Alicia, a vivid picture of her father took shape in Alyssa's mind. "Nay, nay, 'twould be dishonest of me to pretend that he was perfect"—this after her mother had described him as being a handsome, golden man with a fine intellect and hearty disposition. "He had a fiery temper to match his hair," she chuckled, "and could be obdurate as a mule when his will was challenged. I must tell you of the time . . ." and off she would go on yet another story, each of which brought Angus MacKellar more intensely alive in his daughter's heart.

They took a special delight in Alexander, the surprise of Alicia Cairnmore's life. Not only had she found her daughter, but discovered that she had a grandson as well. The circumstances of his birth did not disturb the older woman unduly, since it happened frequently enough. What did disturb her was the look of pain that sprang up in Alyssa's eyes each time the name Sinclair was mentioned.

But it was merry around the board at Cumbray when all the men returned each night for supper. Sir Ralph Cairnmore, Alicia's husband, was a bluff, jovial man of fifty with a whole repertoire of robust jokes to amuse them, some of them distinctly naughty, which caused his wife to blush and clap a hand none too gently over his mouth. He also had a fine singing voice, so they had laughter and song and sometimes even dancing to the skirl of the pipes, and at such times the turmoil in Edinburgh seemed worlds away. But not so far that Luke let down his guard. Sentries were posted on the hillsides around the clock as word filtered back that one royalist after another had been arrested and tossed into the dungeons of Edinburgh Castle, or hung from the battlements of his own stronghold before it was sacked and burned.

Alyssa tried not to think of it during the pleasant evenings in the great hall of Cumbray, watching Alex wield his toy sword and boast to his uncles how he would slay the wicked Lord Morton were he to dare set foot on MacKellar territory. As she exchanged a smile with her mother at the lad's antics, her eyes moved to embrace all the faces about her—Alicia, Nan, Luke, and Stephan and all the others, her family. How intensely dear were those two words, and how complete her happiness would have been had not one very special face been missing.

Would she ever become reconciled to his absence? Would the pain ever go away? Was it possible that a time would come when a whole day would pass without her thinking of him?

It was useless to take comfort in the fact that she had left *him*, her pride intact, before the point came when he left her, as time had proved would have happened. She should be glad she had been spared the final indignity, the shock and anguish of watching him ride away for the last time, leaving her behind in bitter solitude at Lynnwood with nothing but memories to sustain her. Now there was pain, though nothing like it might have been had she given up everything for her lover. Now at least her self-esteem was intact!

Over and over Alyssa tried to concentrate on what she had gained by leaving Lynnwood, while striving to overlook all she had lost. Thank God she'd had a goal of her own to strive for, she thought soberly. And thank God there had been the drive inside her to pursue that goal, and that she had never allowed her great love for Sinclair to come between her duty to herself as a person.

It was difficult to be alone at Cumbray Castle, yet there were times when Alyssa craved to be by herself, much as she enjoyed the companionship and warmth of the family circle. She needed time to think, to come to grips with her new position in life, which would be formalized just as soon as the political situation settled down—if it ever did. She had much to learn about the house of MacKellar, both historically and in a practical sense, and had already begun to take instructions, the beginning of a long process to make up for all the years she had missed.

It was during one of these sessions with her Uncle Luke and Bennington, the chief adviser to the family, that Bennington brought up a subject of vital importance to any great house—the question of arranging an advantageous marriage for Alyssa, one that would stand to benefit the MacKellars most. He went so far as to name several possible candidates, quite frankly and—so Alyssa thought—cold-bloodedly outlining their pros and cons with the air of a man hammering out a crucial business deal. Which in fact it was.

Alyssa was appalled. This was something she had never considered at all! Suddenly she thought of Blake trying to explain to her his reasons for marrying Elizabeth, reasons she refused to even *try* to understand. How different, she mused ruefully, now that she was wearing *his* shoes and had the same weight of responsibility on her shoulders.

At the look of shock on her face, Bennington seemed momentarily taken aback, surprised at her reaction. "My dear lady," he said patiently, the faintest hint of exasperation in his voice, "surely you must realize that you have an obligation to marry well for the betterment of the family."

She desperately needed time to herself to think, to digest the fact that responsibility could sometimes be exceedingly onerous, if not impossible to live up to, and finally she sympathized with how Sinclair must have felt when forced to marry a woman he didn't love. How, Alyssa asked herself miserably, could she bring herself to do it?

That afternoon she slipped away from the castle and rode out into the hills alone, something her Uncle Luke would never have permitted had he known about it. But the family were distracted by a flurry of trumpets from the North Road, signaling the arrival of yet another batch of visitors to Cumbray, for in the political upheaval there was much commerce between the Highland nobility as they sought to keep each other abreast of the situation in the capital. When the stable boys and grooms all ran to the portcullis, curious to see who the newcomers were and hear all the latest news, Alyssa slipped away.

She saddled Belle herself and quickly led her down the lane to the postern gate, selected a key from the ring at her waist—which as Chatelaine of Cumbray she had a right to wear—and quietly let herself out, hoping that in all the activity no one would notice a solitary rider cantering south to the track leading to the river.

She forgot, in her great desire to be alone, that her bright, burnished hair made it obvious who she was.

After a hard, exhilarating ride through the hills, Alyssa dismounted in the protection of a huge boulder on the banks of the Spey, sat down on the mossy earth, and distractedly threw pebbles into the water. The old stubborn mood was upon her, every cell in her body rebelling against the notion of having to wed out of cold expediency; of finding herself a pawn in the great marriage stakes, one of the primary tools the nobility used for gain and aggrandizement. As Bennington had so bluntly pointed out, she had an obligation, and even her uncle had not gainsaid him, though poor Luke had seemed mighty uncomfortable when he glimpsed the mulish expression on her face.

But one thing sank home to Alyssa. As the Chief of a clan she could no longer do what was best for her as a person. Always the good of the clan must come first.

Seizing a rock, she hurled it ferociously in the direction of a tree on the opposite bank of the river, one that vaguely resembled the stooped, gnarled shape of Bennington. She missed and the stone landed with a splashing in the water, sending up a sparkling shower of spray . . . and in the silence that followed, Alyssa heard the crunching footfall behind her.

Gasping, Alyssa spun around and saw him leaning casually against the rock outcropping at her back, his white shirt dazzling against sun-bronzed skin, idly flicking a riding crop against his boots, the gesture betraying his inner tension for all his relaxed pose.

She blinked and started to her feet, certain that he had died and his ghost returned to haunt her. "Leave me in peace!" she choked, backing off toward the direction of her horse. "Oh, Blessed Mother . . . will I never be free of you!"

Misunderstanding, Blake looked terribly hurt at these harsh words. The light vanished from his eyes and he said grimly, "I came here for something that belongs to me, Alyssa."

She gaped at him, realizing that this was no evil vision.
Yet . . ."You—you were in England."

Slowly Sinclair shook his head.

"But—"

"My service to the Queen ended the moment she left the
country. I explained to you," he continued impatiently, "that I
pledged myself to her cause as long as there was a chance that
the people would accept her; until she could be firmly
established on her throne. I no longer believe that to be
possible."

Her senses reeled. "My God . . . ! Then it's truly over?"

He came to her and placed his hands on her shoulders
and gazed soberly at the lovely upturned face, one that seemed
to grow more beautiful with the maturity of each passing year.
All the way back from Dundrennan he had thought of nothing
but her, and it was Alyssa—and all she meant to him—that
eased the crushing disappointment of a goal that had ended in
ruins. True, they had parted in anger that day at Lynnwood, yet
still he had hoped for a warmer welcome than this.

"You must have known I would come back," Sinclair said
tenderly.

"Known you would come back?" Her green eyes flashed
with bitter anger. "Each time you left to follow the Queen I
was left to wonder if I would ever see you again! Each time a
rider approached the manor I died a little, fearing he had come
with the news that you had been killed. Can you imagine"—
her voice cracked and tears spilled over—"how *that* feels?
Nay," she shook her head wildly, "I never could be certain you
would come back to me, Sinclair!" And she added meaningfully, thinking of his marital status, "Especially as you were never
really mine to begin with."

"I was always yours, Alyssa. Always! And I think you
know that in your heart." Blake sighed, his dark eyes pleading
with her to try to understand. "A man in my position must
force himself down many paths he would rather not take. His
own desires must come behind the needs of his clan, or
should."

She looked away, understanding all too well.

"But you always came first in my heart," he went on, his

hands tightening on her arms. "You belong to me, Alyssa, and our son must be with his father." Blake looked deep in her eyes and added determinedly, "I've come to take you home."

Home! How sweet were those words, yet how bitter. More than anything in the world she wanted to be with him, yet there was no going back to the kind of life they had shared, even had she wanted to. "I cannot go with you to Lynnwood," she told him in a small, sad voice. "I must stay on here with my own people."

It was then Blake said gently, "A bastard, however dear you might be to Luke MacKellar, cannot bide with him at Cumbray Castle, Alyssa."

Her eyes jumped back to his face, the word "bastard" ringing jarringly in her ears. But of course he didn't know the truth! Since he had found her so quickly, Alyssa realized that Sinclair must have spotted her riding off when he arrived at the castle, and followed her immediately. Not that anyone at Cumbray would have announced her new status until it was made official. Blake had no idea of who she really was! Because of it, he imagined that she would be willing to continue with their former relationship. For just a second Alyssa was sorely tempted to blurt out the truth, that as the Chatelaine of Cumbray—mistress of the castle—she could no longer be mistress to Sinclair.

Her heart raced as she reminded herself that they were now equals, and as equals nothing stood between them, yet *still* she couldn't speak. The triumphant announcement stuck in her throat, because regardless of her new exalted position she was first and foremost a woman, and unreasonable or not, yearned only to be loved and honored for herself.

When she remained silent, Blake slipped a hand under her chin and raised her face to his. Alyssa could feel his heart thumping, read the tender passion in his eyes, the hungry strength of his body pressing against hers. A great melting weakness undermined her steely resolve, sweeping lofty ideals away in an upsurge of helpless longing, and as he drew her closer she closed her eyes and waited breathlessly for the touch of his lips.

But Sinclair didn't kiss her, not then. Gazing down into

her lovely face, he was thinking that all his life he had lived for
his clan. He had sacrificed and fought for Queen and country.
Now the time had come to do something for himself, but most
of all for the woman he adored. And if it meant a battle with his
family, he was ready for it.

"You will come with me, my love," he told Alyssa huskily.
And when her eyes flew open to meet his, "Not to Lynnwood,
to Augusta. And not as my mistress, but as my wife."

Epilogue

Mary, Queen of Scots, made a fatal mistake in turning to England for help. Queen Elizabeth, who steadfastly refused to meet her in person, saw in her cousin a grave threat to her own throne, an appealing figurehead behind which the English Catholics could gather. Feeling that it was dangerous to allow Mary to roam at will among her people, and for years never able to come to a decision about her cousin's fate, Elizabeth had her moved from one stronghold to another over the years of her long captivity. Mary Stuart's last prison was Fotheringhay Castle in Northamptonshire, and there on the morning of February 8, 1587—after nineteen years in captivity—Mary was beheaded. She was forty-four years old.